Of Royalty and Commoners

A Romance Novel

This book is a work of fiction. References to real people, royal personages, political leaders, events, Intelligence organizations and establishments of various countries, are intended only to provide a sense of authenticity and are used in fictional contexts and circumstances. All other names, characters and incidents in this novel are imaginary ones. They have no resemblance to real incidents or people, living or dead, except by coincidence or in a historical context. The names of some cities, towns, streets, or areas, have been used for authenticity, but only in fictional situations. The author pleads 'literary license' in the liberties he has taken with 'protocol', 'procedures', 'areas', 'events', 'locations' 'chronology', and 'time lines'—for all of which he craves the reader's indulgence!

Of Royalty and Commoners
A Romance Novel

B. B. Dandekar

A Sequel to "Rampaging Lovers" and "The Thar Articles"
(Espionage thrillers\Romance novels)

Let it be said that every commoner has some royal blood within him–and every king some of the commonest of it.

GYAN

ISBN : 978-81-212-1340-0

Price : ₹ 990

First Published, 2016

Published by

Gyan Publishing House
5, Ansari Road
Daryaganj, New Delhi-110002
Phone: 9811692060
E-mail: books@gyanbooks.com

Printed at: G. Print Process, Delhi.

Cataloging in Publication Data—DK
Courtesy: D.K. Agencies (P) Ltd. <docinfo@dkagencies.com>

Dandekar, B. B., 1938- **author.**
Of royalty and commoners : a romance novel / B.B. Dandekar.
pages cm
"A sequel to "Rampaging lovers" and "The Thar articles" (espionage thrillers \ romance novels)."
ISBN 9788121213400

1. Romance fiction, American. I. Title.

PS3604.A53O37 2016 DDC 813.6 23

CHAPTER 1

The pretty girl sitting on the bench seat, of a recessed window overlooking the Avenue, had her back to one thickness of wall and her knees drawn up. She wore a long batik skirt and a plain white blouse; on her knees she cradled a book—Jane Austen's 'Emma'. But a careful observer might have noticed that she had not moved from the open page for the best part of five minutes, because she kept looking down into Fitzjohn's Avenue, in the borough of Hampstead in North-West London. It was a large three bedroom, two bathroom flat, occupying the entire top floor of one of the old-style houses that at one time had the gentry living on upper floors and the servants in the basement—almost like the ancestral home of her great-grandfather, the eleventh Earl of Bromfield, about 20 miles north of London.

Lady Susan—or Susan Samuelson—as she preferred to be called, had remarkably pretty features that were unforgettable, partly because they were unique in their blend in her. She had an oval face, with straight black hair that plunged from behind small ears to past her shoulder—all this came from her father's side—an unblemished white skin with rosy cheeks, that were the envy of both of her sisters, and beautiful large brown eyes—all of which came from her mother's side. In her figure too, she had her mother's tall and alluring build, which, while not being statuesque, was surprisingly beautiful and appealing to those who saw her. Even the scholarly spectacles she wore seemed to befit her. At the tender age of eighteen, and the youngest child in the Samuelson family, she had the complete protection and trust of her parents, her eldest brother, David—the heir to the Earldom and hence the presumptive twelfth Earl of Bromfield—and of her two sisters—Lady Sarah and Lady Ruth. She had no intention of betraying that trust.

While no part of her father's build had entered Susan, it had certainly dominated the future twelfth Earl. Not too tall, not too well-built, not too handsome—that had been the phrase Lady Julia Samuelson had once used, more than twenty-six years before, when describing Colonel Joshua Samuelson MD, of the Indian Army, the man she planned to marry. That is precisely what their son David looked like. A military mustache covered his entire upper lip, the jaw was powerfully built, the hair was jet black, and the black eyes and soft brown skin marked him out clearly to be the off-spring of an East Indian gentleman—of which he was genuinely proud.

"I'll add some colour to the House of Lords, when I sit with them," he said. He already had, because his great-grandfather, the eleventh Earl, was so proud of him, he had, when David was six years old, taken him along and introduced him to all in that august chamber. They were entranced with little David, when he asked, much to their delight, "Are they all going to get a tan like me—or will I be the only one?"

At twenty-four, with a Mathematics Tripos from Cambridge University, he was going to Sandhurst, in the autumn, and—like his father, and grandfather from his mother's side—a career in the Army. He'd tried to drill his three younger sisters in the correct way to salute him when he had his commission, but gave it up as a hopeless cause when they kept laughing so much!

The word "statuesque" could most certainly be applied to the eldest daughter in the Samuelson family—twenty-two years old Sarah. If David was on his father's side, Sarah, for sure, was on her mother's side. She was a stunningly beautiful woman—not a girl anymore—with beautiful brown eyes and straight brown hair down to shoulder length that Emma—the old housekeeper at Bromfield House—would tie into an elegant bun at the back of her head on those occasions when they went for tea parties with the Queen. They were related to the Queen through their grandmother, who had died when their mother, Julia, was five years old, and which grandmother had been, in addition to being related to her, a childhood friend of the Queen.

Julia towered above Joshua when they walked together if she wore high-heeled shoes, and so Julia had abandoned that footwear for flat-heel shoes. Sarah had not, and so, in them, she stood a good six inches above her father. When she hugged him, she would kick off her high heels and now, being barefoot, could hold him as tight as any of the others could.

Lady Ruth—or Ruth, as she preferred to be called—was the athlete of the family. It was a trait that came also from her mother's side. Julia had had the potential to be a great long-distance runner—so her coach at boarding school in Kent had once told the old Earl—but Lady Julia wanted to be a writer not a runner! So while the writing urge had turned up in Susan, the running potential had turned up in Ruth. She had been the captain of the soccer team at Julia's old boarding school in Kent, had many awards for long-distance running—especially the mile at 4:25—and wanted to complete her degree in Exercise Physiology, and coach—where else? but at their old boarding school in Kent.

If she succeeded, she would be, without doubt, the prettiest female coach in the country, because Ruth was exquisitely beautiful with a tall, athletic figure, hair cut short, beautiful blue eyes, that caused Joshua to look teasingly at Julia and inquire—since neither of them had blue eyes—if there had been some period, nine months before Ruth was born, if he'd been away for any length of time? But her beautiful light brown skin—lighter than David's—did speak for the "Indianness" in her, and of which she was very proud. At boarding school in Kent, one of the girls she had just beaten in a race had called her "the daughter of an Indo-Jew", and it was only the quick intervention of the coach that had prevented one girl having her face muddied in the dirt of the track. All the children had been brought up Jewish, with a Bar Mitzvah for David, and Bat-Mitzvahs for the girls, Sunday School (which they hated), and Youth Group (which they loved)—in fact, the whole works!

But all this had happened to Ruth when she was fifteen years old. Now at twenty, she was very mature, and treated such insults with good humor and quiet disdain, because she was not by nature pugnacious. She was tall and athletically built, but with those beautiful blue eyes and pert, aquiline nose—which she had inherited from her mother's side—she carried herself with an elegance that her sisters found difficult to emulate. That elegance, too, came from her mother, who had been the old Earl's hostess at all official functions, and, when required by him, still was.

This was the Samuelson household, a mother and wife, one son and three daughters, spread out in the living room of the Hampstead flat, missing only General Sir Joshua Samuelson, Military Attache to the Indian High Commission in London, whose arrival was eagerly awaited that Saturday afternoon. The Indian High Commissioner had been recalled for consultations to New Delhi to discuss the purchase of sensitive, anti-terrorist arms from a foreign source, and these had stretched out longer than any of them had expected—a full month—leaving the Samuelson family fuming at the inconsiderateness of the Indian Government and the Indian Prime Minister! Joshua would have been forced to stay out there even longer—the Indian High Commissioner was still out there—had there not been a long-standing invitation from the Queen for tea at the Palace that very Sunday afternoon. And so in the interests of foreign relations with Her Majesty, the Queen, the Prime Minister of India and the Indian High Commissioner had relented, and sent him back on a commercial flight to rejoin his family in London.

"Sitting there, Susan, and looking every minute into the street isn't going to bring your father home any sooner, is it?" Julia said. "Come here, darling. Sit with me, and tell me how your day was."

"I know, Mamma," Susan said, addressing Julia in the Indian style, "but I've missed him. I missed him when I wasn't there to see him off—and I miss him now; I'm not ashamed to admit it. You missed him most of all; you were sobbing your heart out for him!"

"I was not. You're not going to tell, Pappa that? Are you? He'll think I'm a little crybaby."

"I already have, Mummy," Susan said cheerfully, now addressing Julia in the English style. "And so have David and Sarah and Ruth. They backed me up, so there's no point in denying it—which I know you wouldn't. There we were, the four of us playing acting charades—David and I against Sarah and Ruth—when we hear the sound of silent crying—oh, so soft, we didn't, at first, even know what it was? Then Ruth said:

'Is Mummy crying?' So we, all of us, crept softly to your bedroom door and, unashamedly, listened at it—and we knew. We rushed in to comfort you, and you know the rest. Weeping like a lovesick girl for your husband! How long have you two been married? Let me see. David's twenty-four, so it has to be at least 25 years. Now I can imagine one of us girls—or even David—weeping at separation from their true love, after a few weeks of marriage—but after 25 years?"

Susan left her bench seat in the recess of the window, and went and sat beside her mother on the sofa, folding Julia's hand in her own.

"Then the four of us held—what would Pappa say?—a 'Council of War', and we decided, unanimously, that we had to call Daddy—and we did."

"You didn't!"

"Oh, yes, we did. There's a four-and-a-half hour time difference between England and India in June—they're ahead of us—so he was in the hotel and just getting ready for bed. Oh, was he delighted to hear from us! We spoke to him, all four of us, for more than an hour—I shudder to think what our telephone bill is going to be this month—but he said he'd wangle something somehow, and he'd be home as soon as he could. Then we reminded him of the Queen's invitation—he'd quite forgotten all about it, so aren't you glad we called him?—and that made him practically whoop with joy, because then he said he knew he'd be home this Saturday."

"So tell me, Susan," Sarah said, coming to her mother's rescue, "why weren't you there to see Pappa off to New Delhi? We were all ready—but you weren't there. So where were you? We would have asked you earlier, but Daddy forbade it! 'She's eighteen', he said. 'She is entitled to tell us when she is good and ready to tell us!' Then I grumbled: 'You didn't make the same allowance for me when I turned eighteen!' Daddy laughed, and kissed me—we were in the car and I was beside him—and said: 'You're right, Sarah. As my first daughter, I was more protective of you than I should have been. I'm sorry. Forgive me?' Tell me—after that—what could I say? Mamma clung to him on one side and I the other, all the way to the airport. But we all, by a vote, decided—if you hadn't already told us—we'd ask you the day Daddy came home—not before—and that is today. So, Susan, why weren't you there with us, when we were seeing Daddy off?"

Ruth said: "Yes, where were you? Daddy waited as long as he could. The driver was getting real impatient and telling Daddy, in Hindi, respectfully, they'd be late and the Indian High Commissioner might be upset—and yet Daddy told him to wait! They'd leave when he said so! So we all waited until, finally, Daddy gave him the signal to proceed. Then he drove like a lunatic, breaking every speed limit. We were stopped twice; it was only Daddy's diplomatic immunity that saved us that day. Finally, the police realised they had better give us a police escort rather than have him kill a few people along the way—and all because of you."

"I've told you," Susan said patiently, wiping her glasses, first breathing on them for clear lenses, "I was taking my 'A-levels' in the college hall at the University of London near Russell Square—which, by the way, I think I've aced. Won't Daddy be pleased!"

"Yes, he will, Child."

"Child?" Susan said.

"An Indian and Pakistani word of endearment for a son or daughter. I was in Pakistan—Karachi to be exact—and I'd gone to see Begum Rehana, the wife of Colonel Rashid Khan who'd been murdered—and they thought Daddy had killed him! She was much older than me—fifty; I was twenty-eight—and she used it for me; the very first time anyone had. I loved her for it."

"Who's 'they'?" David asked.

"Pakistani Military Intelligence. They were out to kill Daddy—for revenge. So I went to see the widow—and she told me she didn't believe for one moment that Daddy had killed her husband—they were like brothers! Though they had fought each other in the war. He called Pappa 'The Lion of Lahore' and Pappa called Colonel Rashid Khan 'The Lion of Amritsar'. We'd been married four weeks—I was pregnant with David, though I didn't know it until a week later—and they were all out to kill my husband! I could hardly allow that, now could I? But it was touch and go, and were it not for Solomon Uncle, I would have been a widow with one child—and the three of you wouldn't even be here with me today."

"Who's Solomon Uncle? Why have we never met him?" David asked.

"Now let me see if I can straighten some relationships out for you all. You do know that Daddy had a younger sister who died young. She had a heart defect. Susan, you are named after her."

They nodded.

"She had a professor of meteorology, David Abrams—and David you're named after him. Well the professor and his student fell in love with each other and they had a few years together—no children—before she died. So David Uncle, in America, is Daddy's brother-in-law. His father was General Sir Solomon Abrams—who saved Daddy's life. It's a long and complicated story—and parts of it are still classified. But Solomon Uncle and Begum Rehana kept Pappa alive—while I ferreted out Colonel Rashid Khan's real murderer in the Thar Desert."

"The Thar Articles?" David said. "I knew it!"

Julia looked at him anxiously. "What do you know about 'The Thar Articles'? It puts India's security at risk and, even after 25 years, it's still classified information. How did you learn of them?"

"Grandfather told me," David said. "He was one of the Directors of MI-6—we all knew that, Mamma—and he realised, last year, that if I was going to be a good twelfth Earl, he'd better take me under his wing and tutor me in some aspects of military intelligence. But rest easy, Mummy, other than these three, blabbermouths, here, India's secrets are quite safe with me."

Julia rolled her eyes to the heavens.

"Besides, tons of people know of the part he played in setting up the route through India, for arms to the Afghan mujahidin fighting the Soviet invasion of Afghanistan; the arms routed through Sind in Pakistan were being sabotaged by the KGB. Daddy was given his knighthood, by the Queen, a few years later, after the Soviets had pulled out of Afghanistan. We were all there—and we were ever so proud of him! What I don't understand, yet, is how an Indian citizen was permitted by the Indian Government to accept the knighthood?"

"Daddy has dual citizenship. The Indian Government, for his services, made an exception in his case. They promoted him to General; the British Government gave him a knighthood; the Americans ignored him; and I gave him four of the most loving, beautiful children in the world! He says he got a good bargain—at least from me—for putting his life on the line. The people who deserve recognition don't always get it. And Begum Rehana is one of them. She could have given PMI the information they needed to find Daddy and kill him—but she didn't! She wanted to keep her husband's trust. That is honour for you—military honour, a military wife's honour, and, I trust, a military child's honour too."

"Ask me anything you wish, Mummy," Susan said quietly. "I'll tell all of you everything. I've nothing to be ashamed of. When I got out of the exam hall, Florenzo was waiting for me."

"Ah ha!" Ruth said. "I knew it. Cherchez l'homme!"

"I didn't know Florenzo was an 'homme'?" Susan said, teasingly. "I thought he was our first cousin—being Daddy's brother's only son—also the childhood friend we've known for all of his lifetime and ours, in addition to being like us half-Indian and half-European, and a very nice boy—if a little aggressive. Is he an 'homme'?"

"I quite agree," David said. "Well said, Susan. And before you start on Rachel, let me say the same for her. She is Joe Uncle's only daughter, our first cousin that we've known and played with and, yes, loved since childhood. If you want to make any remarks about either of them, you ought to do it now—before we see them this evening for Saturday evening dinner. Because they are coming here, tonight, for dinner, and I, for one, am looking forward with great anticipation to having Rachel sit beside me at the table—as she always has for the past umpteen years."

"In addition to which," Sarah said, gravely, "the two of them have seen the four of us stark naked. And we've seen them too—the same way—stark naked."

"What!" shrieked Susan. "When has Florenzo seen me naked? Or me seen him? It's a very bad joke to make in front of Mamma here. What will she think of us? And just when she told us about military honour. Do you think I'd take off my clothes in front of him? You must be mad to say such things in front of Mummy!"

"Mad to say such things in front of Mummy? She was there. All six of us, and Lysa Aunty too. Isn't that true, Mamma?"

"Yes, dear. But Susan doesn't remember because she was four years old at the time. I wondered when she'd find out—and this seems as good a time as any. Would one of you like to tell her about it—or shall I?"

"I think it's best you tell the story, Mummy. She might think we were making it up."

Julia smiled at the thought of it.

"Susan," she said, "do you remember the pond at the bottom of the estate in Bromfield House?"

"Yes, I do. It always had clear water because it was fed by a little stream at the top and drained back into the stream at the bottom; the water in the pond was crystal clear. It wasn't very deep, and you let us swim in it—as I recall—but we always had our swimsuits on; never naked!"

"Yes, dear. But for this one time, when you were four years old—that makes Ruth six years old, Sarah was eight, Rachel was eight too, David was ten, and Florenzc was ten too. You were the youngest which is the reason you don't remember it—but they all do. Well, Lysa Aunty had brought her two over, and I had the four of you, and Emma had put together a picnic lunch with plenty of chicken sandwiches and potato salad and some of her delicious cup cakes, and orange juice. We'd gone over to the pond to have a picnic, and just before we sat down and laid out the goodies, the six of you came to the both of us, stood in a line and asked: 'Mummy, can we go swimming?' Now I really don't know whose idea it was—Sarah or David will tell us in a minute—but the one who was their mouthpiece—was you."

"What? Why me?"

"Because, darling, you were the youngest, and so the least likely to be told off for asking. But today, I'm going to find out, whose idea it really was—because I know it wasn't yours. Out with it David; come on Sarah—you started this story. Whose idea was it? And don't pin it on one of your cousins, because it wasn't their turf; they could not have come up with it."

"It was mine," Ruth said, quietly. "You know I've always been a tomboy. The boys had taken off their shirts and were splashing in the pond—while we girls had to have everything on. It didn't seem fair to me then, though it seems different to me now. So I broached the idea of asking you and Lysa Aunty for permission to swim without any clothes on—and they all went for it without a moment's hesitation. Then, of course, we wanted someone to actually ask the permission—sort of bell the cat—and we settled on Susan. As you say, Mamma, how could you or Lysa Aunty reprimand a four-year-old for asking permission to splash around in the pond without any clothes on?"

Susan looked reproachfully at her Mother.

"And you said 'yes'?"

"Not immediately. Lysa Aunty and I raised the usual objections. I recall me saying: But you don't have any swimsuits on. If you swim with clothes, they'll get wet."

"To which you replied: 'It's all right, Mamma, I'll take them off'. Which is what you proceeded to do. Then Lysa Aunty said: 'But we don't have any towels to dry you all after you come out—for the picnic lunch.' To which David and Rachel both pointed out, almost simultaneously, that we were sitting on two towels, and there were two unused ones in the picnic basket."

Julia looked at Susan, and was relieved to see that the shock of discovering that she'd been seen naked by Florenzo had been replaced by amusement at the incident. After all it was at the tender age of four years—and that didn't count, because she had filled out, in all directions, quite considerably since then.

"Well, Lysa Aunty and I, we looked at each other. Then she shrugged her shoulders and rolled her eyes to the heavens, and asked for permission from one of the Catholic Saints, while I took shelter behind the thought that Moses had been put naked in the little boat to be found by the Pharaoh princess—and we both said 'yes'. After that there was mayhem. Susan was already naked, the five of you followed suit right there in front of us, dumping the clothes, indiscriminately, either in my lap or Lysa Aunty's lap, which made dressing you all up a little confusing. If I recall, and Lysa Aunty might remember it better—feel free to ask her—I helped Florenzo, Sarah and Susan to get dressed, while Lysa Aunty helped David, Rachel and Ruth in the same way. I told Daddy immediately he came home, and Lysa Aunty told Joe Uncle about it too—and they both laughed heartily, and said they'd remind you all of this when you were twenty years old—and get a good laugh at your embarrassment. But I don't think they remember the incident, so unless you want to be reminded and embarrassed, I'd give the subject a wide berth."

"So having now established," Sarah said, "that Florenzo is not an 'homme' but our cousin and our childhood friend, I think we all—especially Mamma—would still like to know what he was doing outside the Hall where you were taking your 'A-levels'? Oh! I almost forgot—congratulations, Susan, on acing those wretched 'A-levels'! I mean it. With my scores, I could never have entered Oxford or Cambridge—only you and David could." Sarah went to Susan, sat beside her on the sofa, and hugged her warmly. David and Ruth went behind the sofa, and kissed Susan on the head.

"Susan," Julia said, "please tell us—but only if you want to; not otherwise."

"Oh, I want to, Mamma. It's being weighing on me too. So what could be a better time than this for me to 'fess' and tell why I wasn't there to see Daddy off? I'd just emerged from the Hall, feeling really good about the exam—and there, right in front of me was Florenzo. So of course I told him excitedly how I'd aced it, and he congratulated me—as you all did—by hugging me and kissing me on the cheek. Then he suggested a light snack and a cup of tea at the restaurant. Well, Oxford Street is not far from Russell Square, and I had plenty of time—so I said, why not?"

"What was he doing there?" Sarah asked. "Did he know you were taking your exam in there?"

"I don't know, dear. Maybe you can ask him when he comes over this evening. I don't mind at all; I've wondered about it too. Maybe it was accidental; maybe not. But he was there, and we were just celebrating my joy, I suppose. Well to make this story as short as I can, we went to the restaurant and Florenzo opened it up with his keys—they were closed after lunch and before opening in the evening for dinner, as they normally do—and so in we went and sat and talked for a few minutes. I told him I was seeing Daddy off, so if he was going to get us a cup of tea he'd better get on with it. So he went into the kitchen and put the kettle on and we talked some more while it was coming to a boil."

"Was Joe Uncle or Lysa Aunty or Rachel or Granpda Romano in the flat upstairs?" Julia asked.

"No. He'd made that quite clear as soon as we entered the restaurant that they were out—Grandpa Romano had gone for some groceries he needed; Joe Uncle and Lysa Aunty were at the movies, and Rachel was meeting with David somewhere."

"Really?" Ruth said.

"Yes," David said. "I'm going to Sandhurst soon; there were things I had to discuss with Rachel—and yes they're private matters which I will be only too pleased to talk about—but not today."

"Why don't you ask me what we talked about?" Susan said, laughingly. "Because I'll be only too happy to tell you that what we talked about was David and Rachel, and how concerned he was about his sister—he didn't think David was really serious about her—and he didn't want her to get hurt. He'd heard that quite a few girls at Cambridge—so Florenzo said—have been throwing themselves at David. After all David is going to be the twelfth Earl of Bromfield. I couldn't confirm or deny anything because nobody tells me anything," Susan wailed in mock sadness.

"Please," David said, "can we get back to Susan? She's all alone with Florenzo—with that Italian blood of his—in the restaurant. Then what happened?"

"That's exactly what Florenzo was saying about Rachel—her Italian blood! But never mind, we won't go into that now. Why is half-Italian blood supposed to be hotter than half-Indian blood anyway?"

They all burst out laughing, which eased the tension in the room. They were not sniping at each other; they were loving siblings—and a doting mother—taking a normal, healthy interest in each other's affairs. And if they couldn't, who could?

"Then what happened, dear?" Julia asked.

"Well, Florenzo didn't like some of the things I said in defense of David. He was upset and angry, and he went off into the kitchen, and the next thing I heard was a terrifying scream. He'd poured the hot kettle of boiling water over his left hand instead of into the teapot! He was in terrible agony, Mamma. So I called Emergency for an ambulance. It took ages to get there. Then we got him to the hospital near Marble Arch where they took over an hour attending to his burns. He may have scars for life on that left hand—but otherwise no permanent nerve damage."

"You poor dear," Julia said, drawing her close with the arm around her and kissing her on the head. "It must have been so terrible for you, but you did the right thing—looking after him until he was in competent hands."

"Well, then we took a cab back to the restaurant, and I put him into bed—fully dressed! I stayed until Joe Uncle and Lysa Aunty came back from the movie, after which I took off, but by then Daddy's Indian Air Force jet had already left for New Delhi."

"So what did you do then?" Ruth asked.

"I came back here—and wept."

Sarah said, "I'm so sorry for being such a bitch about it. Forgive me? But why didn't you tell us earlier?"

"Because Florenzo, specifically, didn't want me too. He insisted on it! I had to honour his wishes too."

"Forgive me, too?" Ruth said. Susan nodded to both.

"What about you, David?" Julia said. "Your sister's pardon for misjudging her?"

"I will, if you want me too, but I've already told her I understood fully—a month ago. Rachel filled me in with all the details of their meeting, that very day, and we had a serious talk about it. I was sorry that Florenzo is so protective of Rachel he can't see straight—pouring an entire kettle of boiling water over his hand!"

Julia relaxed backwards into the sofa. It was not surprising that her girls were so beautiful, because Julia had been a stunningly beautiful woman herself, with brown hair and brown eyes, with an aquiline nose, tall—she towered above Joshua in high heels—elegant and statuesque. Now twenty-five years later, her beauty had not left her; rather it had a pleasing touch of maturity that made her still every bit as exciting to Joshua as on the day he had first met her. The hair had a few streaks of gray—she refused to colour her hair—and there was a hint of a double chin that added charm to the neck. She had put on a few pounds, in the right places, which made her even more desirable. At the age of fifty-three—Joshua was sixty years old—she was once asked, quite innocently, by an MP's wife at a function hosted by her Grandfather, the eleventh Earl, if she was Joshua's eldest daughter? Julia treated the remark with good humor, but Joshua and the three girls were tickled at hearing it, and sometimes teased her about it.

Susan looked at her watch.

"Shouldn't Pappa be coming home now? I thought he'd be here long before this."

"Don't forget, Susan, Pappa is coming home on a commercial flight—not an Indian Air Force plane. He'll be here, darling, don't worry. Commercial airlines rarely keep to their scheduled arrival times," Julia said.

A worried thought crossed into Sarah's eyes. Though she freely admitted she hadn't the best 'A-level' scores—as David and Susan—she was the most sensitive to nuances, and Susan's longing for her father left an anxious dread in her. She longed to ask—and kept silent. But it wasn't only Sarah who was sensitive to the strange vibes that kept her looking worried; Julia, too, knew her children so well that their worries did not escape her either.

"What is it, Sarah? What bothers you? Why don't you ask? Instead of keeping it all bottled up—and I've noticed it at other times too. Does Susan's longing to see her father bother you?"

"No! No! Of course not."

"What then?"

"It's just that—never mind; it's not important."

"But it is, darling. You're my eldest daughter. You've looked after Ruth and Susan like a mother hawk—and I love you for it. Why don't you tell us what is bothering you?"

"Wouldn't it be better if Susan were out of the room?"

"On the contrary," Julia said, "it is essential that Susan be here, because she has to give me her permission to explain away what is bothering you."

"So you know?"

"Of course. And so does Daddy. And so does Susan."

"Mamma, why don't you tell her? I hate to see Sarah suffer on my account. Please tell her—you have my full permission. And if she feels more comfortable, I will leave the room now, so that you can speak freely."

"No! Either you stay and hear me as I talk to all of them—because I'm sure those thoughts and doubts have bothered the others too—or the matter is closed."

"What bothers Sarah," Ruth said, always the forthright one, "is whether your love for our Pappa is not—how shall I put it—'unnatural'? Your extreme concern for him, his well-being, his safety. We too love him—I know I do—but your love is a little 'different'—shall we say?"

Susan smiled. "Unnatural? Different? You had better tell them Mamma before they make themselves sick."

Julia sighed. "The joys of motherhood. Well, sit around and listen. I don't know whether I'll be able to complete it before Daddy comes home, because it is a long story. Perhaps Daddy can complete it when he walks in through that door?"

"Now," David said, "I'm more confused than I ever was. You want Daddy to hear all this?"

"I told you, dear, Pappa already knows it all. It started, about five years ago, when Susan was thirteen years old. We all know how she loves to write. Short stories, plays we've performed, and danced to, and laughed at, and loved. So one day she comes to me with a question. And the question was a simple one:'

'If a bed broke into two, Mamma, would someone under the bed die? Or be cruelly injured? Or just escape with minor injuries?'

"Seemed a simple enough question to me, but I had to know the circumstances: Was the person under the bed a man or a woman? If a woman, was she pregnant? Did Susan—as the author—want him or her to die with a stake of the wooden bed through his or her heart, or did she want him or her to escape with minor bruises? What did the story demand of her as the writer?"

Julia paused. Nobody heard the traffic outside on Fitzjohn's Avenue, or the ticking of the grandfather clock in the room, or the sound of their own heartbeat.

"So I asked if I could read the story, and, reluctantly, she agreed. It wasn't very long; I forget the length of it—maybe ten pages?"

"Twelve, Mamma."

"So I read it, with Susan in the room, and, to say the very least, I was disturbed by it. You have to remember it was a story written by a thirteen-year-old. It was about a man—a very cruel man—and his obedient wife. They slept on a single bed—not a double bed, like Daddy and I have; not a queen size bed—just a single bed. And the reason this very cruel man would not allow his wife to sleep on anything larger is because he would wake up in the middle of the night to exercise his lust on her. 'I am your husband!' he screamed at her when she at first protested. 'Your body belongs to me—day and night!' Even after all these years I still am able to quote from the story. That, darling, is how good a writer you are."

"Thank you, Mummy. Then what happened?" And this from Susan!

"Well, the wife realised he wasn't going to change, and rather than die of sleeplessness, she started to study his sleep patterns. What she found was that he awoke once around 2:00 AM demanded his husband's rights—or whatever—and went off to sleep again. Fortunately for her, he snored, and so she knew precisely when he was asleep again. So what this inventive woman did was to fix a little bed underneath the bed—a thin mattress with a light covering—and using audio ear phones she set her alarm for a quarter to two; no one could hear the alarm go off but her, when she climbed softly onto the bed, gave him his husband's rights—or whatever—waited until he started to snore, climbed back into her bed below the bed, with the alarm set for a quarter to six—he woke at six—climbed back into bed above, gave him his 'whatever' and thus gave herself a reasonable night's sleep."

"Perfect!" Sarah said. "Oh, Susan dear, how do you think of such plots?"

Susan smiled. "It was a mistake I made, which I deeply regret, and will never make again. I wrote what I saw—instead of writing what I know."

They didn't understand. Ruth looked at her inquiringly, but Susan pointed to Julia and waved her on. Susan's face was flushed and tense.

"Well," Julia continued, "this went on for a few months—very satisfactorily to both parties concerned—until one day at the midnight hour, the cruel husband—who had had a drop too much—awoke with a nasty headache, reached for his wife, found her missing from his side, and started screaming and yelling and creating hell, bouncing on the bed in terrible anger—when the wooden bed broke right down the middle."

Julia stopped. She was anxious to finish the story before Joshua was home—it was well past the hour he was expected. The plane was on time; they'd checked that. He had diplomatic immunity, the Military Attache's limousine would be waiting for him at Heathrow; so why the delay?

"So what ending would you three have suggested to Susan?" Julia asked.

"I would have had the wife crawl out from under the bed, uninjured, reach for the small skillet under the bed that she kept specially for such an occasion—and clobber him on the head, and keep on clobbering him until he screamed for mercy!" David said.

"I would have had much the same ending," Ruth said, "except that I would have had her hit him with the skillet—in the you know where, damaging the you know what—so that he'd never again lust after her, or any other woman for that matter, ever again!"

"Oh, dear!" Julia said. "Well, your turn Sarah."

"I don't know. Perhaps, if he'd been shown earlier in the story with some element of humanity in him, when he has that headache, she tends to him—lovingly—and he reforms. He realises what a gem he has for a wife—and they live happily ever after, with his lust at controlled intervals being permitted, in consultation with his wife? After all, Susan, we're all capable of reform, aren't we? So what advice did you give Susan, Mamma?"

"I asked for more time. I then discussed it with Pappa. I asked him to be in the same room with us when I spoke. I told Susan—and correct me if I misspeak, Susan—a story. And, please, when I tell the story now, I don't want any interruptions from the three of you."

David, Sarah and Ruth nodded, wondering what was to come. This was Julia's story:

"There was a very brave Indian Army Colonel, who married a rather simple-minded English girl—who just happened to be from the royal family—though he didn't care for that one bit! He just loved her and he married her. After a brief honeymoon, that was fractured, they were recalled to England because he was on assignment—what and where is not important. At her ancestral home they were put in her old rooms—that had only a single bed in it. She wanted to have it immediately replaced by at least a double bed, but he put his foot down and said: No! So, being very much in love with him, she went along with it—though that first night was one she'll always remember. They slept all entangled; he had his arm over her breast, his hand into her armpit, and his thigh all over her thigh, and his you know what, pressed into her rear. He fell off to sleep immediately; she could not, and when finally, he went into deep sleep and turned over, releasing her, she went right back to doing exactly what he'd been doing—to prevent him from falling off the bed! What a night! Well, to cut a long story short, she got used to it, and found it difficult to sleep without him beside her. He mellowed a little bit when he found she was pregnant with their first child, and agreed to a double bed—no queen size for him, though. Are you all with me?"

They nodded silently.

"It was about six weeks later, they were invited to tea with the Queen. The assignment had been completed successfully by him—he had nearly lost his life—and this simple-minded English girl decided to dress like a commoner. I recall she had on a simple Indian batik dress, and her hair in a pony tail. In their past visits to the Queen she had always had her hair up in a bun and wearing a formal royal gown, as befitting a member of royalty. She didn't want him to be hurt, because the Queen had made remarks—complimenting him on his choice of a wife, no doubt—how his English wife would have made a 'worthy Queen for the Prince of any realm'—remarks he agreed with! But she thought he might be hurt by such remarks, and so to protect him she dressed like a commoner. He noticed immediately, and in order to set him at ease, in the conversation, she said: 'so you think I'm being condescending to you?"

'He said, and I quote, because those few sentences have burned into my mind: 'I have been in two wars, Julia. I sent men into battle who didn't come back, and even though I was there with them on the frontlines—I was lucky; like your Father, they weren't—they come back to haunt me. Even in such nightmares—and I have them Oh! so very often—I would never think you were being 'condescending' to me.'

'It had taken this simple-minded English girl six weeks to tumble to it, that the reason for the single bed was because this Indian Army Colonel was having nightmares of his battles in the wars—of brave men he had 'sent' to their death, of wives he had converted into widows, of children he had made fatherless, of mothers who had lost their sons—and at those times he needed to reach out to me for comfort—not lust! And I had badgered him for a double bed?"

Susan put her face into Julia's shoulder and was weeping unashamedly. Julia, too, was in tears.

"Have any of you had real nightmares?"

"No," Ruth said, quietly. "I can't say for David and Sarah, but I haven't had any. We had two loving, protective parents and a wonderful childhood."

"In a real horrible nightmare, you are not fully awake but you are sweating and shivering and you desperately want it to go away—but it won't! And you reach out to someone—anyone—your wife beside you, and the touch of her warm body, even if she is asleep, brings immeasurable relief and peace to the tortured mind begging for comfort—and I wanted to sleep apart from him? Yes, apart! Because in sleep, and in his nightmares, even a few inches away from me made it seem like there was a mile wide chasm between us that he could not cross—for that comforting touch of any part of my body that would ease him out of his torture and back into sleep."

Julia comforted Susan who was still weeping.

"When I wrote that story, Mamma, how could I have known? I saw a single bed at Bromfield House in the West Wing—your rooms—that could barely hold you! And while there is a double bed in your bedroom in this flat, there has always, always, been a single bed there. I was so angry with Pappa, for what I thought he wanted the single bed for. Why couldn't he have told us?"

"It's not the sort of thing an Indian Army Colonel talks about to his children. He wants to protect them—not have them worry about him and try to protect him from hurt! Why don't you tell them the end of the story, Susan. I'd like that."

Susan dried her eyes on her mother's shoulder and said: "It ended by this rotten thirteen-year-old writer going to her knees before this brave Indian Army Colonel, clasping him by the knees, putting her head in his lap, and sobbing her heart out like a six-year-old baby, while he patted her head and comforted her. She saw the offending pages of the story in her mother's hand, arose with a bound, grabbed the pages from her mother and consigned them to the fireplace, where the roaring fires took that piece of garbage where it needed to go—up the chimney! End of story."

"Not quite," Julia said, with a smile. "Since that very day, Susan's attitude to Pappa became more protective, almost 'motherly'! He noticed it too, and we talked about it. And we came to the conclusion that if that was the way she was seeking solace, and was at peace with herself, who were we to discourage it? Is it 'unnatural'? Maybe. Is it harmful to anyone? No. Does it break any social norms? No, because, strangely, Susan 'mothers' me too! I have to say, I rather enjoy being 'mothered'. Children do it all the time, in later old age, when the parent or parents suffer from senility, or dementia, or other mental illnesses, and revert back to being 'children' again. Provided there is no abuse of the parent, or usurpation of authority, or disrespect—and Susan has always been a very devoted child; our 'baby', as Pappa calls her—why can't children 'mother' their parents? Now, have I answered your questions?"

"Not quite, Mamma," David said. "Why did you agree to the double bed in this flat here in Hampstead?"

"When I first suggested a double bed I wasn't aware of his nightmares! The reason I'd given him was that when you all were little you might want to climb into bed with us—in case you had a bad dream? When I offered to go back to the single bed, Daddy, said: No! He wanted to have pillow fights, and you couldn't very well do that with a single bed. He thought it might be therapeutic for our marriage—or so he said with a twinkle in his eye—if he could whack me with a soft pillow once in a while—and be whacked by me too. So though the bed is a double bed, we always sleep holding each other; either he is cuddling me—or I cuddle him. Do you remember the pillow fights we used to have?"

They all shouted in delight at the thought of those pillow fights.

"Don't I?" David said. "It was always 'boys against girls', if I recall."

"Yes," Ruth said, "and I always resented that when I got older. Why couldn't I partner Pappa? I was as good as any boy."

"Well, Ruth," Julia said, "that was the precise reason. Daddy's a bit of an Indian male chauvinist—and he'd be the first to admit it! Now how could he make both sides even, if you were also on his side? This way we were four against two—because, to him, women are the weaker sex—and by giving me a strong one like you made the battle more even."

"That's right," David said. "He always considered it a 'battle'. He'd get together with me before one of these fights, and we'd plan 'strategy'. And now I see why. He'd take on Mamma and Ruth, leaving Sarah and Susan to be whacked by me. They were fun, those pillow fights; I miss them."

They heard the key in the door as General Sir Joshua Samuelson—to the rest of the world, but a husband or darling or Pappa or Daddy to the five in the room—entered it. With only a cabin airbag; no other luggage of any sort. He dropped the airbag onto the floor and opened his arms to them.

As was their custom, Julia bounded first to him. He folded her tightly in his arms and kissed her lasciviously on the mouth—indifferent to the presence of his four adult children in the room; 'they've had sex education and know all about the birds and the bees', he'd growled to Julia the first time he'd done it, and she had shyly indicated their presence in the room—swaying her from side to side until every part of her, facing him, was one with him.

Julia burst into tears, and at that all four of their children crowded around to comfort her.

After Julia had separated from him, but with an arm still around him unwilling to leave his side, the children took their turn greeting their father.

As was East Indian custom, David hugged his father and kissed him on the side of the head, patting his back in affection. Though David kissed his mother lightly on the lips when greeting her, his kiss to his father was always on the side of the head. Susan kissed him lightly on the lips and then hugged him tight, and he reciprocated the same way.

They had decided a long time ago—when the children became adults—that they would go whichever way their children chose to take, falling in with their wishes in the manner of how they wished to greet a parent; this was Susan's way, and both he and Julia were happy with it.

As it turned out, this time, Sarah and Ruth went Susan's way. The girls kicked off their shoes, to match their father for height, and then proceeded to lightly kiss him on the lips—in the past it had always been his cheek—after which they put their arms around him and hugged him tight, while Susan broke into the broadest of smiles. It was almost as if she had won the day!

Joshua drew Julia by the hand into the bedroom, telling his children: "I need a bath. I'm travel-stained, and that would never do because we have company coming tonight—I believe? Saturday evening dinner, to celebrate my return from foreign lands? Though anybody who is expecting the gifts I'm supposed to have brought back is going to be mightily disappointed—not you five—because….."

"Because we're just so happy to have you back, Daddy," Sarah said.

"I know, dear, but I thought I'd tell you the reason I'm late coming home is because I came from Bombay to London, and my bags have gone from Bombay all the way to Bangkok! Give me an Indian Air Force jet any day. I had to fill out the forms identifying the bags—and so, too, had a long line of other people—and it all took time. But Mamma and I will be out in a jiffy; if anyone does come early—handle the fort will you?"

"Yes, Daddy," David said solemnly, "you can trust your troops to handle any unwanted intrusion while you and Mamma……"

But, mercifully, neither Julia or Joshua heard him because they had entered the bedroom, and locked the door.

"Why did I get the impression outside," Joshua asked, "that we have now three girls 'mothering' us instead of just the one?"

"Because, dear, I just finished telling them about Susan's story—and your nightmares. You don't mind, do you? They thought Susan's 'mothering' of you was, 'unnatural', and I didn't want the other three to have any misunderstandings about their sister—or you."

"No, I'm happy it's all out in the open. The years have passed, and their frequency is much less, so if you want a bigger bed, it's all right by me."

"No!" Julia said firmly. "I've missed you so much this last month, that we might just go back to the single bed—particularly because we don't have those pillow fights any more. I rather miss them though, don't you?"

"Very much! But the children are not little any more, and we have to let them go. I was thinking of them in the plane coming over. They are so alike in the way they love us—I don't think you can say one loves us more, or less, than any of the others. And yet, they're so different. David is the dependable one—the one they all turn to for help and support. Sarah is the most beautiful one, and even though her A-levels weren't the best, she has made very good use of them at the Polytechnic for a degree in civil engineering. She has admission to the Imperial College of Science and Technology for post-graduate work—the D.I.C, then maybe an M.Sc., why, perhaps, even a Ph.D.? She is so incredibly meek and gentle, her strength amazes me. Ruth, in addition to being very beautiful and superbly built, is the most aggressive one—a fine athlete—and so utterly loyal to her brother and sisters that she would fight for them to the bitter end, if she had to! And our 'baby' is both very pretty and a dreamer, and—like you—a good writer, a great scholar, and leaving us for Oxford in the Fall. Oh, how I hate it when children grow up! Ah, well, we have to let them go. Which doesn't mean that you and I can't whack each other with a soft pillow once in a while?"

Joshua went to the bathroom and turned on the water flow, then pulled Julia onto the double bed.

"They'll hear," Julia said.

"I don't care if the world hears! Besides the water is on in the bathroom. They'll just think I'm luxuriating in the shower."

"You think so?"

"No. Do you care?"

"Of course not, darling. I've longed for you, and you know that. The children told me they'd called you in New Delhi to tell you I was crying like a baby for you."

"That they did. It made me feel so good."

"Oh, you cruel, cruel man! Here I was crying my heart out for you, and when you hear of it you rejoice?"

"Well, maybe, there is a little of Susan's cruel husband in me? Do you think that for a half-hour, or so, I could be that cruel, hard-drinking, paunchy, obscene, revolting husband who lusts after his wife?"

"Darling, cut out the rest and just be husband who lusts after his wife because he's been away from her for a month. Because, whether you like it or not, I'm going to be, for the next half-hour, or so, the seductive, nympho of a wife who has just had her husband delivered into her web. Heaven help that poor man of hers who has made her weep for him, and starved her of love for so long!"

The doorbell pealed outside.

"Ignore it," Julia said. "The troops will handle it."

CHAPTER 2

The first to arrive was the eleventh Earl of Bromfield. Though he was ninety years old, he was still active and very much alive; his eyes sparkled when he saw his great-grandchildren. They crowded round him to hug him, taking great care not to knock him over with their exuberance. When he said farewells to them or to his granddaughter, Julia, his eyes watered, but, by common consent, they all pretended not to notice as he dabbed his eyes—for which he was grateful. Tonight he would not be saying farewell though, because, as was his custom, he sent the Rolls with his driver back to Bromfield, and stayed the night with the Samuelsons. He would sleep in David's room—he'd always been given David's bed—with David in a sleeping bag on the floor. David kept one eye open for the eleventh Earl, in case he should need assistance in the night.

The dinner at the Samuelsons, by tradition, would have been on Sunday night when the Italian restaurant 'Romano and Samuelson' was closed for the day. Grandpa Romano was a devout Catholic and his son-in-law, Joe—Joshua's brother—a non-observant Jew. On Sunday afternoon Grandpa Romano attended Mass with his daughter and his grandchildren; Sunday morning was work for everyone; Sunday evening was a reunion dinner with Joshua, Julia and their family. But this Sunday the Queen had invited 'General Sir Joshua and Lady Julia Samuelson and Family' for a 'tea party', and so the dinner had been arranged for Saturday evening, instead of on Sunday. However, as someone had to close up the restaurant on Saturday evening, Grandpa Romano had sent his regrets to Julia and Joshua. He would be able to manage with the non-family staff that worked on Saturdays, but he could not attend their traditional reunion dinner.

The girls and Julia had cooked—as they always did for their reunion dinner—whatever each felt she wanted to cook! No set menu. Three different tastes of three sets of people; English, Indian and Italian. While each liked the other two types of cooking, the four of them—by common agreement—catered to all of them. Susan made Italian spaghetti and meat balls, spicing the meat balls with garlic and other Italian spices—not Indian ones. In addition, Susan kneaded, rolled and baked the flat breads—chapattis. Sarah cooked a lamb biryani, delicately spiced with coriander, cumin, ginger, turmeric, and cardamom powders. The biryani already had the basmati Indian rice in it, but needed a yoghurt sauce—raitha. Ruth went traditionally English, with fried cod—though she did put some spices in the batter—with lightly salted mashed potatoes, creamed with butter and milk. Julia cooked the dessert. Here she had a problem, because Joe had a touch of diabetes and couldn't take sugar. So she made gulab jamuns with a sugary syrup for the rest of them, and bought a sugar-free apple pie for Joe—that she knew he loved.

The doorbell pealed again, and Joe, Lysa, Florenzo and Rachel were at the door. No sign of either Joshua or Julia. David took it in his stride; he was going to be—like his father and grandfather before him—a military man, and such trivial matters didn't bother him. It was a question of urgency—and where was the urgency? The girls rolled their eyes, in amusement, as they heard their father's fairly tolerable singing emanate from the bathroom adjoining the master bedroom.

"Daddy came home only a little while ago," David said evenly.

"Pappa was ever so travel-stained; he felt he had to have a long shower," Sarah said.

"Mummy's in there—seeing to his well-being," Ruth said, blushing red on realising she'd blown it.

"Mamma's making sure he's got the right towels," Susan said hastily, coming to Ruth's rescue.

"Tell me, children," Lysa Aunty said, with a hint of a smile in her eyes, "how long has your father been away from your mother?"

"One month!" The four voices were almost in unison.

"Well, take it from me," Lysa Aunty said, "neither of them is going to be out here very soon, so you might as well heat the food and set it on the kitchen counters."

"On the contrary," Julia said, emerging, fully dressed in a silk blouse with a printed batik skirt that reached to her ankles, her hair in a pony tail. "Joshua's almost done; he should be out in a few minutes. I'm so glad you all could come."

They all hugged each other. Some, like Uncles and Aunts, were pecked on the cheek; the younger ones gave each other, and received, tight hugs that were well received with laughter, and talk, in language that only they could fathom. Movies they had seen, or should see, or should not see—or whatever!

"I hear," Lysa said, "that Joshua was away for a month, and you broke down and cried for him like a baby; the kids had to call him in Bombay or New Delhi or wherever he was? Is that true, Julia?"

Julia threw up her hands to the heavens. "Is nothing secret, or sacred, in this house any more?"

The six children had stopped their talk to listen to far more interesting conversation between their mothers. Even Joe and the old Earl paused to listen in.

"Yes, I did," Julia said smilingly. "And here I was suffering unimaginable agony at his being away from me, but on being told this, by his children, he said, his heart rejoiced. He was actually happy I was suffering! Now, would someone care to defend him—be his lawyer or solicitor and speak up for him?"

"Why don't I speak up for myself?" Joshua said, coming up from behind her and holding her by the waist; then, as she turned around, planting a robust kiss on her lips. "I'll tell you why I rejoiced. After twenty-five years of marriage, the thought does enter your mind, sometimes, as to whether your wife has not a deep, hidden regret about marrying you; whether she doesn't feel that she wants to spend a month by herself away from you; does she really, really feel your absence? Or even though she's, maybe, happily married to you, she would like you to go away from her for another month, or so, every so often? Well, when your wife dispels such insane doubts—and they are insane—from your mind, by weeping for you, tell me, darling, do you want me to cry about it—or rejoice?"

"Rejoice," Julia said. "I'm so happy you did; I didn't see it that way. Thank you, my love."

"Yes," Lysa said, unwilling to give up the argument or to surrender, "it's all very well for men to say that, but did you weep for her?"

"Weep for her? No, I did not. Did I miss her terribly, call her every third day from India, inquire after her and our children—with some other rather nice, if a little naughty, personal talk—you'll have to ask her."

"Mamma, you told us Pappa called you every third day; but you never told us of his 'talk'!" Ruth said.

"I couldn't," Julia said. "Pappa made me cry every time I put the phone down. I must be getting old."

"Don't you believe it, Julia," Joe said. "Lysa cries like a baby even before I've left for India. At least you show British character—until he's out of the house. But in Italy, they bawl for everything, and at everything!"

They all laughed, as Julia motioned them to the table for dinner. The food had been laid out on the counters; so everyone helped themselves during the meal; they had no servants in Hampstead, though the old Earl had several old and devoted servants—almost like family—in Bromfield.

The seating at the table followed a set pattern. Everyone knew the place they were assigned and would not change it for any other.

Joshua sat at the head of the table, nearest the kitchen. Normally in formal dinners, Julia, as the hostess, would have sat at the other end of the table, designed to serve twelve, but Joshua didn't fancy that at all. He wanted her near him, and not 'jabbering away', as he put it, to strangers at the far end of the room. Ruined his appetite! So in formal dinners given by her grandfather she still sat at the other end, but with Joshua sitting next to her—as the old Earl had the seat opposite to her at the far end of the room.

Tonight the seat at the far end of the room, opposite Joshua was occupied by the eleventh Earl himself, making for the unusual situation of two men at the heads of the table.

Julia sat next to Joshua; Lysa sat next to Julia. They were very old friends—besides being the wives of two close brothers—and they had much they could talk about, including their children, though that was better done in private.

Lysa was on the short side and rather heavily built. She had exciting Italian features of a light-brown, clear, complexion, with black hair cut short, beautiful black eyes with long eyelashes and a small nose and mouth. Even in her youth she had been on the heavy side, with a body that made her very attractive to Joe, who had always fancied heavier women—and still fancied his wife.

Sarah sat next to Lysa, with Rachel beside her. They were the same age, and Rachel needed Sarah to distract her, because David, who was on the other side of her, unashamedly tried to command her entire attention. The person who helped was the old Earl because David was next to him too, and David had to make sure the eleventh Earl was well-provided with food and drink.

Rachel, like her mother, was also not too tall, and a little on the heavy side; she freely confessed to David that she loved good food, and working in a restaurant didn't help any! He'd assured her and reassured her that he liked her just the way she was; none of those super thin models for him—no thank you! But, unlike her mother, she had long black hair that was tied into an elegant bun at the top of her head. Also, unlike her mother, she had large lips, an aquiline nose and large cheeks that turned fully rosy when she blushed. And the nearness to David made her blush very often—a fact that was not lost on either mother at the table in the room.

That made one side of the table.

On the other side of Joshua, the place was assigned to his brother Joe. Joe looked like Joshua in height and build, but he sported a thin mustache and a goatee beard, unlike Joshua who had a thick military mustache on his upper lip, and no goatee. But like Joshua, he wore spectacles that he wiped by breathing on the lenses for cleaning of the eye glasses, a habit that Susan, over the years, had acquired from her father and from him.

Next to Joe was Ruth. They had a lot in common to talk about because Joe, in his youth, had been a long distance runner too, and so they spent many a close moment talking about times and personal records and lost opportunities for winning some of the big races. It was Ruth's ambition, in the mile, to bring her personal best down to 4.18 which would place her in the world class of women milers. No woman had ever run the 4:00 minute mile—and many believed no one ever would! It was one of the reasons that Ruth made fried fish on the days that Joe Uncle came over—Joe Uncle loved fish!

Next to Ruth was Susan, and—no one quite knew how he'd been assigned that seat—next to her was Florenzo.

Florenzo was almost entirely Italian in his looks and bearing—everything from his mother's side. The handsome Italian features with heavy sideburns, dark eyebrows—almost threatening in their ferocity—the light-brown complexion—lighter than Joe's but darker than Lysa's—the aquiline Roman nose and firm mouth. From his grandfather he had height; from his father a slim build. He was tall and wiry—lean but muscular—quite unlike his mother Lysa.

The seat next to Florenzo—in between him and the eleventh Earl—was reserved for Grandpa Romano, the Italian patriarch of the family. Today it was vacant.

The food disappeared as everyone helped themselves; all the cousins had white wine—a fruity riesling—chosen by the girls; Joshua, Joe, and the eleventh Earl had a scotch and soda with their meal, and Julia and Lysa had a glass of sherry. The food and drink flowed fast and free—so did the conversation.

"Florenzo," Joshua said, "I heard you burnt your hand with boiling water the day I was leaving for India? I do hope it is better now. Will there be any permanent scars on it?"

Florenzo placed the back of his hand on the table for all to see. The scar had started to heal and was only very faint.

"So tell us, Florenzo," Ruth said, innocently, "what were you doing outside the Exam Hall when Susan was taking her A-levels? Was it accidental or did you go there to meet with her?"

"Why don't you ask her?"

"We did. She doesn't know. She said to ask you."

There was a moment of deliberation.

"I went there to meet her."

"Oh! May we ask why? As a result of your meeting with her she missed seeing Pappa off at the airport."

"That is precisely the reason I went to meet her!" Florenzo said vehemently. "All of you were so hell-bent on seeing Uncle Joshua off, no one even bothered about poor Susan. I felt sorry for her."

"You what?" Susan said, quietly. "Poor Susan? You felt sorry for me? Do you know that Pappa waited almost an hour for me, and when I didn't turn up—thanks to you!—they had to drive like lunatics to the airport—to a fuming Indian High Commissioner and a waiting Indian Air Force plane. They got stopped, twice, for speeding on the Motorway. Fortunately Pappa has diplomatic immunity and so, finally, the police thought it better to give them a police escort than have them kill themselves—and others. And you felt 'Sorry' for me?"

"Easy, Susan dear," Joshua said evenly. "I don't think Florenzo quite meant it that way. Did you now?"

"No, Uncle Joshua. Not that way at all. I just thought we had some time, before you left, for a quiet chat."

"Oh," Ruth said, "what did you talk about?"

"That's personal and confidential," Florenzo said, airily. "I don't wish to discuss it. May we change the subject?"

"Wait a minute," Susan said. "My sister just asked you a question. Either you answer it—or I will. There are always two persons in any conversation, and what might be 'personal and confidential' to one is not, necessarily, the same to the other. Now, Florenzo, either you tell them or I will—because I think the family has a right to know."

"That's so right, Susan dear," Lysa said. "We are all family—the only one either side has. I think of the four of you as being mine, and I'm certain your Mamma thinks of my two as her own. So please tell us. What was it that prompted Florenzo to come to meet you outside the Exam Hall, and what was it that made him so upset he poured an entire kettle of boiling water over his hand instead of into the teapot? Since then, I have told you, personally, and I will be pleased to tell you, publicly, before all our family here that I am so very grateful to you for being there and being with him until he came back from the hospital, with his hand in a bandage. You saw my reaction when we came home and saw him? I started bawling! And Grandpa Romano was no better. Only your Joe Uncle kept his head—and thanked you before you left. What did Florenzo ask of you that you couldn't give?"

"Ask of me? That I couldn't give?" Susan repeated, mystified. "Oh, no! Lysa Aunty, that's not what we were talking about."

Susan took a deep breath. "Florenzo was concerned about David's keeping company with Rachel and his 'closeness' to her. He thought I ought to advise David to keep away from her—and I told him to take a hike! I told him I would do nothing of the sort—Rachel was a big girl who could look after herself, and my brother was the future twelfth Earl and had more honour in his little finger than he, Florenzo, had in his whole body! That really got him riled up—I was upset too—and the rest you know."

All eyes now turned to David and Rachel. The old Earl who had been listening in avidly to the talk—but keeping out of it—now reached forward and patted his great-grandson on the shoulder. It was a gesture of support for his heir—and the honour of the Earldom.

"I don't see what the problem is," David said, quietly. "Rachel and I like each other's company. We take in an occasional movie—when Florenzo gives her time off from her duties at the restaurant—then some dinner after that, where we talk and discuss the movie—among other things—after which I see her safely home to the flat above the restaurant, kiss her goodnight at the front door—and that's all. What is Florenzo's problem?"

"Let me say my piece too," Rachel said. "We have grown up together—all six of us—since childhood. We are cousins and you could say we are 'flesh and blood'. I like David's company. I feel safe and secure when I am with him because I know I will come to no harm. It is a warm and trusting feeling! Is there something very wrong with that? Does he hold my hand when we walk—yes. Does he kiss me on the lips at the front door—yes. In fact, I'll do it right now!"

And before anyone could say a word, Rachel turned to David, put her hand round his head, pulled him towards her and kissed him, very gently, on the lips. And he responded likewise.

"There! Close relatives and very good friends do kiss on the lips. Mothers kiss sons on the lips; Mamma kisses Florenzo. Fathers kiss daughters on the lips; Pappa kisses me. David is my cousin and my very good friend, and if I kiss him on the lips, I don't suddenly become a trollop—do I?"

Everyone sitting around the table—except Florenzo—beamed at her in delight, but only Joshua said:

"No, dear, you don't. But I am going to play Florenzo's advocate for just a minute—and against my better judgment! He worries about you. Joe Uncle and I had a younger sister, Susan, who has since died. We were terribly worried for her safety and happiness, I can tell you. Julia Aunty met her too, and they got on the way you get on with Sarah and Ruth and our Susan. Florenzo's fears arise, perhaps, from the fact that you are not giving yourself a chance to meet other men; of going out with other friends; of finding someone really special—as I found Julia Aunty, and as my brother found your mother."

Rachel smiled at him. "Joshua Uncle, I am 22 years old. I've just finished a degree in English and Philosophy at the same Polytechnic that Sarah got her degree from. Now she's off to Imperial College for post-graduate work—and I will cook, clean and wait at tables in the family restaurant. Sarah and I had friends at the Polytechnic—we went out with them, always responsibly, I am pleased to report. I have met other men. It's not as if David is the only man I've known from the cradle to the age of twenty-two—is it now?"

"No," David chimed in smiling broadly. "And it's not as if she doesn't, right now, meet any Italian men either. There's this terribly handsome, Italian waiter—that Florenzo and Grandpa Romano have just brought over from Italy—who works with her in the restaurant. He doesn't speak much English, so Rachel has to take the orders from the customers, and he then serves the food. When they work, they're always together."

"Oh, David!" Rachel said, putting her arm in his and pulling him tight towards her. "Don't tell me you're jealous of Alfonso?"

She pointed an accusing finger at Florenzo. "Now look what you've done!"

They all laughed, including Florenzo who threw up his hands in mock despair, abandoning them both to their fates. But David was not going to let such an opportunity pass without gain.

"Actually I was going to raise the question with you, Florenzo, but I didn't quite know how to broach it. Now that you've laid all of your sister's life in the open—on the table so to speak—I've a request to make of you. Please, could you give Rachel at least one morning off from the restaurant? You work her seven days a week!"

"Doesn't she have Sunday off—like the rest of us?" Joe asked.

"Pappa," Florenzo said, "you have Sunday off—the rest of us don't. We all—except you, that is—go to Mass on Sunday afternoon. On Sunday morning, Grandpa Romano and Mamma go off to the meat and produce market for fresh lamb and vegetables. I struggle with the accounts and the stock inventory. Rachel and Alfonso clean up the restaurant and the flat. That includes mopping all the floors, cleaning all the tables and chairs and booths—you don't know how incredibly messy customers, especially little children, can be with Italian food and all the sauces we serve. Then, when Grandpa Romano and Mamma come back, Alfonso, by law, gets the evening off. Which puts all four of us in the kitchens again preparing for Monday's servings. Tell me, Pappa, when do I give Rachel time off?"

They were all silent. Susan almost knew what was coming.

"Unless," Florenzo said, not looking up from his plate, "unless, one of Rachel's other female cousins offered to help out? This spaghetti and meat balls are excellent! With a little twisting to the recipe—Grandpa Romano is the final authority on what is served at the tables; after all we have a reputation to preserve—I think it would be just fine. She will have to mop the floors and clean the tables too—and do all that Rachel does," he added hastily.

Rachel appealed to Susan; Susan nodded with a smile.

"If you mean for me to help out on Sunday mornings, I'll be happy to—if Rachel has the morning off—before our reunion dinner here, that is."

"Susan, dear that is terribly kind of you. I'm not sure Lysa Aunty and I should impose on you in this way. Hell, if you have to mop the floors, I'll do it myself instead," Joe said. "Lady Susan is not mopping any floors in my flat or in our restaurant!"

"No imposition, Joe Uncle. Freely offered by me to help out my brother and my cousin—who is also our dearest friend."

"Then come for lunch with us; be part of our family there, as we are here, today, a part of yours," Lysa said.

She assented, with some misgivings. But this was not the time to raise them.

There was a lull in the conversation as Julia served the dessert. Little glass bowls were passed to her end, and she scooped two of the gulab jamuns into each of them—for starters—with some of the sugar syrup. Joe, of course, made a wry face at being excluded from the 'gulab jamuns feast', as he put it, but graciously accepted a whole sugar-free apple pie.

"So aren't we all going to tea with the Queen tomorrow?" the eleventh Earl asked. "I've received my invitation; I trust you have yours?"

Julia nodded. She would have preferred an avoidance of the subject; Joe and his family, not being royalty had not been invited.

"Which is why I wanted to ask you, Mummy," David said. "Could you, please, call the Palace, so we can take Rachel along. I'm sure she would love to meet Her Majesty, the Queen."

"Oh, could I? I'd love to!" Rachel said. "You can teach me to curtsy."

"Quite impossible!" Florenzo said. "Why are we having this argument all over again? Tomorrow is Sunday. Since I have no help, except Alfonso—and he gets the afternoon off—and Susan is not available to help us, you cannot go. Monday we open for business as usual—for lunch at eleven—or have you forgotten?"

Rachel was silent.

They all knew that Grandpa Romano had placed the labour-side management of the restaurant in Florenzo's charge; Grandpa Romano and Lysa had charge of the kitchen and the menu, while Joe looked after the cashier's desk and the receipt of money. So while the restaurant name had been changed to 'Romano and Samuelson' out of respect for his son-in-law and the name that his daughter and his grandchildren would carry, the restaurant was still his very own. He and his wife had started it more than thirty years ago, when, with their only daughter, they had come to England. His wife had died soon after Joe had married Lysa twice, first in their Catholic church in West London, and then in a synagogue in East London, where Joe—not too well off—had worked in a furrier's shop.

"Never mind, dear," David said consolingly. "You will meet the Queen one day, I promise you."

"Unless," Florenzo said, "Susan would like to change places with Rachel for tomorrow?"

"No!" David said with unusual firmness. "Lady Susan has an invitation to tea with the Queen tomorrow, and that is where my sister is going to be! I'm sorry I brought it up. Matter closed."

The eleventh Earl, Joshua and Julia, their daughters, Lady Sarah, Lady Ruth, and Lady Susan, and Rachel too, all looked at David, and at each other, with the greatest of unabashed delight.

He would make a worthy twelfth Earl!

As they were leaving, Florenzo whispered to his mother: "He doesn't love her; I was only testing him."

Her response was a sharp slap on the back of his shoulder with the palm of her hand that sent him trundling down the last three steps to the landing—faster than he'd anticipated.

"You keep out of your sister's affairs, young man, or Pappa and I will disown you!"

It had been their usual practice, since childhood, that Florenzo and Rachel stayed over for a Sunday night 'slumber party' with their cousins. The old Earl took David's bed, and David and Florenzo, in the past the very best of friends, slept in sleeping bags on the floor. They didn't really fall asleep, but waited until they heard the old Earl snore gently, when they crept to the girls' room, tapping it gently before entering it. The girls awaited them and then the six of them, whispering quietly, would have a glass of milk or orange juice—David did not care much for milk as a drink—and two types of biscuits, that Julia made sure they had plenty of in stock in the flat. The next morning, David or Sarah took Florenzo and Rachel back to their flat above the restaurant, well in time to prepare for the opening of the restaurant, for business on Monday, at eleven in the morning.

Today, because the reunion dinner had been changed to a Saturday, Florenzo was missing. The routine for Sunday had already been outlined by him as 'hectic' and he would not stay for their 'slumber party'. He would have preferred that Rachel come home along with them as well—but his father overruled him.

"You may control the labour in the restaurant, Florenzo," Joe said, "but elsewhere, Rachel is my daughter, and I'll be damned if I let you say where she goes or where she stays!"

So the five of them—four grown girls and one grown man—sat round in a circle like twelve year olds, reliving lost childhood and nostalgic memories of years past. About half an hour later, the girls cleared away the paper plates and serving dishes—now empty—while Susan took the empty bottle of orange juice and the almost empty milk bottles to the kitchen.

On the way back she noticed the light still on in her parent's room.

David was on his way out to his bedroom, but she motioned him, silently, to come back into the girls' room again. He did not understand, but he complied.

Susan called everyone together.

"I feel really bad," she whispered, "that we did not have a coming-home present for Daddy. But I've got a wonderful present for him—right now—if you all agree, that is."

"Present for him? What present?" Sarah said. "We've nothing to give him that he doesn't already have."

"A pillow fight," Susan said.

All of their eyes lit up with anticipation—except Rachel's, who did not understand.

David explained: "You take the softest pillow you have, so that no one is hurt. It's always been boys against girls, ever since I can remember Pappa showing us the game. More like a 'war' he explained to me—being the soldier that he is. Each one—honour bound—counts the number of 'hits' he or she makes on the 'enemy'. Got it? Hits on the hand of the enemy don't count because the free hand is like a shield that wards off the hits from the body. Hits on the back, front, head, and legs do count. Then we total up the number of hits the boys have and the number of hits the girls have; that declares the winner. The time limit is 15 minutes of sheer mayhem. We can climb on the bed, chase each other across the room—but we cannot leave the room. The flat underneath us is vacant, so we can make as much noise as we want to—there will be a lot of laughing and giggling, I assure you. Great Grandfather is so fast asleep—I heard him snoring before I left—so he'll not awaken. Then after that comes the fun part where we all 'make-up with the enemy'—but you'll understand all that before long. We'd better get going before their light goes off. That it's on means they are still awake, and probably reading—they love to read in bed, and so do I."

"But the door to their bedroom may be locked?" Rachel said.

"No. The door is never locked, except when they are doing—you know what. The rest of the night it is always open, because, in childhood, one of us might have a bad dream, or something like that, and come to them for comfort. So the door was always unlocked; we'd go in and snuggle up into bed with them, sometimes all the way into the morning. But the light has to be on before we go in—for a pillow fight."

It was on.

"I'm in my nightdress," Rachel said.

Sarah rolled her eyes to the heavens. "Do you think they are sleeping in their best suit and formal gown—or in dressing gowns and robes? Rachel, they're dressed for bed as we are—Daddy is like David here in his pajamas, and Mummy is in her nightgown like you or I. We've, all, seen them before that way a zillion times, because when we were ill, they'd—both of them—spend the whole night with us. We loved them for it then—and we still do."

"But Rachel doesn't have to come in with us, if she feels uncomfortable in her nightgown in front of them," David said. "We'll understand—and so will they."

"I'm in," Rachel said quietly. "Oh, yes, I'm in there with you all. One for all, and all for one!"

David opened the door, and then with a muted whoop, out of consideration for a sleeping ninety-year-old Great Grandfather—and each armed with a soft pillow—they stormed into the room, taking both Father and Mother by pleasant surprise. Joshua, ever the military man, rolled off the bed, grabbing his pillow as he did, and, whacking Julia with it almost as soon as he had a hold on it, he got in three good whacks, before she responded with her athleticism by rolling off the bed on the other side and out of his reach.

After that it was a free-for–all.

Julia and Ruth concentrated on Joshua. Ruth, particularly, had an agenda she wished to fulfill—a demon she wished to lay to rest—by showing her father that she was every bit as good as any boy in the fight! Her height, athletic build, dexterity, and eye and leg coordination—she was after all a 'miler'—enabled her to pile on the hits, until she saw that her mother, was just standing by, and letting the two of them slug it out without coming to her assistance, so that her father could never say: "yes, dear, but it was two against one!"

It was fairly even, the battle between them. Ruth was taller than Joshua, and so she managed quite a few hits by coming down towards his head, and when his free 'shield' hand was uplifted to defend himself, she swooped low and hit him several times in the waist and legs. But Joshua, being a military man, was able to evade many of the hits by stepping backwards adroitly, closing in around her when her striking hand was lowered to get a few hits in himself.

Their respect for each other's abilities, in battle, rose immeasurably—which is all that either wanted from the pillow fight.

At the other end of the room, David was having a rough time, besieged, as he was, by three opponents. Rachel, he thought, might be an easy target because she had no experience of that 'war'. He was soon disillusioned. She was about the same height as he was and with excellent eye-hand coordination, she countered every one of his strokes with her 'shield' hand, playing as in a team, and allowing Sarah and Susan to clobber David from behind almost at will. And when he turned to them, Rachel got in stroke after stroke until finally, in despair, he threw down his pillow and stood like a statue, accepting the hits from all three with a cheerful smile—until Rachel actually came to his defense by, throwing down her pillow and using both of her hands as shields to protect him from the hits of his sisters.

The fifteen minutes were over; Julia called for a 'truce'; the girls had a runaway victory over the boys—it wasn't even necessary to count the hits.

Then came the ritual of 'making up with the enemy'—which had been religiously done in childhood, with them as little ones. But, of course, they had not had a pillow fight in twelve years!

Would they follow the same ritual?

Joshua and Julia decided to leave it to their children in the room.

What the parents did was to lie on the bed towards its centre, close, in each other's arms—as they had done, in years past, at the end of such pillow fights.

The rest was up to each of their children, to act as they wished—as individuals.

Susan followed her childhood practice of slipping into the bed behind her Father and hugging him tight, her hand around his waist. The last time before, that she had done that, she had been six years old. She would always be the 'baby' of the family.

David had last slipped into the bed behind his mother and held her by the waist when he had been twelve years old. This time, Sarah slipped in close behind her mother, with her arm around her mother's waist, but stretched out to hold her father's hand.

Ruth did precisely what she had done in childhood; she lay down on top of both her father and her mother spread-eagling her arms around the both of them, as if to protect them from harm.

David, wordlessly, lay down on the bed, on his back, at their feet, feeling their bare toes—of all of them—dig into his side. He raised his hands above his head and closed his eyes.

Rachel stood for one long, anxious moment, uncertain of what she ought to do.

There had been lot of laughing and giggling as the girls got into bed with their parents. It came abruptly to an end—with the silence in them all. There was an unanswered question in the mind of each of them.

What would Rachel do? They almost knew, or at least hoped, it would be so.

Rachel got into the bed, at the foot of it, easing herself, gently, on to David, face downwards, so that her body flattened his, and was flattened by it. He lowered his hands around her and hugged her tight. She raised her head and kissed him on the lips as she had done at the dinner table; then she snuggled contentedly into him.

Joshua and Julia permitted themselves a faint smile. They knew that it was coming. Her on top of him.

What better place for it to first occur than at the foot of their own bed, with not only them, but with all his sisters in bed with the two of them?

They all broke into conversation with each other—except David and Rachel who savored the moment, not wanting it to be disturbed even by their speech.

"This was our welcoming-home present to you, Daddy," Susan said, tightening her arm around her father's waist, and digging her head into his back.

"Oh, what a wonderful gift! Couldn't have asked for anything better," Joshua said. "Thank you all. Your gifts will be here, when my luggage comes back from Bangkok. I hope we'll have many more of these—that is so long as you all want to? For fights, such as this one, you all will decide—how we have them, when we have them, how we 'make-up with the enemy', or whatever."

"Well, dear," Julia said, with a laugh, "after that drubbing that you boys received at the hands of us mere girls, would you care for a realignment of the teams for pillow fights in the future, because I'm sure we'll have them once in a while—at least until the girls are married."

"Oh," Sarah said, "and why not after then?"

"Because, dear, you'll then have families of your own—for pillow fights. But that may not be for a while yet, so we can realign the teams, at least for now, for fairer play. Go on, Pappa, I'll even give you the first pick, then I'll pick, and so on. So who's your first choice for team partner?"

There was no hesitation in Joshua's first pick for a worthy partner. Years of Indian—and military—male chauvinism 'passed' away in a single word:

"Ruth."

"I'll take David,"

"Sarah."

"Susan."

"What about Rachel?" David said, anxiously. "We don't want to leave her out, do we?"

"No, of course not," Julia said. "When she is with us, we'll let her choose. If she's mad at you why she could choose Pappa's team so she can clobber you good and proper, and when she's feeling soft and tender towards you, why she could pick ours."

"Oh, please," Rachel moaned, "why do you leave such decision-making to me? If I pick Joshua Uncle's team, David will think I'm mad at him, and if I pick his team, he'll go strutting all over—like a peacock—and boss me around for a week!"

They all laughed as Joshua and Julia eased them out of the bed, and sent them away to sleep.

CHAPTER 3

The Queen had called the party at 4:00 PM. At precisely 3:30 PM, the Military Attache's limousine, chauffeur-driven, pulled up outside the house on Fitzjohn's Avenue. Susan, who was at the recessed window seat, called out "It's here!" and they, in full blown regalia, walked as daintily as formal gowns—some strapless and some backless, covering Lady Julia and her daughters from the shoulder to the ankles, except in Lady Ruth's case where it was still a formal gown fit for presentation to the Queen, but extended to only just below her knees—would permit.

The men were dressed no less formally. General Sir Joshua Samuelson was in his full Indian military general's uniform with all his ribbons—but no holster and no gun! David, too, was in the formal military uniform of a new entrant to Sandhurst.

Joshua dismissed the driver, sending him back to the High Commission by a cab, and elected to drive the limousine himself, with Julia and Susan on the front bench seat with him and the other three in the seat behind. On the excuse that their gowns would get 'all crushed and crumpled' Sarah and Ruth took the window seats, squashing poor David in-between.

Normally the Queen would have invited them for tea. Julia thought it odd that the invitation in this case had read 'party'. She was soon to find out why.

In all the years that the children were growing up, they had been invited very many times to tea with the Queen. Julia's mother, in addition to being related to the Queen, had also been her dearest friend. When her friend lay dying, the Queen promised Julia's mother to look after Julia, who was then just five years old.

Over the years the Queen had come to love Joshua, as a son-in-law as well, particularly when she found out, at their very first meeting, that they both had an abiding interest in the novels of Jane Austen. They were both very knowledgeable too of the nuances in her works, and had spent much delightful time in discussion and discovery.

The tea party had always been just for their family alone, in a small cosy room in the Queen's chambers.

Not this one! This was held in a small banquet hall, and there were more than twenty people in the room. The Queen was already in it, and most—if not all—of the guests had arrived and were drinking, not tea, but a British white wine, that went down surprisingly smoothly. Staff were serving exotic appetizers—like Indian samosas—and the counters had already been laid out with British fare that ranged from 'roast beef and Yorkshire pudding' to 'shepherd's pie' and 'fish and chips'. This last entrée was quite simply because the Queen liked a bit of fish for her dinner, and the Chief Chef at the Palace was well aware of it.

They curtseyed to the Queen and the Duke; Joshua and David bent low over their outstretched hands. They were the last to arrive, so Julia was able to ask in a whisper: "Elizabeth Aunty, what's the occasion?"

The Queen smiled roguishly.

"Julia, my dear, your mother would have wanted it, and I am delighted to give such a party, where some of my grandchildren—and they are my grandchildren, Julia; I promised your mother that—can meet other eligible young men and women, shall we say?"

"This is a surprise, Elizabeth Aunty. You, in the role of a matchmaker? On second thoughts, you would make a great matchmaker! After all you are "Mother" to us all. This party now takes on a meaning I hadn't thought of before. I'd better go and keep a "motherly" eye on my brood. You've done what Mummy would have wanted of you; I had better now go and do what she would have wanted of me."

The party guests consisted of those she knew—even if slightly—and those she did not know at all. Of the ones she knew well, the first person who caught her eye was Cecily, her childhood friend from boarding school in Kent when they had both been teenagers. Cecily saw her too and rushed over as they hugged and kissed each other. Cecily was Julia's age—a young fifty-three—but as different from Julia as one could imagine two close friends to be.

Cecily was small in both height and build, with delicately formed features and a face that was radiantly beautiful, in the classical shape of the nose and the mouth and the small ears. The skin complexion was very fair with long blonde hair that was tied into a classical bun—not unlike Sarah's—at the top of her head. She had been married for almost twenty years to the Earl of Rathbone, who had died five years ago in a tragic car accident on the motorway. She had two children—the present Earl of Rathbone, a shy, retiring, young man of twenty-two, Lord Albert, and Lady Jane, a tall, slim, willowy, blond, and, like her mother, of almost model-like features and beauty. Jane could have easily been a super-model—many an agent had tried to interest her in the profession—but she had chosen to be instead an agent herself—a literary agent. She had a flat in London, and she and the Samuelson girls were great friends. They often went out on shopping sprees together, much to the 'pretence' dismay of their respective parents when they came home with the richness of their 'spoils'!

Lord Albert had intended to enter the British Army—as his father before him—but his father's tragic death had forced on him the duties of Earl of Rathbone, and an estate in Oxfordshire. He was a handsome man, tall and gaunt, with a military moustache not unlike General Samuelson's, and with the same military bearing that Susan's father had. Lord Albert had a degree in Philosophy from Oxford University, and it was, perhaps, his insistence on seeing all sides of any question, that kept him out of most conversations, because while his mind, which was brilliant, thought out the issues, others with more fleeting time span attentions and superficial insights had moved on to other topics. This had happened once too often before, and so, in despair, he had almost ceased to enter most conversations, listening to the views of others while not contributing any of his own. Susan found that rather disconcerting. So one fine day, while taking a walk through the grounds of the estate in Oxfordshire, she broached a philosophical question on the Nature of God and the conflict between evil round us and a meaning and purpose to the universe. She proved right! There was a silence, almost as if he expected her to lose interest in her own question, but when she continued walking in total silence, he expounded his own theories, that, he explained apologetically, resolved the conflict—at least to his own satisfaction. She could not get him to stop talking! Since then she found herself defending Lord Albert's 'tongue-tied' shyness as wisdom and not a form of 'dumbness'.

Lady Jane took a particular interest in Susan's creative writing, and though, with her connections, she had several successful writers on her list, she had been unable to get Susan's work published. Susan was unconcerned about it—she spent more time consoling Jane when a rejection slip came through, than the other way around—because she had a mother's example that failure to be published did not imply she couldn't be a wonderful human being and a warm and loving person. Jane was now persuading Susan to write a novel; Susan had taken that advice seriously, and work on it had begun. When asked when it might be finished, Susan rolled her eyes in mock despair and raised her hands to the heavens, as if only it might know—certainly not she, the poor author!

The second family that the Samuelson's knew very well was Viscount Edward—Cecily's brother—and his wife Begum Naseem Banu, and their two children, Lord Joseph (he preferred the biblical name of Yusuf) and Lady Rehana. Both brother and sister were long-distance runners—Lord Yusuf in the mile and Lady Rehana in the 800 m—and they naturally gravitated towards Ruth. They had all met each other several times before at each other's homes, on the track, in relays across the country, by invitation, because of their nationally recognised times in their chosen races.

Lord Yusuf was a very tall, very thin boy with jet black hair—like his Pakistani mother—and a black moustache and sideburns that merged into a trimmed, short scruffy beard. He had black threatening eyebrows, a semitic hooked nose, and while he had been born in England and educated at one of the finest boarding schools in Sussex, he still adored his mother's Muslim roots. As did Lady

Rehana, who had the exotic quality of a Pakistani beauty with a light-brown skin, but with green eyes, an aquiline nose and large lips—all of which came from her father's English side.

They were so busy comparing notes on the running regimen they had tried to maintain over the spring—and moaning of having fallen so woefully short of their expectations—that they did not notice the not-too-tall, stockily-built man, with red hair, a well-trimmed moustache, kindly eyes behind coral frame spectacles, and a little older than they were, who—with a glass of wine in his hand—had stepped up behind Ruth.

He tapped her on the shoulder and she turned around.

"Lady Ruth?" he said.

"Yes. Do I know you, Sir?"

He smiled: "No, Lady Ruth. But I know you—from the running track, at the London University relays, two years ago. Does that count for an introduction?"

She laughed. "It might. Depends on whether you were cheering me on, or waiting to see me fall."

"Oh, Lady Ruth! How could you say a thing like that? I was cheering you on; you were winning the mile with an almost unheard of time of 4:20, when you slipped and fell. I don't know how you felt, but I have to make a confession—I cried! A grown man like me, but I had a lump in my throat and tears in my eyes. It was one of the saddest moments of my career as a spectator at the track meets. Since then I've seen you several times—you have been devastatingly perfect—but this is the very first time I've had the opportunity of meeting you, and may I say how thrilled I am."

He put forth his hand; she extended hers, but instead of shaking it, he raised her hand to his lips and gently kissed it.

She blushed.

"Look here, you," Yusuf said, "I don't know who you are, but even if this is the Queen's party, you can't barge into a private conversation that my sister and I are having with Lady Ruth. So will you now please buzz off?"

"Yusuf," Ruth said sharply, "don't be so rude! I'm sure the gentleman meant no harm. This is a party where we circulate and mingle—and that is just what he was doing, weren't you, Sir?"

He smiled: "No, Lady Ruth, I came over with the express purpose of saying hello to you. So perhaps your friend is right. I was barging in, and I do apologize. Forgive me," and with a slight bow and an even slighter smile, he turned around abruptly and retreated to the far end of the room. There were a line of chairs set against the wall—probably laid out for elderly guests who might find standing all the time a little tiring. He sat on a chair facing her, and raised his glass of wine to her. She responded likewise, much to Yusuf's anger.

"What bloody cheek!" Yusuf said. "You don't even know his bloody name. Who does he think he is—a bloody French nobleman—kissing your hand in that disgusting way? Better wash it before you eat, Ruth, in case he has salivated all over it!"

"Oh, you are mean," Ruth said. "Why do you dislike a man you've only just met—not two minutes ago?"

"Because he fancies you—though you're too naïve to see it. Not that he'd have much of a chance, would he now, Ruth? Short—you're taller than he is, and in high heels, you positively dwarf him!—stockily built, flaming red hair, glasses! Tell me, Rehana, do you think you could fancy a man like him?"

"I don't know," Rehana said slowly. "David is short and I've always fancied him, though he has never given me any encouragement. Why, Ruth?"

"Because he's already 'spoken for' shall we say?"

"Oh, I didn't know that! Who to?"

"I can't be sure—and feel free to throw yourself at him, if you so choose—but he fancies women heavier than us. He's very fond of our first cousin Rachel Samuelson—but then who can say?"

"But could you go for such a man?" Yusuf persisted. "You'd be ashamed to be seen with him in public!"

"Well, Daddy is shorter than Mummy, and they've been very happily married for 25 years. In fact, if I could have a marriage as theirs, I'd die a very happy woman."

"I'm sure I could put on some weight for David. I am about a year older than him, though," Rehana said, with such a serious face, that Ruth burst out laughing.

"Oh! And what about your dreams of being the 800 m world record holder? You put on a few pounds, and you can say good-bye to competitive running."

"I've been meaning to ask you, Ruth," Yusuf said, changing the subject abruptly. "Rehana and I train on Saturday mornings at the Athletic Tracks on Hampstead Heath. Would you like to run with us?"

"I'm sorry, but on Saturday mornings, the family attends Services at the Hampstead Reform Synagogue. Then we have a light lunch, before cooking for the Sunday reunion dinner. Two of us cook on Saturday; the other two on Sunday. I'm on Saturday. My father's brother, Joe Uncle, and his family—and, yes, Rehana, that includes Rachel—all get together with my great-grandfather, the eleventh Earl, after which she stays over for a slumber party with us girls—and David. I'm sorry, I wish I could be more encouraging, but I can't."

Rehana smiled. "You never know. Tomorrow, I start to splurge on food! Where will running get me? What can I do with records? On the other hand, David, is some catch." But they knew she was only pulling their legs. Rehana was a fine actress!

"But surely the family can spare you, for an hour or so, after the service and before your preparations for your next-day dinner?" Yusuf said, as persistent as ever. "The Tracks are only a mile away from the Synagogue. I've run it before."

"I suppose so; I'll have to ask. Why do we need an hour? Half an hour of hard running is all that I do."

"Well," Yusuf said, sheepishly, "Rehana and I usually go to a Pakistani café round the corner for a cup of tea and some pakoras. We thought you might like to go along with us. If you like Indian food, you'll love our cooking too. A little spicier, I'd say, but no different."

"You're on," Ruth said. "I may say anything against Rehana putting on a few pounds, but I'm not averse to good food myself!"

Ruth turned around to look for her stockily-built admirer; he was talking to her father. A few minutes later he left the room. She felt a pang of disappointment, but seeing the old Earl sitting by himself against the wall, she went and sat with him.

Sitting in a chair along another wall was an older lady, perhaps fifty years old, attended by a young man—her son. They seemed to know no one in the room, and so the young man was keeping his mother company, making sure she was well-provided with food and drink.

Standing by herself in the centre of the room was Sarah, a glass of wine in her hand.

The Queen saw the picture, excused herself from Viscount Edward and Begum Naseem Banu and came over to Sarah.

"My dear, will you permit me to introduce you to a very old and treasured friend of mine, Lady Sophie, and her son, Lord Jacob, Duke of Trenton?"

The Queen took Sarah by the hand and led her over to the older lady against the wall. Sarah curtseyed.

Jacob was taller than Sarah, built like a rugby player, and very handsome, with blue eyes, black hair with sideburns and a well-trimmed beard; yet looked shy and diffident, as if he didn't think he was good enough for her. Lady Sophie motioned Sarah to sit beside her.

"You are the most beautiful woman I've ever seen, my dear," the Duchess said, waving her son away.

"Thank you, ma'am," Sarah said, blushing.

"Tell me, dear, are you Jewish?"

Sarah got up with a bound. She had not been expecting so forthright a remark, especially after the earlier compliment to her beauty. It was almost as if the Duchess was pointing out a contradiction in terms—how could a Jewish woman be so beautiful?—and the remark was offensive to her father's blood, and to her.

She would have curtseyed once more, made her polite apologies, and left the Dowager Duchess of Trenton, but the older lady put out her hand and held Sarah's arm.

"I'm sorry," the Duchess said. "Were you offended by that question? You misunderstand me. Forgive me for being so forthright. Please, would you sit beside an old woman for ten minutes—no more—while I tell you a little story? Then you can avoid me the whole evening—if you wish. The food has been served, but they'll all start eating in about ten minutes. Please?"

Sarah was a gentle girl, brought up to respect her elders; meek and gracious—as her father had said about her. She smiled and sat beside the Duchess, who held her hand and would not release it.

"My father was the Duke of Trenton. I am his only daughter, and so my son, Jacob, is now the present Duke. My own husband, who was—like your father—a colonel in the army, died five years ago."

The Duchess of Trenton smiled easily and paused for a few moments. She was so anxious to detain Sarah that she had been speaking rapidly, and was out of breath.

"Please," Sarah said, "please don't rush yourself. Even if they start the food line, I will get a plate for you and a plate for me—with whatever you wish on it—and you can tell me your 'story' in a leisurely way; we have no ten-minute deadline."

"Thank you, dear. The Queen, was so right when she talked to me about you. Not only are you the most beautiful woman I have ever met; you are also the most gracious."

Sarah blushed again. Her hand was still held by the Duchess; the older lady would not release it.

"My father married a very beautiful and charming lady from the royalty—the daughter of the Earl of Brenwich—and he was desperately in love with her. They had parties, lived life to the full, entertained foreign visitors and dignitaries. She was the perfect hostess and he adored her! One day she eloped with a French nobleman, who was a guest at his castle in the north of Scotland—and his world collapsed."

She released Sarah's hand, to search for a lace handkerchief in her purse.

"For two years he was as if in a dream—of low self-esteem, anger against women, and self-pity. He kept blaming himself. What had he done that she had run away from him? Could it be that he had not loved her enough? Or could it be that he had not provided for her as her French lover could? When the divorce was final, he tried—and failed—to put his life together again in the castle; the memories overwhelmed him. So he bought a huge flat in London. We still have it."

The line had commenced for the food service on the counters. Both the Duchess and Sarah opted to wait to eat, until the story was over; her son seeing them occupied refrained from approaching his mother.

"One late evening he was walking the streets of the East End of London, aimlessly, when he felt hungry. He saw what appeared to be a very small, low-class café, probably Polish, but there was an appetising aroma emanating from the front door—so, in he went. It was about ten at night; they closed half an hour later. He sat down at a table in one corner after ordering his food at the cashier's—there was no waiter or waitress service—and looked around.'

'He was the only customer in the café at that late hour. The owner, a tall, elderly man, was manning the cash register, taking the orders, and calling out to customers when their food was ready. A thin, emaciated girl, perhaps seventeen years old, wearing a scarf, was mopping the floor preparing to complete her duties before the owner closed up for the night. She mopped the rest of the floor while he was eating, and when she saw he had almost finished, she approached his corner.'

'Please, Sir,' she said, politely, 'may I mop under your table? If you could just lift your legs for one moment, while I get underneath, I would be done.'

'She must have been very pretty once, but the cheeks were hollow and the eyes sunken.'

'He kept his feet down, looked her in the eye, and said, sourly: 'You close at 10:30. There are still fifteen minutes more. Wait until I have left the café!'

'She leaned against her mop and looked back at him, a faint smile on her lips. No anger, no dismay, no hard feelings; just a smile.'

'You are right. Please forgive me. I'll be back when you have left.'

'She put the bucket and the mop to one side, and left the room. The café owner, in the small café, had seen, and heard, the exchange. He came over and sat down beside my father.'

'She has an old and sick mother that she has to go home and feed; so I let her go early when there are few customers. They are refugees from Auschwitz; they came only a month ago.'

'My father was so ashamed, he walked out of the café, food uneaten. The next evening he was back again, at the same time. Only this time, as soon as he saw her mopping the floor, he beckoned her over, raised his feet and invited her to mop under them. She thanked him, mopped under his feet—and left early for the night.'

'This happened a further five nights in a row.'

'On the seventh night, he called the café owner over, then called her over, and invited them both to sit at the table with him. The café owner sat; she leaned against her mop, but remained standing.'

'He is like a father to you; I can see that,' my father said. 'So what I say to you, I would like to say in front of him. Is that alright?'

'She nodded.'

'You don't know me; I am the Duke of Trenton. I married the daughter of an Earl—I loved her very much—but she ran away with a French nobleman. I am now divorced. I've decided to marry at the other end of the social scale—the commonest of the commonest of the common. Will you marry me?'

'She laughed. 'So you think I am the scum of the earth, do you? Perhaps I am. I was repeatedly raped by Nazi prison guards at Auschwitz—I have nothing to offer you that has not already been taken from me.'

'Except your love? I want you to promise me only three things—that you will love me, be faithful to me, and bear me children to carry on the family name. Is that too much to ask for in a marriage?'

'She seemed to soften.'

'I'll marry you, but you must promise me three things too. That you will love me, be faithful to me, and that our children will be brought up Jewish. All my family—my father, brothers, sisters, Uncles, Aunts, cousins, friends, everyone, except my old mother, and she too is dying—died at Auschwitz. But my Jewish children will prove—at least to me—that they did not win. Yes?'

'The rest happened so quickly, even my mother has lost track of how fast it occurred. First, my father produced a ring—not his first wife's ring, but a simple gold band he'd picked up that morning—went down on one knee and slipped it on her finger. Then he handed the surprised café owner one thousand pounds—at that time it was an enormous sum of money—to make arrangements for the wedding in the nearest synagogue, then he bundled her into the car he had outside and drove her to her room, where he called an ambulance and admitted her mother into a private ward in the nearest hospital. The girl whose name was Miriam—he found out that day—protested she had no money for the hospital or medical expenses, but he overruled her. Remember, Sarah, this was before National Health Insurance in England. Then he took her, not to his flat, but to a nearby good hotel and lodged her in there—and the rest is my history.'

'They were married in the synagogue in the East End of London. The café owner gave the bride away. The synagogue that could hold a thousand, held only six people—the bridegroom and the bride, the Rabbi, the Cantor, the mother of the bride, and the café owner."

'They had only one daughter—and you are looking at her. The doctors advised Father that, after those repeated brutal rapings, Mother ran risks of severe complications, and dying, if they had other children. So Father refused to have any more. Even I was a miracle—shall we say?"

"What happened to your Grandma?" Sarah asked.

"Oh, she survived! She lived with us for many years after my parents were married. She played with me until I was about twelve years old—so she lived for at least thirteen years after their marriage. The Polish café, named 'Kanska', on Silver Street, still survives. The original café owner—the one who helped my parents to marry—has long since died, but his son and daughter carry on as usual; even the furniture in the café is still the same. Jacob and I go in there, most Friday evenings, when we are in London, and I sit in the exact same chair that my father sat on when he refused to allow my mother to mop under his feet! Now where is that boy of mine?" the Duchess exclaimed.

Sarah, smilingly, pointed to where her son, Jacob, was sharing both a laugh and a glass of wine with Lady Jane at the far end of the room.

"He is well occupied, ma'am. But you are not. Come with me while I introduce you to two of the finest ladies in the kingdom. The one is my mother, Lády Julia; the other is Lady Cecily, mother of the Earl of Rathbone."

She took the old lady by the hand and led her towards the two friends who had been conversing in low tones about—who else?—but their children.

Sarah introduced them, then seeing the Queen standing all alone; the Duke was with her great grandfather, the eleventh Earl of Bromfield, discussing the House of Lords and cricket scores.

"Thank you, Elizabeth Aunty, for introducing me to the Duchess of Trenton. It was a most stimulating talk."

The Queen smiled. "I thought you'd enjoy her story. There is no royalty and there are no commoners. In the end there are only people with upbringing."

Sarah noticed that the Queen had her plate empty.

"Elizabeth Aunty, may I get you something? Some appetizers, or a glass of wine, or some dinner?"

The Queen burst out laughing. "Did I say something a moment ago about upbringing? You've only proved my point. Ruth was here first, asking if this old lady needed anything—and I had a cupcake. I do so love those cupcakes—and so does Julia. She always has, ever since childhood. Then Susan was here next, inquiring if she could bring me anything—and I had a glass of wine. She's so sweet, my Susan, I do hope she finds happiness. And now you're here inquiring after me too. Well, Sarah, I will have two of those delicious Indian samosas that my chef knows you all love. I asked him to tone the spices down for present company—and he has done us proud."

"So do you think David will be along shortly? Inquiring after you?"

"If I was a betting woman—except at Ascot and the Derby—I'd lay a wager he'll be along. Please be sure not to tell any of your sisters or your brother about our little conversation, will you? I feel with you, Sarah, that I can share confidences."

"Thank you, Elizabeth Aunty, I feel honoured."

Sarah looked to Lord Jacob, the Duke of Trenton, and felt a mild pang of disappointment—that she quickly suppressed—at seeing him still engaged in close conversation with Lady Jane. Perhaps, he liked her sort of woman—tall, slim, willowy, a super model type of body, unlike Sarah's, who because of her height, was not heavy like Rachel, but had a body, marvelously well-built, to attract the sort of attention that her mother, Julia, had garnered in earlier years.

It was just a fleeting emotion. She wished both the Duke and Lady Jane the very best of happiness in life—should they seek it together.

The afternoon was drawing to a close. The desserts had come on; rhubarb pie, ice creams and sherbets, even Indian gulab jamuns floating in heavy sugar syrup that would, by their sweetness, have set any mouthful of teeth on edge. Of any crowd—except of course the Samuelsons!

Sarah cast one last glance at Lord Jacob and Lady Jane and turned away. She had some solace from seeing David bringing his Queen a bowl of two gulab jamuns, urging her to try one. She did—and asked him to bring her two more. David was sure that gulab jamuns, once the choice dessert of Indian Maharajas, had found their way into the list of royal desserts!

The Queen flashed a triumphant smile, of one who'd won her bet, as she beckoned Sarah to come over. Soon the Queen would be standing with the Duke, as her guests lined up to say goodbye to their Sovereign.

Sarah came immediately. "You were right, Elizabeth Aunty," she whispered. "David served you, as we all did, and I'm so very happy you won the bet."

"That's not quite the reason I called you over, dear," the Queen said. "I notice you've been casting rather anxious glances at you know who, talking to you know who."

Sarah blushed a deep red. "Oh, Elizabeth Aunty, was I so transparent? What must you think of me?"

"On the contrary, dear, I have the highest regard for you; I've told you that already, and I'll repeat it as often as you wish. All I wanted to say is that sometimes things are not all they seem to be. I've had the most delightful conversation with your mother and Cecily Aunty, and you will hear some of it from your mother, I am sure. I've made them an offer for you, but if you feel you don't want to, don't hesitate to say no. It is not an offer from your Queen; it is an offer from your Elizabeth Aunty."

And the Queen gave her a light hug, before she went to join the Duke, as their guests—and her subjects—said goodbye to their hostess—and their Queen.

CHAPTER 4

They were in the Military Attache's limousine on the way home when the parents started, what the children called their 'inquisition'! Privately they enjoyed it, because each of them could listen in to the inquisition of the other three. Everybody's everything was out in the open, and all of them could feel free to join in.

"Well, David," Joshua said, "did you enjoy the afternoon?"

"No, I did not. Well, it was okay; nothing special; nothing worth remembering, I don't think."

"Oh," Julia said, "was it because Rachel couldn't come?"

"Yes. I'm beginning to dislike Florenzo intensely. He was a good friend of mine—so I thought—until recently, and now he's gone all prickly and mulish."

"Well, you can't blame him, David," Susan said, soothingly. "He's only trying to protect his sister from being hurt by you—as you would try and protect any of us three, if you thought we ran the same risk, would you not?"

"I suppose so," David said miserably. "But why can't he trust me to be honourable to his sister? I mean her no harm. We're very fond of each other—we always have. We enjoy being with each other; why his anger?"

"Two very good reasons," Ruth said. "First he hasn't been brought up to the same standards of honour as was insisted upon by this military general driving this battle wagon!"

They all laughed.

"Why, thank you, Ruth. But if you really want to know how a battle tank should be driven, you should have been there with Mummy and me—and my old Havaldar Mansingh—while returning home from a Fort in the Thar Desert, after Mamma had saved my life by uncovering the murderer of the 'Lion of Amritsar'! Pakistan Military Intelligence thought I'd killed him, and were after me for revenge. Mamma saved me; then drove that battle tank into India."

"I don't believe it," Sarah said.

"You'd better believe it, dear," Julia said laughing, "and I nearly upturned it at the speed I was going, with Daddy showing me his turret-turning skills, chasing a fictitious enemy in the Thar Desert."

"So what is the second reason, Ruth?" David asked.

"Because I don't think—and correct me if I am wrong—that Rachel is as open about it with her family as you are with us. For instance I could ask you right now, in front of those who love you the most: are you, unofficially, engaged to her?"

"We've talked about it," David said without the slightest hesitation. "But she doesn't want to."

"Oh, and why not?" this from Susan. "Has it anything to do with Florenzo and me?"

"No, dear," David said comfortingly. "I would never try to bargain away—not that I even could—your freedom for my happiness. Never!"

"Thank you, David. I didn't think you would. But if it isn't that, then what is the problem facing her?"

"Grandpa Romano."

They understood—all of them. Grandpa Romano was a devout Catholic. A marriage to a Jewish man, even if he was to be the twelfth Earl of Bromfield, was unacceptable.

"But Lysa Aunty—his only daughter—flouted him and married Joe Uncle," Ruth persisted. "If she could do it, why can't Rachel?"

"Because Joe Uncle made some concessions that I am not prepared to make," David said quietly.

"Such as?" Julia asked.

"Such as the children being brought up Catholic, and not Jewish. Mamma, you made those concessions to Pappa, when you two got married, did you not?"

"Yes, dear."

"Was it gut-wrenching for you?"

"No, dear. I talked to Grandfather about it—he was the only one I had—and he asked me one simple question: 'Do you love him?' I said: Yes, I do—those were practically my marriage vows! 'Well', he says, 'I rather fancy seating a Jewish twelfth Earl in the House of Lords. So promise me an heir to the Earldom and I'll dance at your wedding, even if you're marrying the garbage collector!'"

"Thank you, dear. I trust I was a little better than the garbage collector?" Joshua said mildly.

"Yes, you were, my darling. But not by much," Julia said, teasingly. "What it means is that everyone has some issues they consider important—and over which they will not give in. For Grandfather it was having a twelfth Earl—I could have died an old maid, and then where would the Earldom be? For Daddy, it was having you all brought up Jewish."

"And for you, dear? What was your issue over which you could brook no compromise?" Joshua asked. He knew the answer, but he wanted their children to hear it.

"Marrying you, dear. I had never been in love before.'

'The thought of losing you was unthinkable! Besides making the marriage work—against the odds—was a challenge, I relished. And the odds against it working were fearsome. Ethnicity, religion, culture and country, royalty and commoner—even height! Most people didn't give us more than five years—yet here I am, twenty-five years later, still crying when this cruel, cruel husband of mine leaves me for a month."

"You've left me a lot to seriously think about," David said. "Why don't you now ask Sarah how it went for her?"

Sarah told them the entire story, from the time the Queen called her over, to the time she'd led the Dowager Duchess to her mother and Cecily Aunty.

They were fascinated by the tale.

"Arranged marriages were done all the time in India, in early days," Joshua said. "Sometimes the bride and the groom had seen only photographs of the life-partner before the day of the marriage. And the marriages seemed—at least most of the time—to work out pretty well."

"So tell me, Sarah," Julia said, "what did you think of her son, the Duke of Trenton? He seemed to me to be a fine young man. Tall, handsome, and superbly built!"

"I didn't get a chance to even visit with him," Sarah said, trying desperately to speak without emotion. "He was so taken up with Jane, I hadn't the heart to break in on them."

"Ah, well, maybe the opportunity will arise later," Julia said. "But he is Jewish, and if bringing up the children Jewish was so important to his grandmother—and I can see why it was!—then the old Duchess isn't going to let it go."

"Why didn't you break in on them, Sarah?" Ruth said. "There was this young man—well not so young—who broke into the conversation between Yusuf, Rehana and me, and certainly got my attention. Was Yusuf mad though! Told him in the most impolite of terms to buzz off; I felt quite sorry for him. I meant to go up to him, later, and apologize for Yusuf's rude behaviour, but he'd left early. Weren't you talking to him, Daddy?"

"Oh, you mean Major William Sqigby? Yes, we had a delightful talk all about your times in the mile. He felt you were already a world class miler—and so did I. So what's cooking between you and Yusuf?" Joshua said, laughingly. "No man can even talk to you without that young man flying off the handle? Must be serious."

"Oh, Daddy! That's just Yusuf. Though he has asked me to train with him and Rehana on Saturday mornings for about an hour—after Services at the Hampstead Reform Synagogue. I'd be back well in time for the Saturday cooking, for our Sunday evening dinner. Would that be all right with Mamma and you?"

"I don't see any problem. Do you Mamma?"

Julia shook her head. "No, dear. Train all you want. We'll be there for the London University relays."

"By the way," Ruth said, "and I'm just reporting the conversation, Rehana expressed an interest in David. I told her he fancied heavier women, and was already 'spoken for'—what an old-fashioned term, I couldn't believe I was even using it, but it seemed so appropriate. It didn't seem to deter her. Said she was going on a food splurge to catch his eye, and to heck with her world class running in the 800 m. There's love for you, David. A woman who is willing to let herself go to the dogs—just to catch your eye!"

They all laughed, because they all knew Rehana and they knew she had a great sense of both wit and humor; she didn't mean half the things she said. As to the other half, whether she meant them or not, they had no means of knowing. She was deeper than she appeared, even to those who knew her well—besides being a great actor!

Which turned all attention to Susan.

"So how did you enjoy our Queen's party, Susan?" Joshua asked.

"Enormously, Daddy," Susan said. "I had a long, long talk with Jane—before your Lord Jacob—decided to monopolize her….."

"He isn't 'my Lord Jacob'," Sarah interrupted with a laugh. "It's just not within me to be aggressive in such matters, and so—and I say it without self-pity—I am condemned to die an old maid. On second thoughts, that's not such a bad deal is it? I get to live with Daddy and Mummy for the rest of my life…."

"No, dear," Julia said, "for the rest of their lives—because when we die, and we will, you'll just have to live alone for the rest of your life. I'm not sure you'd care for that, would you now? No children?"

Sarah pulled a face. "Probably not. Ah, well, we'll see. Why don't we go back to Susan. We're not letting her off the hook, just because she's the 'baby' of the family!"

Susan laughed. "I don't want to be let off the hook. I want to bore you with all the details of how Jane keeps egging me on to write a novel—when I can't sell even a short story or a poem I've written. Her dear older brother refuses to open his mouth and say a single word; just keeps looking and salivating, as if he'd like to eat me for his breakfast—or whatever."

They all howled with laughter, so hard that Joshua, who was laughing harder than anyone else, ran over the curb, before getting back onto the road again.

"And yet," Susan said, after she had dried her eyes, "I know he can talk at length, because I asked him, once, about the Nature of God and he went on for a full ten minutes—I couldn't get him to stop talking! But does that mean his wife—whoever she is—will have to discuss the Nature of God at every breakfast they have together—or eat in silence?"

"Far better they eat in silence than quarrel at the breakfast table every morning—as some couples do," David said darkly.

"Susan, let me have the last word," Julia said, as they drew up outside their building on Fitzjohn's Avenue in Hampstead, "Suppose a good man has a disability—say he is a mute—does that rule him out as a suitable partner to everyone? To some, perhaps, but there could be one understanding woman who could love him enough to make light of his disability—and they could still be very happy together, couldn't they?"

"You're right, Mamma. I'm sorry, I was poking a little innocent fun at him. I'm sure when he finds out— and he will because I'll tell him—he won't give me a second thought."

"In any case," Julia continued, mischievously, "in defense of my dearest friend Cecily's only son, I can't see him having you for breakfast, or whatever. He might, with your permission, possibly, nibble on your big toe, but that would be about all."

There was another howl of sustained laughter.

"And, Susan dear, when you tell him about the little innocent fun you were poking at him, do be sure to tell him about your mother's remark too," Julia said. "If he has any sense of humor, he might be tickled—not upset."

They were a normal, educated, cultured, Indo-British family coming home after an afternoon tea party with their Queen.

Such an evening for the Samuelsons was not yet over, however. The highlight of the evening came when Joshua remarked: "How about a cuppa for us all, girls?"And Julia said: "David will set the table—as usual."

So David set out the cups and saucers, the teaspoons, paper napkins, the sugar bowl with its own teaspoon, and the two milk jugs—one with two per cent milk for the children, and the skim milk for their parents—and finally a plate of the delicious almond macaroons, they all loved, that Susan had baked for them.

The girls alternated between the one who made the tea for everyone, and the two who washed and dried the dishes after tea was over. Today it was Susan's turn to make the tea, Ruth's turn to wash, and Sarah's turn to dry, while their parents prepared for the onslaught of their inquisition—by their children.

Because it was now the children's turn to grill their parents!

"So what did you talk to Cecily Aunty about, Mamma?" Susan asked innocently—an innocence that their parents had learned to distrust.

"About all of you—what else?" Julia said.

"Oh, any specifics?" Ruth asked.

"Plenty! We played matchmakers there at the back—even the Queen joined us for a while. I thought she was most distraught at having to leave us when the juicy tidbits were being discussed, but the royal equerry came up with a cable, from the President of some South American country coming here, that needed a quick response. She even told us to stop talking—sort of everyone go silent—until she came back, but of course she knew we wouldn't."

"So why are you leaving us hanging on the cliff, Mummy? Who were you discussing?" Susan said.

"You, dear."

"Me? What is there to discuss about me? I'm going to Oxford in the Autumn—your old college, remember?"

"I know, dear, and I told Cecily Aunty that at eighteen you were too young for marriage and you certainly didn't want to be tied to an engagement for all the time you were at Oxford. Well, Lord Albert's mother doesn't see it that way; he's desperately in love with you."

"Really?" Susan said, a little annoyed and a little amused. "His mother knows he loves me, but I don't? Seems a trifle odd to me. Well, Lord Albert had better find himself someone else—hadn't he?"

"Yes, dear. That's exactly what I told Cecily Aunty. If he has anything to say, he should say it to you—and get his answers from you; not from me. I'm just preparing you for just such a meeting."

"Thank you, Mummy. Better to be forewarned, eh, instead of being caught unprepared?" Susan who was sitting next to Julia, leaned over and rubbed her head into Julia's shoulder.

"Can you believe that?" Ruth said. "The 'baby' of the family gets the first offer! Isn't that wonderful?"

"It isn't going to happen," Susan said, firmly. "So stop, all of you, dreaming of bridesmaids' dresses and matching shoes, or whatever!"

Joshua who had been silent until now, said: "Well, said, Susan. I'd like to see that first novel published—before the responsibilities of an engagement so weigh you down, as they did Mamma, that you have no time to dream. Wouldn't you like to know of my talk, about Ruth, with her Mr. Squigby?"

"To start with, Daddy, he isn't 'my' Mr. Squigby. I don't think the others care much for hearing what he had to say about me."

"Oh, we do!" Sarah said. "So just give us the truth of Mr. Squigby's infatuation with Ruth, Daddy, in his own unvarnished language."

They all laughed at Ruth's pretended discomfiture; she more than the others couldn't wait for her father to proceed.

"He's not what he seems," Joshua said quietly. "For one thing he's definitely not royalty—so why did the Queen invite him? His father was a Jewish tailor in the East End; his mother, who was not Jewish, worked as a cook in a royal household. They both worked very hard to put him through college and Sandhurst. He's a major in the British Army—a self-made man. I liked him, but he couldn't take his eyes off the three of you, laughing and chatting away, in your corner of the hall. He admires your running prowess, Ruth—

but that may be all, dear. I don't want you to be hurt, my love, which is why I'm telling you all this."

"Thanks, Daddy. I'll not be hurt; I'm so hard into training, to compete with those world class runners, I just don't have the time, or the energy, for anything else—with anyone."

"So did you discuss, Sarah at all?" Ruth asked. "Or did she go scot-free?"

"No, she doesn't go scot-free," Julia said. "In fact, it was the Queen, who asked if Sarah could be—after finishing her post-graduate work at Imperial College—her Lady-in-waiting. That is great honour for Sarah, but I tried to tell Her Majesty—and she understood—that if Sarah did her Ph.D.—our very first non-medical Doctor!—she might go into teaching as a lecturer in civil engineering at some university or polytechnic. How proud we would be of her!"

"Thank you, Mummy. I may not be the best in exams, but I love research and the Ph.D. would be so exciting. Yes, my future life is laid out for you all to see—so don't feel sorry for me. There's only one person who is permitted to feel sorry for me—and that isn't any of you."

"Oh?" David said. "And who might that person be?"

"Why, me, of course, silly!"

That brought another round of sustained laughter.

"As it turns out the Queen's interest in Sarah is tied in with her interest in David."

This time even Joshua appeared startled.

"Oh? What was the Queen's interest in David about?"

"Not David, dear, but Rachel. She asked about the twelfth Earl's 'plans', as she put it, and I felt I had the duty to keep her fully informed. And I did. The very first question she asked was: 'Why isn't the girl here? Why didn't you bring her? I'd like to meet her'. So I waffled a little, and hedged a little I'm afraid, about how much hard work it was to run a restaurant, so we couldn't get her away, etc, etc. But Her Majesty gave me one of those withering looks—and I knew she'd seen through me—through and through! Then our dear Elizabeth Aunty softened and said: 'You know what I really need is two Ladies-in-waiting. What about Sarah and Rachel? Sarah could help Rachel around me. Of course, you'll need to talk to her parents—then let me know.' Now that's a personal invitation from the Queen—your Joe Uncle will put his foot down, with Florenzo, you'll see."

"There's something odd about what Elizabeth Aunty said to me," Sarah said, slowly. "She was talking about Lord Jacob's interest in Jane—I think? She said: 'Sometimes things are not all they seem to be.' I wonder what she meant?"

Julia heaved a sigh. It was not a pleasant task she had been given—by her oldest, dearest friend from boarding school in Kent. But she had to tell what she had been begged to do.

"I can tell you what Elizabeth Aunty meant, Sarah, because Cecily Aunty told us all openly—so that no one would get hurt. And Jane wants it that way too. Jane wants a partner, a loving, lifelong, partner to love and to hold and to keep—but it will not be a man. So when Lord Jacob finds that out, and if he pursues her, she will tell him, he will be either devastated if he is truly in love with her, or relieved that he has been let off the hook—I can't say which. That is also what Cecily Aunty wanted me to make you all aware of—so that none of you, nor Jane, gets hurt either."

There was a shocked silence in the room. The girls had known Jane since childhood. Never once in all those years had any of them ever suspected even for one moment the truth about Jane. Their first response was to express disbelief. But when the girl's mother—at the express request of the girl—was asking them to believe it, how could they deny it?

"I don't think it makes any difference, whatsoever, in our relations—at least mine—with her," Susan said. "We have been closest together because she is my literary agent; never once has she made any advances that would be considered inappropriate."

"We've gone shopping with her," Ruth said, "umpteen times; tried on dresses and slips—and, yes, unmentionables too—together, as girls who are friends will often do; not once by word or act has she given any of us cause to be offended or even alarmed."

"That's a sign of her character and upbringing," Joshua said. "Julia, my darling, please tell our girls how Jane wants them to be with her?"

"She'd like for you to be natural with her, to discuss the matter—anything and everything—with her so that it's all in the open, and to treat her as your friend—as you have always done in the past. That is what Cecily Aunty wants of us, and I don't think that is too much to ask, is it?"

"No," Sarah said, "and I think I speak for my sisters too. That is the right and proper way for us to treat a girl—who has been our friend since childhood. Let me, ask you, David, did you suspect anything? All the years we were growing up?"

"No," David said, colouring a little. "But that is because ever since adolescence, I've always fancied 'heavier' women. You've made no bones about telling everyone that yourselves! So Jane, being so tall and slim and willowy—though very beautiful—never did come onto my horizons. Rachel used to be jealous of Jane sometimes; threatened to go on a diet. I'd reassure her time and again, I fancied her and not Jane. I won't tell Rachel though; it's always good to have a competitor—particularly if she isn't a competitor!—in the picture, to keep the pot boiling, so to speak?"

"Oh, you cruel, cruel man," Julia said, laughing. "I know where you get those genes from—and they aren't from me."

"Well said, David, my son," Joshua said, also in laughter. "Women need to know there are plenty of fish in the sea."

"Aren't men terrible?" Ruth said. "Why we have anything to do with them is beyond me?" But, sitting as she was, on Joshua's side, she turned and nuzzled her head into his shoulder, even as she made the remark.

"Yes," Susan said, "but are they any different from us? Don't we make the loved one jealous, by pretending we have an interest in someone else? Take Yusuf and your Major Sqigby, Ruth. Your hands are not quite as clean as you would like us to think."

"How many times do I have to tell all of you," Ruth said, laughing, "that he is not 'my' Major Squigby? And with a name like that too? Who would want to be called 'Mrs. Squigby'?"

"I have the last word," Sarah said, "because my hands are clean. I've never played one man off against another, simply because," and she moaned in mock sadness, "I haven't had even one man seriously interested in me—let alone two."

They laughed with her.

Little did Sarah know how wrong she was soon to be!

CHAPTER 5

A different scenario was being played out in the private breakfast room of the old Earl's suite of rooms at Bromfield House. The Earl preferred his breakfast in his private suite than in the big dining room, at a table that could have, and at one time had, seated forty.

"Who is there for breakfast with me?" he'd moaned to Tomkins and Emma, when they had mildly suggested it might be more appropriate for the Earl to keep up his traditions of old, when, even with Julia, his five-year-old granddaughter, he had breakfasted at the table in the dining room downstairs.

So it had been agreed that when any of his family was with him, they'd breakfast downstairs; otherwise it was in his room, where he could be more comfortably dressed—at the age of ninety—in pajamas and a dressing gown. It had also been agreed that at that time in the morning, other than Tomkins, his butler of old, and Emma, his equally old housekeeper, none were permitted to disturb him at breakfast in his rooms.

So it was that morning, as the old Earl was having his breakfast of a soft-boiled egg, two slices of toast with real butter and marmalade; none of these synthetic margarines for him—and if the butter killed him he was old enough for it!—and a pot of hot tea, when the disturbance came in the form of a light tap on the door.

Since Tomkins was already in the room, attending to his needs—perhaps, a fresh cup of hot tea, my Lord?—it would have to be Emma—and so it was.

"I'm sorry to disturb you, my Lord," Emma said, coming into the room, without hesitation, "but there's a gentleman—or a servant to my thinking—outside who wishes to see you."

"Emma, you're old and I'm old—and so is Tomkins—but none of us is so decrepit that we do not know the difference between a gentleman and a servant. So which is it to be?"

"Well, my Lord," Emma said, with a smile, "that depends on who you ask. If you were asking me, I'd say he was a servant—and a miserable one at that!—but if you were asking the Prime Minister he'd say he was a gentleman. So, my Lord, who are you asking?"

The old Earl threw up his hands, in mock despair, and appealed to Tomkins. "Tell me, Tomkins, why does Emma choose to play word games with me this early in the morning? And at breakfast time too! What have I done to offend her? Could it be that she asked for a weekend off last month, and I denied it? Said PM was having dinner here that weekend! Or could it be that she wants a new set of dining room crockery for guests—it is getting rather old, but I didn't deny it; I only said I'd think about it! Or what? Do you have some enlightenment to offer me on her baffling choice of words, Tomkins? Either one is a servant or one is a gentleman, regardless of who I ask—her or the PM!"

"Not quite true, my Lord," Tomkins said, with one of his rare smiles. "If you were to ask Emma, she would confirm, without hesitation, that the person waiting downstairs for an audience with your Lordship, was one of your servants. On the other hand, if you were to ask the Prime Minister of England, he would confirm, without hesitation, that the person waiting downstairs for an audience with your Lordship, is a Member of Parliament, an MP, and hence—at least to the PM's way of thinking—a gentleman."

"Oh! So you mean—it's James downstairs, wanting to meet with me?"

"Yes, my Lord."

"Then why doesn't she say so? Instead of going on and on, in this roundabout way, about servants and gentlemen?"

"Because my Lord, I suspect she wants to keep her servant waiting downstairs as long as possible—to give your Lordship a chance to finish your second cup of tea—before receiving your summons to call him up."

The old Earl gave Emma a smile, wagging his finger at her.

"Devious! That's what you have become, Emma— devious in your old age."

"Yes, my Lord, I am happy to say. May I request permission to be in the room while you talk to James?"

"Me, too, my Lord?" Tomkins said.

"Oh, and why, if I might ask? You don't think I'm going senile so as to let James lead me by the nose, do you?" And the Earl laughed.

"Heaven forbid, my Lord," Emma said, "but we know James, shall we say, a little better than your Lordship does?"

The Earl nodded. "Bring him on, Emma, and the both of you can be my watchdogs—if you so wish—to see that I don't give the kingdom away."

Emma ushered James into the room.

The problems between James—a servant, who had been hired at Bromfield House, as a boy of sixteen to run errands, more than thirty-two years ago—and Emma, the housekeeper, had arisen when Lady Julia, then twenty-one, had driven down from London to see her grandfather. It had been Lady Julia's practice to strip off her glove; then offer her ungloved hand to the reception line of servants waiting to greet her arrival at Bromfield House. Emma—who had doubled as her governess and as her 'mother' too—strongly protested the act. Servants might be out working in the gardens or the kitchen; their hands might be unclean! Lady Julia refused to budge. So a compromise was reached. Lady Julia, if she came unannounced, would have a cup of tea and a muffin with old Crabtree at the gate lodge. In those ten minutes, the servants were hastily rounded up, made to wash their hands with soap and hot water, had their hands inspected by Emma and Tomkins—after which Emma inspected Tomkins' hands and he, hers.

It seemed to satisfy all parties, until James, just employed, hearing of the ritual remarked:

"Who's to say that 'er ladyship's 'ands are all that clean?"

That had nearly had him fired! Emma had marched him straight up to the old Earl, who listened to both sides, gravely, and then passed judgment.

It was not so serious as to get the lad fired, but he could not stand in the reception line, for Lady Julia, unless he followed the housekeeper's instructions.

The matter had ended a little differently, though. On Lady Julia's next visit, James, not being permitted in the reception line, hid in the shrubbery outside the gate lodge, to have a look at 'er ladyship'. He saw her, tall, elegant and very beautiful, with the grace and charm that was part of her royal upbringing. Overcome with 'puppy love' he had raced back to Emma and begged to be allowed to stand in the reception line for Lady Julia. She had made him wash his hands, twice, inspected them front and back, before reluctantly ordering him to the very end of the line.

And when Lady Julia had extended her ungloved, outstretched hand to him, he had bent low over it and kissed it.

The boy had become a man in service—as a servant—at Bromfield House. Until he'd gone into a small 'motor mechanic' business for himself, made a little money—and decided to go into politics, standing as member of parliament for Bromfield. He'd been soundly beaten twice, but each time he'd made friends, even as a loser, until in the last election—much to everyone's surprise, including his own—possibly propelled by the mood of the country, he'd been elected as the Labor member from the constituency of Bromfield.

He was a handsome enough man, medium height, stockily built, with receding hair that was turning grey, but which he dyed, rather threatening eyebrows turning grey, which, too, he dyed, and a general overall disrespect for anyone and everyone because, in some obscure way, he felt that it made him more noticed and important.

He came into the room, and signaled dismissal to Tomkins and Emma. They stood their ground. The old Earl, seated at his breakfast table—now cleared of everything from the Earl's breakfast—motioned him to a chair opposite. It was too far away to offer hands in a handshake, from either side.

"Well, James, congratulations on winning the seat from Bromfield," the eleventh Earl said. "What brings you here to see me? As you know, I'm conservative, though, as a rule, I keep out of local elections—love of Queen and country—and I kept out of this one too. So I can't contribute to your campaign chest, I'm afraid. Principle and all that."

"Oh, no, your Lordship! I wasn't here for money. I've made quite a bit in the 'motor mechanic' business to fend for myself and my boy, Richard."

The Earl raised his hand as if to inquire: Then why are you here?

"It's about my boy Richard. He's got his 'O-levels' now. Several attempts, but he has perseverance. I'm very proud of him!"

"And so you should be," the Earl said.

"What I'd like is for him to be employed in some sort of Personal Assistant job—to your Lordship, that is. He'd take care of all the boring jobs like answering telephones, attending to your personal correspondence, being a 'grandson' to you!"

"I'm afraid that's impossible, James. I already have a young man—who has a degree from the Polytechnic—who comes in two days a week and helps me out. Wonderful boy; we're all ever so proud of him."

James decided to try a different tack.

"My Lord, twenty-six years ago, when I was twenty-two and Lady Julia was twenty-seven—a mere five years older than me—I rather thought that, given different circumstances, Lady Julia might fancy me. I certainly fancied her! But society was very different then. She was royalty; I was a commoner and your servant."

Emma advanced towards James, but the Earl waved her back.

"Let him say his piece, Emma."

She made a wry face, but stopped four paces from him.

"So you thought Lady Julia might fancy you?" the Earl said, in a quiet voice. "How interesting?"

"This was about the time, she had that unhappy love affair with the gentleman from South Africa—and before that Indian Colonel stepped in to "console" her, on the rebound. And I said to myself, if she could marry a 'wog', why not me? I mean, at least I was white; her children and your great grandchildren would have been white! Now my boy Richard is prepared to ignore that part of the 'wog' Indian blood in Lady Sarah—we'll say no more about it."

"Go on."

"Well, society has changed since then; I'm not your servant anymore, but your MP! And my son fancies Lady Sarah. I think she'll fancy him too, once she gets to know him better—as your PA. Now, as you know, my Lord, there is a rising sentiment in the House of Commons to abolish the monarchy and all royalty—too much of a tax burden on the British taxpayer—but if there was to be this union between our two families, the Labour government would be able to squash that sentiment—and you would be doing the Queen herself a great service. Think of that—the headlines in the tabloids: 'The Earl of Bromfield saves the British Monarchy!' So what do you have to say to that? Is it a fair deal?"

"Tomkins, would you please ask Jonas to come up?" the old Earl said, mildly. "Do you think Jonas would do, or should I call for his son?"

Emma smiled her broadest smile

"Jonas would do very well, your Lordship. What do you think, Tomkins?" Emma said, turning to Tomkins, who had on another of his very rare smiles.

"Jonas would do just fine, my Lord," Tomkins said. "Shall I call for him?"

"Please do."

"Who's Jonas?" James asked, anxiously.

"One of our grounds men; his son has the degree from the Polytechnic, and is my PA."

"Ah, I thought you would see the light my Lord. You are summoning Jonas up here to tell him his son is no longer to be in your service, as your PA—and has been replaced by mine? Very sensible."

Emma burst out laughing.

"What is she laughing at?" James asked, annoyed. "She will have to go when Richard moves in with you and Lady Sarah. He'll make it a condition to the marriage. We don't want any senile, old hags around here, do we now?"

Bloodshed was prevented only by Tomkins ushering in Jonas—one of the grounds men. Jonas was six feet, four inches tall, and even though he was seventy years old, he'd kept himself in perfect physical condition. The biceps swelled in the arm sleeves of the tight tee shirt he wore. He had a tough beard that was closely trimmed and well-kept, with military handlebar moustaches. He'd been in the British Army in earlier years, as a master-sergeant—and he had the greatest of respect for General Sir Joshua Samuelson of the Indian Army, who had met him as a doorman at India House and recommended him to the old Earl, for employment.

James remained seated. Tomkins must have informed Jonas of what was transpiring in the Earl's private dining room, because Jonas advanced towards James. The Earl bade him desist.

"James, this is Jonas. He will escort you quietly to the front gate; if you resist, I will give him instructions to beat the stuffing out of you before throwing you out. You bloody bastard, you come into my house, speak disrespectfully of my granddaughter, Lady Julia, speak disrespectfully of my great-granddaughter, Lady Sarah, speak disrespectfully of my grandson-in-law, General Sir Joshua Samuelson of the Indian Army, speak disrespectfully of Her Majesty, the Queen of England—and all of it before two reliable witnesses here—and you have the effrontery to sit there and smirk? Now get out of my house, before Jonas catches you, or you are dead meat!"

Jonas advanced towards him.

"He spoke disrespectfully of my Lady Sarah? She is like my own granddaughter—as a child I gave her rides on my shoulders, as I did Lord David, and Lady Ruth, and Lady Susan—and this bastard has chosen to insult her? Give me permission, my Lord, to beat the stuffing out of him anyway; I will go to prison with great joy!"

But before he could reach James, the MP bounded out of the chair with surprising agility, dodged around Tomkins—Emma would have tripped him up for Jonas, by sticking out her foot, but Tomkins let him pass— and was out through the door, with Jonas close behind him.

That was the last they saw of Mr. James Apples, MP.

Jonas came back, a little ruffled and crestfallen, but he was seventy years old, and, as the eleventh Earl really wanted, there was no violence committed in Bromfield House that day.

"Tomkins," the eleventh Earl said, "I think this calls for a little celebration, doesn't it? Bring up a few bottles of our best champagne, for Emma and you and Jonas—and me, of course. We'll drink toasts, individually, to all of the lovely people Mr. Apples chose to insult in this room today—and then each of you can also add all on your lists, that you wish us to raise our glasses to."

That Saturday morning, Ruth attended Services with the family at the Reform Synagogue in Hampstead. It was a ritual the family enjoyed. They had formed friendships over the years with other Jewish families. It wasn't very close to where they lived on Fitzjohn's Avenue, being set, almost in isolation, on the western edge of Hampstead Heath. It had been at one time a two-storey mansion of the gentry, but the family, falling on hard times, had sold the building to a group of Eastern European Jews who had pooled their resources to buy it. Converting it into a synagogue had been easy. The architect just gutted the inside of the building, leaving the two-feet thick, solid brick walls supporting the roof above. The windows, of what had been the upper storey, had been blocked in with decorative brickwork, thereby giving the interior a 'religious' look. The inside was very plain, with bench style seating and—being a Reform congregation—no balcony for the women. Men and women prayed together at all times, and on all Holy days. It was an elegant synagogue though, because the benches were cushioned with soft padded fabric to make the long hours of seating during the festival days, reasonably bearable! The 'Bima', where the prayers were conducted by the Rabbi, was against the far side, with the scrolls enshrined in a decorated wooden cabinet set into the wall.

There was no reserved seating, but by going a little early, the Samuelsons had an almost 'reserved' pew, right in the first row, to the left of the Bima. Sometimes, if the girls were to be a little delayed, Joshua and David would drive along early; each would sit at one end of the pew, placing four prayer books between them, effectively reserving the pew for the Samuelson family. It was a friendly synagogue; most of the women and men knew each other from years of praying together. Newcomers to the neighbourhood were welcomed, not only to the synagogue, but to homes as well.

Saturday morning Services were designed not only for the Sabbath, but for Bar Mitzvahs and Bat Mitzvahs as well, after which the entire congregation retired to an elegant Jewish restaurant—whose owner was a member of the congregation—several blocks away on Finchley Road, for the reception.

Ruth, with prior permission, skipped the reception, leaving a few minutes before the service was to end, to meet Yusuf and Rehana at the gates of the Synagogue. She tripped down the front steps and out the gates; they crossed the side street that ran in front of the Synagogue, directly onto the Heath itself. There they put on their running cleats; the girls stripped off their skirts, to their running shorts underneath, and then they all jogged along running trails to the Athletic Tracks, on the southern edge, about a mile away.

Hampstead Heath has everything anyone could possibly wish—to get away from the hustle and bustle of city life—to find refuge in. It lies about four miles from the heart of London and to the north of it. About 790 acres in area, its lowermost corner lies in the southeast, near Gospel Oaks Tube Station and Mansfield Road. The Eastern edge of the Heath has most of the recreational facilities on it, and Ruth and her siblings had often made use of them. The prime attraction for them had been the bathing ponds—the Highgate and Kenwood Ponds.

Ruth had been more attracted—even as a child—to the Athletic Tracks that were located just a little to the south and west of the main Pond areas.

There was, however, yet another area of the Heath that had pond and water facilities, west of the Athletic Tracks and a little to the north of it. The children had used these ponds too—particularly David, when he'd decided to take up fishing. Joshua and he would often leave the girls to their own devices on Saturday—generally a shopping spree with Julia—then they'd take their fishing tackle, drive up to the Athletic Tracks that had parking facilities and toilets too, and make their way, past Parliament Hill, to the two fishing ponds, to greet old friends, who'd found that it was the only place in North London where one could possibly catch a live fish! The fish they caught were then proudly taken home, where Julia, with tongue in cheek, would make a special 'fish dish' that provided barely a morsel to them all, but which all the girls would gleefully proclaim was the best fish they had ever tasted! The girls did this just before they spread out their morning's shopping before their father, who reciprocated by then saying they were the best dresses, he had ever seen, and could they, please, put them on immediately—and that included his wife too—so that he could admire them all in their 'loot', before the credit card statement came?

And in that vast expanse of green, that was Hampstead Heath, there were walking trails and jogging trails and bike riding trails, and benches for the weary, and low hilly tracts and shallow vales, and gorse, heather, grass and trees—for enjoyment, relaxation, deep meditative thought, or just a spot of shut eye!

This was just 'warming up'; they talked even as they jogged. Not so when they were on the tracks themselves; there Yusuf and Ruth, who ran the mile, used Rehana as a 'pacer' for the first 800 m—which was her middle-distance race—then Yusuf, being the faster, became the 'pacer' for Ruth. She was down to 4:22—not quite world class as yet, but pretty close to it.

After half an hour, they crossed over to the road on the other side of the Heath. It seemed to be a Pakistani neighbourhood, because both Yusuf and Rehana met passersby they knew. Born in England and educated at English boarding schools, neither of them spoke any Urdu and understood little of it, Yusuf moaned to her.

At the corner of the street, facing the Heath, Yusuf indicated the Pakistani café they were headed for. The front entrance faced the Heath, but there were other exits at the rear of the building.

Yusuf and Rehana knew most of the young people in the café; some of the girls wore a scarf; others did not. Yusuf ordered three cups of hot tea and a plate of onion pakoras—shredded onion dipped in spicy batter and deep fried; they were delicious!

There was a burly Pakistani monitoring the entrance, collecting money at the cashiers till, and breaking up occasional arguments between friends. Behind him, to one side, was the door to another small room.

"A prayer hall," Yusuf explained, "for those who wish to pray. Rehana and I don't—Father's influence, I suppose—but some of the more orthodox ones do use it. But this room is like a Youth Group Meeting Hall; you have one like it in the Hampstead Reform Synagogue too, don't you?"

Ruth assented readily. Belonging to the Jewish Youth Group had always been—for her and her siblings—great fun.

Two young Pakistani men came up to them, pulled a couple of chairs to their table, and started conversing with Yusuf in English—and to each other in Urdu. Yusuf indicated Ruth, as if to point out that it was impolite to speak in a language she did not understand; they apologized and proceeded in fluent and flawless English—with a cultured Oxford accent—to inquire about their training? Any improvement in their times? Would they be coming every Saturday?

Their names were Khaled and Ahmed.

Ruth looked at her watch and stood up.

"I have to leave," she said. "Cook my dish today for the Sunday evening reunion dinner."

They smiled, and Yusuf saw her to the door.

The shortest way home would be along the southern edge of the Heath—this she'd jog with cleats, before donning running shoes—then across Rosslyn Hill Road to Fitzjohn's Avenue, where she'd turn towards home.

She had gone about half way down the Heath, when she heard her name called from behind. It was Major Squigby. He'd been running hard to keep up with her 'easy jogging' and he was out of breath and coughing wildly. She stopped, seated him down on a bench nearby, asked him to breathe hard—and not talk!

"I'm sorry," he said, when he could speak. "I hope I didn't startle you."

"You did, not by calling my name, but by nearly dying on me after you did! You're not in very good shape, Major Squigby, for you to try to keep up with me."

He apologized again, and this started another round of coughing—until she put her finger to his lips and forbade him to speak!

When he had recovered, they resumed their walk towards Rosslyn Hill Road and Fitzjohn's Avenue.

"I had to see you," he said. "We don't have much time, because you'll soon be home, and I wanted to speak to you privately."

"What about?"

"You've just been with Lord Yusuf and Lady Rehana at the Pakistani Youth Group Meeting Hall, I believe?"

"That's right."

"I wouldn't go there again, if I were you."

She stopped short.

"Why not?"

"I'm sorry, I can't explain."

"Major Squigby, I will go where I choose, meet with who I choose, and do exactly as I choose. Unless you can give me reasons, and evidence, I can accept, to persuade me to act otherwise."

"Please, is not my word good enough that what you are doing may be very harmful to you?" he pleaded with her.

"I'm afraid not. I don't even know who you are. You are breaking up my friendship with a brother and sister I like very much. We have been friends since childhood, because their father, Viscount Edward, is Lady Cecily's brother, and Lady Cecily and my mother, Lady Julia, were at boarding school together in Kent, since their teenage years. They go back a long way! Major Squigby, I do not dump my friends on the word of a total stranger—who may have ulterior jealous motives for the advice he is giving. Now I have a dish to cook for our reunion dinner tomorrow, with all the family, and I am late as it is. I wish you goodbye."

And Ruth put on a burst of speed for the remaining distance on the Heath that left Major Squigby, literally, standing in his tracks—as she disappeared from view.

Susan and David went together on that Sunday morning to the Italian restaurant—Susan with some trepidation; David with great anticipation of a fine, relaxed morning with Rachel. It would be relaxed—he was sure of that—because there was no secrecy to it any longer. Everyone knew he was taking her to a morning movie show. There they would sit close, very close to each other, savoring each other's presence and touch; she would put her head on his shoulder and pull his arm into her side and breast. After the movie, they would saunter along, arm in arm, to their favourite café—that had the merit of not being elegant! They could seek out a quiet corner, discuss the movie, and, as the restaurant was neither Indian nor Italian, enjoy a cup of hot tea and some Greek pastries, baklavas, that Rachel loved.

Passersby assumed they were a recently married couple, though closer inspection would have shown the absence of wedding bands—or even engagement rings—on either of them.

Susan, on the other hand had no clue of what was expected of her—and whether, when she did find out, she would be equal to the task of satisfying Florenzo, let alone Grandpa Romano! It wasn't that she felt incompetent in any way to do the work she had elected to perform, so that Rachel could have some time off with David.

It was their attitude to her that made her uneasy.

Take Grandpa Romano; would he consider he was giving up a Catholic granddaughter to the Jewish faith, and receiving a Catholic granddaughter-in-law instead? A sort of religious exchange—one for one? His great-grandchildren from his granddaughter would be Jewish; those from his grandson would be Catholic?

She had to very quickly disillusion him of such ideas.

Or Florenzo; did he merely seek help on Sunday to keep the restaurant working efficiently when they opened on the Monday morning? Or was he ensuring that, with proper tutelage by Grandpa Romano in the nuances of Italian cooking, he would acquire a good cook—and a wife as well?

She had to very quickly disillusion him of such ideas.

But before working on the other two, she had to disillusion Alfonzo of a few ideas as well!

Alfonzo was a very handsome man; even she had to admit that. He came in about the same time as David was leaving with Rachel. She ignored him, and though he tried to kiss her on both cheeks—Italian style—she fought him off, put her arm in David's arm, and the two marched out the front door.

So he kissed Susan on both cheeks instead, grinned sheepishly, and brought out two buckets and two mops.

"We mop floor, together, yes?"

"No," Susan said. "You take your mop and bucket, and mop the flat upstairs; I'll do the restaurant and the kitchen floor here."

"But Rachel and I, we do mopping together. Easier!" he said, in broken English.

"You heard what I said?" Susan said, with a dangerous edge to her voice that precluded any dissent.

He glumly took his mop and bucket and went up the stairs, muttering something in Italian—all of which, mercifully, she didn't understand.

Joe Uncle, who had heard the exchange, came down the stairs with his own mop and bucket, gave her a great big smile of welcome—and disappeared into the alcove that led to the 'Men' and 'Women' Washrooms. At home, the five of them—Daddy was exempt, though David was not—took turns to do the two bathrooms in their flat on Fitzjohn's Avenue, and she would have done what was expected of her here too; nevertheless she was grateful to Joe Uncle for his kindness.

Florenzo, sleeping late on Sundays, was the next to come down the stairs, from the flat upstairs. He saw that Susan had just finished up mopping the floor of the restaurant, had put away the mop and bucket and washed her hands with soap and water—preparatory, she thought, to helping Grandpa Romano in the kitchen. Florenzo called out to Susan:

"Could I have my breakfast now: one fried egg, over hard, two rashers of bacon, two slices of toast with butter and marmalade, and a pot of hot, regular, not decaf, coffee; you'll find what you need in the kitchen."

"What?"

"You heard me? Breakfast! Best thing that happened to mornings; could you prepare my breakfast? Oh, I forgot—milk and sugar, for my coffee, on the tray."

Susan smiled sweetly at him.

"Grown man like you, and you don't know how to make your own breakfast? Why, even David—and he's the twelfth Earl, and he will have all the servants he wants—knows how to get his own breakfast."

"That's not what we agreed to," Florenzo said. "You agreed to fill in for Rachel and do everything she did on Sunday morning—and she always gets me my breakfast on Sunday morning," he ended triumphantly. "So, into the kitchen with you, my girl—snap to it!—and bring me my breakfast pretty quick, because I'm hungry," he said, smiling at her equally sweetly.

"Really? Well she's your sweet sister—which I am not. I'm only the hired help, and I don't cook breakfasts for a lout like you. Besides, I've had my breakfast, and when I make a cup of tea for myself, why I might just make you a cup too—if you ask nicely, that is; not otherwise. So if you want breakfast—you get it!"

"Well, that's the very last time, Rachel gets Sunday mornings off, my girl," Florenzo said, airily.

"Fine! And that's the very last time, my entire family ever dines at your lousily-run Italian restaurant," Susan said heatedly. "Or any of the people we know—all the Dukes and Duchesses and Viscounts and Viscountesses and Earls and—why are the wives of Earls called

Countesses anyway?—and all the Barons and Baronesses, and all the Lords and Ladies at Court—you can say goodbye to their business—you lousy worm—if Rachel doesn't get Sunday mornings off. And I don't cook your breakfast!"

"Are you calling me a lousy worm?"

"Did I compliment you? You're not fit to be a bloody worm; even worms have more honour than you!"

Their voices had now risen, as they were heaping insults on each other. Florenzo called Susan a 'royal bitch'; Susan called Florenzo a 'lazy lout', an 'insensitive clod', and a 'no-good dimwit'. And each had a few more choice words and colourful language for the other. Susan, with her command of the English language, scored the initial points, until Florenzo started to swear at her in Italian—to even the score.

That brought Joe Uncle, Lysa Aunty and Grandpa Romano into the room—including Alfonzo from upstairs.

The situation was explained, simultaneously, by both Florenzo and Susan, in a babble of both Italian and English—at which Grandpa Romano sat on a chair and put his head in his hands, while his shoulders shook; Lysa Aunty and Joe Uncle sat side by side in a booth and burst out laughing, and Alfonzo leaned against his mop and winked at Susan, which wink was not lost on Florenzo, who decided then and there he would fire Alfonzo as soon as he could!

Florenzo thought he would appeal to Grandpa Romano, who raised his head out of his hands to reveal he was laughing harder than them all.

"Are you sure," he asked Susan, when his laughter had subsided, "that you do not have Italian blood in you? You remind me exactly of my wife—Lysa's mother. She gave me hell for forty years—and I miss her still. I prepared breakfast for her every morning, so don't think Italian men are all like him."

"Susan, you are right," Lysa Aunty said. "Joe, our first-born is an 'insensitive clod'! Who would ask a Jewish girl to fry him two rashers of bacon for his breakfast?"

Joe agreed. "I think Grandpa Romano, you and I will have to reassign Susan's responsibilities on Sunday mornings. The three of us all agree we would like her to come?"

They agreed.

"I think that Grandpa Romano does need Susan's assistance in the kitchen—as Rachel used to help him."

The others agreed. They ignored Florenzo who was drawing attention to his role as the 'Labor Manager'!

"I think Alfonzo and I can do the mopping of the floors and the bathrooms; no need for Susan to do that."

The others agreed. Joe Uncle continued: "Lysa, you will get Florenzo's breakfast—unless you want to instruct him on how he can get it himself?"

"He will get it himself—or go without breakfast," his mother said, heartlessly.

Florenzo moaned; Susan laughed. This so upset Florenzo that he turned, viciously, to his grandfather.

"Grandpa, didn't you tell me about one of your grand nieces in Milan, who wants to come to England? A very beautiful girl and so well-built—you showed me her photograph; I was dazzled by her! Well, could we arrange for her to come over and help us? Then we wouldn't need Lady Susan to come over at all, would we now?"

"That," said Susan, "is the first intelligent thing you've said all morning. No, I mean it. She will make you a very good wife—get your breakfast every morning—and make a very good Italian cook, and so be a worthy daughter-in-law, which I could never be. I'm going to Oxford in the Fall for a degree in English; then I plan to be a writer. Would I make breakfast for a husband I love and respect—of course, I would! And my children too, but not for someone who thinks of me as his servant—and treats me like one."

There was a silence; Florenzo was frothing at the mouth, but his family ignored him. Lysa went up to Susan and folded her in a warm and tight embrace.

"But you will always be our wonderful niece; we will love you always—Joe Uncle and I—and you are always welcome in our home—as are the rest of your family. Will you remember that?"

Susan hugged her Lysa Aunty back; went across to Joe Uncle and hugged him; then went across to Grandpa Romano and folded him in a tight embrace that caused his eyes to water. She felt the teardrop on her cheek.

"Come into the kitchen," he said, gruffly, "we have Monday's menu to cook for our customers."

CHAPTER 6

The events that had transpired, for all of the children, were conveyed to other members of the family—but only selectively. Even in as close knit a family, as the Samuelsons, some secrets had to be maintained—if only for the safety, or happiness, of the others.

The old Earl dropped by, and then closeted himself with Joshua and Julia, though Sarah was included. He related the rather upsetting interview with James. Of the three, the person most upset by the news was Julia.

"I had no idea all these years that he 'fancied' me," she said, almost in tears, to Joshua. "I treated him as I did any of the other servants. Why would he have any such other ideas about me?"

Joshua put his arm around her.

"Darling, your behaviour to the servants was impeccably gracious—as only you could be. I don't think you should be upset, or wonder how you could have behaved differently. We act the way we were brought up; we can hardly be responsible for the emotions we arouse in others, by being our natural selves, can we now? I wouldn't give it a second thought. I can see why Emma would have wanted to horsewhip him, though!"

The Earl laughed. "Rest assured Julia, he has no such ideas now—after Jonas chased him down the stairs and out through the front door and down the driveway to outside the gates. But if his son ever comes anywhere near my Sarah, I want to know—and Jonas wants to know!"

Julia was still a little concerned that Joshua, not being then in the picture, might—without saying it—still be curious about their 'relationship' from twenty-five years ago. He sensed her frustration, because he said:

"Darling, the relationship between master and servant is probably the most sensitive of all relationships, and more misunderstood than any other between two human beings. I had a servant girl once. She was sixteen years old; I was Colonel of the First Rajput regiment stationed in Ajmer. She was an orphan when I found her. I took her in, was like a father to her; she cooked and cleaned for me—until my Havaldar fell in love with her. I got them married, underwrote all the expenses—they were too poor to even get married! When we went into war with Pakistan, I saved my impetuous Havaldar's life by refusing him permission to attack an enemy battery with two hundred of our men—until I had the report from the advance scouts, I'd sent out into the night. They came back with the report that the enemy had brought in heavy artillery during the night—so I sent in my battle tanks instead, and we wiped out the battery and won the day, without a single life being lost.'

'My servant girl worships me—as a god! She prays, every night, to her other Hindu gods, for my safety, because I had decreed life for her husband."

The talk between Ruth and her parents was even more confidential. She related the events of Saturday morning—particularly the rather mystifying behaviour of Major Squigby.

Joshua and Julia listened quietly. Suddenly, Joshua disappeared into the Master bedroom, closing the door behind him. Ruth would have followed him in, but Julia held her arm and patted the sofa next to her. They talked desultorily for about twenty minutes—with Ruth getting ever more anxious—until Joshua emerged from the bedroom. He sat on the other side of Ruth; she was between them.

"Ruth," he said, very gently, "I talked to the Director of MI-5—you don't need to know who he is. You know that Mamma and I were both in Intelligence—I was Director of IMI, Indian Military Intelligence, for many years; Mamma was with MI-6 for about a year. It took a few minutes, but I got the confirmation I suspected. Your Major Squigby is a field agent with MI-5."

"What!"

"Yes, dear. MI-5 is concerned with the internal security of these islands. I think you should take his advice seriously."

"Why didn't he tell me on Saturday morning that he was with MI-5?"

"Because no agent likes to blow his cover. In IMI or MI-6, the phrase was that 'a blown cover was akin to committing suicide!' That is why he didn't tell you."

Ruth got up with a bound.

"Are you telling me, Daddy, that Yusuf and Rehana, Viscount Edward's children, are plotting something against the Crown? That's ridiculous! Major Squigby's just infatuated with me; he can't stand me being friendly with Yusuf—and I just won't take it! I told him: 'If you have any evidence, let me see it'—otherwise he should stop bothering me. Mamma, don't you think that was the right response from me—before he slings mud at the characters of two of my dearest friends?"

"Yes, dear, I think you did right. We'll say no more about it. Don't worry the others—David, or Sarah or Susan—about this matter. Please?"

Ruth nodded and left the room.

But the confidence that produced both tears and laughter—tears in Susan and laughter in the rest—came when Susan confided to the entire family at four o'clock tea, that afternoon, of what had transpired at the restaurant that morning.

"I cannot believe," Susan moaned, "that I could use such language with Florenzo. I've disgraced the family, Pappa and Mamma. You've taught me always to be civil and gracious—like Sarah is—and here I go calling him the most atrocious names! I'm so ashamed of myself."

Trying hard to keep a straight face, Joshua asked: "So what did you call him, dear?"

"Well, he called me a 'royal bitch', and then I ploughed into him. I called him a 'bloody worm', a 'lazy lout', an 'insensitive clod', and a 'no-good dimwit'!"

At which her entire family burst into howls of unrestrained laughter, which they found difficult to control.

"It's not funny," Susan said, plaintively. "Joe Uncle and Lysa Aunty and Grandpa Romano also burst out laughing. That got Florenzo so upset he asked Grandpa Romano about his grandniece in Italy, and how he'd love to marry her, or have her as his maid or to cook his breakfast, or whatever—and so he's now spoken for. Well, I think maybe it is funny—that I helped him make up his mind on someone."

But yet more surprises were to come that very evening at their traditional Sunday evening reunion dinner. This time the table was full—Grandpa Romano came as well; Florenzo helped him up the stairs to the flat.

As usual, as they ate, they talked, sometimes to the one sitting beside or opposite, sometimes to the entire party around the table.

The seating arrangement was still the same as usual, and so Susan was next to Florenzo, with Rachel next to David.

It was Florenzo who started the conversation that dealt with the person uppermost in their minds—the grandniece from Italy! She would soon be an addition to their families, sitting, as they were, around this same table. Joshua searched in his mind as to where the extension piece of the cherry table was?—that would allow fourteen persons around it. He thought it might be under one of the beds; he'd have to have a look for it.

Florenzo produced, with a flourish, a photograph of Grandpa Romano's grandniece—and then tinkled on his wine glass with a fork, to draw everyone's attention.

"I'm so happy to announce," he said, "though Susan may have already told you about it, that I'm engaged to Roberta, my cousin twice removed, I think, who will be joining us shortly in England. We called her yesterday, after Susan left; I proposed and she accepted. The wedding will be in Italy, and of course you are all invited to it. I have a photograph of her here, if any of you wishes to look at it."

There were congratulations from everyone, and a demand for the photograph to be seen by one and all. So Florenzo passed it round the table starting with the first person on his left—Susan.

Roberta was a rather heavily built, not very tall girl—almost like Rachel—with a fine complexion, short dark-brown hair, beautiful black eyes, and a sexuality that came through even in the photograph. The face was lively, the eyes were laughing, the sensuous lips were parted in a smile. A very beautiful Italian girl, who, Florenzo informed them all carelessly, knew everything about cooking the most exotic Italian dishes, and would be a great asset to the restaurant.

They all looked at the photograph with appropriately gushing remarks to her beauty and liveliness—in which Susan joined in wholeheartedly, praising not only her looks and figure, but how wonderfully she would suit Florenzo and be a worthy partner in his life. For some reason, this praise seemed to annoy Florenzo—rather than please him—as if he expected Susan to be both dejected and critical rather than overjoyed and effusive.

After Florenzo, it was David's turn to tinkle his glass of wine, to draw their attention to Rachel and him.

"We've talked about this," David said, turning to Rachel, "and, darling, feel free to correct me at any time. We both feel that this is the most appropriate place and time to make the announcement; so here goes."

He reached into his shirt upper pocket and drew out an engagement ring—a platinum band with a large central diamond, surrounded by a cluster of smaller rubies. He showed the ring around to the family.

"My family will recognise this ring—it belonged to Great Grandma. It has been reset, but has been in the family for four hundred years. Every Earl of Bromfield, who gets engaged to be married, uses it. And when Great Grandfather knew I was serious about Rachel, he gave it to me this week. Not as the twelfth Earl, Rachel, but as David, I'm asking you: Will you marry me?"

"Thank you, David, for asking me. I've wanted to marry you since I was twelve years old—so why have you waited so long? Of course, I'll marry you, my darling."

And Rachel turned to David, ignored the ring and proceeded to kiss him in a manner that left no doubt as to her intentions of being fully and completely married to him before long. He would have gone down on one knee to put the ring on her engagement finger, but that was precluded by the fact that she was sitting beside him, and by the fact that she had her hand around the back of his neck and her lips about three inches away from his own—and showed no intention of letting go.

Grandpa Romano glowed: "All that Italian blood in her," he said, proudly. "They don't make them any hotter than that in any other country in the world!"

The rest of the Samuelson families—from both sides—burst into joyous clapping and applause at this public engagement that the future twelfth Earl and his new bride had chosen to carry out before them. Joe and Joshua, close brothers, smiled and raised their wine glasses to each other; Julia and Lysa held hands at celebrating the union of their two children—an event that the both of them had dreamed of since the children had been playing with each other, sharing their gifts of chocolate with each other and, yes, even squabbling with each other, since childhood.

None of them asked the crucial question, uppermost in everyone's mind.

How would the children be brought up? Jewish or Catholic?

Perhaps that problem would be solved in later life?

Not as far as Rachel was concerned; that was not the way she ran her life—nor the way she wanted her husband to run his—always in doubt!

This time she tinkled her wine glass with her fork to draw their attention. She looked proudly at the ring on her engagement finger, before she spoke:

"I know that the question uppermost in your minds—including that of my father, who is Jewish, and my mother and Grandpa who are Catholic; Florenzo did not count in my deliberations, and never has, I'm very happy to reassure all of you of that!—is the religious identity of the children. David is Jewish; I am Catholic; Our children will be brought up Jewish."

Florenzo raised his hand as if in protest, but she silenced him—almost dismissed him—with a wave of her hand.

Why, she is Lady Rachel, Countess of Bromfield already! Julia thought delightedly.

"My thinking has been very simple on the question. I have two parents—one Jewish, the other Catholic—and I love them both very much. My parents have two children, Florenzo and me. While there was some possibility that Florenzo and Susan might get together, the answer to the question, for me, was difficult. What if Susan were to insist on her children being Jewish? Mother and Grandpa would have had no Catholic grandchildren. But what if Florenzo had insisted on his children being Catholic—and I had gone the same way—then Father would have had no Jewish grandchildren. Now it seems that Susan—by telling Florenzo where exactly he stood in her affections—has made my decision so much simpler, because Florenzo's children will be brought up Catholic, giving my Mother and Grandpa Romano Catholic grandchildren; my children will be brought up Jewish, giving my Father Jewish grandchildren. Problem solved; matter closed."

"Even King Solomon could not have pronounced a more just judgment than the one you've just given, Rachel," Joshua said, "and for that I thank you."

Joshua got up from his seat, went behind Rachel's chair and kissed her lightly on her head; Julia did the same—and Sarah, Ruth and Susan were not far behind. David sat basking in their joy—and his own—until he felt Lysa Aunty and Joe Uncle, his future in-laws, do the same to him—welcome him into their family.

That Sunday night reunion dinner turned into an engagement party that went on late into the night.

As they had done on past occasions, the men pushed all furniture in the living room to the walls on the sides, rolling up the carpet, leaving a dance floor in the centre of the room.

The girls—including Rachel—in the meantime cleared the dinner dishes, washing them, drying them, and putting them away.

The elderly folk sat on the sofas alongside the walls, initially, with a glass of port or sherry—the old Earl and Grandpa Romano found, surprisingly, they had a lot in common to talk about. But when the dancing commenced, they all joined in, so that six men and six women, all members of one large family, danced half the night away.

CHAPTER 7

Ayrton Hall of the Imperial College of Science and Technology, in South Kensington, London, has an historic architectural crest, carved out of stone, above the entrance, that is the envy of many of the older historic buildings in London.

Sarah did not know about it, until she was about to enter the building, when it arrested her eye, and she stopped to admire it.

It was early summer, not the first day of term, yet she was checking her mail—in a 'pigeonhole'! Ayrton Hall was far from being a pigeonhole, but along one wall of the main entry hall were the pigeonholes that held the mail for the many thousands of students—many of them from overseas, and so receiving thousands of letters from parents, wives, and family—that would have been impossible to deliver, addressed as they were to the named student, c/o 'Imperial College', London. Sometimes no other address, but just that: c/o 'Imperial College, London'.

There were not too many students checking their mail in early summer. Normally, all of Sarah's mail would be delivered to the flat in Hampstead, but there were some acquaintances, professional societies and work-related people to whom she had given the Imperial College address, and she felt that at least once in a while she ought to check her mail, while passing Ayrton Hall.

The mail was put into alphabetical pigeonholes. Some of the alphabets such as P and Q might be lumped together—how many would have a last name beginning with Q?—; others like A and B had pigeonholes to themselves.

There were no letters for her; plenty of letters from overseas addressed to names like Srinivasan or Singh, postmarked from India—which she could recognise because of her part-Indian heritage—and a whole host of other unpronounceable names from almost every country in the world. Foreign students, who had come for post-graduate work, or research, to Imperial College, treasured their mail from home.

There were not too many students at that time of the day—late evening—looking through the pigeonholes for mail; some delightedly finding a letter or two; others turning away disappointed.

Except one student—a handsome, turbaned Indian student—who kept looking through the pile of letters in his hand, going through them again and again, as if in disbelief that he had none.

He was not a Sikh; the intent of the turban was not to cover long hair. His hair was close cropped, and his turban sat high on his head like a crown, with the trailing edge riding majestically on his left shoulder. He had a well trimmed mustache and short beard, cleft in the middle that spoke of some pride in his heritage. He was tall—taller than Sarah—thin, but powerfully built, with a strong nose and mouth, and when he opened his mouth to express his dismay at the absence of any letters for him, he showed white, flawless teeth.

Sarah was a kind person, gracious, and unhappy at the unhappiness of others—even strangers, particularly from foreign lands. They were lonely and homesick, and being deprived of letters, from home, must surely make them even more miserable.

She went up to him.

"Forgive me intruding, but you seem upset. Does something bother you?"

He seemed startled; no one in cold England had ever come up to him and inquired after him—whether happy or unhappy. Most strangers left him alone. He was already lonely; being left alone made him even lonelier.

"I have had no letters from home for a month. My mother cannot read and write, but my father can, and they promised me a letter at least once a week. I've been here a month—no letters! What has happened to them? Are they ill—and so do not want to write because they do not want me to be upset? But I'm upset anyway—not knowing!"

"Well," Sarah said, "let's see how I can help you. First what is your last name—the surname, as you say in India."

"Oh, and how do you know that?"

"My father is from India. My mother is English and I have her skin complexion—of which I am very proud—but I am also very proud of being half-Indian. I've been to India with my parents several times—to visit Grandma when she was alive. My Grandfather died before I was born, so, unhappily, I did not get a chance to know him. But why are we talking about me? We were talking about your problem—of no letters! So what is your name?"

"Devinder Mansingh."

"And you have been looking in the pigeon hole for 'Mansingh'?"

He held out the pile of letters to her—all under the last name beginning with M.

"Odd," Sarah said, a frown wrinkling her brow, "now where have I seen that name or something like it? If I was Sherlock Holmes, I would deduce that the only pile of letters I've been through, because my last name is 'Samuelson', are under S—so whatever seems familiar must be under S. I've got it!" she almost screamed in delight. "The sorters have split your name in two. You can't blame them; perhaps the address is not too legibly written, but I've seen a bunch of letters under Singh, and I'm almost certain there is a name that begins with M before each of them."

She retrieved her pile of letters from the S pigeonhole, and very quickly found no less than six letters that could have been misread by a non-knowledgeable person as addressed to Devinder Man Singh. The fact that Singh was such a common Indian-Sikh name had almost made it inevitable.

She handed him the letters; he practically tore them out of her hands—then retreated to a bench in the far corner of the entry hall to eagerly devour them.

She smiled at his joy, feeling part of it too, smiled again softly to herself, and slipped out of Ayrton Hall to return to South Kensington Tube Station, thence to Finchley Road Tube Station—and home.

The term would not commence for at least another three months. In between spending the summer with her sisters and brother—David would be leaving for Sandhurst, and Susan for Oxford in the Autumn—she had little time to check her mail in Ayrton Hall. But one day, passing the Hall, she went in and looked through the pile of S last names, and found to her surprise a handwritten envelope, sealed, no stamps on it—as if it had been privately placed in the pigeonhole. It was a letter from Devinder. It read:

"Dear Miss Samuelson,

I write this letter in shame! I am ashamed that after you were so helpful, and gracious, in finding all the lost letters from my family, I sat down to read them immediately instead of first at least thanking you for your kindness! What must you have thought of me? If you can find it in your heart to forgive such abominable behaviour, please could you drop by the Union Cafeteria at four o'clock in the afternoon, which is when I have an hour's tea break every single day, and permit me—as an act of contrition—to buy you a cup of tea? I may then at least be able to concentrate on my class work for the Advanced English class I am taking, because now all I see is your very beautiful face before me—and what I also see is the disgust you must have felt at having helped such a thankless Indian!

Please forgive me, I beg you,

Devinder"

The letter was dated more than three weeks ago. The grammar, the syntax, the construction of the sentences, all spoke of English learnt as a foreign language. There were many, many Indians, with English as their native tongue, who spoke it far better and more fluently than she did—but not Devinder!

It was ten minutes past four—she had finished for the day and was on her way home. She decided to humor him—at least this once—by having tea with him and setting his mind at rest that she had not been upset by his 'abominable' behaviour.

He had not been expecting her—he had waited for her for three weeks, and she had not shown up—so he wasn't quite sure she was in the Union Cafeteria on his account. Perhaps she was meeting a friend—after all he did not own rights to the Cafeteria, every afternoon at four!—and it would be only more offensive to her for him to assume that she had come to meet him. That is the way he thought, so she had to approach his table and stand at it, with a smile, before he erupted from his seat, took her by the arm to the serving line for a cup of tea—she offered to pay, but he insisted on paying for it.

After he had expressed his apologies once more, and she had waved the incident away as of no consequence, they settled down to getting to know a little more of each other. Sometimes she would ask the questions about him, and he would reply at length; sometimes, though more shyly, he would ask about her, and she replied freely to his inquiries.

They found they had a lot in common—in their Indian heritage.

Devinder Mansingh, was a Rajput who came from Marwar in Rajputana. It was an important railway junction—and so, sometimes, the town was referred to as Marwar Junction. His father had been in the Indian Army and was now retired; his mother had more humble beginnings being a servant, cooking and cleaning, in the household of a military officer—and was illiterate. They had taken out huge loans to send their son to England, for a Master's Degree in Mechanical Engineering—for which Imperial College was world renowned!

That is what she gathered from their conversation.

Her first name was Sarah—he had asked the question shyly—and she was the eldest daughter of an Army man too, who was working with the Indian High Commission. She took the opportunity to tell him that the High Commission, located in a building, called 'India House', had a first-class Indian cafeteria on the top floor of the building—she had eaten there several times herself—and the food was absolutely delicious and very cheap; she recommended he try it. Maybe she could treat him to lunch there one day? After all he had paid for her tea—had he not? It was only fair, she should be permitted to return the favour. He assented, without hesitation. She wanted to get her Master's Degree in Civil Engineering, and then, possibly, go on to a Ph.D. and a teaching career—if she was capable of it.

That is what he gathered from their conversation.

As it turned out, for the both of them, the next day was free for lunch, and they agreed to meet outside Ayrton Hall; then take the tube from South Kensington to Holborn, and a short walk to Aldwych. The food was delicious; Sarah took two trays, and asked him his preferences. He was a Hindu and did not eat beef though he ate chicken and lamb; so he was not a strict vegetarian as his parents were. She piled the dishes on the trays—a self service—much against his protestations that the food was too much. She told him he looked a little thin, and needed fattening up, adding a dessert for each of them—gulab jamuns—followed by hot tea with milk and sugar—British style.

They had a leisurely lunch; then strolled back from Aldwych to Holborn, so they could take the right tube lines—she to Hampstead and he to South Kensington, where he was living with two other Indian students in a bed-sitter on Queens Gate Terrace. They did not hold hands though their shoulders bumped several times in a friendly sort of way; once he put an arm round her waist to prevent her from falling off the curb when it suddenly came to an end and she appeared to be unaware of it.

That evening, at dinner time, she decided to tell her family about Devinder. Rachel was there too—but now Rachel was part of the family; besides, being the same age, the two of them, since childhood, had always been the closest of friends.

For two compelling reasons she felt the need to keep her family informed of her friendship with Devinder, and as yet it was just that—a friendship.

The first was that her siblings had kept the family fully informed of what was going on in their social lives. She had known about David and Rachel for ever! She knew about Ruth's Mr Squigby—though each time Ruth strenuously denied he was 'her' Mr Squigby. She knew of Ruth's friendship with Yusuf. She knew of Susan's tongue-tied Lord Albert, Earl of Rathbone, and she knew of Susan's fiasco with Florenzo. It seemed only fair that they should be aware of her friend.

There was another reason. For one brief moment, she had panicked, in India House, while having lunch with Devinder.

Her father worked in the office of the Indian High Commission, in India House. He ate his lunch in that same India House cafeteria. What if he had been there at that very hour, and had seen her there with Devinder? What would his reactions have been?

Would he have come over to their table, smiling at greeting one of his children, while she, shamefacedly, would have introduced Devinder—and then gone into a whole litany of explanation as to how they had ended up also, having lunch together, in India House?

Or, if he had seen her, would he have ignored her, avoiding eye contact, taken his lunch tray and sat at the other end of the large cafeteria—with his back to them—so as not to embarrass her?

But in either case, what would he have been thinking? That after giving her life, bringing her up through all the illnesses, falls, and tears of childhood, fed her, clothed her, educated her, and, more importantly, loved her into womanhood, she had treated him as an utter stranger—as a nobody in her life—praying that he would not notice her, or, if he did, not come up to her so as not to embarrass her?

That was unbearable; it was unthinkable! She would not stand for it any longer—the family had to be told.

And that is precisely what she did at the evening dinner. Fortunately everyone was there—including Rachel, who it seemed was spending more time at their house than at her own. Her mother, Lysa, rolled her eyes, and told her pointedly that she looked forward to the day when David, and their children, would spend more time in the restaurant than at his home!

Dinner was over, and they were having a dessert of Indian halva—a milk cake—when Sarah tinkled her water glass and said: "I want you all to know where I had lunch today—and with whom. I had lunch at India House with an Indian student, Devinder, who is doing his postgraduate degree in Mechanical Engineering. I met him only a short while ago, but I helped him locate his mail from home—he was looking under M for Mansingh, but the sorter had placed the letters—six of them—in S for Singh. That led to him inviting me to a cup of tea at the Union Cafeteria, and then me inviting him, today, to lunch at India House."

She looked round the table with a teasing smile.

"And before you all jump to rash conclusions, let me disillusion you. He is a friend—and no more."

Joshua looked at Julia, while the others were firing a battery of questions at Sarah, who answered them with equanimity and graciousness.

Yes, she liked him. He was a very nice boy, very polite and simple; nothing devious about him: This was in answer to Ruth.

He was tall—taller than her—very slim and wiry with a turban that he wore on his head: This was in answer to David.

No he did not have long hair—that was for Sikhs; he was a Rajput: This was in answer to Rachel.

Joshua started out of his seat, but Julia restrained him with a hand on his arm.

Yes, he knows Daddy is Indian, and I am half-Indian; it delighted him! I don't think he knows I'm Jewish, though—the matter never came up: This was in answer to Susan.

She wasn't quite sure what his father did. She thought he had been in the Indian Army at one time, and was now retired. His mother had been in the employ of an Indian Officer of the same regiment. He did mention she spoke a little English, but could not read or write: This was in answer to Joshua.

"Am I in love with him?" Sarah repeated the question—from her mother. "I don't know; I'd tell you if I knew. I've never been in love; perhaps Pappa and Mamma and David and Rachel—particularly Mamma and Rachel, because they are women in love—can tell me what it feels like for a woman to be in love?"

David said: "Do you find yourself thinking of her very often? Do you reach for the telephone to call her—even though you just finished talking to her a few hours ago—but restrain yourself because you say: What will her family think of me?"

Rachel said: "Do you find your heart aching—feeling miserable—because he is going away for a while, or because he has been away from you for some time?"

David said: "Do you resent her spending time with other men—yes, I mean simple jealousy!"

Rachel said: "Do you truly and genuinely want to do the best you can for him, to make him happy?"

Joshua said: "Do you think that you could never be happy with anyone else—but her!"

Julia said: "Does your heart skip a beat when, after a long absence, he comes near you—and touches you?"

Sarah burst out laughing. "Is this some sort of quiz game? Four or more yeses, out of six, means I'm in love; three yeses means I'm about to fall in love; two yeses, or below, means I'm not in love?"

"You could almost say so," Rachel said. "The human heart does not lie to its owner. It may lie to others, but it cannot lie to itself."

"Thank you, Rachel—and all of you too. I am a scientist and an engineer. On the basis of the six criteria that the four of you have so thoughtfully placed before me, I can truly and honestly say, with great conviction, that I am …."

She looked round the dining table; the silence made her smile. They were her family and they loved her, and they had every right to know what her heart was telling her.

".....not in love. I cannot, truly, say 'yes' to even one of the criteria you gave me. Not one single one!"

This is when Joshua spoke up.

"I'm glad you made that clear to us, Sarah. For I would never do anything to hurt you—you know that."

She nodded, smilingly.

"Now we have to make sure that he is not hurt. Is he in love with you?"

Sarah raised her hands to the heavens.

"How can I say, Daddy? He has never said he loves me—he has not tried to hold my hand; he has never made any other sort of verbal advances to me. I don't know. How can I know?" she ended piteously.

He reached with his hand across the table to her, and she held it. "Never mind, dear, you don't need to know. Sarah, you were there, weren't you, when Great Grandfather told us about his little 'incident', shall we say with Mr. James Apples MP?"

Sarah nodded again.

"What incident?" Susan said.

So the whole story was repeated once over again to the others in the room. It fascinated them; it held them spellbound that servants could aspire to relationships or marriages way above their social status and reach.

Only this time Joshua added: "The name of my Havaldar was Mansingh. It is a fairly common name, and perhaps I couldn't be more mistaken. The name of the servant girl, the orphan of sixteen that I employed to cook and clean for me—and treated like my daughter—was Rupa Devi."

Sarah was almost in tears, not for herself but for the effect it would have on Devinder, to find out that his mother had been a servant girl in the employ of her father. Would he be so filled with anger she had hidden the truth from him—though until a few minutes before she had not known the truth herself—that he would hate her, and possibly all women?

"What shall I do, Pappa?" she moaned. "Please I need to know what to do?" She stumbled toward him.

Joshua folded her in his arms and calmed her down.

"I'll tell you what you—and I—have to do. First we have to establish, beyond any doubt, that this Devinder is Havaldar Mansingh's son. That, you have to do tomorrow by asking him, casually, what is his mother's name? That should be easy enough. Work in Mamma's name. Say: 'My mother's name is Julia; what is your mother's name?' Can you do that?'

She nodded, miserably.

"Good! Then, as in any military operation, there are several options—depending on the answer.'

'If his mother's name is not Rupa Devi, you might want to continue for awhile with things as they are—until you have sorted out your own emotions, considered the ramifications of your actions, and talk to Mamma and to all of us again—if you wish.'

'If his mother's name is Rupa Devi, invite him promptly over for lunch the day after tomorrow, which is a Saturday—remember for lunch not dinner!—and then leave the rest to Mamma and me."

"What! You want to meet him? Heap insult upon injury? Pappa, you don't mean that, do you?"

"My darling girl, have I ever let you down? Would I start letting my eldest daughter down in my old age? Trust me, sweetie, everything will be just fine—just find out first whether his mother's name is Rupa Devi."

"Yes, Daddy, just so long as you don't think you're fighting a war—with Devinder as the enemy!" she said laughing, easing the tension in all of them around the table.

The next day—a Friday—Sarah met Devinder at precisely four o'clock, for tea at the Union Cafeteria. He paid for the tea, and she thanked him for it.

When they were seated, he talked about difficulties he was having in the Advanced English course he was taking. Not that the course was too academically challenging—oh no! It was just that the lecturer was a Scotsman and spoke with such a heavy accent, Devinder couldn't understand much of what he'd said in class.

"Why can't they all speak like you?" he moaned.

She laughed, and reassured him that like everything, the human brain was capable of great adaptation—especially at their young age—and in just a few lectures, his accent—and his lectures—would become more intelligible; it was only a matter of time.

That cheered him up considerably.

"What would I do without you, Sarah?" he said.

Which brought her back with a bump to the mission at hand. It was like a military operation to her father—and it was fast becoming that way to her too!

"Devinder," she said, "I know so little of Indian women. What are they like? The ones I've seen have been all so beautiful. The colourful saris, the long hair, the jewellery they wear—it's all so mysterious to me. Even their names!"

"Well, their names—first names, I mean—can depend on which part of the country they come from. For instance, South Indian names are quite different from North Indian names—or from Bengali names. Even in North India, there are so many regions with different languages—even scripts—that name identification can be a real headache! The country is much more integrated now than it was, say, 50 years ago."

"Now, Devinder," Sarah said, "you've got me even more confused. So let's start with basics, say Rajput names."

She decided it was time to take the plunge!

"My mother's name is Julia. What is your mother's name?"

"Rupa Devi."

"That's a beautiful name. What does it mean?"

"Rupa means 'beautiful'; Devi means 'Goddess'. A beautiful Goddess! She is that to me. I will finish my degree; go back to India—England is too cold for me—and look after them for the rest of their lives. My brother is a farmer, so he is not too well off, and my sister has married a clerk in the railways, and can barely survive with her three children—so it will have to be me."

"Of course," Sarah said, warmly. "Children should look after their parents in their old age—and not only with money. Sometimes they need us to be nearby and hold their hand—as they did ours in childhood. Talking of parents, mine have invited you for lunch tomorrow, Saturday at 12:00 noon. Can you come?" She paused.

"Oh, please say yes! I told them of you, and where you come from, and my father—who I told you is Indian—would love to meet you; my mother too. Will you?"

"Yes, but my hesitation is because I know so little of the English; I might behave inappropriately, or hurt them unintentionally."

"Behave naturally, and you'll be just fine," she said reassuringly. "Besides, you know me."

Devinder rang their doorbell the next day at precisely 12:00 noon; Sarah, who had seen him from the window seat overlooking Fitzjohn's Avenue, opened the door to him and folded her hands in front of her chest in the Indian 'namaste'—and he, delightedly, responded in the same way. He felt 'Indian' in their home already!

Introductions followed in quick order. As it turned out Joshua was also awaiting his arrival because he held out his hand and introduced himself first:

"I'm Sarah's father," he said. "Let me introduce the rest of the family to you. This is my wife, Sarah's mother, Mrs Samuelson. And this is our eldest son, David, and his fiancée, Rachel—who is also my younger brother's daughter. They have known each other since childhood—and find that they can't do without each other! We're very proud of them both. This is our second daughter, Ruth, who is a long distance runner—her race is the mile—and she's world class, and we're all so excited to see if she can make the Olympics! And this is our youngest daughter, Susan, who is going to Oxford this term—the term at Oxford starts later than at Imperial College—and she wants to be a writer, and we're all so proud of her too. And on to lunch!"

The table had already been set for lunch. Rachel had obtained a special dispensation from her parents to be at the Saturday lunch—Saturday was a busy day at the restaurant, but Joe and Lysa had hired temporary help since Rachel's engagement to David.

The dining table had been 'shrunk' to seat eight; the seating arrangement planned to make Devinder most comfortable. Joshua and Julia were at the head of the table, at each end. Devinder sat next to Joshua, with Sarah beside him, and Susan beside her. On the other side of Joshua was Ruth, with Rachel beside her; beside Rachel was David, placed next to his mother.

Julia, on being complimented by Devinder on the excellence of the Indian cooking he was enjoying, took delight in explaining to him that she had only prepared the dessert—gulab jamuns—that he had yet to taste! All the Indian dishes on the table were prepared by the girls. Sarah had made the lamb biryani, Ruth had made the cauliflower and potato vegetable, and Susan had made the chappatis. The cucumber, tomato and onion raitha was Rachel's contribution—she was having a go at Indian cooking herself.

After he had complimented each and every one of them individually on the excellence of their cooking, including Julia on the excellence of the gulab jamuns, and declaring himself unable to eat another morsel—Sarah had been persuading him to enjoy seconds of every dish, or whatever pleased him—Joshua tinkled his water glass with his fork to draw their attention.

"I have a little surprise for Devinder," he said. "It was really Mamma's idea—so she gets the credit for this one—which is why I'm glad we're having Devinder over for lunch and not dinner."

He stopped as if inviting them to guess the surprise, but none of them could—not even Sarah.

Joshua brought the phone to the table, and switched on the speaker phone, so that the conversation would be heard by all in the room.

"We are going to call Devinder's parents in Marwar Junction, so that they will get a chance to talk to him which, being a parent myself, I know they will enjoy more than anything else in the world."

"But, Sir, how do you know their number?" Devinder asked, in amazement.

"You'll find out in just a moment," Joshua said, with a smile. "They are four and a half hours ahead of us; it is about 2:00 PM here so it must be about 6:30 PM there. Both Havaldar Mansingh, Devinder's father, and Rupa Devi, Devinder's mother, should be at home now. I certainly hope so."

They were.

Joshua explained about the speaker phone so that both parents at the other end knew they had an entire family listening in—in addition to their son.

Their joy was unbounded!

"General Samuelson," Havaldar Mansingh said, "what an honour it is for me—and Rupa Devi—to hear your voice! I never thought I would see you again—after that ride in the Army battle tank that your good Lady drove in the Thar Desert!"

"Lady Julia is here, and she will tell you herself, whatever she wishes."

"Havaldar Mansingh and Rupa Devi, we're delighted to meet your son, Devinder. He is a real gentleman and a Rajput! When our daughter, Sarah, told us about her friendship with Devinder, we thought you might like to have a few words with him—to hear his voice—and you can speak with him as long as you wish—in Hindi. Please do not be concerned that we do not speak the language; we quite understand. You might want to give him news about his brother and sister and their families too."

It was not a brief conversation—but neither was it an overlong one—possibly because Devinder's parents had concerns about their Colonel Saheb's long-distance bill! Joshua's interrupted the conversation, at times when they might hang up—he spoke and understood Hindi—to reassure them, repeatedly, that it was of no consequence, but they finally brought the telephone call to a close, thanking all of them individually—General Saheb and his good Lady Memsaheb, and Miss Sarah, and Miss Ruth, and Miss Susan, and Mr David, and his wife-to-be, Miss Rachel—for their concern for their son, and pleading for their protection over him.

Devinder's face registered total surprise and joy. He had never, in his wildest imagination, ever dreamt that he would be able to speak to his parents; he thanked them profusely as he left.

Sarah saw him to the door, and down the stairs to the main entrance of the building.

"May I ask you one question?" he said, smiling.

"Feel free to ask anything you wish," she replied, with an equally warm smile.

"Why didn't you tell me you were Lady Sarah?"

"Would it have made a difference, Devinder? I don't think so."

"My Rajput honour now stands between us. My mother and father would disown me—I would disown myself—if I were anything to you but the humblest of your friends."

"The military honour that my father instilled in all of us children, Devinder, has always told me that if neither of us is dishonourable, any two people can be good friends. Sure, when husband or wife comes along, and children too, or distance separates us, that friendship may become only a warm memory, and relegated to years past, but until that time I would be honoured to be considered your friend."

"So when did you find out that Mother was a servant in your father's house—that he looked after her like his daughter—and that he saved my father's life too?"

"Yesterday! When I asked you your mother's name—on my father's instructions."

"That makes me feel much better. It means that all the time we were friends, you were not pitying me—or playing the noble, charitable Lady of England!"

She laughed. "Far from it, Devinder. I saw you were miserable because you had no letters from home—and I wanted to help."

"You are truly gracious, Lady Sarah, and I wish you every happiness."

"You are truly a fine friend, Devinder, and a noble Rajput, and I wish you the same."

He folded his hands in a namaste of farewell. She responded likewise.

She then put forth her hand and he shook it warmly.

She found the family anxiously awaiting her return up the staircase. The cheerful smile on her face reassured them that their Sarah had not been hurt—neither had Devinder.

She went up to her father and wagged her finger at him.

"So Daddy, you were counting on his Rajput honour to rescue me—weren't you? That was the reason for the phone call to Marwar

Junction. And what Plan B, Daddy, did you have if his Rajput honour had failed him? Wasn't that a big risk you were taking?"

"It is like a battle plan, Sarah. When I took men in to battle, was I not taking a very big risk on their lives?— and mine too, because I was always on the frontlines with them. Most times the plans worked; sometimes they didn't. Did I have a Plan B? Of course."

"So, Pappa, what was it in my case?"

"You haven't guessed?"

"No."

"You. Your good sense; your realistic appraisal of the chances of happiness for the both of you—not just you alone. You're not a selfish person, Sarah—far from it. You would consider his happiness too in any decision you might make. But before we went to Plan B, the family had to know whether you were truly in love with him or not—and you answered that for all of us."

"So tell me, Pappa, what exactly did his mother have to say to him in Hindi? She went on for ever so long. I kept watching his face, and his changing emotions towards me—from friendship to deep respect—came through, though I didn't understand her words."

Joshua laughed. "You know it already, dear. She just recounted the tale exactly as I told it to you and Great Grandfather; exactly as we told it to the family here. Then she said: 'Colonel Saheb never laid a finger on me when I was his servant girl, and if you lay one finger on Colonel Saheb's daughter, don't bother to come home, because you will have disgraced our honour! You will not be welcome in this house.'"

"Oh, dear! That was harsh."

"Well, it was more a threat. Had you two been in love and decided to go ahead, Rupa Devi would have come around to accepting him—a mother's love will not be denied—even when Rajput honour is at stake! Fortunately, for Rupa Devi, he was not in love—and neither were you."

"Would you all like to know what settled it in my mind? That I was not in love."

They eagerly assented; all sat around the table.

"The essence of all the questions that you posed to me, to determine whether I was in love with him or not, can be distilled into a single word—just one word."

There was a silence in the room, as she waited for any one of them to come up with the word. They had played games, about love, with her; now it was her turn!

"The word is 'yearning'. All your questions asked the same of me—did I yearn for him? Take all the people we know to be in love. When David feels like calling up Rachel every few hours and restrains himself because he is unsure of how her family will take it—he yearns for her. Rachel misses David so dreadfully—she is here more than in her own house! When Mamma cries like a baby every time Pappa leaves her for a month—it is because her heart yearns for him. Pappa called Mamma every three days—because he was missing her! Missing someone is yearning for them. Without yearning there is no love! And I had no yearning for Devinder. So I was not in love like David or Rachel or Mamma or Pappa."

Julia threw up her hands in mock horror.

"The next time, Pappa leaves me for a month, and I feel the need to cry for him, I'm going to lock myself in my bathroom, and turn the shower on full—so that none of you can hear me. Is nothing ever secret in this house anymore?"

"Mamma dear," Ruth said, "that is what we have been telling you and Daddy for years now—since adolescence—but did either of you ever pay any heed? There are no secrets in this house—thank God! You know what I really fancy tonight—if Rachel can stay over—is a good pillow fight, with the new teams. No more boys against girls! Rachel, don't you feel like giving David a few good whacks? And don't spare him, dear. You will have to be on the opposing team to David, because, remember, dearest sister-in-law-to-be, we have to make up with the enemy!"

It would be a fun-filled conclusion to an exciting day.

CHAPTER 8

They had all missed Saturday morning Services at the Hampstead Reform Synagogue that Saturday morning because they had invited Devinder for lunch—and the lunch had to be cooked.

So Ruth had also missed training with Yusuf and Rehana that Saturday morning. She accepted it philosophically, determined to go next Saturday for training with her friends.

She was in the living room, her long legs, in running shorts, up on the armrest of the twin loveseat sofa she was lying in, her head propped up by two pillows against the other armrest, reading a 'romance' paperback; despite her tough exterior she loved to read such novels by writers who would die—so Susan had told her—'unheard and unsung'!

"Very likely, my dear Susan, but at least they have given me several hours of pleasure by their work; should I honour them less because the literary book reviewers and critics ignored their work as 'trash'?"

She had reached the climax where her heroine, rejected in love and disappointed with life, was contemplating entering a convent for an order of nuns in the French Alps, when Joshua and Julia entering the living room, stopped, saw a tear roll down Ruth's cheek, and smiled at each other. They had a child who could feel; a warm and loving daughter, who, like their other three children, wouldn't ever let them down!

That she would, next year, complete her degree in Exercise Physiology at the London Polytechnic, and was a world-class miler, was reason to admire her; their love for her was independent of it.

"Ruth," Joshua said, "you have no lectures this afternoon, I believe?"

"Yes, Pappa, or is it 'No', Pappa? I have no lectures."

"Will you be in this afternoon? At say 2:00 o'clock?"

"If you want me too. I was planning to go for a jog later to the Athletic Tracks on Hampstead Heath, but I can delay that. What is it?"

"We are going to have a visitor. Mamma and I would like you to be in—if that's possible. If not, I'll call him and postpone the visit."

"No, I'll be in. I can always go jogging later, after he has left. Who is our visitor?"

"Major Squigby."

"I'm sorry, Daddy, but I think I will be out, when he comes. That man is persistent—isn't he? Can't get through to me so what does he do? Get through to my parents!"

"On the contrary, he says he is coming here only because you invited him to visit with you."

"What? He's lying through his back teeth. Throw him out, Daddy!"

Joshua smiled. "Didn't you tell us that he met you on Hampstead Heath?"

"Yes."

"And that you insisted on his evidence being placed before you?"

"Yes."

"Well then, when he has it, he considers that you invited him to present it to you. He didn't know how to reach you; he waited for you the whole of last Saturday morning, on Hampstead Heath, but we had Devinder over, and you didn't go to the Tracks, or come back on Hampstead Heath. So he called Mamma, and she suggested this afternoon—your afternoon off from lectures at the London Polytechnic. What would you like me to do? I can call him and tell him you've changed your mind, and have no wish to see any evidence collected by the Crown. Shall I do that?"

Ruth swung her legs off the armrest, placed the book on the cocktail table in front of the sofa, went up to her father and hugged him; then hugged her mother too.

"I'm sorry, Daddy and Mummy, for being so abrupt. I really am. I'll be happy to have 'your' Major Squigby come by this afternoon; I'll go jogging after he has left. It shouldn't take him long to have his say and leave?"

Major Squigby came by promptly at 2:00 PM. He shook hands with Sir Joshua, bowed low over the outstretched hands of, first, Lady Julia, and then Lady Ruth.

Silently, without preamble, he drew from one pocket of his long overcoat a small tape recorder; from another of those cavernous pockets he drew out sheets of typed paper. He placed the objects on the cocktail table, and then sat down on the twin love seat sofa Ruth had occupied half-an-hour before. He invited them all to sit; though it was their house, he appeared to be in complete control of the proceedings.

Ruth thought: 'Just like a government bureaucrat!'

He cleared his throat. Little did she suspect how nervous he felt—or what he would not have given to disappear through the floor. Julia did, so she went, silently, to the kitchen and brought him a glass of cold water, which he drained. He flashed a smile at her.

The daughter did not understand him, was his lonely thought, but at least her mother did!

"Lady Ruth," he said, addressing her, "you asked me for evidence to validate our suspicions that a terrorist act is being planned in the Pakistani Café that you were in with Lord Yusuf and Lady Rehana. I asked you to disassociate yourself from him; to your credit you refused."

She was about to protest his change of heart, but he silenced her with a wave of his hand.

"You may think of me as you wish; that is your right, but by the same token I trust you will permit me to think of you as I wish—because that is my right too."

He smiled at her, and she yielded him his rights—without protest.

"One does not yield up one friends—or lovers—without convincing proof, that they may not be all that we had thought them to be. That does you credit. I work for MI-5; you are aware of that."

She was about to protest his use of the word 'lovers'—but decided to let it pass. He could think as he pleased!

"So you see I'm only fulfilling my responsibilities to the British public by trying to protect them from harm—and you are a member of the British public."

"Thank you. Your concern for me is touching. Now may we get on with this evidence that you say you have? Please?"

He nodded, handing over to her the typed sheets of paper. The heading read:

TRANSCRIPT of RELEVANT TAPINGS at the CAFÉ

Parts of the transcript had black lines over them so that they could not be read. She presumed they were classified information, and had been deleted on that account. She rejected them.

"Transcripts can be doctored," she said, sweetly. "You know me very little, Major Squigby. Let me hear the taped recordings, or please, don't waste my time."

"I was only trying to protect you," he said. "That accounts for the black lines on the transcript."

"Thank you, but I don't need your protection. You have used that word before, and it rather grates on me."

"Very well," Major Squigby said, but she saw a smile on his face, instead of the anger she had presumed her remarks would arouse; she thought that was odd.

"First," Major Squigby said, "I'd like you to listen to this conversation—just so that you can identify a voice you might recognise. Because if you cannot recognise the voice—and some people do have poor voice recognition, just as some people have poor face recognition—this session is at an end, and I will leave without your hearing the rest. Is that understood, Lady Ruth?"

She nodded. It was a female voice, and it said:

"I have to leave. Cook my dish today for the Sunday evening reunion dinner."

"Why that's me!" Ruth said, sharply.

"Quite right, Lady Ruth. So you do have good voice recognition. We can now proceed with the rest of the tapings."

"How did you tape me?" Ruth asked.

"Confidential, I'm afraid."

"Either you level with me, Major Squigby, or I will, very politely, exit by that front door for my afternoon jog—which you have so inconveniently disrupted. Now, how did you tape me?"

He looked at her with great admiration. Never in his experience had he come across a woman so strong and so entirely sure of herself, she could take on MI-5—and insist on her rights.

He looked at Sir Joshua in silent appeal.

"Don't look at me, Squigby," Joshua said, sadly. "It has to be that royal blood in her."

"Don't look at me, Major Squigby," Julia said, with equal sadness. "It has to be that military blood in her."

They all laughed.

'At least,' Ruth thought, 'he has a sense of humor!'

"We have Pakistani informants. Men and women of great character—and courage; British citizens who are loyal to their Queen and country. They hate these jihadists and fundamentalist radicals who would destroy the relationship between different sections of our citizenry. One of them—who will be nameless—has been frequenting the Café for eight weeks in a row. Why eight weeks? Because there are eight square tables, with four chairs each, in the Café. He has a 'bug' stuck to the underside of each table—so that no matter where anyone sits, we monitor all conversations. And we do it legally—because one of the participants has been previously involved in such activity; we have a court order permitting us to monitor the Café. There! Does that satisfy your sense of British justice, Lady Ruth?"

"It does."

"Now I'm going to play a series of taped conversations from the Café; you will almost certainly recognise some voices—you may not recognise others. May I suggest you refrain from talking or asking me any questions until you have heard all of the tapings, after which you—all of you—are free to ask me any questions you wish. Is that agreed? This request for no interruption is so that I do not have to switch the machine on and off."

They assented. Major Squigby switched on the tape recorder and settled back, his eyes on Ruth. She found it disconcerting, but she listened carefully.

"Well, did you make contact with her?"

"Yes."

Ruth started involuntarily. Even in that one single word she recognised the voice of Lord Yusuf. Major Squigby's face was inscrutable.

"And?"

"She has promised to come and train with Rehana and me."

"Good! So how long do you think you will take to break her down?"

"I don't know. Several weeks, maybe?"

"We don't have several weeks!"

"Well, to ask her for the Bentley—which is her mother's car—I need to get, shall we say, 'friendly' with her?"

"Yes, but you're a handsome guy, Yusuf. And a runner like her. She'll fall for you in no time at all. Just work on her. All we want is the Bentley!"

"I know, I know, that's all you want. But that's not all I want. I want to fornicate with the bitch first. A Jewish bitch! Then we get the car—but not before I fornicate with her. You understand, Ahmed?"

"Fornicate with the bitch as often as you want—and good luck to you—but just make it quick. We can't hang around, forever, waiting for you to get your cock in!"

"Give me a time line. What is the date? Ali will take a while to get the four bombs ready. So when is it to be?"

"Yusuf, I don't know. The orders will come from above; it is not in my hands. You and I will know the date in advance—though not by much. Maybe a day or so in advance. Will that be enough?"

"If you wanted her Mini, it might do, but if you must have the Bentley, it will take longer."

"We have to have the Bentley. How are you going to fit her body in the Mini, Yusuf—have some sense! She's a tall girl; when she's dead, we could cram her into the boot of the Bentley—never in the Mini."

"I'll try to set it up, but I need to know the date in advance."

"I'll speak to the guy who calls the shots. Leave it to me. I'll get back to you."

The tape recording came to an end.

For Ruth, it seemed her world had come to an end. She had been genuinely fond of him. Like her, he and Rehana were runners. There was a fellowship among runners, that few, who were not runners themselves, could appreciate, or even understand.

The tears welled up into her eyes and down her cheeks. No sobs, just the unhappiness of a girl who had been faithful in her friendship, only to find that others could be cruel and inhuman. Would she be ever able to trust again? Would she ever be able to befriend again?

Major Squigby was about to rise from his seat, go across to her and sit beside her to comfort her; Joshua, sternly, and silently, forbade him to rise by almost the authority of a military command with his outstretched arm. Instead, Julia went and sat beside her daughter, put an arm around her, and let her weep, softly, on her shoulder.

Major Squigby rose, picked up his tape recorder and the transcript, and would have silently left the room.

"Where do you think you're going?" Ruth asked, recovering herself almost as rapidly as she had dissolved into tears.

Major Squigby turned around.

"I'm sorry," he said, "I had no wish to intrude on your grief. Please forgive me. But if the tape recording has persuaded you to keep away from Lord Yusuf and the Pakistani Café, then at the very least I have served some purpose in life."

"On the contrary," Ruth said, wiping her eyes on her mother's blouse in the region of Julia's collar bone; then turning around to face him. "I plan to get even closer to Lord Yusuf. I will intensify my training to make absolutely certain I get together with him and Lady Rehana every single Saturday—even encourage him a little, perhaps by letting him hold my hand?"

"What!"

The exclamations of surprise came not only from Major Squigby—who practically sprang towards her—but from Joshua and Julia as well.

"Well," said Ruth, now completely recovered and in charge of the situation, "you do want to know the date when the terrorist attack is planned, don't you? If he needs Mamma's Bentley he will have to give me sufficient time for me to make the arrangements for it. In fact after Yusuf, I will be the first to know."

"Impossible! Out of the question! We'll just pick him up as soon as we hear chatter about the date—and that will abort their mission! Sir Joshua and Lady Julia, your daughter can't be serious about continuing to associate with men who are planning to rape her, kill her and stuff her body in the boot of your Bentley?"

"Major Squigby, tell me, do you think I have less courage than your Pakistani informants who risk their lives on a daily basis to protect Queen and country? Besides, it has now become very personal."

"Please, Lady Ruth, I beg of you, please, stay away from him!"

Then Major Squigby did something that none of them—least of all Ruth—expected him to do. He went down on his knees in front of her, reached for her hand, caressed it with his cheek, then moved it to his lips and kissed it. Then, in front of her parents, he put his head in her lap and on her bare knees, while she stroked his hair, in shocked and—as she freely admitted to them afterwards—delighted surprise.

Joshua and Julia would have left the room, but Ruth motioned them to stay.

"Major Squigby," she said, gently. "My father, was Director of Indian Military Intelligence. He and my mother had been married two weeks, when he was called on to find out why arms—being sent through India to the mujahidin in Pakistan, who were fighting the Soviet invasion of Afghanistan—were not reaching their destination. This was on a route that Pappa had set up with Colonel Rashid Khan of Pakistan. Mamma, who for a year was with MI-6, went with him, and saved his life by finding out the real murderer of Colonel Rashid Khan; PMI thought Pappa had done it, and were out to kill him. They risked their lives, two weeks after marriage, for Queen and Country. Mamma didn't know it until a few weeks later, but she was pregnant with David! Do I have less courage than they have?"

Her eyes, now dry, sparkled. She chided him.

"After all, Major Squigby, I have royal blood from one side and military blood from the other. They said so themselves; you heard them, did you not? Come now Major Squigby, when I have you to protect me—and I apologize for being so rude to you about that word 'protect'; it will forever be enshrined in my vocabulary as one of the sweetest words in the English language—why should I worry?"

Major Squigby got to his feet. He was embarrassed by his actions, but she seated him beside her, and held his hand.

"You will be careful! Please?"

"Yes, I will."

"And you will carry a gun with you? Do you know how to use a gun?"

"Yes, I do. Pappa taught all of us how to use a gun when we were very young, and in India. But I cannot carry a gun."

"Why not?"

"Because when I train, I run—and so does Lady Rehana—in a running body bra and running shorts. There would be no place to hide a gun, I'm afraid."

"I see."

He thought about it for a moment. It was as if Joshua and Julia were not even in the room.

"But Ruth could have a 'bug' planted on her, could she not?" Julia said softly.

"Of course!" Major Squigby said, looking in gratitude at Julia for the suggestion. "Lady Julia could have it sewn into the inside of the waistband of your running shorts. So you can communicate with us at all times. Please!"

"Yes, of course. I am neither foolhardy nor foolish. A 'bug' it shall be—as Mamma suggests. One condition to the 'bug'?"

"Lady Ruth, please ask anything of me that you wish: If it be in my power to give it to you—I will."

She smiled. "That you stop calling me 'Lady Ruth'.

"Ruth' will do just fine."

He smiled, as he assented, rising from beside her.

"Where do you think you're going?" she asked.

"I thought we were through?"

"No, we're not. Didn't you say we could ask you questions after listening to that dreadful tape?"

"Yes, of course. What would you like to know?"

"Is Rehana involved in all this?"

"Ruth, I don't know. We really don't know. So please be very wary when you are with her."

"I will. Next question. Do Viscount Edward and Begum Naseem Banu know about Yusuf's involvement with jihadists?"

"Yes, they do. As you well know, Viscount Edward is the Director of the South East Asian Bureau of MI-6. We had to tell him. It took all our persuasion to prevent the Viscountess from calling in her son, playing the evidence—this very tape—in front of him, and then thrashing him with her sandal! Begging your pardon, General, but people from your part of the world are very excitable."

"Don't I know it, Major Squigby?" Julia said, making an attempt to roll her eyes to the heavens, and not succeeding very well.

"Please, Ma'am, would you call me, 'Will'? I'd be so honoured."

"Will, it is," Julia said.

"So to answer Ruth's question fully, the only condition they both made—Viscount Edward and the Viscountess, I mean—is that they be present at the 'kill'. And to that we agreed."

He collected his tape recorder and his transcript, for the second time that afternoon.

"Where do you think you're going?" Ruth asked again, innocently.

"Home. Why do you ask?"

"Well, you've done a lot to protect me—and notice I'm using the word myself. Now I'm going to do something to protect you."

"Oh?"

"I could not believe that a man running barely 50 yards came so near to coughing himself to death—and frightening the daylights out of me in the bargain! So Will, dear, you and I are going for a little jog. Nothing very strenuous, I promise you. I'll slow down to a nice, easy pace for you. Half an hour to start with—and we'll build up both distance and pace as time goes by. Then I'll bring you back here, let you cool off, and offer you a cup of tea and some cookies that Susan has baked—she bakes the most delicious almond macroons—after which I will permit you to leave. Is that agreed?"

He could not believe he was hearing what he was hearing!

"With the greatest, greatest of pleasure!"

"Major Squigby," Joshua said, laughing, "beware! The good Lord might grant you what you've been praying for. Don't ever complain to me that I didn't warn you."

They all agreed, for Ruth's safety and the peace of mind of her siblings, that no disclosure would be made to them. Ruth met Yusuf and Rehana for training, the next Saturday morning. She slipped away a little early from the Services in the Synagogue, meeting them, as usual outside the gates. They crossed the side street off North

End Way, into the Heath, where Rehana and she stripped off their blouses and skirt, tying the two pieces of clothing round the waist. They were down to running body bras and running shorts, as they took off for an easy jog down the Heath, south towards Mansfield Road, where the athletic field and tracks were located.

In the waistband of Ruth's running shorts, Julia had sewn a tiny 'bug'. They had deliberated where it should be placed. At first they thought the side or back of the waistband would be most comfortable, but Ruth dissented.

"If he puts his arm around my waist, Mamma, and he might well do that, he'd feel it immediately. Far better it be placed in front."

And so it was placed almost directly above her navel. They had tested it, and though the range was limited, Major Squigby, in the safe house across from the Pakistani Café, monitoring the Café, had a reception loud and clear to anything she said or was said to her.

In the Café, they sat as usual at one of the tables and ordered their tea and pakoras. They had barely finished, when Rehana rose suddenly.

"I'm going to leave a little early, Ruth," she said. "Yusuf wants to talk to you something personal; I'd only be intruding."

"Oh! What?"

Rehana laughed. "You'll find out soon enough, dear."

"So what did you want to talk to me about; so personal that Rehana had to leave?"

He came straight to the point.

"Ruth," he said, "do you trust me?"

"Of course. I've known you since childhood. We've played together all these years; we're both milers—what a question to ask?"

"If I asked you for something—that is yours to give—would you give it to me?"

"Well," Ruth said, slowly. "Now that does depend."

"On what?"

"On what the request is? If it is against my moral or ethical principles—or even my values—the answer would be a regretful and polite 'No'. If, on the other hand, you wanted a small loan of money, say, I would give it to you without asking questions on what the money was for. Does that make sense?"

"Yes, dear, it does."

"So what is it that you want from me that is mine to give? Unless you ask you'll never know, will you?"

He took a deep breath.

"Could you loan us a car—and your services—for a day. Just one day."

"Oh, sure! We have a Mini for the use of us four children. We have an erasable bulletin board in the kitchen, and we all just write down the day we want it, and the time. Then, if there is an overlap, we carpool—dropping each other off or picking each other up—without any problems. It's worked very well all these years—even when Susan got behind the wheel!"

"No! No!" Yusuf said hastily. "We need a bigger car; the Mini would be too small."

"Why? Why do you need a bigger car? What is it for? Where will I be driving you? When is it you're going to need it?"

"Khaled, Ahmed and a third man—you don't know—are leaving for Pakistan soon. They need a car to drive them to the airport. I'll be coming along to see them off, of course; they're very old friends of mine. They are going back forever! Even if each has only two bags to check-in—that's at least six bags—with three airbags, it's quite a lot of luggage. It would never fit in a Mini, would it now?"

"No, it would not," Ruth said decisively. "What you need is a full-size car. Why don't you rent one? It's not too expensive, and if you're going to see them off, why you can drive it back; you don't even need my services."

"I'm afraid it's not as simple as that. You see they're flying back home on a private jet owned by a Pakistani businessman. He flies in and out of the country at his will. So they haven't a clue when he's coming and when he's leaving. Apparently—so they tell me—he grew up in the same village as Khaled's and Ahmed's parents did, and so he's taken an interest in them. When he found out they wanted to return, he offered to help with jobs, and the flight back home. They don't know the date they're flying back; so how can they reserve a full size car? Say they get a phone call from this man's secretary saying be at the airport at such and such a time on the very next day, and they are unable to rent the car? Sometimes even rental car companies don't have cars to rent in this autumn tourist season, particularly in London—at short notice? If they aren't there on time, he isn't going to wait for them! There go their chances of a free flight back home and jobs awaiting them—all because they took a chance on being at the airport on time. If we can arrange a full-size car— guaranteed!—their problem is solved."

"I see."

"I would like to help them, Ruth. I've known them for years. Mamma and Pappa both drive mid-size cars—Mamma drives a Honda Civic; Pappa a Ford Cortina—with rather small boots, or I'm sure they would have helped."

Ruth felt it was time; she had protested enough. Major Squigby, in the building across the street, must be pulling his hair out in handfuls, begging her to agree to Yusuf's request for a full-size car. She didn't mind Major Squigby losing his hair—lots of very nice men were bald—but his anxiety was a cause for concern!

"Well, Yusuf, Mamma has a full size Bentley. It's got a huge boot. It's more than 27 years old, but it works just fine; besides they don't make cars like they used to—the size, the luxury, the reliability of the engine. Would you like me to ask Mummy, whether she can spare it for a day? I'm sure she'll say 'yes', but she'll need advance notice, to make sure she has no shopping plans, or a visit to Cecily Aunty's place, or whatever."

"Could you, Ruth? I'd be ever so grateful! So can we have it at a day's notice?"

"Impossible! Have you gone mad? I'm asking my mother to give me the use of her car on one day's notice? Take a hike, Yusuf—and tell your friends to take a hike too! I'd be ashamed to tell Mamma she gets one day's notice to change her plans. Don't you think she has to inform other people, she can't make it? She might have plans to see Grandfather at Bromfield House. What does she do—call him and say: 'I can't come tomorrow, because Ruth has to have the Bentley, because Yusuf's friends have to go to the airport'?"

"All right! All right! Don't keep on about it. I'll find out what is the maximum notice they can give. If that suits you, we'll go with your Mamma's Bentley; if not we'll just have to make other arrangements."

Ruth yielded up talk of the Bentley. How much truth there was in Yusuf's tale of the Pakistani businessman and his private jet, Major Squigby and MI-5 would have to investigate—it was beyond her capability. But there were other avenues she would like to probe—within her purview. She knew that Major Squigby would like her to leave the Café as soon as possible, but some of the dangers that he had outlined, for her, were very personal—and only she could get some answers out of Yusuf on those issues.

"So tell me, Yusuf, why did Rehana have to leave? There's been nothing personal that you've discussed with me at all."

"Rehana had to leave because I don't want her to know about Khaled leaving. She has a soft spot for him, and it might hurt her."

"Is she in love with him?"

"I don't know."

"Because if she loves him, his leaving without even saying goodbye would be very cruel and more hurtful than if he was just honest with her."

Ruth stopped for a moment. The next question rattled Yusuf more than she'd anticipated.

"Has she given her body to him? Lost her virginity to him? Is she pregnant by him?"

"No! How can you even think about her in that way? She is a well-brought up Muslim girl; she will be a virgin until her wedding night!"

"I'm very glad to hear your views on the subject, Yusuf. Really happy! You're right, well-brought up Muslim girls—or Jewish ones—don't go around giving themselves to men they hardly know, or think are in love with them, or think they are in love with. But there are exceptions—and I didn't know whether such an exception would apply to Rehana."

Yusuf looked up sharply, and with interest.

"Oh? What are the exceptions where a well-brought up Jewish girl might make exceptions to keeping her virginity until her wedding night?"

"Well, Yusuf," and though she was addressing Yusuf, were her remarks for Will as well? "I can't speak for all well-brought up Jewish girls; I can only speak for myself. But say I was engaged to a soldier, and he was ordered out onto the battlefield in some far off country for a long tour of duty that might see him come home to me—and then might not. I would seriously consider giving myself to him—if he wanted me. Suppose I withheld myself from him, and he died, the regrets I would have would punish me for the rest of my life. On the other hand, suppose I did give myself to him, and he died on the battlefield, wouldn't the thought of that one last night with me, make his last few hours on Earth that much more bearable? And then, wouldn't that thought sustain me for the rest of my life? Every circumstance is an individual one. There are no set rules; I wish there were."

Yusuf got up at once. "I have to go," he said. "I'll keep you informed on the date we're going to need that Bentley. Just make your Mamma aware that you may have a need for her car—in the near future."

Ruth waited until he'd left; then went across to the man at the cashier's till. "May I enter the other room?"

"No," he said, gently. "Keep away from this café too!"

Ruth and Will had made arrangements to meet every Tuesday and Friday, for Will to lay out before Ruth the relevant taped conversations that had taken place in the Café from Saturday afternoon onwards. That would keep her more knowledgeable for the track session on the next Saturday.

But at Will's insistence, they were not to meet in public. So Will's training sessions—much to Ruth's regret—were put on hold by Will, until this 'matter' had been settled.

So on Tuesday afternoon, Ruth, as usual, put on her running gear—her body bra and an 'unbugged' pair of running shorts—and jogged down to Finchley Road. She crossed the road at the traffic light, past the tube station entrance, jogging down the line of terraces that stretched, sometimes in straight lines and sometimes in shallow curves, as the lay of the land had dictated to the original planners of that part of Hampstead.

She slowed down as she entered Compayne Gardens, as if to catch her breath, but at No. 33, she turned left swiftly into the building. She went up the stairs to the top floor, but before she could knock the door opened.

"You must have a sixth sense," she said, as she entered.

"No," Will said, smilingly, "I was just watching, and, waiting for you, looking out through the living room windows that look down on Compayne Gardens. A yearning to see you the quickest moment possible?"

Ruth started at the use of Sarah's word. He did not notice because he was looking appreciatively at her outfit.

"Very fetching," he said.

"Thank you."

"And congratulations on the way you handled yourself with Yusuf on Saturday. A professional agent couldn't have done it better. I have a lot of information to report to you."

Ruth looked round the room. It was the first time she had been in Will's flat. It was a bachelor flat that amply personified the character of the one who lived in it. Quite simply put—it was in spotless condition!

It had been meticulously cleaned, everything was in its proper place—the books were in the library cupboard, the kitchen sink had been cleared of the lunch dishes that had been washed and put away, the bed had been made—she peeked into the bedroom to find that out—the dining table had been set for two, sitting opposite to each other, the temperature in the room was a little on the cool side, but coming in as she was from a run, it seemed refreshing to her. Was it in this condition because he knew she was to be visiting his flat for the first time?

He must have read her thoughts because he said:

"No, it isn't always this neat every single day; I sort of put it into shape for you. But it is in pretty good condition, most of the time, because I like it that way."

The door to the study was closed. She indicated it with a raised look of her eyebrows, and he acquiesced.

She was surprised by what she saw. It seemed like she was in the control room of a front line army base. There were six computers lining one wall of the study; each had a swiveling chair in front of it. There was one additional main computer that was on the office desk, with on office chair in front of it, with filing cabinets lining the other walls of the room. And there were files—literally hundreds of them—strewn on the tops of the cabinets and even on the floor of the room, beside the main desk.

Yet, everything was still neat and orderly.

"I can't tell you much, Ruth, much as I would love to, because you don't have security clearance—as yet. I have put in for it, urgently, arguing that the very least MI-5 can do for a woman who can put her life on the line for Queen and country, is to give her security clearance!"

"Thank you, Will. I don't need to know. All I will surmise is that you are the Section Chief of MI-5 for this area, that there are at least six safe houses—like the one opposite the Pakistani Café—and that they are all linked to you by those six computers, while you are linked to headquarters by the computer on the office desk."

"Tell me, dear, why did I even bother to apply for security clearance for you?"

She laughed as they left the study; he closed the door behind them.

On the cocktail table in the living room, she saw the tape recorder; there was no transcript. He invited her to sit where she pleased. He was uncertain of where she might want him to sit. She sat on the sofa; patted it beside her, for him to sit.

He switched on the tape recorder.

She reached out and held his hand. Their hands, fingers intertwined, lay between them, adjacent to and touching her bare running thigh.

The tape recorder came on. There were two voices; one was Yusuf, the other she recognised as Khaled:

"So you've got the Bentley—as the getaway car?"

"Yes, but she asked a lot of questions first; why we needed the Bentley? I had to tell her; she's an intelligent girl. She wants the date too. So you'll have to get it."

"You fool! You told her everything; about the Pakistani businessman and his private jet?"

"I had to. Only the truth was credible. Anyone else going to the airport rents cars or takes cabs—except people fleeing the country. Do you have the date?"

"Ah, well, what's done's done. They'll have to tell me and Ahmed, at the very least, the night before."

"That isn't good enough. I can see her point of view too. She thinks she's giving you all a ride to the airport in the Bentley—she doesn't know she's going to be in the boot herself! Why do you say you'll know at least the night before?"

"Because that's the procedure. We know the target only the night before. Everything is ready; then in the night we plant the bombs. Next morning, at the right time—which is also given to us the night before because we have to set the timers—the bombs go off; then in the getaway car—the Bentley, in this case—we head for the airport and back to Pakistan. For the next operation, they'll use a different set of people."

"But you told me Ahmed was there for the last operation—when the Sloane girl had her throat slit from ear to ear?"

"That was unusual. Many will handle a gun when it comes to the killing; not too many will use a knife—not the way Ahmed does, with positive enjoyment of the killing. Others are sick all over; not Ahmed—he gloats!'

'I asked him once about it. Seems he was jilted by a white girl in his youth—he has hated them all, ever since. We had to have him for the Sloane girl, and we'll need him for your Jewish bitch as well. By the way how are you getting on—with getting inside her? Some progress I hope; you may not have much time."

"Not too well. She's a virgin and wants to stay that way; she's orthodox Jewish in that way."

"Well, then, we'll just have to hold her down; you rape her, then Ahmed does his thing on her, then we stick her in the boot of the car, with the luggage—make sure the car is filled up with petrol—and we take off."

Ruth fingers tightened round Will's; his on hers. She leaned her head against his shoulder, and shuddered. The spasm of fear passed. She straightened up.

"Would you like me to stop?" Will asked, gently. He shut off the tape recorder. "We can always pick it up later."

She shook her head.

"I'll be alright, Will. Just hold my hand! I cannot believe there are cruel men like this in this world—men who would slaughter me like one of their goats."

"You can still back out, my love. We'll pick the three of them up; on the basis of what we have, we could incarcerate Yusuf and Khaled for a short while, and Ahmed for a very, very long time."

"No! They'll only abort the mission and surface with others somewhere else. No! We have to get the entire cell—the top man and all—before they leave the country."

He nodded miserably, as he switched the machine on again.

"So what is the procedure going to be? Tell me Khaled, in case she asks me questions. I can't say: 'I don't know, I don't know'; it becomes fishy after a while!"

"It's really quite simple. We learn of the date a few days earlier; I'll insist on it. We learn of the target and the time for the bombs to go off, the night before. That morning, you make sure she and the Bentley are outside the Café about half an hour before the bombs are due to explode. That will give you sufficient time to rape her, Ahmed to kill her, time to load her into a sack and then into the boot, time to put all our luggage in as well—and time to take off for the airport. We don't have to be near the target when the bombs go off—in fact, we had better not be, because they'll be looking for people like us. We'll hear all the good bits—how many killed; how many seriously injured—on the BBC. There, now have I filled you in properly?"

There was no answer, so it must have been Yusuf acknowledging with a nod.

"Do you have any clue as to what the target might be?" Ruth asked. "From the procedures they follow, it doesn't seem that Yusuf will know the target until the night before their operation—and by that time the bombs will already have been planted and we will be unable to prevent the attack. We will certainly be able to apprehend them—but preventing them taking innocent lives should be our first priority."

Will frowned. She was right—and he knew it.

"Our people have researched it—as best they can. If it is on next Saturday, the Queen is scheduled to open an addition to the Children's Mercy Hospital in Bayswater. If it is on Sunday, the only high-profile event—and they do try for the maximum publicity by going for high-profile events—is the Prime Minister attending a concert of the London Orchestra at the Albert Hall in South Kensington. If it's Monday, there is a flower show in East End of London. On Tuesday, there is nothing that is high-profile. On Wednesday there is a London Book Show of self-published writers at Earl's Court. On Thursday, the Communist party is holding a big rally in Hyde Park—these open air events are the biggest headaches! And, finally, on Friday, the Liberal Party is holding a Town Hall meeting in Camden. Then we're into next week; for that they're still working on high-profile events in the City. It ain't easy, Ruth!"

"What did you think of the information I forced out of him about the Pakistani businessman with the private jet?" Ruth asked.

"Anybody would wonder why they could not rent a car to get to the airport? Why do they need a privately owned, full-size car? Unless they have to have a guaranteed, available, getaway car at their disposal, at very short notice; one that will take them all, and the luggage—and me. And for which the money trail doesn't lead back to Mr Businessman!"

"That was very clever of you, dear," Will said. "We made inquiries at Heathrow. They have a complete log of the planes that fly in and out. There was a business jet that was in—and out—at the time of the last terrorist attack and the Sloane girl's murder. And the same business jet flew in two weeks ago; its 'take-off' date has not yet been fixed. We're keeping an eye on the jet; if necessary we'll immobilise it where it sits."

Ruth leaned back against the sofa; Will leaned back too. They were still holding hands against her bare thigh—neither wanted to yield up that delight. So they sat, and sat, and sat; finally, Will said with a laugh.

"Dear, I don't want to get up because I'll lose the touch of your hand and your thigh. And you don't want to get up—I think—for the same reasons. Why don't we make a deal?"

"Oh," she said, blushing a crimson red, "and what sort of deal are you prepared to offer, Major Squigby? One that will entice me to move from the comfort of this sofa—and its delights?"

"That instead of sitting opposite to each other at the dining table for a cup of tea and some cupcakes—bought I'm afraid; not homemade, and not as good as the Queen's!—that we sit beside each other, and that each gives the other full permission to lean across to the other for the comfort of whatever is within reach—be it hand, or thigh, or waist or shoulder?"

"What a wonderful idea, Will! But I am agreeable to the deal, only if you agree to a tight hug when I leave—which does bring my breasts into play as fair game—and a non-tender kiss on the lips as well. Do you agree, Major Squigby?"

"Done, Lady Ruth!"

"Though I have to tell you, Sir, that my tight running body bra may be very fetching to look at, but it is not the right upper garment that would afford you—or me, for that matter—the fullest pleasure from the softness it so harshly conceals."

CHAPTER 9

Yusuf's call came that Thursday. No one was at home, when Ruth answered it.

"This Saturday. Can you get the Bentley?" he asked.

"One minute," Ruth said.

She put her hand over the speaking end of the telephone, waited for one full minute before she uncovered her hand, and went back on the telephone.

"Yes, Yusuf, Mummy has said that'll be fine. I can have the Bentley to take your friends to the airport. What time is their flight? What time do they want to leave? What time do you want me there outside the Café?"

She appeased her conscience by arguing that since her mother had already agreed that Ruth could have the Bentley, anytime of day or night, only subject to them—and Major Squigby being informed—she wasn't lying by not speaking for one minute!

Besides, according to Jewish moral law, was it acceptable to lie to a man who intended to rape and then murder you?

"Great! Well they want to leave some time in the morning. Can you be here outside the Café by 9:30?"

"What about our training? I'll have to miss Services—but we've all done that before, once in a while; we did it when Sarah's friend Devinder came for lunch one Saturday and we all had to cook for him—so why don't I park the Bentley at, say, 9:00 outside the Café? The three of us will then go to the Athletic Tracks, get some training in, for half an hour or so, and then we do whatever your friends want. Yes?"

Yusuf sounded doubtful. "Couldn't we just skip training for a day as well?"

"No!" she said, firmly. "I'm doing a lot for your friends; the very least you can do is to let Rehana and me get our training in."

"Rehana! She won't be coming to the airport with us; there isn't place for her in the Bentley."

"I can see that, but she can still be with us for the half hour or so before, can't she? I'll call and ask her to come."

"No! I'll ask her. All right, all right! We'll meet at 9:00, at the Athletic Tracks; just make sure that the Bentley is filled up and outside the Café, when you come." And he rang off.

She then spent a busy twenty minutes on the phone to Will and her father—as she had promised—keeping them informed.

Major Squigby had a very busy afternoon that Thursday, keeping several government and police departments informed of the imminent threat of a terrorist attack on Saturday morning—target unknown, exact time unknown. What they did know was that the attack was to be in London. Without inciting panic, the terrorist threat was raised, internally, to red alert.

Citing national security, the Home Office did not inform the news and public media of the threat.

Saturday was the day when the Queen was to open the addition to the Children's Mercy Hospital in Bayswater.

The Prime Minister asked for an urgent meeting with Her Majesty, to request her to postpone the ribbon cutting ceremony for a few days, until the matter had been resolved. The threat to her life was very real; it was a matter of National Security!

Her Majesty graciously, but firmly, declined.

"Prime Minister," she said softly, "we will not permit foreign terrorists—who are no better than bandits and ruffians—to dictate to this country, where their Queen will go, and when she will go, to where she wants to be. I have promised to cut the ribbon for the addition to the Children's Mercy Hospital in Bayswater at 10:00 o'clock, on Saturday morning—and that is where I will be. I will do my job; you must do yours. I wish you good day, Prime Minister."

At 9:00 on the Saturday morning, Ruth driving the Bentley parked outside the Café. She did not know if it was open or not, and whether there were people inside it or not; instead very rapidly, she stripped off her skirt and blouse, flinging them into the Bentley, and, in her running gear, crossed the side street on which the Café was located, into the Heath.

There she sat on the grass to await Yusuf and Rehana. Only a few minutes later their Mini pulled up. Rehana seeing her on the grass, waved to Ruth; then stripping off her blouse and skirt and flinging it into the Mini, she ran to meet Ruth. Yusuf disappeared into the Café.

"Where's Yusuf?" Ruth asked casually. "Isn't he going to train with us?"

"Oh, yes. He'll be with us in a minute. He has some business—wouldn't tell me what it was—in the Café. He'll be out shortly.

They sat for more than forty-five minutes, waiting for Yusuf, talking about their childhood—Rehana was older than Ruth, but they had been good friends since childhood, because Ruth's mother, Julia, and Rehana's Aunt Cecily, had been best friends since their teenage years in boarding school in Kent. There was a close bond between the girls, not only as runners but as women who truly were fond of each other.

"So I hear that David is engaged?" Rehana laughed. "That's the story of my life—always the lady-in-waiting! I don't know what it is to be in love."

"Yes, David is engaged. And now they can't seem to go anywhere without each other. He's at Services this morning, with the family, in the Synagogue—and she's there too. She's more at our house than hers; Lysa Aunty is always moaning to Mummy about it—how she's lost a daughter, not gained a son! You'll like Rachel. She is nice to be with, and fun to be around. And she loves David! The yearning that Sarah called true love; you can see it in her eyes when David walks into the room or when he touches her. Even I didn't know what it was—until a few days ago."

"Oh! You're in love?"

Ruth blushed. "And you will be too, one day."

Ruth reached out and held her hand. Rehana was surprised, but pleased, and reciprocated by warmly tightening her fingers around Ruth's trembling hand.

At 9:45, Yusuf came out of the Café and signaled them to come on over. They strolled leisurely towards Yusuf and the Bentley.

"I'm sorry, I couldn't train with the two of you," he said, avoiding looking at Ruth. "Now Rehana, dear, it is time for you to take the Mini and go on home. Ruth and I have to talk over some personal matters in the Café."

At that instant, a figure appeared around the corner of the street and rapidly approached them. It was Major Squigby. Ruth held out her hand to him, and he shook it warmly.

"Lady Ruth," he said, "what a pleasant surprise. And Lady Rehana and Lord Yusuf too! We meet again. Almost as at the Queen's party."

"Yes," Yusuf said harshly, "and as that party you are now intruding on us in a private conversation. So why don't you just disappear?"

"I will—if Lady Ruth tells me to disappear," Major Squigby said, quietly. "Do you, Lady Ruth?"

"On the contrary, Major Squigby. Words cannot express how delighted I am to see you at this moment. I'm afraid, Yusuf, you won't be able to fornicate with this Jewish bitch after all," she said, without emotion.

Three things happened almost simultaneously after that—and very rapidly.

A Rolls pulled up behind the Bentley, its front fenders touched the Bentley lightly; in it were Viscount Edward and Begum Naseem Banu.

Begum Naseem Banu was older than both her husband and Julia—almost sixty years old. But her looks belied her age. She must have been at one time an extraordinarily and exotically beautiful woman. She had a slightly hooked, semitic nose, with luscious lips bordering large cheeks, her charm enhanced by that agelessly mature look. Even the wrinkles in her eyes and the double chin appeared becoming. She was tall, but heavily built—which was her only concession to age.

Viscount Edward Andrews on the other hand was tall, lean and gaunt, with a clean-cut boyish face and with creamed and carefully parted blond hair; the sharp eyes were piercingly blue. In earlier years, people meeting them as a couple for the first time had mistaken him to be her eldest son, which delighted her, because that is the way she had always treated him—and he loved it!

A military jeep pulled up in front of the Bentley, then backed up so that its rear fenders touched the Bentley lightly. That Bentley wasn't going anywhere!

At the very same time, about one hundred uniformed policemen poured out of the safe house, rapidly going through the alleyways to the rear of the building, blocking off all exits from the building.

Begum Naseem Banu, yanked Yusuf by the arm into the open rear door of the Rolls; Rehana and Ruth piled into the front seat beside Viscount Edward. Rehana, confused, her eyes fearful, held her father's arm and pressed herself to him. Major Squigby stationed himself behind Yusuf, but did not attempt to hold him.

"Now, you little twerp," Begum Naseem Banu said, angrily, "you'll tell us all what is the target of today's bomb attack—and the time it's set for!"

No reply. She slapped him hard across the face. He only laughed.

"You can hit me all you want, Mamma, but you're getting nothing out of me. It may be too late anyway."

The Begum reached into her handbag and drew out a long, thin bladed dagger with a jewel-encrusted handle.

Yusuf laughed again.

"You can kill me Mamma, but I won't tell—and neither will those you've arrested inside. We are jihadists; we serve a higher cause!"

This time it was Begum Naseem Banu's turn to laugh out loud. "Kill you? You're not worth killing, you miserable son of mine—

how we ever conceived you, your father and I will never know! No, I'm not going to kill you. You believe in suicide bombers—you jihadists—don't you? Well you'll have the pleasure of seeing your mother commit suicide in front of you. I'm going to count to three. You're going to tell me where the target is and the time when the bombs are set to explode. One."

Silence.

Yusuf thought he could back out of the open door and run for it, but Major Squigby, had him now in an oft-rehearsed army hold Yusuf could not break. The Major's arms were around Yusuf's chest and neck, making him keep his eyes pinned on his mother.

"You can't be serious, Naseem!" the Viscount shouted from the front seat. He opened the front driver's side door, and tried to open the rear door of the car, nearest to his wife—but she had it locked.

"No, Mamma!" screamed Rehana, in terror. "He isn't worth it!"

Even Ruth said: "Naseem Aunty, please don't do it. Please!"

"Two." Silence.

Naseem unbuttoned the front of her blouse to reveal voluminous breasts held tightly together by, and overflowing, an equally voluminous bra. With her free hand she flung the two sides of her blouse apart.

"I am the daughter of the Maharajah of Cholistan, an ancient kingdom in the Thar Desert. You and your fellow jihadists do not know how to live like men—let me show you how a Queen dies. Three."

She raised her arm backwards to plunge it into her chest, with full force, when Yusuf screamed:

"The Hampstead Reform Synagogue at ten o'clock! You are all too late anyway."

Ruth and Major Squigby looked at their watches.

It was five minutes to ten.

Ruth threw open the front passenger door of the Rolls, dragging Rehana with her.

"Quick," she shouted. "The Hampstead Reform Synagogue; you know the way. Pace me—the fastest you've ever run in your life. The fastest ever!"

Without waiting for her reply, Ruth raced across the street and into the Heath.

Rehana was ahead of her very rapidly. As an 800 m runner she was capable of much faster speed than Ruth, in the shorter distance. She was running so fast, Ruth had difficulty keeping up with her—but then wasn't that the job of a pacer? Rehana thought of Yusuf, as her legs pumped faster and faster on the running trail they had jogged so many times before. It was the only way he could be saved from certain and long-term incarceration—if she and Ruth could save the two hundred or so innocent Jews at prayer in the Synagogue. It was like running with a tiger on your tail, except that the urgency was even more because she was running not to save her own life—but the lives of others.

At 700 m her leg strength began to give out; at 800 m she collapsed on the ground, and rolled out of the way, as Ruth skipped over her and overtook her, without a break in step, or looking back.

Now it was Ruth's turn to run the fastest she had ever run in her life, or at any meet, or in any race.

She thought of her family—her entire family: Pappa and Mamma, Sarah and Susan, David and Rachel—all sitting on that front pew, and she was flying over the ground as if it was meant to be. Her heart was pumping blood as never before; she did not hear her beating heart. Her lungs were pumping air with heaving, gasping breaths; she did not hear her thumping lungs. And her brain was releasing, out of her fear, the hormone adrenaline in massive, massive quantities into the blood stream, that made it all possible.

There was no tiredness in the fast-flying, long, graceful legs that relentlessly beat the ground, and surged her onwards towards her goal—the Hampstead Reform Jewish Synagogue. Four hundred yards away from it she saw the roof—it was still in place! No orange flames erupted from it—yet! That was all it took to energize her even more, so that she was covering the last quarter-mile in the same time as she had covered the first quarter mile with Rehana.

She didn't care for her speed. She had no thoughts of breaking the world speed record for a woman miler, or being the very first woman to have run the mile in under four minutes—they could keep all that! All she wanted was to reach that Synagogue before it exploded into flames before her!

She came to the edge of the Heath, raced across the road, up the five steps, through the open doors, down the centre aisle to the first pew, and collapsed into her father's arms crying: "There are bombs in the building, Daddy; get everyone out!"

After that Joshua took over—ever the military man. He thrust Ruth into David's arms saying: "David take the family out, and go with them; that's an order!"

Then he shouted as loudly as he could above the singing of the Cantor: "There are bombs in the Synagogue! Everyone out! Don't panic! But don't delay! Hurry!"

He then went to the Rabbi—who was eighty years old—to rush him out of the building. The Rabbi grabbed the Torah; the Cantor grabbed the Haftorah, and joined the short line of worshippers making for the exits.

"Thank God," Julia whispered to Joshua, "there was no Bar or Bat Mitzvah today. There would have been three or four hundred instead of just two hundred or so today—God has been merciful!"

"Why aren't you out of the building?" Joshua snapped.

"Because, dear, sometimes in a rush, a mother could forget a sleeping baby placed beside her; in her hurry to get her older children to safety—she forgets the little one. Why don't you take one side of the aisle—say the right side. I'll take the left side. All we do is look down each row and meet at the front."

He nodded, with a smile. Trust Julia to think of such things—she would have made a great military Colonel!

Julia rapidly passed from row to row looking to the end of it for a bundle. And in the second last row, she saw it. A wrapped up little bundle. She raced down the pew, prepared to abandon it if it was a large purse or a shopping handbag.

It was not. It was a little baby, who opened its eyes and smiled at her. She grabbed it to her breasts and made for the front entrance. She could never have waited for Joshua—not with a baby in her arms; Joshua would have forbidden it too!

Outside, a line of policeman—Will Squigby had been busy on the phones too—held the line of Synagogue-goers in safety, on the Heath, on the other side of the street. The mother was trying, unsuccessfully, to break through the ranks, shouting for her baby. When she saw Julia come out to the top of the steps, she ducked under the line of hands holding them at bay, and raced towards the Synagogue—a policeman in pursuit.

She reached Julia just as the policeman reached her. Julia thrust the baby into her arms—the baby now crooning softly—while the policeman seeing the contents of the bundle, helped her carefully down the steps to safety.

Joshua was not quite as quick as Julia.

On the very first pew, closest to the door, but at the far end of it, he saw a man—sleeping. He'd had enough experience to know that men do fall asleep, at prayer, in a synagogue. He rushed down the pew and shook him awake.

It was a homeless man who had taken shelter in the Synagogue, as soon as it had opened, possibly because he'd found a comfortable seat, and a warm place, in which to close his eyes.

"You! Come on! Out of this building!" Joshua said.

"Oh! Come on, Guv'nor. I wasn't doing no harm. Just getting a spot of shut eye. Give me a break, Guv'nor."

"Out! There are bombs in this building!"

The man laughed and winked at Joshua: "I've heard that one before too, Guv'nor."

There was no time to lose. Joshua decided to try a different approach.

"Look," he said, quietly. "You exit this building with me, now, and I'll give you fifty pounds outside. What do you say?"

"Cor, Guv! For fifty quid I'll run out of it for you!" And thrusting Joshua aside, he ran down the pew and out the front entrance.

Julia did not like it at all. Joshua should have been there ahead of her. There could not possibly be two babies left behind in there—could there? Then she saw a homeless man run out of the building—closely followed by Joshua.

She had turned towards the front door, the homeless man was racing down the steps, Joshua was almost with her—when the Synagogue exploded behind them.

The towering orange flames shot upwards igniting the wood roof, hurling the debris high up into the air raining it down on the street and the surrounding area below. It was good that Major Squigby had ordered the street closed to traffic at both ends of it.

But the blast of hot air had nowhere to go—except through the front doors. The windows on the upper story had been bricked in; those on the ground floor were shut and barred, though some of the slats in the shutters had been left open to let in the light. Some of the window panes did crack under the blast of hot air, but they held. The front doors were open, and as the blast erupted through, like the exhaust of a massive jet engine, it caught Joshua in the back and Julia from the front—propelling them, both, like missiles, down the steps and onto the pathway leading away from the Synagogue. Julia landed on her back, tearing the muscles of one shoulder. She screamed in agony, while the medics from the waiting ambulances rushed to her help. Joshua landed on his front. His left cheek hit the ground first and a sharply pointed piece of gravel punctured his flesh and tore at it, as he slid down the pathway. His cheek was bleeding copiously, but the medics, with a local anesthetic, stitched it up; he refused further hospital treatment. He would have a permanent scar down his left cheek for the rest of his life.

Joshua's and Julia's first concern was Ruth. She was sitting on the grass still recovering from her fierce run up the Heath from the Athletic Tracks to the Synagogue. She saw Rehana come slowly down the path and, getting to her feet, rushed to meet her.

Rehana had seen the towering flames erupt out of the Synagogue roof and assumed the worst; her joy when Ruth told her no one had been killed, made her pacing all seem worthwhile. No one could possibly know what her 800 m time had been; she had probably broken the world record.

No one could know what Ruth's time in the mile had been either. In five minutes flat, she had run just over a mile, and her father and mother had emptied a small synagogue—saving a tiny baby and a homeless man in the bargain. Had she broken the world record—even possibly done the impossible, of being the first woman ever, to run the mile in under four minutes?—not on a track but in the most pressure-driven of circumstances ever imaginable? No one would ever know.

But that didn't matter to either of them. One did not run for records or fame or glory—one ran for this!

The homeless man came up to Joshua.

Joshua assumed that he had come for his fifty pounds, reached into his inner coat pocket for his wallet, pulled out fifty pounds, and handed it over with a smile.

At first the homeless man refused to accept the money.

"Cor, Guv," he said, "you saved my life; I don't need to be paid for it—do I now? Thank ye!"

He had turned away, when a thought struck him. He came back.

"Tell me, Guv," he said, "does that priest of yours help in the soup kitchens?"

"Our Rabbi? Oh, yes. We have a responsibility to feed the poor. He and the Cantor and some members of the congregation—I don't have the time, but my girls help out once a year—they help in the soup kitchens, both with providing food and service. Why do you ask?"

"Well, Guv, if you could give me those fifty pounds, and I go and gift it to him for the soup kitchens, why the next time I'm eating there, I can look around and say to myself—though I wouldn't tell my buddies anything—I'm helping to feed you hungry lot! Would make me feel real good."

Joshua smiled. He emptied out his wallet for fifty pounds—and then three hundred and fifty more.

"That's an excellent idea, my man. Here take this lot—the whole four hundred. Give it to the Rabbi for the soup kitchens; as our thanks—yours and mine—to the good Lord for his deliverance on this day."

The Samuelsons stood and watched as the homeless man approached the Rabbi. There was a brief exchange between them, the homeless man pointing to Joshua. The homeless man handed the money over to the Rabbi, waved to Joshua and his family, then ambled down the Heath to, presumably, the first vacant bench he could find, to complete his interrupted sleep.

CHAPTER 10

A week later, the Samuelson family prepared for their reunion dinner on the coming Sunday evening, but the menu was a little different—as were the guests who would be eating it.

Sarah, as usual, still opted to make the lamb biryani.

Instead of fried fish, however, which was Joe Uncle's favourite food from years of eating in pubs, Ruth opted to make a chicken casserole with potatoes and onions. The reason was not that Joe Uncle had fallen from favour; it was because he was not going to be there. But Major Squigby had been invited and his favourite dish—Ruth had, in casual talk, obtained the information out of him—was chicken casserole with potatoes and onions! There would be *raitha* for the biryani, but not made by Rachel—because Rachel was not going to be there. The *raitha* would be made by Joshua instead.

"Oh, yes, let Daddy make the raitha," Susan said, heartlessly. "Men need to know how to cook too—what if Mother and we girls decide to go on strike—who's going to feed him? How's he going to survive?"

Joshua laughed. "I will make the raitha, Susan, but if you all decide to go on strike haven't you heard of the words 'eating out'? Besides, I'm not sure, dear," he said, addressing Julia, "whether it isn't enshrined somewhere in your wedding wows: 'Thou shalt feed thy husband for all the days of his life'? And if it isn't, for old timers like me—it should be!"

Susan would have made the chappatis, because Lysa Aunty loved chappatis—but Lysa Aunty wasn't going to be there—so she opted for the cauliflower and potato vegetable instead, because Rehana was going to be there, and Susan knew she loved it.

Julia would make the gulab jamuns as before, because she knew that whoever was there it would be well-received; besides she made the gulab jamuns because they were Joshua's—and her own—favourite dessert. Sometimes, she argued with herself, one had to cook for oneself!

The reason for the change in the menu was a phone call received two days earlier—from Lysa Aunty.

Roberta was flying in on Sunday evening, and their entire family was going to Heathrow Airport in two cars to receive her.

Rachel was going as well. Could Julia spare David from her Sunday reunion dinner?

Julia laughed heartily on the telephone.

"Lysa, dear," she said, "David is not a 'Mamma's boy'. Not anymore. Not since the age of fourteen. He's free to come and go, eat with us or not eat with us, be with us or not be with us—as he pleases. And the same applies to all the girls as well. That they do choose to be with us, and eat with us, gives Joshua and me a secret delight—we must have done something right!—but they're always on their own, even though they live with us. Now for that part—living with us after the age of eighteen—you'll have to blame that Indian father of theirs more than you can blame me. He insisted on it! 'When they get married, they can move out', he'd growled, when we first discussed it. If any 'child' had insisted on moving out, I would have supported it—but not one of them did. So, secretly, I was pleased Joshua put his foot down on that issue."

"So you mean, I have to ask Rachel to ask David to come to the airport with us?"

"Absolutely! You've got it. And if she asks him—shall we say—'nicely', I can't see how he could refuse. The only genuine reason he might demur—and that is because I know my son—is if he felt that the very first meeting with Roberta should be strictly a 'family' affair. And he doesn't know whether Florenzo fully accepts him, yet, as part of your family—or even wants him to be there when he greets, for the first time, his bride-to-be on English soil."

Julia heard Lysa yell at the other end, and smiled.

"If Florenzo doesn't accept David as a member of this family, he had better start looking out for another restaurant for himself and his Roberta!"

"Mamma," Ruth had said, "since we're going to be six persons short for Sunday dinner, could we possibly invite others for it—at least just this one time?"

"Yes, dear," Julia said guilelessly, turning her head away, so that Ruth could not see the smile dancing in her eyes. "Did you have anyone in mind? Someone special? Or just a friend, maybe?"

"Oh, Mamma," Ruth said, blushing red, "you're playing games with me! You know who I mean."

"Yes, dear. Your Major Squigby, I presume?"

Ruth nodded.

"I also notice that—unlike as in the past—you haven't protested the use of 'your' in front of the gentleman's name. Put it in another way, Ruth. Your Mamma makes the seating arrangements—and as I have always put Rachel beside David, do I now put your Mr. Squigby always beside you?"

"Yes! Oh, yes! His name is Will, by the way, so we don't have to keep calling him Mr. Squigby or Major Squigby all the time."

"You're serious about him, then?"

"Yes."

"Is he serious about you, darling?"

"Yes. We haven't talked too much about the future, but both of us feel the 'yearning' to be with each other when we are away from each other—what Sarah so rightly defined, in a single word, as love."

Julia folded her daughter in her arms and hugged her.

"I'm so happy for you, darling. I will let Daddy know about this little talk of ours—he'll be delighted; he has always liked Major Squigby—but when you choose to tell your brother and sisters, is up to you."

"When I invite Will for Sunday dinner, may I also include his younger brother, Samuel?"

"Samuel? Were they brought up Jewish?"

"Yes. As Daddy told us on that first day when we met them at the Queen's party, his father was a Jewish tailor in the East End of London; his mother worked as a cook in the household of some royal princess, many, many years ago—humble beginnings."

"Darling, that has never bothered us. In Sarah and Devinder's case, it wasn't his humble beginnings that was the stumbling block; it wasn't his race or religion—your father is both Indian and Jewish—it was more what paths their lives would take in the future, if they got married. Would they live in England—with him pining away for his family in India? Would they settle in India—with Sarah miserable? Even Rupa Devi saw that. Sarah is a very practical person; an engineer! She saw the 'yearning' wasn't there, and did the right thing by not encouraging it to develop—because, as in arranged matches, it can develop over time. You have no such stumbling blocks—and the 'yearning' is there already—so you, my brave, lovely daughter are spoken for!"

"Isn't that a very old-fashioned way of saying I've made a commitment?"

"Yes, dear, but isn't it so much more romantic? Tell me, who do you want me to put Samuel next to, at the dinner table? What are his interests? If he is into science and engineering, Sarah and he might have something in common. Or is he into literature and philosophy, when he will be more at ease with Susan?"

Ruth laughed. "None of the above, Mamma. He used to be a middle distance runner in his college years. He's now in his late twenties and works in a bank in the City; perhaps we should put him next to Rehana?"

"Oh, you scheming matchmaker! Yes, just let's do that. Why shouldn't Naseem Aunty have a few headaches to deal with—why do they all have to come my way?"

"You mean you've already invited all of them?"

"Yes. Rehana and you saved all of us in the Synagogue, but it was only possible because Naseem Aunty forced the target and the time out of Yusuf. She deserves our thanks too—as do you and Rehana."

Which decided the order of seating at the dinner table that Sunday evening.

The old Earl could not come. He had an urgent meeting with the Queen on Monday morning, and so he did not have the luxury of spending Sunday night at their flat in Hampstead; he had to be in Bromfield.

Joshua sat at the far end—the Earl's usual place—but this time, for a change, Julia sat at the other end of the table, as in a formal dinner, but nearest the kitchen. To Sir Joshua's right sat Viscountess Begum Naseem Banu. Beside her sat her daughter, Lady Rehana, and beside her sat Samuel Squigby, a banker from the City.

Beside him, and so next to her mother, was Lady Sarah.

Lady Julia had, on the other side, Viscount Edward. Next to him was Lady Susan, then Lady Ruth and, finally, next to her was Major Squigby, who was also beside Sir Joshua, at the other head of the table.

Dinner was a lively affair, the white, fruity riesling went down very well with Sarah's lamb biryani. The conversation was free and animated; the laughter was uninhibited—yet no one spoke of, or even mentioned in passing, the events that had transpired the previous Saturday. It was as if the subject was taboo.

Ruth and Will found their knees touching—quite by accident—under the table. Rehana and Samuel, after a little shyness on both sides, found that Samuel's past love of, and participation in, middle distance running, and Rehana's present love and participation in it made for a bond neither had believed possible on first finding themselves seated next to each other.

Rehana was a tall, slim, very beautiful woman, with a light-brown skin, green eyes, pert nose and large lips. The dark-brown hair would have cascaded in a straight waterfall past her shoulders, but she had tied it into an elegant bun at the top of her head, for the occasion.

Samuel Squigby, on the other hand, though tall and slimly built—unlike his older brother—had a dark grey moustache that was trimmed short, a rather florid face, intelligent eyes, and a ready smile, but with the first symptoms of a spare tire around his midriff. Rehana's first reaction to Samuel was: He needs more exercise!

The dessert had been served; soon the evening would come to a close. Joshua tinkled his wine glass with a fork.

"'Tis time for toasts, ladies and gentlemen. Let me give you the first; then each of us can propose as few or as many as he or she wishes, until we run out of toasts—or we run out of wine! We stand for the first toast; then we remain seated."

He stood up: "The Queen—our Elizabeth Aunty!"

They all stood up and toasted the Queen.

"I'll give one more—then I'll yield the floor," Joshua said. "To my lovely wife of over 25 years, who last Saturday showed me how the life of one baby could be so precious—more precious than her own. Lady Julia!"

Julia said: "I'll give the next toast. To my wonderful husband of over 25 years, who showed that the life of even a homeless man could be so precious. General Sir Joshua!"

Julia said: "I'll give one more then I'll yield the floor. To a woman, herself a Queen, who showed to her son—and to all of us—the courage she has, in her willingness to die for a just and noble cause. I give you Viscountess Begum Naseem Banu!"

"I'd like to give a toast," Naseem Banu said, with a smile at Julia. "To two girls, who showed the world that they could accomplish the impossible against all odds—and do it together. A Jewish girl and a Muslim one. I give you Lady Ruth and Lady Rehana!"

"I'll go next, if I may," Ruth said. "To a man who decided to protect a rather headstrong girl—without her knowledge, without her consent, and against her wishes—and all in the performance of his duty. I give you Major William Squigby!"

"I'll go next," Will said. "To the most wonderful girl in the world, who was willing to run the risk of being raped and then murdered to save the lives of innocent people—and who has captured my heart! I give you Lady Ruth! Darling, will you marry me?"

The proposal took her by surprise; she turned a crimson red. The applause gave her a few seconds to recover herself.

"Yes, my love, I will marry you." She turned towards him and kissed him full on the lips.

He took a ring from his inner pocket—a plain silver ring that belonged to his mother who had served as a cook. Given to her, with love, by his father who had been a poor tailor in the East End of London. Their late marriage had lasted 30 years. Ruth loved it and kissed it; then displayed it to the family around the table.

They crowded round her congratulating her, hugging her, kissing her as was appropriate. Her sisters, Sarah and Susan, clung to her, and she to them.

They thought that might be the end of the evening, but they had not counted on the one man who would not allow it to end, with matters unfinished, or words unspoken—Viscount Edward Andrews.

He tinkled his wine glass with his fork to attract their attention.

"We are all family," he said. "Cecily's friendship with Julia goes back a long, long way. I know the questions that are uppermost in your minds—and mine too—and we cannot possibly part without laying them bare on the table—at least as much as we know."

There was a silence in the room. Viscount Edward took another sip of his riesling.

"Yusuf," he said. "What has happened to him? What will happen to him? What has the investigation of the incident revealed to us? How will it affect my family—and possibly yours? I'm sure these are all questions uppermost in your minds. Major Squigby—Will—and I talked about this, and we both feel that you all—more than anyone else in the whole wide world—have more right to hear the truth. So I will give it to you, and then Will and I will answer any questions you might have."

He paused. "If I leave out any details, it is not that I don't trust you all—even my own wife and daughter—but because of the oaths I took as Director of the South East Asian Bureau of MI-6; they prevent me from revealing them. Will, if you have anything to add, feel free to do so."

Will nodded.

"Yusuf was arrested, together with seven other men, in the plotting and commission of the terrorist attack on the Hampstead Reform Synagogue last Saturday. Let us talk of the others first—then we will talk last of Yusuf.'

'Three were arrested inside the Pakistani Café—Khaled, Ahmed, and Ali, their bomb maker. A Pakistani businessman named Suleiman was the mastermind behind this attack—and the last one too, where Katie Sloane was murdered by having her throat slit from ear to ear. We thought it might be Ahmed—who is a ruthless killer and delights in murdering white women—who might have killed Katie, but we had no evidence. Fortunately we did not try him for it! I say 'fortunately', because he would have got off last time—no evidence—and then invoked 'double jeopardy' to get off this time. But since we did not try him then, we can try him now, and with the tapes that we now have, as evidence, I think he will get imprisonment—without parole—for the rest of his life. None of them will be executed, because that makes them martyrs to their stupid cause, and we will not assist them in that. Life imprisonment is more a deterrent than execution."

Edward stopped and looked to Julia, pleading, for more wine; she refilled his glass immediately.

"The bomb maker will also get life imprisonment, for his involvement in the last attack and this one; so that takes care of him. Khaled may get a lighter sentence—but that does depend on the legal defense he can muster—misled young man, unaware of the consequences, etc. etc. What was of greater interest to us is the mastermind, the Pakistani businessman, whose private jet was impounded at Heathrow—as material evidence used in the commission of a crime. It has yielded an enormous amount of significant information on his terrorist cell, on the correspondence he had with other terrorist cells, on the way in which these operations are financed—the money trail that leads all the way to the Taliban in Pakistan. That we have taken up with the Pakistani Government. It also led to the arrest of three others in this country—his personal secretary, his accountant, and his driver. We have deliberately not, overtly, confronted some of the other cells, because they will disappear and regroup again—which would not help us much. Rather we are monitoring them, and, if we get the opportunity, we'll put informants into their cells, so that we can nab them when they do consider acts of terrorism against the British people." He looked around the table.

"Which brings me to Yusuf. He is under house arrest at an undisclosed location—even Naseem Banu and Rehana don't know where—but I have visited with him several times in my official capacity—not as his father—and I've persuaded him to give evidence for the Crown, in the trials of the other seven. So it is for his own protection that he is being held incommunicado. I suspect that if he cooperates fully—and he shows every intention of doing so—his solicitor and lawyer will make a 'plea bargain', as the Americans say—a deal—that should get him a suspended sentence with conditions—he cannot leave the country; his passport has been impounded as well. Any questions?"

"What will happen to Yusuf after the trial?" Rehana asked, fearfully.

"Well, that does depend on him," Viscount Edward said. "He will be monitored. He would like to go back to Pakistan, except that Pakistan doesn't want him! They have enough problems with their own radicals, without having one of ours! Honest Muslims in this country will be afraid to associate with him for fear of being tainted and watched—and I don't blame them one bit! His best bet would be to rehabilitate himself in British society; perhaps, marry an honest Muslim girl who knows of his past and can forgive him for it. Mamma and I have hopes for him, Rehana—and so should you."

He looked round the table; there were no further questions. He continued:

"Finally, as has been done before, the Queen has stripped him of his rights to the Viscount's title—she informed me of that personally, which I thought was very gracious of her—so that the Viscount's title will now go to Rehana's eldest son."

"Oh, no, Pappa!" Rehana cried. "I don't want what is his!"

"I'm sorry, dear," Viscount Edward said, gently, "but it is no longer his. If you do not accept it for your son, it will languish, and a line that has extended continuously for generations—over 300 years—will come to an end. Is that what you would want for your mother and me?"

Rehana hung her head, and was silent. Samuel touched her hand that was lying on her lap, to comfort her; she held on to it.

That surprised them both—Rehana more than Samuel.

Viscountess Naseem Banu, sitting next to Lady Rehana, saw her daughter hold Samuel Squigby's hand, and smiled to herself.

CHAPTER 11

That summer—it was sometime in early July—Susan, by dint of some very hard work, completed her novel. She was very adept at the computer, as most of her class were, and so she had the novel on a back-up disk and on the hard drive of the common laptop the girls shared in their room. David had the privilege of a separate room—and hence his own laptop, though he invited his sisters to make full use of it when he was not on it. Each had their own passwords, and so none of them could invade the privacy of a sibling.

The matter came to light, at dinner one evening, when Susan casually asked if she could have the Mini, the next day, to go in to London. She had put in for it on the erasable bulletin board, and, since no one else had asked for it, she presumed it was okay.

"Why are you going into London, dear?" Julia asked.

Susan smiled. It was not an inquisition. She had been the last to obtain her driver's license, only after her eighteenth birthday, and the family—particularly her mother—was anxious about her taking the car into London, on her own, without someone sitting beside her. So Susan had picked a day when she knew no one wanted the Mini—as a test case to see the family's reaction.

"I could give you a ride in the Indian Embassy limousine that comes for me, dear," Joshua said, "and you can find your way back home on the Tube."

"I find, I've got to go to South Kensington to check my mail at Ayrton Hall," Sarah said, not looking up. "I'll come with you. Drop you off and pick you up back again. Anytime you wish, dear; you pick the times."

"I forgot, I'll be meeting Will in Oxford Street; is that where you're headed?" Ruth said. "We could all go together?"

Susan burst out laughing.

"Oh, you are all so transparent, it's deliciously funny! The 'baby' of the family has to be protected from the cruel London bus drivers and cabbies. So David, why haven't you just found out, this very minute, that you and Rachel are meeting up—where else but at the restaurant, which we all know is just off Oxford Street?"

David made a wry face. "Rachel can't make it tomorrow. Apparently Florenzo wants Roberta and Rachel to develop strong 'bonding', as sisters, and he's taking the two of them off on some sort of grocery shopping spree for the restaurant—cauliflower or cabbages or whatever—and I'm specifically not invited."

"I'm sorry, David," Susan said, "I didn't mean to hurt you—or any of you. You're all so concerned about me and instead of being grateful to you all, I'm poking fun at you. I'm sorry—though Daddy, you get no apologies from me."

"Oh? And why not, dear?"

"Because all of them offered to be with me, or take me there—and bring me back. While you would have abandoned me to take the London Underground on my way back—fighting horrendous crowds on my way home. Didn't you think that your youngest child might have deserved more humane treatment?"

Joshua and Julia laughed simultaneously; they looked at each other and nodded.

"What?" asked Susan mystified. "Is there something you haven't told us?"

"It can't be," Sarah said. "David and Ruth and I know everything of your past."

"Everything?" Julia said.

"I think so," David said.

"Have you ever asked us, or have you ever been told, where we fell in love with each other?"

Even David forgot his pain of separation from Rachel as they begged their parents to enlighten them 'on where they fell in love with each other'!

Joshua waved to Julia to continue; this was their story, but it was hers to tell.

"You know that I worked for MI-6 for a year. My assignment was to protect a meek, East Indian doctor, an MD, with a practice in Hampstead, from Slagter, a South African hit man, because this meek doctor had—or so they thought he had—some information that the South African Government desperately needed to have. Well, this meek doctor, who worked for Indian Military Intelligence, wasn't easy to protect because he didn't want to be protected! He wanted Slagter to come after him—for reasons of his own. So I engineered a chance meeting with him—in South Kensington of all places—and since we both lived in Hampstead, I asked him if I might join him on the way back?"

Julia paused, winking at Joshua—a wink that was not lost on any of their children.

"Why did I wink at your father? Because as it was—the honest truth—at that time, I wasn't in love with him at all. My instructions were to protect him until I'd wormed the information out of him; then I could drop him, and let Slagter have him!'

'The Bentley was round the corner, but we would have been in Hampstead in no time at all—and I wanted the longest possible way back home for more time to know him—maybe get to know him well enough to arrange future meetings.'

'So I suggested the Tube. It was the rush hour and—as Susan has so rightly pointed out—the crowds are horrendous. Twice I tried to get him on the train with me—twice he got left behind. The third time, I was on; he was caught in the doors that wouldn't close. The station man wanted him off the train—I said, 'No'! The station man said something to the effect that 'this train ain't going anywhere lady unless he gets off'! So as an agent of MI-6, I did what I had to do—I put an arm round him, pulled him towards me—and on me—and the doors closed behind him.'

'I will never, as long as I shall live, ever forget that tube journey from South Kensington, on the Circle Line, to Baker Street. We were squashed up against each other, and each succeeding station made it even closer. I was standing on his foot; to ease that I asked him if he could move his leg ever so slightly, so I could slide my foot in—it ended up by his thigh being between my thighs, and mine between his. Then a burly labourer was beside this meek doctor, and his elbow was digging into the doctor's ribs. To protect himself......"

"I'll swear to it to my dying day," Joshua interrupted.

"Yes, dear, though the children can believe it or not as they choose."

"What did the meek doctor do?" Susan asked.

"He raised his hand; the train took a sharp turn round a bend, and the palm of his hand ended up firmly clutching one of the two that we women have, and him unable to move it—so he says."

"What?" exclaimed Sarah, in mock horror. "He had his hand on your.........?"

"Yes, dear, but I had my thigh between his thighs. And the nice thing was that after the initial shock of it—and some guilt—neither of us wanted our bodies anywhere else except exactly where they were—in that crowded tube train. He apologized profusely, but he couldn't get his hand out—and I didn't want it out!"

"And the rest," Joshua said, "is history—your history. If it wasn't for that unforgettable train ride in the London Underground, we might not be having this conversation together at all. So I have absolutely no hesitation in abandoning any of you to travel the Underground, provided you find someone respectable and worthy of you to take the train ride with—as your mother did with me."

"When I took that train ride, dear," Julia said, darkly, "I didn't know that you were either respectable, or worthy to take the train ride with me. It could have gone either way."

"I don't know what you mean, Mamma," Susan said.

"Look at it this way, dear. If a rank stranger—or almost a stranger, even under difficult circumstances, puts his hand where he shouldn't……."

"Or her thigh where she shouldn't," Joshua said.

"Quite right, dear. Or her thigh where she shouldn't, you can have either of two reactions. You may forgive them the act, but at the first available opportunity, you turn round, silently, and walk away. Sarah defined 'love' as 'yearning'—and she is quite right. But yearning arises after love has already arrived. What is the emotion you have when it is about to arise—the moment you fall in love? I'll define it for you in a single word too—it is 'awareness'. Suddenly, Daddy and I became 'aware' of each other in a way that, had we not had some guilt about our body postures—his hand and my thigh—we might have wanted that train ride to last for a long, long, time—say three times round the 'circle' of the Circle Line! Or at least until the office rush had abated, when people might have looked askance at the East Indian gentleman and the white woman standing—for no good reason—in close proximity, in each other's arms, with his one hand you know where, and her thigh, you know where."

"I think I know what you mean, Mamma," David said a little shamefacedly. "It's like when Rachel and I go to the movies. I'll look at a movie and say: 'How about that one?' And she'll say: 'No, David. That's only ninety minutes. The other one is two hours long!' And we go for Rachel's pick. I don't think I need to explain why we go for the longer movie, do I?"

"I think I, too, know, Mamma, what 'awareness' is all about. And since we are all 'fessing up', I might as well tell you my story. Will and I were sitting on his sofa while he was playing the second part of those dreadful tapes. Some of what Yusuf and Khaled were saying was so dreadful, I reached out to Will for his hand and he held it. I was in my running shorts, our hands were between us, and the back of his hand was digging into my bare thigh.'

'Will had set the table for a cup of tea and some cup cakes—for us after we had heard the tapes—with chairs opposite to each other. Neither of us wanted to leave the sofa for the table! We sat there, and sat there, and sat there, until Will laughed, and said something to the effect: 'Ruth I'll make a deal with you. Neither of us wants to leave this sofa; but if I rearrange the chairs so that we sit side by side, and each gives the other full permission to reach over and touch the other on hand or shoulder or thigh, could we move over there?'

'And I said, something to the effect: Provided we add two more to that list: a tight hug when I leave—which brings my breasts into play as fair game—and a non-tender kiss on the lips!"

Joshua looked at Sarah and Susan. Susan was listening in with wide open eyes—these confessions from her mother and David and Ruth—and eagerness to hear more; Sarah was looking a little sad.

He leaned across and touched her on the arm.

"Sarah, my love," he said, "falling in love or 'awareness', being in love or 'yearning', can all arise even after marriage. We have known one way; in millions of other arranged marriages, in India and elsewhere, these exact same emotions can arise after marriage and be just as lasting and fulfilling—sometimes more so—as in any love match."

Sarah smiled: "Thank you, Daddy. Please don't worry. I have a career. I'm going to get my Ph.D., teach structural engineering at some University or a good Polytechnic; be a fulfilled woman. But thank you."

"So why don't we come back to my original question to Susan?" Julia said. "Why do you need the Mini to go into London? If it's business related; we'd love to help. If it's an assignation, we'll keep out of it."

They all howled with laughter—Susan included.

"No, Mamma, it's not an assignation. I've just completed the first draft of my novel, and I promised Jane I'd let her have a look at it; maybe she might suggest some changes, before she sends it on its rounds."

They all congratulated her with peals of delight.

"May we read it?" Joshua asked, cautiously. "Or is it to be a surprise—buy your copy if you want to read it, and that's final!"

"Oh, Daddy, would I ever charge any of you for the misery of reading it? The problem is I don't have a print copy. I've got a disk—that I'm taking to Jane—and it's on the laptop. You can read it on the laptop if you wish, but at the moment it is only a draft. Maybe, you all might like to wait until it's more finalised?"

"That's very sensible, dear," Julia said, "but maybe you can satisfy our curiosity a little bit by telling us something of the story? What is it about? Or more appropriately—who is it about?"

Susan blushed.

"It's about a family—not us!—but a suburban middle class family, set in London, where three of the grown children have different aspirations as to where they want to reach—and find they don't have the will, or the means, or the talent that it takes to get them there. Except the fourth child—the youngest—who thinks they are all wasting their time, and the sole purpose in her life should be to make as much money as possible. The damaging effects that such ambitions—or lack of it—have on their parents, and on each other, make up the essence of the story."

Joshua burst into spontaneous applause, clapping his hands; the other followed suit.

"Tell us more about the fourth child," David said. "How does she plan to make her money? Does she want to be educated? Or skilled at some trade? Or what?"

"She is not a nice person," Susan said, quietly. "A trollop, actually. Now! Before you jump to any conclusions, let me say that just because I might make one of my characters into a tart, doesn't make me one. Mamma, please tell them about a writer's imagination, and the way writers can project themselves to write, convincingly, about people they've never known or even met."

"Yes, dear," Julia said, "they can; otherwise all any writer could write would be his or her autobiography—and not a story more!"

"What about your conviction to write only about what you know—and not what you see?" Ruth asked.

Susan smiled sweetly. "Well, I do know a lot of young people—starting with three round this table—and a few more we've known who own an Italian restaurant, and a few more we met at the Queen's party, don't I? Characters are always composites—a little bit of this one, and a little bit of that one, and some more from a third guy or gal—and you have someone who comes to life on the written page. So will you see some of yourselves in some of mine—maybe? But I'll leave you all to spend many fruitless hours probing the intricacies of my mind, should that interest you. To be honest, all my experiences may be buried so deep into my subconscious, even I might not be able to disentangle them. Far better to enjoy the novel and leave it at that, without analyzing and dissecting each character for which real life person supplied what, to make the 'lunatic' who jumps out of the pages of my novel. Now who's coming with me tomorrow to Lady Jane Literary Agency in London?"

There were no offers.

Suddenly, in ten minutes, she was no longer the 'baby' of the family; she had become—at least to her siblings—an adult, who could take care of herself fully, whether it was on the written page, or in a car on the streets of London. She did not need their protection; it was they who needed protection from her!

Joshua said quietly: "You're on your own, dear girl. You have to face the London traffic some time; I've sat with you before; you drive very well—and defensively."

Julia grimaced, but agreed with Joshua—in principle.

David excused himself; he was taking Rachel for a late morning baklava and a cup of coffee.

Ruth excused herself; she was meeting Will for a cup of tea and a cupcake at a local café.

Sarah excused herself; she would be reading in the girl's room, if they needed her.

Susan sat with her head between her hands; her father and Mother beside her. And she wept inside.

"I've upset them all," she said, sadly. "They, who've loved me so much—I threw all that love away, for what?"

"Don't feel that way, darling," Joshua said. "They'll come around. The life of a writer is a lonely one—because people don't understand all the emotions and characters that flood through your mind. They misunderstand you. If you write, realistically, about whores they think you're a whore, or have been to whores. If you write about betrayal and revenge they say: ah! he must have known these emotions himself—how else could he write so knowingly about them?"

"But I was just writing fiction," Susan lamented.

"Precisely, dear," Julia said. "I know how you must feel. I knew a writer once—a very good writer—who wrote so realistically about a married women, but in love with many men, her husband, on reading her first novel refused to read any more of her work. She had a choice—give up writing the way she did, or have her husband withdraw himself and his emotions from her."

"So what did she do?"

"She couldn't give up her writing. He withdrew his emotional and physical love—playing out her fantasies with real women! She died a very lonely woman—sustained only by the people in her head. She didn't divorce him because she loved him; he didn't divorce her because he needed the financial security she afforded, but she might as well have been dead to him."

"Is that what is going to happen to me? Is that what happened to you, Mamma?"

"Darling, this man sitting beside you—my husband—could not have been more supportive. He told me: 'Love me, dear, and I will never probe the loves you have in your mind. I'm a soldier; I fight real men—not fictional ones!' Your brother and sisters—don't worry about them; they'll come around, but be very careful that the man you love and marry is as supportive of you, and your art, as this military general has been of me."

Julia leaned across and kissed Joshua on the lips long and lovingly.

"Now, I've a question to ask of you two," Joshua said. "What would you say if I was to grow a beard with sideburns, to hide this deep and permanent scar on my cheek? I see people looking at it—it's as if their eyes are drawn to it—and I think, to some of them, it looks gross and distracting; possibly even disgusting? Don't misunderstand me; I don't care about the scar—but I do hate to disgust others."

Susan started out of her chair.

"What! Grow a beard to hide your scar—because you think we can't look at it without disgust? Oh, Pappa! How can you even think that way? To us, it is your badge of honour—to be worn with pride. A homeless man—and two hundred Jews—are alive today partly because of that scar!"

She bounded across the table, kissed him gently on the lips; then smothered his scar with kisses, starting at one end near his eye and ending at the other end near his chin.

"And I can do no better than our 'baby' can," Julia said, with a laugh, as she repeated the performance, except that the kiss on his lips was not quite as gentle or tender as Susan's had been.

"I'll go and talk to Sarah for a while," Susan said. "Try to make peace with her. She's too kind-hearted to shut me out for long."

"Let me make a suggestion, Susan," Julia said. "Run off another disk of your novel, and leave it beside the computer—for anyone who has the interest in it to read it. Pappa and I most certainly will. Sometimes the novel you read, is nowhere near as 'demonic'—and could be even funny and heart-warming—as the one you've imagined it to be. Make sure you label the disk with the title of your novel. By the way, dear, what is the title of your novel?"

"A Family at War," Susan said.

She disappeared into the girls' room; they heard the sounds of laughter, as Sarah and she made amends.

Julia took Joshua by the hand, and indicated the bedroom.

"My lips have already shown their love and devotion to your scar, Joshua, but there are two other parts of my upper body that have a fierce longing to show that same love and affection for it—and the face that carries it. Shall we, my darling?"

He arose with alacrity.

"Though I have to warn you, General Samuelson," she said, teasingly, "that you do run the risk of being smothered by them."

"Thank you for warning me, Lady Julia," he replied, with a laugh, "I look forward, with great anticipation, to the bwyb!"

CHAPTER 12

Susan had no difficulty driving the Mini into Central London. It was a working day and the traffic was very heavy, but she navigated the Mini with ease to one of the side streets off Oxford Street, where parking on the street was permitted, before walking the rest of the way to Lady Jane Literary Agency.

The Agency was located in a newer office building, with solicitors and real estate agents rubbing shoulders with investment bankers and literary agencies; Susan passed two others, before coming to Jane's door on the second floor.

Jane was seated at her desk that was covered with piles of manuscripts on both sides, towering over and threatening to spill over onto a laptop computer at the dead centre of the desk.

There was a tall, thin, beautiful woman, with short hair and a winsome smile seated on one of the two chairs on the other side of the desk.

Jane introduced them.

"Susan this is Winnie Benthall—one of my more successful writers; Winnie this is Lady Susan, daughter of one of Mother's oldest, and dearest, friends, Lady Julia Samuelson."

"Ah, Royalty! Welcome to the club. We could do with more of you," Winnie said.

"I've read one of your books," Susan said. "Dealt with the lesbian scene in London—and very sympathetically too. I presume…"

".. that I am a lesbian too? Is that the question you were going to ask me? No need to be embarrassed, dear," Winnie said, smiling. "Yes, I am—and so is Jane; are you?"

Susan shook her head. "I'm sorry, but I'm not."

"A pity, dear, I could go for you," Winnie said, smilingly. "Ah, well, I have to be off. Nice to have met you."

Jane saw Winnie to the door.

There was a sofa on one side of the room, behind the desk, and Jane invited Susan to sit with her on it.

Susan produced the disk of 'A Family at War' much to Jane's delight.

"So you finally got it done—the first draft, I mean. Wonderful! I have two 'sleeping partners', shall we say, whose opinions I value a great deal. Between the three of us we read all the manuscripts sent to us by aspiring writers. Three quarters of them we reject out of hand, with a note saying that their work is not something we handle, which is just a polite way of saying—go somewhere else; please don't send us any more of your work! To the other quarter, and even that is several hundred a year, we offer suggestions to the writer on how the manuscript could become—if not better—certainly more salable. If the changes to the manuscript meet with our approval—and they don't always do—we proceed to do the rounds with it, carefully selecting markets we think are best suited to the manuscript. And then, sometimes, just sometimes, we do strike lucky with a new writer. The established ones, with publishers demanding sequels, why, we just pass their manuscripts onto the publishers, and let the editors at those houses work directly with the author, on the final draft of their work."

Susan said: "If you've got an established reputation as a literary agency that handles lesbian work, why are you wasting your time with my novel—there's not a shred of lesbianism in it."

Jane smiled: "No, I'm not doing you a favor, Susan. The fact that I am establishing a reputation as an agency that handles lesbian work—bothers me! I'd rather be a well-rounded agency with different types of fiction—even some non-fiction or scholarly work. And so I'm going to make a special, serious effort for your novel—for my sake as well as yours. Now, how are you placed for lunch? Business expense—treating a client to lunch—and deductible on my income tax. Oh, please say yes!"

"Yes."

"Great! Let me get my coat and we'll go to a fine Italian restaurant just around the corner, that belongs—so you all told me, when you recommended it to me years ago—to your Uncle's family? I've eaten there ever so often, and the food is delicious."

Susan wished she could sink through the floor and disappear. But David, Sarah, Ruth, and she, had recommended it to Jane on one of their joint shopping sprees—in happier times. Now there was Florenzo to contend with, and even more of an unknown was Roberta.

The restaurant was almost empty for which Susan was grateful. Lysa saw her immediately and came over to greet her. Joe Uncle was at the cash register and waved to her; Florenzo was not to be seen. Alphonso and a not very tall, heavily-built, Italian girl with short, dark-brown hair, a fair complexion—not swarthy as Florenzo was—and beautiful black eyes, framed by long eyelashes and deep eyebrows, were serving appetizing food to an elderly couple and three grandchildren in the other corner of the room.

Lysa folded Susan in a warm embrace. She smiled at Jane; she knew Jane very well because Jane had eaten there so often.

"My dear Susan, thank you for coming—the food's on us! We never charge family—and you are my family. Order anything you wish, dear, it's on the house."

"No, Mrs. Samuelson," Jane said hastily. "Susan is my guest for today—please let me do the paying. It's deductible on Income Tax. There will be a third person joining us—my brother Lord Albert, who is in town."

Lysa smiled. "Lady Jane, I will be happy to charge Lord Albert and you; but I cannot in all conscience ever charge one of my favourite nieces—when Sarah and Ruth come they become my favourite nieces too!—so why don't we compromise? You pay for Lord Albert and yourself; I pay for Susan. Yes?"

So they agreed. Roberta came with the menus to the table. She spoke broken English, but it was sufficient to get their orders right. She looked at Susan with great interest. Florenzo had filled her in with some of the details of what had transpired at the restaurant—he thought it better he put in his side of the episode, before she heard the story from Alphonso or anyone else. There was an uneasy silence; Susan put her head into the menu—she knew perfectly well what was on it—but the morning was proving to be more traumatic than she could handle.

Particularly, when Lord Albert walked in through the foyer and marched straight up to their table. Susan rose to meet him—he was after all the Earl of Rathbone. She would have put out her hand, but he put his arms around her, pulled her to him, and kissed her on the mouth. Jane smiled in approval; so did Lysa.

Florenzo, who had just walked out of the kitchen to be with his beloved Roberta, saw the kiss and shrieked in surprise—a cry that was not lost on Roberta, who turned crimson. Susan would have moved her mouth away, after the first kiss, but hearing Florenzo's cry—and seeing the look of anger on his face, standing as he was behind Albert's back, annoyed her. So she put an arm round Albert's neck and planted a second kiss on his mouth—as if kissing him back in return.

Untangling of tangled signals, as they occurred, proved well-nigh impossible!

Florenzo on seeing Lord Albert kiss Susan assumed that she had deliberately brought Lord Albert, Earl of Rathbone, here to flaunt him before Florenzo, to show Florenzo for what he was—only the 'labour manager' of a restaurant! That was his cry of anger.

Roberta thought: 'Florenzo still loves her and has brought me here to England to flaunt me before his Susan!' So she turned crimson.

Susan thought: 'He still thinks he owns me? He has no rights on me—I'll do as I please!' That was the reason for the second kiss.

Albert was in heaven with Susan's return kiss; he didn't care about signals—tangled or otherwise!

'Oh, dear God, I've blown it!' Susan thought. 'Whatever came over me? To make me do a thing like that—plant a second kiss on his lips?' She saw her Lysa Aunty give her a wink—and then disappear into the kitchen. Susan knew exactly where she was headed—to the telephone, to call up her good friend and sister-in-law, Julia, to give her the good news that an engagement would soon be forthcoming between her youngest child and the Earl of Rathbone.

This has to be set right, was Susan's next thought, and the very first thing to do was to not sit beside Albert—but across him. She managed that very adroitly by the simple manoeuvre of sliding round Albert's tall body, to plant herself almost on Jane's lap, causing Jane to move hastily into the booth, opening up the seat beside her for Susan.

But Albert, who had been given a stern lecture by his mother and sister on the behaviour that someone he was trying to court might expect from him—which was the reason for the first kiss—was not to be denied either.

Roberta had delivered only two menus to the table—Albert had not been there when she had done that—one on each side of the booth. Jane had her menu; Albert had the second; Susan had none. So in common courteous consideration, Albert leaned across to Susan and shared the menu with her, touching her hand lovingly, as he pointed out dishes she might enjoy.

For once, Albert refused to keep silent, as was his custom. That was another of the stern warnings delivered to him by his mother—who had called her childhood friend Julia—for some insights on how her eldest son, Lord Albert, could endear himself to her youngest daughter, Lady Susan.

She found it strangely unnerving to find Albert in complete command of the conversation—and talking intelligently—on various topics that ranged from the movies of the day to the chances of the Liberal Party in the next forthcoming elections.

To her surprise, Lord Albert leaned across the table, urging her to come up close to him—and when she did, not wanting to hurt him—he whispered: "I'm going to stand as a candidate from the Liberal Party for a seat in the House of Commons—like Lord Benn did so many years ago." His constituency would be his family seat in Oxfordshire.

While she was eating, her mind thinking frantically on how she could extricate herself from the mess she had created by a single kiss on the lips—to her surprise, David and Rachel walked in through the front entrance, saw their party, and came over to their table.

David had always liked Albert; Albert was two years younger, but they had been to the same prestigious public school, though, after that, Albert had gone to Oxford and David to Cambridge.

Rachel! She was the only one who could get her out of the mess.

Susan grabbed her arm, marched her off to the flat upstairs, sat her on the bed, and told her the whole sorry tale.

Rachel laughed until the tears rolled down her cheeks. The humor in the situation began to strike Susan too—as a writer—so they both lay on the bed and laughed, while the party downstairs didn't quite know what to make of it.

"What do I do, Rachel?" Susan moaned. "Albert thinks I'm in love with him; Roberta's mad as hell, because she thinks Florenzo and I are still pining for each other; and Florenzo—I don't care what he thinks! But what do I do?"

Rachel dried her tears. "Wait till I tell David, the mess his youngest sister is in. Knowing David, he'll laugh harder than I did. But I'll tell you what to do—that is if you're asking me?"

"Please! Oh, please?"

"Don't worry about Roberta; she has a sense of humor too. I'll take care of her. Don't worry about Florenzo—it'll teach him to treat women better. But Lord Albert, Susan, is your first priority. Clear it up immediately. Ask him to take you home in his car. David will take care of your Mini. I'll tell them you're not feeling too well and want to leave at once, and Lord Albert—the gentleman he is—will rise immediately and offer to take you home. Give me the keys of the Mini."

And that is what they did. Rachel went downstairs and announced to the party that Susan wanted to leave for home immediately. Would Lord Albert see her home?

He sprang to attention as Susan came down the stairs and without a word of inquiry or demanding any sort of explanation, he escorted her out of the restaurant.

They drove to Hampstead in silence for most part of the journey. He had reverted to his usual silent self. Finally, she could no longer stand the silence, and she said: "Albert, I'd like to apologize to you."

"Oh? Whatever for?"

"For giving you quite the wrong impressions in the restaurant."

He laughed: "You mean that second kiss? Is that what you're apologizing to me for—because you didn't mean it?"

"Yes."

"Well, don't apologize, dear girl. I'm a philosopher, remember? I'll remember one of the two kisses we had—forever! Not the one I gave you—that will be tinged with guilt because I'll never be sure whether you welcomed it—but the one you gave me."

"Why?"

"Was that the very first kiss, on the mouth, that you've given to any man—outside your family?"

She nodded; then realised he was driving, with eyes on the road, and hadn't seen her nod, and said: "Yes."

"That's why. Such an honour! How could I forget it?"

"Albert, I'm eighteen years old. How can I give you a commitment on anything—let alone marriage. Because that is what you want from me, don't you?"

"Yes."

"I don't know what love is. Those who do have told me there is an 'awareness' that arises when you fall in love, and then a 'yearning' to be with the loved one—and I haven't felt either."

He seemed surprised at her definition of 'love'.

"Really? An awareness of the partner when you receive her very first kiss? And a yearning for her when she is away from you? I was never really sure how I felt; now I know! Thank you for making it clear for me."

She sighed.

"Albert, I'm going to get a degree in English from Oxford—Mamma's old college. Then I want a career as a writer. You want a wife to bear you children and look after them, and run the huge estate you have in Oxfordshire—while you go into politics! Tell me, could two people be more mismatched?"

He smiled: "You're so right, Susan. Say no more about it. Think no more about it. I'm sorry, I've upset you. Please forgive me. There! We're already home; you'll forgive me if I don't come upstairs to your front door—or attempt to kiss you goodbye?"

"Thank you, Albert, for being such a gentleman. I will always respect you. I do wish you would open your heart to other women—more worthy of you than I am."

The disk, and a two page letter from Jane, came in the mail to Susan about a week later. The letter from Jane was just a single page. She was attaching a thoughtful critique of 'A Family at War', by her sleeping partner, whose opinions she trusted implicitly. She didn't know whether Susan would even want to attempt a revision—or if one was even possible—so fundamental and deep-rooted were the changes required in her manuscript, for it to be suitable for Lady Jane Literary Agency to undertake its sale. She apologised, etc etc.

Susan was in tears as she read the second page that was typed and unsigned, and had listed the objections to the novel in considerable detail.

This is what the critique said:

While the writing style is commendable, the novel lacks the characterisation that would make it salable.

All of the characters—save one—are shown as ruthless men and women, selfish and uncaring, who have no compunction, whatsoever, in riding over the feelings or fine susceptibilities, not only of strangers but of their own loved ones!

The father is depicted as boneless, spineless, gutless; the less said of him the better.

The mother is depicted as selfish, and concerned only about who will support her, financially, in her old age.

The three older children are depicted as so obsessed with their ambitions, they have no time for their parents, or for each other.

The only realistically portrayed character is the youngest daughter—a tart—who shows some humanity when she offers her 'services', for free, to a poor, lonely, elderly man who cannot afford to pay her.

Strangely, she is the only one that we—as the readers—want to know more about; we couldn't care less about the other five—whether they live or die! Certainly we wouldn't waste any more time on them.

The only realistic part of the novel is its title; it is truly a novel about 'A Family at War'!

This novel is not salvageable. Suggest we reject.

While Susan's first reaction had been tears, her next reaction, when she had read the critique twice, was anger. Anger against all publishers, editors, literary agents and their reviewers—particularly them that could not, themselves, write a single page; yet made their living tearing up the work of others! She then extended her anger to include all thin, willowy women, and all lesbians.

It didn't take her very long—after another look at her novel on the laptop, but from a different set of eyes—to grudgingly concede that maybe the reviewer had some valid objections to the work.

So that evening, after dinner, she shared the critique with her family, and Rachel, with an apology for having riled them up, without reason, since they could see that in no way had she portrayed any of them in her novel.

Maybe she had portrayed herself—but only as a tart!

They all, including her mother, laughed at her characterisation of herself.

"You know dear, you weren't far wrong in thinking of yourself as a 'tart'; I've often thought of myself that way."

"What!" shouted Joshua. "Impossible! Not even in your wildest imagination would you ever think of yourself as a 'tart'."

"Are you quite sure, dear?" Julia asked, teasingly. "A tart sells her body for an agreed sum. Do you agree?"

"Yes."

"A writer sells her imagination for an agreed sum?"

"A ballet dancer, or a pianist, sells her talent for an agreed sum," Sarah said.

"A railway porter sells his strength for an agreed sum. Does that make him a male gigolo?" David said.

"Some professional milers sell their speed for an agreed sum," said Ruth.

"Doesn't a wife sell herself—on a permanent basis—to her husband for her 'keep'?" Rachel said. "I'm only asking?" she added hastily.

"The list applies to almost anyone at all who earns a living," Julia said. "Except that the oldest profession in the world sells what most ethical or moral standards would frown upon—but, for some, it is a living, and, sadly perhaps, the only one they have."

"Well," Susan said, sweetly "thank you all for abandoning me to the wolves, when you all thought I'd reviled you in my book. Wouldn't even sit beside me on the cruel streets of London. I'm so hurt—I could cry," she ended up laughing, to make sure they knew she wasn't hurt in the least.

Instead they all burst out laughing, Joshua and Julia included.

"What?" asked Susan. "What is so funny, about what I just said?"

"Should we tell her?" Sarah asked.

"No, I don't think so," Ruth said.

"Maybe we could just give her a hint?" David said.

"Yes, let's just do that," Rachel said.

"What are you all talking about?" Susan said, now knowing something was afoot.

"Tell me, Susan," Julia said, "didn't it strike you as odd that David brought the Mini home without knowing where you'd parked it?"

"I never thought about that. On second thoughts, David, how did you know where it was parked?"

"Because we saw where you parked it," David said.

"We? Who's we? And how did you see where I'd parked it?"

"Because we weren't going to allow our 'baby' sister to drive for the first time, alone, in the cruel streets of London, without keeping an eye on her, could we now? So with Pappa, Mamma and Sarah in the front seat, and Ruth, Rachel and me in the back seat, we all piled into the Bentley, and keeping two cars behind you, we kept an eye on you all the way to Oxford Street."

"You didn't!"

"Oh, yes, we did. Mamma drove. When you parked, Rachel and I got off, and Mamma took Pappa to India House, and the others home. Didn't you think it also odd that Rachel and I would turn up at the restaurant at the precise time you and Albert and Jane were having lunch?"

"And whose bright idea was this, so I can castigate her?" Susan asked.

"Mine. Whose else could it be?" Ruth said. "Since the terrorist attack on the Hampstead Reform Synagogue, I've become paranoid about keeping you all safe. I'm sorry, Susan. Forgive me?"

"Forgive you? I was just coming over to thank you, and say how much I love you all."

And Susan went over to Ruth and hugged her from behind, kissing her on the top of her head; then followed that with a hug to everyone around the table.

David excused himself: "I have to see Rachel home; I won't be long." He extended his hand to Rachel.

Ruth excused herself, laughing: "I'm meeting Will at his flat; then we're driving to the Heath where we'll meander—yes, hand in hand—until it's time to come home."

Joshua excused himself: "Take care of yourselves—all of you. I'm off to the East End of London where I'm giving a lecture on 'Military Strategy in the India/Pakistan Wars' at a meeting of the East End India Club—whoever they might be. It's a series of lectures every Friday evening."

Julia excused herself: "I'm going with your father to make sure he doesn't lose his way going there—Daddy's terrible when it comes to finding the right roads!—and more importantly, doesn't lose his way coming back home in the dark. He doesn't see too well at night."

Susan looked at Sarah.

"I know you like to read, Sarah. But do you think you could read in the living room so that I have you around me. I don't want to be left alone with my thoughts."

Sarah smiled and assented, brought her novel from the bedroom, and settled herself in the sofa opposite to Susan. There was silence for a while. Finally, Sarah put her book aside and said: "Susan, can I put in my two pennies worth on your novel?"

Susan turned eagerly to her. "Oh, please do! I can't seem to think straight as far as my own work is concerned—probably no writer can. Have you read the first draft?"

Sarah smiled guiltily: "Yes," she said. "Almost everyone of your family has—I saw Daddy and Mummy read it together; Ruth read it after me, and David and Rachel read it last."

"And?"

"None of us liked it. Oh, Susan, please don't be upset! But let's be constructive about it. May I make a suggestion? Why don't you portray your characters on people you know—us."

"But I thought you'd all be offended by that."

"Far from it, dear, we'd be flattered if you made us out to be who we are—flawed, imperfect, but human? Shall I continue? Or would you rather I just sit here and read without saying another word—just being near you, which I always, always, will."

"No! No! Please, help me, Sarah, as if you were helping your drowning 'baby' sister! Is that too much to ask?"

Sarah smiled, came and sat beside Susan and said:

"Well, here goes. Let's take each character in turn, shall we? Let's take the father first. He's spineless, boneless and gutless. Take Pappa—do you think he is spineless, boneless and gutless? He's been in two wars—on the frontlines! His adversaries—not his own men—called him 'The Lion of Lahore'! But he's so human that even to this day he has nightmares of the men he took into battle who didn't come back. And risks his life for a homeless man in a Synagogue. That's a father who anyone can respect—and wants to read about.'

'Take the mother—selfish—whose only interest is in knowing who will take care of her in her old age. Take Mamma! Could you possibly wish for a mother more caring than her—I think not. Her ambition was to be a writer too, but that wasn't as important to her as having us. And a baby's life was more precious than her own! In both Pappa's and Mamma's case, seconds counted, because the Synagogue exploded behind them as they came through the front doors. They could very easily have abandoned both the homeless man and the baby to save themselves—instead they ran the risk of being incinerated, getting the other two out.'

'Take the daughter who wants to be a ballet dancer. She betrays her family and her best friend for her art. Take Ruth! She was willing to run the risk of being raped and murdered to save the lives of two hundred innocent Jews. Do you think she has no ambition? She wants to make the British Women's Olympic team in the mile—if that isn't ambition, I don't know what is!"

"Or take you, Sarah. You want to get a Ph.D. and then teach—yet you, besides being so beautiful, are the gentlest, kindest, most gracious woman in the world. Oh, Sarah, how could I have been so blind?"

Sarah blushed: "I was hoping you wouldn't think of me, but thank you for doing so. We all have our flaws; I know I do."

"Oh? And what are your flaws, Sarah dear?"

"I don't think I have the courage that you all have—the courage to fall in love. I shrink from it because I feel so diffident about making someone happy. What if I can't? What if I can't meet their expectations of me in love—or in bed? Will they hate me forever—even as they stay tied to me by meaningless marriage vows?"

Sarah wiped away a tear, and this time it was Susan who did the consoling. When Sarah had recovered she asked: "Do you want me to continue?"

Susan dissented, smiling: "Let me continue. Take the son—as ruthless a man as ever had the misfortune to grace this earth. And take David! He wants to go to Sandhurst—be an Army officer—then enter Military Intelligence like Daddy and Mummy and Will. He has ambition too, but as our eldest brother, no one could have taken more responsibility for all of us, his siblings, than he has. There was a time when he was sixteen and I was ten—and Daddy and Mummy were away—I'd go to him with any problem I had, and he always had time for me. What are his flaws? I think they stem from Daddy, really. The military man in him! I hope for Rachel's sake that he learns to be less of a military man than he is."

The key at the door told them that one of the family had returned—it was David.

As he entered, they burst out laughing. He looked inquiringly at them. "What's so funny?"

"Daddy has a phrase; it comes from India: 'Think of the Devil and the Devil appears!'" Sarah said.

David laughed too. "Why, thank you, dear sisters. Now will you do me a favour and tell Rachel I'm a personification of the Devil himself? She is constantly lamenting there isn't enough of the Devil in me!"

He paused: "I presume you were discussing Susan's novel?"

They nodded.

"Then may I add my two pennies worth too?"

"Please do," Susan said, "and don't spare this poor writer. Our sister here has given me hell."

"Sarah? Given you hell? Impossible! Now if you'd said that about Ruth, or even Rachel—who has given me hell on more than one occasion—I'd believe you. But Sarah?"

"If you've finished banishing me to that miserable class of people, who can't seem to say a bad word about anybody," Sarah said, laughingly, "tell us what you felt about 'A Family at War'?"

"Susan, you are writing a novel—not a short story or a novella or a novelette. Why do you limit yourself only to one not-so-likeable family in suburban England? Bring in more characters, more classes, more diversity, more ethnicity, more romance, more honour, more emotion, more of everything. Even Royalty! How many writers you know, Susan, can go to our Queen's party and call her 'Elizabeth Aunty', may I know?"

"Or be the sister of the twelfth Earl of Bromfield?" Sarah put in.

"Thank you, dear. The basic thrust of your novel itself has to change; how do different people, from different races, religions, and classes, all search for meaning in their lives, and still remain warm and human—and sometimes not! That is what is lacking, dear. But your style is excellent, your writing is crisp and lively, you have—my dearest 'baby' sister—a way with words! There, I've said what I wanted to say; now flay me—I'll sit here quietly and listen to all you have to say."

"Flay you?" Susan said. "I have only two words I want to say. But there is something I want to do to the two of you first."

She hugged them both tight and said: "Thank you."

She released them both, then marched straight away into the girls' bedroom. They heard the sound of the disks—two of them; the one she had, and the one left beside the laptop—being thrown into the trash can. They heard the 'beep' of the laptop as it was activated.

Sarah and David smiled at each other.

Susan, the writer, was at work again.

CHAPTER 13

Two invitations were received, almost simultaneously, by members of the Samuelson family.

The first of them was for Sarah. She had gone to Ayrton Hall to check on her mail in the pigeonhole for 'S', as was her custom every two weeks, and found an impressive, official-looking, embossed envelope with the seal of the Indian High Commission in London.

It was an invitation from Shri (Havaldar) and Shrimati Mansingh of Marwar, India, inviting Lady Sarah Samuelson and Family, to attend an engagement reception for their son Devinder to Premlata, daughter of the Indian High Commissioner in London, that Sunday, at India House, at 6:00 PM.

There was an RSVP card, with its own smaller envelope. There was also a handwritten note from Devinder, begging her to attend.

Sarah thought about it for exactly one minute, before she wrote 'Regrets' on the RSVP card, inserted it into its own small envelope, cancelled the address on the front side, wrote 'Devinder Mansingh' on it instead, and placed it in the pigeonhole for 'M', where Devinder would be sure to find it.

The second invitation was received at the Hampstead flat. It was addressed to General Sir Joshua Samuelson, Military Attache to the Indian High Commission. It too was an impressive, official-looking, embossed envelope with the seal of the Indian High Commission in London.

Joshua turned it over in his hand as he examined his mail at the dinner table. It had been delivered earlier in the day, but Joshua had been at work.

"It's an invitation," he said. He looked at Sarah. "Devinder's getting engaged."

"I know, Daddy," Sarah replied, calmly. "I found a similar invitation from Devinder, in my box at Ayrton Hall. It was from his parents to me and family. There was an RSVP card, and I've sent my regrets."

Joshua smiled. "Well, dear, this one's different. It's from the Indian High Commissioner and his wife inviting General Sir Joshua and Lady Samuelson and Family to attend the engagement reception for their only daughter Premlata to Devinder, youngest son of Havaldar and Shrimati Mansingh of Marwar, India. It's at 6:00 PM, this Sunday, at India House."

"So why is this one different, Daddy?"

"Because, dear, for that one you sent your regrets; for this one I can't. Now I know why you might feel awkward about attending his engagement reception, but don't you think that will send the wrong message to her—we're not concerned about him now—that maybe something had been brewing between the two of you—when there wasn't. Besides, you're my daughter and you are as brave as any of us around this table. You're not going to keep running away from him all your life, are you?"

Sarah sighed. "I'll come, Pappa, but Susan and I were discussing this only the other day; sometimes we wish you'd been just a cowardly father—as some others have—so that we could, just sometimes, have been cowards ourselves too!"

Joshua laughed. "Sorry, dear," he said. "There should be a register, somewhere, for unborn children waiting to be born, where the unborn child can stipulate: 'Absolutely not a Colonel in the Indian Army for a father! Will take a garbage collector—but not him!' But for this life, my love, you're stuck with me."

They laughed, Sarah included. Then she said, teasingly: "I don't know, Daddy, but I might have stipulated: 'Absolutely must have the granddaughter of the eleventh Earl of Bromfield for a mother; for a father, any man she chooses—including, even let's say, a Colonel in the Indian Army?—will be acceptable.'"

Joshua smiled. "Touche, my darling daughter. How right you are. I keep thinking of you all as my 'troops', forgetting what a debt we all—me included—owe to this dear lady beside me for having chosen me as her husband." He leaned over and kissed Julia gently on the lips.

"You don't have to come, Sarah," he said. "I can always make my apologies to the High Commissioner and his wife. Be yourself! You're my eldest daughter—not a soldier under my command. If I've come across to any, or all, of you, over the years, as a military colonel and not your father—I apologise."

"Oh, Daddy, I was only joking; you know that I wouldn't change you for all the cowards in the world! And I'll be there with you, holding aloft the honour of the Samuelsons—even if it makes for the most embarrassing of evenings."

"We will, of course," Joshua said softly, "be going in full Indian regalia?"

They all groaned—including Julia—as he fully expected them to do.

"What are you all groaning about?" he asked. "Why is it that when you go to a party given by our Queen, you all go in formal gowns—all dolled up—but when it comes to a reception by the Indian High Commissioner, all of you want to go dressed as the wife and children of an Indian slum dweller?"

They all hooted with laughter at his description of the clothes they might be wearing to the reception.

"I think," Sarah said, "that what Pappa means is that we do not give equal importance to the Indian side of our blood. For instance we live in England."

"Whose fault is that? They live here so we've lived here," David said.

"We don't speak any Indian languages—Hindi or Marathi," Sarah said.

"Whose fault is that?" Susan said. "They never encouraged us to learn any."

"We don't wear Indian outfits as a matter of normal wear—like we do jeans, or skirts and blouses, or dresses," Sarah said.

"Indian outfits are just not designed for the athletic woman," Ruth said. "Can you imagine me trying to run in a sari?"

Joshua threw up his hands in mock horror. "Come as you choose," he said. "But if I disown you when the High Commissioner comes to greet us, don't blame me if I look blankly at all of you and say: 'I haven't a clue who they are; find my wife first, and then check with her which of these scruffy children are mine!'"

"You wouldn't!" Rachel said. She'd been sitting silently listening to the light-hearted exchanges between this Indian father and his children. She had an Indian father too, but he had never insisted on her wearing a sari. "I'd love to wear a sari; I don't know how. And I don't have a sari or a sari-blouse or a petticoat skirt."

"We can soon remedy that," Sarah said. "You're smaller than we are, but there are pretty new outfits—almost never worn—that we've outgrown; I'm sure we can find a sari that you like—Benarasi silk or nylon."

"Daddy, you did say 'Indian regalia', didn't you?" Ruth asked. "We can wear Punjabi Salwar Khameez? Does that meet with your approval for the reception?"

"Oh, sure, Ruth. I know you prefer that because it gives your legs the freedom of a runner. The Salwar Khameez, with a long muslin or silk cloth across the breasts, for modesty, was the royal outfit of the court of Moghul Emperors in India. They are an important part of Indian history—and their dress code, with Indian women, has outlived them."

"Please, will someone show me how to wear the sari?" Rachel said. "I presume, I am coming?"

"Of course you are," Julia said. "You're like our daughter—you always were. That day, for your information, and Florenzo's, the Queen asked for you!"

"I started to make excuses—very busy, cooking Sunday evening for the restaurant opening on Monday, etc.—and the Queen gave me one of her withering looks; Her Majesty doesn't miss a thing."

Julia turned to Joshua.

"Darling, I'll need your help to put the sari on. I've forgotten quite a bit. Will you?"

"It is a truth, universally acknowledged," Joshua said gravely, "at least in male Indian circles, that the wearing of a sari by a woman in the presence of a lover or husband, can take an awful long time."

"'Pride and Prejudice', Daddy," Susan said, laughing. "The very first sentence! I forgot you and Elizabeth Aunty are well-versed in Jane Austen."

"I only say it, to give Mummy plenty of time to get ready."

"And before any of you, especially Rachel, jumps to the wrong conclusions," Julia said, "the woman, before she wears the sari, already has on a blouse, and a long petticoat—from her waist to her ankles—on top of her unmentionables. So, yes, my darling husband of twenty-five years, we'll start real early with wearing the sari so that we are both happy people."

"Does David know how to help me put a sari on?" Rachel asked shyly.

"Of course, I do," David said. "And if I don't get it right the first time around, we have, always, been instructed to try, try, and try again, until we do get it right. And that's precisely what I'll do—so we'll have to start even earlier than Daddy and Mummy!"

"We'll just have to make sure Lysa Aunty doesn't walk in on their act—otherwise we'll have some very exciting Italian histrionics," Julia said.

"I don't think Mamma would mind—but Florenzo would. Fortunately, Roberta is keeping him on his toes—so he's been leaving us alone. As Pappa Joshua has said before: 'We'll let the troops handle it!'"

"I presume by troops, you mean Sarah and me?" Susan said.

"No. I meant Ruth. She's the only one who can be out here, keeping an eye on the street, because she's not wearing a sari. I presume it takes about three minutes to put on the Salwar Khameez?"

"Less," Ruth said, "but on second thoughts, I think Will should be given a crash course on how to put a sari on his beloved—me! I've changed my mind, Daddy, I'm all for the sari bit. Why should I miss out on all the fun?"

Julia looked despairingly at Joshua.

"See what you've started? Our daughters, who are engaged to be married, want to imitate us, an older couple and married twenty-five years. Is that fair? I don't remember you helping me with the sari when I first learned to put it on."

"On the contrary, my dear, you have a very selective memory. When my mother first taught you how to put a sari on, I was in the room with you, because she said, quite rightly: 'when I'm gone who else will help you but Joshua?' Of course, I was the model son in her presence—I kept my hands to myself."

Julia laughed.

"You're right. And when we were downstairs—and remember we were engaged, not married—she whispered to me: "You might tell Joshua you don't know how the blouse goes on as well—and let him figure it out for you."

"I can't believe this," Susan said. "Grandma actually was in on the conspiracy? You'd think most mothers would be protective of their sons from the evil, scheming wives their sons had brought home!"

Julia laughed again.

"Not my dear mother-in-law. Her one fear was that I might see the living conditions in India—not quite Bromfield House—and walk out on her son. Don't forget she had known me only two days, when the incident occurred. I spent hours reassuring her, Joshua and I truly loved each other—and nothing, but nothing, was going to tear us apart. She died a very happy mother, after seeing all four of you; Susan you were about two years old when she died. I loved her very much—my own mother had died when I was five years old—and she loved me too."

As it turned out, Ruth was not in the living room, in a Salwar Khameez, guarding the front door. She was in with Sarah and Susan putting on a sari as well. She had not intended to, but on one of her walks with Will—as a member of the family he was coming to the Indian High Commissioner's reception for Devinder and his fiancée,—she had mentioned the dress code for Indian women, and found to her surprise that Will wanted, very much, to see her in a sari! He'd seen Indian women in saris in Hampstead, and he had even fantasized how Ruth might look in one. So she smiled and said, he would for sure, see her that Sunday in a sari, so that his fantasies of her might not be fantasies any more.

The telephone rang. Susan who was nearest the phone answered it.

"It's for you, Mamma. Elizabeth Aunty, personally, on the line."

"Oh!" Julia said as she went to it. "I wonder what Elizabeth Aunty wants?"

"Julia," the Queen said, "Put me on the speaker phone so that all there can hear me. Look, dears, I know you are all going next Sunday to the reception being given by the Indian High Commissioner. Am I right?"

"Yes, Aunty, you're right. Their daughter is getting married; it is her engagement reception."

"Yes, I know. I've been invited too, but I can't accept—much as I'd like to be there with you all. Protocol! I'd be attending every reception of every ambassador in London—and I can't. So, please, will you represent me—all of you?"

"Of course, Elizabeth Aunty. We'd be honoured."

"Good! I'll call the High Commissioner, give him my regrets, and inform him that Lady Julia and her family will represent me instead. Thank you, dears. I hear Major Squigby has now won Ruth's hand?"

"How did you know, Elizabeth Aunty?" Ruth asked.

The Queen chuckled. "I have my methods, dear," she said, "but do tell Will his mother baked the finest pies!"

So on that Sunday, at ten minutes to six in the evening, General Sir Joshua Samuelson, in full Indian Military uniform, with his wife,

Lady Julia on his arm, his son, in the uniform of an entering cadet at Sandhurst, his son-in-law-to-be also in British Military uniform, his three daughters and one daughter-in-law-to-be, in colourful—and expensive—Benarasi silk saris, with exotic, and real, 22 kt gold Indian jewellery of necklaces and earrings, stepped from their three cars onto the curb outside India House. With valet parking for the occasion, they could walk right into India House.

Julia was the only one who did not have a gold necklace; hers was a double-string of matching real pearls, presented by Joshua's mother to her, at her marriage to Joshua. She had other gold jewellery—some of the pieces Rachel was wearing were Julia's that had, in Indian tradition, been earmarked for Rachel on her marriage to David—but the pearl necklace was Julia's favourite piece. As they entered the banquet hall of India House, the family was the cynosure of all eyes.

General Sir Joshua Samuelson with his elegant wife, Lady Julia—tall, elegant, alluring and agelessly beautiful, with her hair tied in a bun, and wearing a green and gold silk sari, wrapped round her hips and legs, with pleats tucked into her waistband; then draped round her breasts, over her left shoulder, round the back of a gold blouse, and tucked into her waist. She had worn flat-heeled shoes that were hidden beneath the sari, only the painted toenails peeping out as she walked, holding Joshua tight, his arm in her breast.

Behind them came Lord David, the twelfth Earl of Bromfield, with his cousin and fiancée, Rachel, on his arm, held equally tight—the example being set by his parents ahead. Rachel, very beautiful, not-too-tall and a little on the plump side, suited David perfectly in their walk. She had on a gold-yellow silk sari with black embroidery that matched her long black hair, now tied in an elegant bun, and a gold blouse that had belonged to Sarah in earlier years and fitted Rachel surprisingly well. Rachel was a little apprehensive; it was the first time she was attending such official receptions—but David only held her tighter to reassure her.

Behind them was Major Squigby with his fiancée, Lady Ruth. Here the difference in their heights was noticeable, but they ignored it. Ruth had worn flat-heeled open shoes—as her mother had—and

Ruth, like Julia, was not one to stoop, and so they did make an odd couple—as her parents did in front—to others, perhaps, but not to each other! Ruth had chosen—from her collection of saris—a blue sari, to match the blue of her eyes, with gold embroidery. Her light-brown skin spoke volumes for the 'Indianness' in her, and, like her two sisters, she was very comfortable with both sides of her. She had short hair and so she had chosen a 'choker' gold necklace that fitted her high on the neck.

Behind them came Sarah and Susan, also arm in arm.

Sarah had the sort of beauty that turned heads when she entered the room, with beautiful brown eyes and straight brown hair; she could best be described as statuesque—an elegance that she had inherited from her mother. She had picked a red silk sari with gold embroidery on it, that went with a gold blouse, all of it a blaze of colour, that with her beauty and elegance dazzled the eyes of every young man in the room—causing many a skipped heartbeat!

Susan, tall and alluring, with oval face, rosy cheeks, unblemished white skin—that was entirely from her mother's side—and straight black hair—entirely from her father's side—that plunged past small ears, had chosen a yellow sari with black embroidery to match the colour of her hair. She had on coral-frame spectacles that were a little larger than she needed for her beautiful black eyes, but sitting high up on the bridge of her nose, they centred her eyes to perfection.

The tables were reserved seating, with names of the parties on them—General Samuelson and Family had a table for eight, which suited them admirably, because there were eight of them.

Light strains of Indian classical music came from the orchestra in one corner of the room; behind each table was an Indian 'bearer' or waiter—in full Indian regalia complete with a turban and a trailing end that came past one shoulder.

He saluted Joshua smartly, and Joshua returned his salute—until he looked into the bearer's face.

"Why, Ranjit Singh," Joshua said. "This is a pleasant surprise; I didn't know you worked at India House?"

"I'm in the kitchens mainly, Colonel Saheb—no! now it is General Saheb!—but for occasions like Miss Premlata's engagement reception, we are all pressed into service. May I say, Sir, how delighted I am to have been assigned to your table, to serve you and your beautiful family."

Joshua smiled, as Ranjit Singh helped the ladies to their seats.

Joshua waved around the table: "My beautiful wife, Lady Julia; my son Lord David and his fiancée, Miss Rachel; my daughters Lady Sarah, Lady Ruth and Lady Susan, and Lady Ruth's fiancé, Major Squigby. This is Havaldar Ranjit Singh of the First Rajput Regiment, stationed in Ajmer; we've been in two wars together, and a finer soldier you are unlikely to find anywhere in England."

"Not true, Colonel Saheb—may I continue to call you Colonel Saheb?—Havaldar Mansingh, with his wife Rupa Devi, is here—the High Commissioner flew them both out for the engagement reception. After all it is their son Devinder that Miss Premlata is to marry."

"I knew who she was marrying but I did not know Mansingh would be here. Quite like old times, eh! Ranjit Singh."

He took their orders for beverages; before leaving he hesitated before his Colonel.

"What is it Ranjit Singh?" Joshua asked, kindly. "Is there something you wish to say?"

"It is to Lady Julia—if I may be permitted, that is?"

"Go ahead. You have my permission."

"Memsaheb Lady Julia, soon we will all be busy, and I will not be able to tell you what I have been wanting to say to my Colonel Saheb's wife for twenty-five years—because the opportunity has never arisen. Today is a miracle, because it has! May I?"

"Of course, Ranjit Singh. What is it that you've been wanting to tell me? I'm the only wife he's ever had."

They all—including Ranjit Singh—laughed.

"May I say, Memsaheb, that this husband of yours, my Colonel Saheb, is one of the bravest men in the Indian Army—'The Lion of

Lahore'! He was on the frontlines with us when he took us out to the battlefront—not hiding behind us in the rear, as some of the other colonels did; he treated the lives of his soldiers like they were his own life. He saved my life by refusing to let Havaldar Mansingh attack an enemy battery with two hundred men—I was one of those two hundred men; then I was a sepoy! When he left for England, I didn't even thank him for it. Mansingh and his wife, Rupa Devi, thanked him, but I couldn't; it has been weighing on me for years. Today I have done it!"

Ranjit Singh spoke fast to get whatever was within him, all out into the open; turned round and abruptly left to fill their orders for beverages.

There was a silence around the table.

Joshua said plaintively: "What's going to happen to me when Mansingh and Rupa Devi turn up to greet us—and they will. Didn't Sarah say this was going to be an embarrassing evening? Didn't you say, Sarah, that you and Susan would prefer your father to be a coward—once in a while? What better evening than this for us to be cowards? Come on, Sarah, you and I will leave, quietly, before the evening begins. I'll take you to an Indian restaurant and we'll have some father\daughter bonding? What say you? Let our troops—your mother, and siblings, and their loved ones—hold the fort!"

Sarah laughed, as did Julia.

"No, Pappa. Today you pay the full price for being one of the bravest men in the Indian Army—'The Lion of Lahore'! As Susan will find out—if she becomes a famous writer—you have to pay for everything in the end—even courage, or the goodness in you. And today the both of us have to pay for it. What makes it so bearable, Daddy, is that I am not alone. Come, sit here between Mamma and me; we'll each hold one of your hands to see you through it."

"More likely, Sarah wants her hand held when Devinder, with Premlata, comes to speak to her," Susan said, laughing. "Will he flaunt his bride-to-be before her? Show his pity for Sarah that she does not end up an old maid? Make pointed remarks that Sarah wasn't the only fish in the sea, and the one he's caught is no less than the one and only daughter of the Indian High Commissioner in

London? I don't know him well enough to know what line he is going to take—Sarah knows him better than we do."

"So, Pappa," Ruth said, "why did Ranjit Singh ask to address Mummy? Why not directly thank you?"

"Because he knew that I would cut him off the instant he started, with some curt reminder that 'the ladies are waiting for their drinks!' But he also knew that, as his Colonel, I would never interrupt his conversation with my wife, because that would have been grossly discourteous to her! Nuances of Indian culture, shall we say? Those regrets have been bottled up within him for a long time—the speed at which he wanted to get them out shows that," Joshua paused.

"I have also to initiate you all—Mummy knows this one—into the method a servant will greet a master," Joshua continued. "The servant—male or female—will bend over to touch the feet of the master; then draw the hands to the chest. What a caring master—like Mummy or I—will do, is to put our hands forth to the servant before he or she is half-way down, touch the servant on both shoulders and draw the servant upright again. Did you get that? I just mention this in case Devinder's parents—particularly his mother Rupa Devi—feels it necessary to make obeisance to all of us. Ah! Here they come."

He was referring to the party that had arrived at the head table. The Indian High Commissioner, his wife and daughter, accompanied by Devinder, Havaldar Mansingh, and Rupa Devi—the guests of honour—all were seated at the head table, and the food service began.

The food was served in a 'thali'—a round stainless steel, serving tray—that contained several smaller round, stainless steel 'watis'—cups without handles—that contained the rice, the dal, two vegetables, some pickle, some raitha, and, if non-vegetarian, an extra wati of either chicken or lamb—no beef! Indian breads—chappatis, puris or naans—were served separately on the table, in unlimited quantities.

The food was excellent, the conversation delectable, the evening—despite Joshua's and Sarah's misgivings—thoroughly enjoyable—until all the food was eaten. Between the clearing of the main meal and the serving of the dessert—gulab jamuns or rasgullas—the High Commissioner tinkled his water glass with his spoon and the microphone immediately drew the attention of the guests to the head table.

Silence reigned.

The High Commissioner welcomed them all to the evening's reception in honour of the engagement of his only daughter Premlata to Devinder, doing post graduate work at the Imperial College of Science and Technology and son of Shri and Shrimati Mansingh of Marwar, Rajasthan, India.

After the applause had died down, he went on to say that, while the dessert was being served, their families would walk down to the tables, greeting the invited guests individually, introducing themselves, and being introduced to guests and their families.

Their table was one of the first to be reached.

Devinder had not seen Sarah. He had received an RSVP with her regrets; he wasn't looking for her. What made it more difficult for him in the large hall was that she was in a sari—which is the very last outfit he would have expected her to be in.

He was almost upon her when he saw her, and he shouted out in uncontrolled pleasure: "Sarah!"

She smiled, but did not respond.

Joshua stepped into the breach: "Your Excellency, may I present my family? This is my wife, Lady Julia; our son, Lord David, the twelfth Earl of Bromfield, and his fiancee, Rachel; our eldest daughter, Lady Sarah; our second daughter, Lady Ruth, and her fiancé Major Squigby; and our youngest daughter, Lady Susan."

The High Commissioner introduced his wife and daughter. "Does Devinder know one of you? Which of you is Sarah?"

"He knows us all, Sir. He and Sarah are at Imperial College—though in different departments. He has also been to our house for lunch. A delightful boy! And our heartiest congratulations to the happy couple on their engagement."

His Excellency would have pursued the matter of his future son-in-law's acquaintance with the stunningly beautiful, Lady

Sarah—out of mere curiosity; not suspicion—were they not saved by Rupa Devi who, on seeing her Colonel Saheb, rushed forward to do obeisance to him and Lady Julia. Havaldar Mansingh followed suit—leaving the High Commissioner and his wife gaping in surprise. Premlata smiled at Sarah, extending her hand; Sarah shook it warmly.

The High Commissioner and his wife, Mr. and Mrs. Menon were South Indians from Madras, and so much darker in shade—as was their daughter—than the North Indians like the Rajputs or the Punjabis.

The three of them were also all on the short side, slim and lightly built. In intellect they were brilliant! Premlata had been educated at Harvard in Business Administration—at that time her father had been the Indian Ambassador to the United States. She was a very pretty girl with delicate features, a small nose and mouth, black hair—like Susan's—that if unbraided would have reached to her waist. Instead it was tied into a single pigtail that was then wound into a bun at the back of her head. On the center of her forehead she had a round red mark just above her nose and between her eyebrows.

Mrs Menon reached out to Julia, who led her to the vacant chairs, and they sat down; Sarah seeing her cue, sat beside her mother and entered into their conversation. Devinder would have moved to the vacant chair beside Sarah, to engage her in conversation, but Susan slipped into it first and engrossed herself also in the talk between the two older women, effectively cutting out all access to Sarah.

Joshua kept Mr Menon busy in small talk, preventing Mansingh or Rupa Devi from further display of loyalty to their Colonel Saheb; he secretly enjoyed their devotion, but this was not the time for it! Joshua couldn't be quite sure how much Mr. Menon knew about their past associations, or his Master/servant relationship with Rupa Devi.

Ruth and Rachel weren't going to be left out of the 'act'. They, very gently and politely, led Havaldar Mansingh and Rupa Devi to the four other vacant chairs at the table, drew the chairs out so that they could all sit facing each other, and politely inquired if they were enjoying England? It had turned a little cold; were they warm enough?

They spoke in English to both Mansingh and Rupa Devi; he translated for her. But she was not listening to them about the weather. Her eyes were flitting between her son and Sarah—on whom her son's eyes were riveted.

She thought: Why, if my son is good enough for the only daughter of the Indian High Commissioner—who is Colonel Saheb's Saheb—did I think he wasn't good enough for Colonel Saheb's daughter?

The answer when it came to her caused her to smile in relief, and the reassurance that she had been right in her thinking. It was because both Mansingh and she had a debt of obligation to the Colonel Saheb that could never be repaid! They had no such debt to the Indian High Commissioner. Her son's history, and his future, had been written long before he had been born—in the life of a sixteen year old girl plucked from poverty and nurtured into womanhood by the Colonel Saheb, and in the life that the Colonel Saheb had decreed for her husband—by saving it on the battlefield—otherwise Devinder would not even have been born!

In the case of the Colonel Saheb's daughter, it was a question of Rajput honour, ingrained even among the poorest of Rajputs; in the case of the Colonel Saheb's Saheb's daughter, no such honour was at stake.

Havaldar Mansingh must have been thinking along precisely the same lines, because he smiled at Rupa Devi and nodded; the Colonel Saheb's daughter had to be protected, for the sake of her happiness—no matter what it took—even from their own son!

The boys, David and Will, zeroed in on Devinder and Premlata, who seeing herself the centre of attention of all the young men at the table, turned on her charm, leaving Devinder alone and miserable. He kept looking towards Sarah but was unable to establish eye contact.

Why, he said to himself, is this my engagement reception; yet I am feeling so wretched? Seeing Sarah in a sari had aroused hidden emotions within him. If he, he argued with himself, was good enough—and his family background was good enough—for him to have 'snagged' the only daughter of the Indian High Commissioner in London, why had he been found wanting and so unsuitable—even by his own father and mother!—for the daughter of the Military Attache to that same High Commissioner?

Premlata was a remarkably intelligent girl, showing her ability to converse on topics as diverse as nuances in Indian cooking to the state of the British economy.

Time being short—they had so many other tables to visit in the banquet hall—Mr. Menon made his excuses, collected his party and made to the next table. Sarah made sure that no matter which table they were at, her back was always turned towards them.

Sarah and Joshua looked at each other in elation. The family had stepped in and carried out a 'military operation' of the highest caliber—so smoothly and efficiently—Joshua doubted if he could have planned it any better himself!

Courage after all was not so trying a virtue.

The dessert was served, and while waiting for their hot tea or coffee; the girls went to the powder room for powdering their noses and small talk; the men disappeared in the direction of the bar, to celebrate the success of the evening—it had not ended in a disaster, and that was success!—with a glass of sweet white wine for the girls, a glass of sherry for Julia, and scotch and soda for themselves.

Julia was sitting all by herself when a short, dumpy Indian woman, in an expensive Benarasi silk sari and bedecked with 22 kt gold jewellery, came and sat beside Julia. She introduced herself:

"I am Mrs. Varma," she said, sweetly, "wife of the Deputy Indian High Commissioner."

She came straight to the point.

"You have very beautiful daughters!"

"Thank you."

"Are they married? Or engaged?"

"Well, my son David is engaged to his cousin, Rachel, who is with us today, and our daughter, Ruth, is engaged to the Major in the military uniform; the other two are neither married nor engaged. Why do you ask, Mrs. Varma?"

"I'm asking about the tall, very beautiful, elegant girl in the red sari and the gold blouse. Is she married or engaged?"

"You mean, Sarah, our eldest daughter? No, she is still single. Why do you ask?"

Mrs. Varma leaned confidentially towards Julia.

"I have three sons. My eldest boy—he is almost thirty years old—is not married. He has been looking at Sarah—did you say?—for the past two hours, as if no one else existed in the hall! I think we can arrange a match between them. Yes?"

"No. An arranged match may be the done thing in India—and it has its uses even here in England—but my daughter would not agree to it; she has to meet the boy, get to know him, like him—then perhaps..."

"Why don't you bring her over to our table? We're right in the front—there. We should, rightly, have been at the head table, but Mr. Menon said there wasn't enough room for all seven of us—I have two daughters too. Yes?"

"You want me to bring my daughter over to your table—to meet your son?" Julia said, trying to keep a straight face.

Mrs. Varma lowered her voice confidentially.

"Protocol! My husband is the Deputy Indian High Commissioner, while your husband is only the Military Attache. I'm sure you understand."

"Perfectly, Mrs. Varma."

Mrs. Varma beamed. "So where is Sarah?"

"She has gone to the powder room with her sisters and her sister-in-law-to-be."

"So you will come; I'll tell my son you are willing—to let them get together, did you say? Sarah will not find my son wanting—if you know what I mean."

Before Julia could reply—and had just saved herself from bursting into outright laughter; she had no wish to hurt Mrs. Varma—she saw Mr. and Mrs. Menon rush towards her, Mr. Menon ahead of his wife.

"Oh, Lady Julia! Why didn't you tell us? Why didn't General Samuelson tell us? Oh, we're so embarrassed!"

"Tell you, what, Your Excellency?"

"Her Majesty, the Queen, called more than two days ago; I did not receive the message until two minutes ago—my Personal Assistant will just have to go! Why did you not tell us that you and your family have been deputed by Her Majesty, the Queen, to be her personal representatives at this reception? What an honour it is for us to have you; you and your family could have been easily accommodated at the head table. Our sincerest of apologies. Will you forgive us? Please!"

Julia extended her hands to them. The Indian High Commissioner bowed low over her right hand; Mrs Menon took her left hand and curtseyed.

Mrs. Menon saw Mrs. Varma gaping with open mouth, and nudged her sharply:

"Curtsy to Lady Julia! What are you waiting for?"

Mrs. Varma curtseyed to Julia, turned round and scampered away. Joshua passed her as he and the boys were returning with their drinks on two trays. At the same time the girls returned from the powder room.

Mr. and Mrs. Menon returned to the head table; Mr Menon's PA would soon be on his way back to India!

"What was that all about?" Joshua asked, casually. "What were Mr. and Mrs. Menon doing at our table again? And why was Mrs. Varma here?"

Julia smiled at him: "Of no importance, dear."

He understood. It had been their code for twenty years—ever since David was four—to say: 'Don't ask me now, dear; ask me when we're in bed together and alone'!

The only problem with that was that their four super-brilliant children had cracked their code long, long ago, and knew perfectly well what it meant. Now their 'war plan' would be how to worm it out of their mother or father, without appearing to do so. They had worked it out, to perfection—the various lines of approach that could be used. Some were successful with their father; some with their mother. Both parents had their Achilles heels.

In their father's case, the one person he would confide in would be Joe Uncle.

In their mother's case, the one person she would confide in would be Lysa Aunty.

In both cases, Rachel would have to be brought in, to assist in the operation.

She had done it before, knew what to do, and enjoyed doing it!

CHAPTER 14

The very next day, Julia was at home doing the laundry when she heard the doorbell peal loud and long.

She was doing the 'knit-delicates' that day, going round from room to room, collecting them in the hamper she carried. She started in the master bedroom collecting Joshua's socks and her unmentionables, then to David's bedroom for his socks, then to the girls' room for a further whole pile of unmentionables.

She heard the doorbell peal a second time; it was Lysa at the door and she was pretty upset. She had been crying.

Julia thrust the hamper of soiled clothes aside, and led Lysa to the twin sofa in the living room.

"What is it, dear?" Julia said.

"She's leaving him?"

"Who's leaving who?" The anxiety was unmistakable!

"Oh, not Rachel and David—they'll stay together forever—thank God! Roberta's leaving Florenzo. She and Alphonso are going back to Italy."

"Alphonso? Don't tell me!"

Lysa nodded sadly. "I blame Florenzo. He doesn't know how to treat women. A girl comes new from Italy to England; she's missing her family, lonely and homesick, and instead of giving her all the comfort she needs for her to fall in love with him—he instructs her on her duties in the restaurant! First he loses Susan and now Roberta."

"He never had Susan, Lysa," Julia said gently. "You can't blame him for that. She would never have been happy with him, running a restaurant. She's aced her 'A' levels, is going to Oxford for a degree in English Literature—to my old college, actually—and then wants to be a writer. She doesn't want to be stuck in a kitchen cooking lasagna or spaghetti and meatballs—which is what Florenzo would have her do. Don't misunderstand me, Lysa dear, I love Florenzo—as you love Susan—but that's not the life either of us would wish for her—would you now?"

"No," Lysa said. "You're right. Susan was not for him; Roberta was! Now what excuses do you have to make for my son—for losing her?"

"It is that combination of Indian and Italian male chauvinism—and poor Florenzo gets it from both sides of the family—that make his attitudes to women the way they are."

"But David doesn't treat Rachel that way. He treats her as if she is piece of rare fine china! Makes me think, why wasn't I treated that way?"

"Because David is also a military man—his father is that way too. I was going to do the laundry when you came. If it had been Joshua, seeing me with the laundry hamper in my arms, the first thing he would have done would have been to take it from me and carry it to the laundry room. Tell me—don't you think I can carry a laundry hamper from one room to another? He doesn't even think of it that way; to him it is chivalry! David is the same way. If he had seen me with the laundry hamper that is exactly what he would have done too."

"Makes you feel good?"

"It does, actually, I'll admit. But not all Indian or, for that matter, Military male chauvinism is quite as endearing."

"Oh?"

"When we were first married, and Joshua and I were going anywhere together in the Bentley, he would always drive—Indian or Military male chauvinism? I wanted to drive, and he rejected the idea. For heaven's sake, I thought, it is my bloody Bentley! I know it better than anyone else. Why shouldn't I drive when we are together?"

Julia's eyes twinkled. "So one day, as we were going out, I handed him the keys of the Bentley and said sweetly: 'You drive, dear.'

'Don't you want to drive?' he said.

'No,' I said. 'I can see that you're the better driver; we are going into London, and you're afraid that I'll have an accident and that you might end up getting injured or—even worse—killed. So to set your fears at rest, I'll let you drive—every time.'

'As I knew he would—he exploded!'

'Me? Afraid of getting injured or killed? Have you gone mad? I'm a soldier, for heaven's sake! If I was afraid of getting injured or killed, I wouldn't have gone into the Indian Army, or been in it for twenty years!'

'Then he saw the twinkle in my eyes—I'd kept my face averted from him until then—and he laughed, wagging his finger at me.'

'You've found my Achilles heel, haven't you, Julia? Well, you're right, dear. Any time we have an argument all you have to do is to give in, saying: Yes, dear, I don't want you to be afraid!'" Julia smiled. "But he had found my Achilles heel too, because, I've never, in twenty-five years of marriage, ever used that ploy again to win an argument. Others? Yes. But not that one!"

They laughed. Julia could see that Lysa was feeling better already.

"Let's have a cup of tea, Lysa and some of those delicious almond macroons that Susan bakes. You'll love them. I can do the laundry later. There's so much I want to tell you about Devinder's engagement reception at India House yesterday evening. Has Rachel filled you in on anything, so I don't repeat stuff you already know?"

"Rachel? I hardly see my daughter anymore! She's more in your house than in mine. Thank God for that; at least one of my children has found someone to love."

While they were having tea, Julia gave Lysa all the information about the previous evening, including how Sarah and Susan had prevented Devinder from attaching himself to Sarah, and how Ruth and Rachel had prevented Devinder's parents from revealing any past relationships between them and Joshua, thereby avoiding questions from arising in the minds of their hosts, the Indian High Commissioner and his wife, Mr and Mrs Menon.

But it was only with their second cup of tea, that Julia told Lysa all about her encounter with Mrs. Varma, the wife of the Deputy Indian High Commissioner, and the strange matchmaking proposal that she, Julia, had received for Sarah.

"I think, sometimes, Lysa, that all Indians are mad, and ask myself, what lunatic community have I married into? Then I look at Joshua and my brood—and I say: Thank God for that; what would I have done with them?—without their honour, and their traditions, and their customs and yes, even their endearing lunacy!"

Lysa pushed away the plate of macroons—she'd had two already.

"I'd better not, Julia. I'm getting fat."

"Eat!" Julia said. "I've put on a few pounds too. Most Indian husbands like their women on the heavy side—none of these super thin models for them."

Lysa helped herself to two more. Then she laughed.

"I know that—and so does Rachel. She swears the only reason she keeps David's love is because she's fond of good food—as he is."

"Talking of Rachel, Lysa, make sure in conversation with her—casual like—that you drop the gossip about Mrs. Varma and her eldest son's interest in Sarah."

"You want me to?"

"Oh, yes!"

"Why?"

"It's a long story that goes back to the time when David was four years old. If Joshua or I had some adult or important information to give to the other, and one of us asked for it in front of him, we had a coded message for each other: 'Of no importance, dear!' That meant: 'I can't tell you now; ask me for it when we're alone or in bed'. Get the picture?"

Lysa nodded.

"The system worked for a while, but the children are so intelligent they broke the code—and then devised devious methods of obtaining the information, without Joshua or me tumbling to it. Of course, I had been an MI-6 agent and Joshua was Director of IMI for a while—and so it became a game, because we knew they'd broken the code. So now we know, they know, when there is 'secret' information, we are withholding from them, but they don't know, we know that they know. Got it?"

"More or less," Lysa said, wrinkling her eyes in amusement.

"So not being secretive parents we pass on the information to them any way that makes them feel good. In this case, they will use Rachel to pump you—just go along with it. That is, if it's okay by you?"

"I'd love to! Why should you all have all the fun? Parents in a spy game versus their children! I like that; I'll let Joe in on it. He'll love it too. Come to think about it, Rachel has pumped both Joe and me in the past for some gossip that you or Joshua might have passed to us—I never thought she was being a spy for David."

"I don't think they use the word 'spy' any more, dear, even in the agency. It's always 'agent'. Much more dignified, don't you think?"

They had finished their second cup of tea, ravaged Susan's almond macroons, when Lysa got up to go.

"Thank you, Julia. Talking to you always makes me feel better."

"You're very welcome here anytime, dear. So fill me in before you leave. What's going to happen to Roberta and Alphonso?"

"Roberta has moved in with Alponso—into his bedsitter; his landlady gave him permission. They're going back to Italy. They offered to work overtime to earn their fares back to Milan, but Joe and I just decided to give them their fares—as a wedding present. After all Roberta is Pappa's grandniece. And keeping them working in the restaurant is only going to make Florenzo feel much worse—the tension between all of them will kill me! As you may have guessed, we will not however—not even Pappa—be attending the wedding. Florenzo will hire three Italian girls to take the place of Rachel, Roberta and Alphonso. So Rachel is yours."

Sarah was unaware of the matchmaking offer, made for her, from Mrs. Varma for her eldest, thirty-year-old son. It was just as well, because she was not feeling very sympathetic to Indian males in general, and one in particular.

The only Indian man who aroused the warmest of feelings in her heart, was her father. That had been a sterling performance from him, and the family, in protecting her from Devinder, at the engagement reception. That a General in the Indian Army was willing—for the sake of his daughter—to act like a coward, and flee the banquet hall at India House, with her, only caused her to admire his courage even more.

It took a lot of courage for a brave man to be a willing coward.

The problem had arisen when she had gone as usual to check her mail in the pigeonhole at Ayrton Hall. She had now reached a stage when she dreaded even checking it; but she did, and groaned.

There was a hand-written note from Devinder, begging her—pleading with her—to meet him in the Union Cafeteria at 4:00 PM the next day. She thought about it, and decided she would go, but would not involve her family in any of her decision-making. This she had to do by herself, for herself.

He was there, at his favourite table at one end of the room, head down, downcast and morose. Rather than have him buy her cup of tea, she went to the counters, bought two cupcakes and a cup of hot tea.

She was a little early; it was ten minutes to 4:00 PM.

It was worse than she had expected—much worse.

He had been engaged two weeks—and he wanted to break his engagement to Premlata.

"She is not what I expected," he moaned to Sarah. "She is so unlike you. She is domineering and bossy and demanding, and thinks that because she is the daughter of the Indian High Commissioner she can have her own way in everything. She is a spoiled brat! Please help me, Sarah." He reached out his hands to her on the table.

Sarah had a cupcake in one hand and a cup of hot tea in the other—and so she ignored his hands.

"Devinder," she said, kindly, "I cannot advise you on how you should run your life; talk to your parents—they are still in London. All I can do is to tell you without the slightest of hesitation—or regret—that I cannot and will not be a part of your life. I am not in love with you; I never was. I was kind to you, but that is part of my upbringing—to be kind to others."

He looked at his watch.

"You did get engaged to her. There must have been something about her that made you think you could be happy with her?"

"You and your family—and my parents—had just told me you were not for me. I went along to India House for dinner to soothe my aching heart. It was the dinner hour; the cafeteria was packed. There was only one seat vacant—at a table for two. She was at the table. I asked her permission and sat down; we got talking. She seemed like a nice person then—not pushy at all."

"Pushy? In what way?"

"In any discussion we have—be it on anything—she is always right! How can I live with a woman who is always right?"

Sarah saw the light. Her face lit up in a smile.

"My brother and my brother-in-law-to-be talked to her at your engagement reception. Their assessment of her was that she is an extremely intelligent woman! She has a Master's Degree in Business Administration from Harvard University—no mean achievement. She was very well informed and could talk knowledgeably about many subjects. Is that why you find her so 'pushy'? Because she knows more about most subjects than you do—except Mechanical Engineering?"

She laughed. He seemed offended by it.

"That is no reason to dump a woman, Devinder," she said, gently, "because you feel intellectually inferior to her? Be proud of her! Let everyone know that she is the most intelligent woman you have ever met—certainly far more than I am—and how thrilled and pleased you are that she has consented to be your wife!"

He looked at his watch again. He did not speak.

So she continued: "In days gone by, Devinder, when women were not educated, they admired their husbands for their intellect, their knowledge and superior education; why can't you do the same now for your wife?"

It is when he looked at his watch for the third time, that she tumbled to it.

She rose hastily to her feet, pushed the second cupcake towards him, collected her soiled paper napkins and litter into her tray, and dumped them into the nearest trash can, before coming back to the table.

"Where are you going, Sarah?" Devinder said. "Please stay; for a little while longer?"

She folded her hands in front of her chest in an Indian 'namaste'.

"This is goodbye, Devinder. The cupcake is for you. It is Indian custom to sweeten the mouth of the person you are parting with—and I am parting with you. You are expecting Premlata here any minute; am I right? She will see us both together, and then you will spin her some story of how madly I am in love with you, causing her to break the engagement. Because you don't have the courage to face her, and break it yourself? That is why you called me here today—and that is despicable."

Sarah turned round abruptly, and before he could say another word, she raced to the front entrance of the Union Cafeteria. She was on the sidewalk, outside the building, when she saw Premlata on the other side of the street, at the traffic light, waiting for the lights to turn green, and for the pedestrian crossing sign to signal to pedestrians it was safe to proceed. So Sarah turned sharply up the sidewalk, away from her, to the next intersection and the next traffic light, before finding her way to South Kensington Tube Station; then onto Finchley Road Tube Station.

After that it was a short walk to Fitzjohn's Avenue, and the safety of home.

CHAPTER 15

Susan's new novel—it wasn't a second draft of the old one—was completed by the end of September. It had been radically altered. It still followed a family, but it brought in whole new avenues of race, religion, class distinctions, masters and servants, Indians,—she had to have them, she told her father!—English,—she had to have them, she told her mother!—royal blood and common blood; in fact she threw in every type of diversity she could think of—changes in plot too, as new ideas flooded into her head, almost as she wrote. In one scene she even threw in the kitchen sink! She made her characters human. This time she did not go down to London to see Jane and hand over the disk of the novel; she mailed it to the Agency, quietly, and tried to forget all about it. She didn't even mention it to the family; hardly any point in getting their hopes up—or their feelings all riled up—when nothing would come of it, and a rejection letter from Jane would be back soon, in the mail, to her. That is what she thought.

So Susan was very surprised, when ten days later, she received a warm and cordial letter from Lady Jane Literary Agency.

First, Jane congratulated her on the new novel—they would be very happy to represent her in finding a suitable publisher for it.

Then she apologized for not having given Susan more encouragement, even as she rejected the first novel. She was glad that Susan had seen fit to incorporate some of the suggestions—on the humanity of her characters—of her sleeping partner's review of the first novel; it was quite obvious to her, however, that Susan had gone way beyond anything either Jane or the reviewer had suggested or imagined possible—and done it superbly!

They were so impressed with it that, breaking their own rules, they planned simultaneous, multiple submissions of the manuscript to some of the major—and some of the not-so-major, but reputable—publishing houses in London.

Susan still withheld the information from her family. Jane, in the past, had made submissions of her poetry and short stories to literary magazine after literary magazine, without any success; her novel would go the same way. But a flicker of hope in her—and she tried hard to quench it—would not be quenched.

So no one was more delighted than Susan, when she received a phone call from Jane, bubbling over with excitement, that her first novel had been accepted. It was one of the smaller houses, but it was a good start; sometimes small houses became big houses on the authors they nurtured.

Could Susan come down to Lady Jane Literary Agency the next day at four in the evening, to approve some minor editorial corrections from her editor? The contract would come later.

Thinking that 'there's many a slip 'twixt the cup and the lip', Susan still refrained from alerting any of her family to the possibility that they might have a published author in their midst.

This time she did not put in her request for the Mini, on the bulletin board, opting to take the Tube instead.

At Lady Jane Literary Agency, as she fully expected, she saw Winnie Benthall in the room. But Jane and she were not sitting across the office desk; they were on the sofa, holding hands. They did not withdraw their hands, as Susan entered. Jane motioned Susan to one of the two chairs across from the sofa.

As she had also fully expected, Lord Albert was comfortably ensconced in the other chair, his lanky, gaunt frame fitting comfortably in the seat, though his legs were dangerously outstretched to anyone crossing his chair. Susan stepped over his feet. He withdrew them hurriedly, and apologized for his feet being where they were.

After discussing the minor editorial changes suggested by her editor, and a glowing endorsement of the Literary House that had decided to invest in her, Jane apologized again for rejecting, without encouragement, Susan's first submission.

"You shouldn't apologise for your review," Susan said, addressing Winnie—Jane's lesbian partner.

They had openly displayed their love for each other; it seemed churlish for Susan to disregard their lesbian relationship.

"Many of the comments you made about the inhumanity of my original characters, except the youngest daughter—the 'tart'—were well-merited and very useful to me. Please don't apologise; you wrote the review as you saw it—and it is I who should thank you for setting me straight. But it was my sister, Sarah, and my brother, David, who expanded my vision and made me rethink the diversity that I know about—I was now writing about what I do know!—which has made the new novel what it is. So, 'Thank you'."

Winnie looked at Jane in surprise.

"Why is Lady Susan looking at me? And thanking me? What on earth is she talking about?"

"Aren't you Jane's sleeping partner? The one who reviewed my first submission?"

The three of them burst into uncontrolled laughter. Susan was almost offended by the outburst.

"What?" she asked, quietly. "Why are you laughing? What have I said that is so funny? Maybe I have a hidden talent for writing humorous books?"

Jane put her hand out and touched Susan on the knee.

"I'm sorry, dear. Yes, you're right. Winnie is my 'sleeping partner'. We do sleep together; it is a warm and, I hope, a permanent relationship. But Winnie did not review your first submission. That was done by my 'business sleeping partner'. He has money invested in Lady Jane Literary Agency, but he does not control it, plays no part in running it, and does not take any of my profits—though he could, if he wanted to."

"I'm sorry," Susan said, smiling. "Well, then, please convey my sincerest thanks to your 'sleeping business partner' whoever he might be."

"Why don't you do that yourself right now," Jane said. "Just turn to your left and say what you have to say to Albert."

Susan turned to Albert and smiled at him.

"Thank you, Albert."

She got up from her chair. "I have to leave," she said. "Give me a call when the contract arrives, and I'll come down to sign it."

Albert got up hurriedly as well; she would have to cross his long, outstretched legs.

"May I take you home, Lady Susan?" he asked. "I did enjoy our last ride to your house. No obligations! Perhaps, we can discuss your novel? The diversity in it is so enthralling! Sarah and David suggested that? I'm so ashamed of myself for not suggesting those same ideas. It has made your new novel truly brilliant!"

"Flattery, Albert, is always pleasant to a budding writer's ears—but it will get you nowhere."

Jane and Winnie laughed at his discomfiture.

"But, yes, you can give me a ride home, if you wish," Susan said, feeling a little sorry for him.

They were almost at his Rolls, when Susan said:

"Albert, I have an errand I have to run in South Kensington. Are you pressed for time? If not, could we go there first?"

"Of course, dear. The more time I spend with you, the happier I am. Now, please don't reprimand me for saying what I feel."

"I will never reprimand you, Albert, for saying what you feel—on condition that you do not reprimand me for doing what I feel. Is that an agreement?"

"Oh, yes! And what is it, Susan, dear, that you want to do at this very minute?"

"I just told you. I want to run an errand in South Kensington."

"South Kensington, it is," he said cheerfully. "Just ask whatever your heart desires, and we'll do it."

"No questions asked?"

"No questions asked."

When they were on Oxford Street, he asked: “Where in South Kensington?”

“The Tube Station.”

“And what errand would you have to run in the Tube Station?”

“Didn’t you just agree? No questions asked.”

“Quite right, dear. My lips are sealed, but tell me what you want to do when we get to the Tube Station because I have to park this Rolls somewhere. What are we doing when we get to the Tube Station?”

“Take the Tube, of course.”

“Won’t it be crowded?” he said, mildly.

‘I pray that it is!’ she said to herself silently.

“Where are we going?” he asked. “I’ll need to know, to buy the right tickets.”

“Leave it to me,” she said.

She bought two day passes for unlimited travel on the Underground. As she had intended, they had reached South Kensington Tube Station just as the rush hour was at its height. Crowds of office-weary Londoners came pouring down the escalators and elevators as if fed by some unseen hand into a gigantic mashing machine, ending up on already overcrowded platforms in both directions.

Susan had elected to travel on the Circle Line towards Baker Street. The crowds massed in around them. He was taller than her, and fought to be at her side, and she did all she could to sidle up to him, so even on the platform they were touching—her shoulder against his arm.

“I presume,” he said, gently, “that you have a reason for why we are here, or doing whatever it is we’re supposed to be doing?”

“Absolutely! You’ll find out when we get on the train.”

“Will we be able to get on the train? It’s awfully crowded here—and the trains will come in pretty full.”

“You’re so right,” she said, smiling up at him. “As always, dear.”

The first train they missed. By dint of much pushing they were able to fight their way to the front edge of the platform—for the next train.

On the next train, he got on; she couldn't. The passengers pouring out of the compartment separated them; he got off.

On the third train, he got on again. Grabbing her by the waist he hauled her into the compartment and to the side of it, while the mass of bodies around them threw her into his arms.

He was against the partition wall that separated the seats from the doorway; she was up against him. The pressure against her back from everyone around her was comforting. She had Albert where she wanted him. Now it was only a matter of doing the right things.

She deliberately stepped on to his toes.

"I'm sorry," she whispered. "Do you think, Albert you could move your left leg ever so slightly so I can step off your toes?" He tried by shuffling his feet allowing her to slide her leg between his.

His thigh was between hers; hers between his. Neither could escape the pressures on each other—of the wall at his back and the people behind her—as the train accelerated down the tracks to Gloucester Road.

He was sweating with anxiety that she might misunderstand his posture or the position of his leg; she decided it was time to allay his anxiety and let him in on the purpose of the train ride. But she had one act more!

"Albert," she whispered, "I have this handbag of mine slung up on my shoulder. It's digging into me, and is very hurtful; do be a good chap, and bring your hand up to take some of the pressure off me, will you?"

"Are you sure? I have no wish to offend you?"

"Absolutely sure! In fact, I'm getting more sure every minute."

Hesitatingly, he raised his hand as if to ease the handbag away from her breast; she flattened herself against him at the precise second his palm was hovering over her generous breast, and he ended up by cupping it, pressing hard the now erect nipple. He would have pulled his hand away from the touch, but she placed her hand over his hand and pressed it into her.

"Albert," she whispered, "do you love me?"

"You know, I do. Very much!"

"Then why, may I ask, instead of making love to me, you are fighting to be away from me? Your hand is on my breast—it was my doing. Your thigh is between my thighs; mine is between yours. That was my doing too. Make love to me. You say you love me; then love me!"

After that there was no stopping Albert. He smiled as he realised the purpose of the journey. It was for her to discover whether he could arouse an 'awareness' in her. Would the closeness of his body, his hand on her breast, his thigh between hers, arouse in her the same emotions that had arisen within him, so many years before?

His love for her had arisen a long time ago—at the same time as her indifference to him.

She had been twelve years old, a voracious reader; she had an entire library of books bought out of her own pocket money—books of girls at boarding schools in England and Switzerland, books by Louisa May Alcott and Susan Coolidge, and others—with every available minute of free time spent with her nose—and her eyes—in books. There was a price to pay—she needed glasses. She was sensitive at first, because she was fast developing—at least in her body—into a woman. But she had to agree to wear them, so that she wasn't kept away from her beloved books.

The first time Albert had seen her in them—he was sixteen at the time—was at Bromfield, when Cecily Aunty had brought him and Jane over to spend the day with them.

Not intending to be cruel—though he realised after he had made the remark that he was—he had said: "Henceforth, I'll call you 'four eyes' Susan! Lady 'four eyes' Susan, if you wish."

She wept at his remarks.

His mother, hearing the remarks and seeing her cry, made him apologize to her, publicly, in front of all the children, and the servants around as well.

He had decided, then, that he would never try to joke with girls; his remarks had been very cruel. Far better he stay silent and let others do the talking—at least he wouldn't offend a girl—the way he had offended Lady Susan. Far better they think him 'dumb' than for him to be shamed in front of them—as before Lady Susan.

Over the years, he had not forgotten the incident; neither had she. Was that the reason she had ignored him? Was it fair to hold a remark—possibly spoken by a sixteen year old boy in his own insecure world—against him for so many years? Was that the reason she had fought even the idea of having any feelings for him, though he had on more than one occasion expressed his love for her? Was it that incident that could be the reason for his lack of speech in female company?

She felt so ashamed of herself, for having made him suffer, for so many years, for what had been intended, possibly, as an innocent remark. She had meted out to him a punishment that had lasted six years—and could, possibly, last his lifetime. She put her free hand round the back of his head, drew his head towards her, and kissed him on the mouth in a manner that left him in no doubt as to her intentions—unlike the kiss she had planted on his lips, in the restaurant, the last time.

Now neither could be restrained. They didn't care for the people around them—most ignored them; others smiled benignly—all they both wanted to be was as close to each other as possible, and squashed as they were, by the people around them, that closeness was easy to maintain. They had no idea where they were—and didn't care. The crowds still hemmed them in—they were grateful to their fellow travelers—but it did restrict Albert in what he wanted to do, so he whispered in her ear: "Darling, do you think you could move the handbag to the other shoulder?"

"Why, my love? Is your hand getting tired of being where it is?"

"Tired? Of being where it is? No! I could keep it there forever."

"Oh? Then there must be another reason. I won't ask if you don't want me to—and I'll do it."

"No! No! There should be no secrets between us. I want to fondle the other breast."

"Sort of be fair to the both of them?"

"Yes, but that's not the only reason."

"Why then?"

"I'm afraid I am in a dream. Like last time. You kissed me on the lips, and I was in heaven. Then twenty minutes later you said it was a mistake and wouldn't happen again. Suppose you change your mind about what's happening now? I'll live with regret the rest of my life—I swear it—that when I had the chance to fondle both your breasts, I settled for only the one of them. There, I've told you—now do you hate me for it? Will you punish me like the last time, I hurt you?"

"Hate you? Punish you? No, darling, I love you—for wanting them both. Lord Albert, Earl of Rathbone, I hereby give you full permission to fondle one or both of my breasts, as you may choose. Proceed Sir Albert! There now you've been anointed. Wait until the next station comes. If it is on our side, there will be a moment's relief for me to move the handbag."

The platform was on their side, and as the passengers exited, she swiftly moved the handbag from one shoulder to the other. Albert took the hand on her breast and put it around her waist to draw her up close; he took the other hand, that had been around her waist, up to her breast. This time her response to his touching and fondling, and the pressure of her thigh between his; his between hers, sent waves of pleasure surging into her; into him to. She did not attempt to enhance it by kissing him on the lips—that would have been a distraction—instead, she put her head on his chest and clung to him, as a fireball erupted within her.

When she opened her eyes, they were on South Kensington Tube Station. She had been planning to ride with Albert from South Kensington to Baker Street—as her parents had done twenty-six years before. But neither had paid any attention to the stations they'd passed—and had not cared.

They'd completed one full circle of the Circle Line, and the office crowds had thinned considerably.

She took him by the hand, quickly, and they exited the train.

"Why did we get off here, Susan?"

"Because this is where we started out from, my love, and we have to pick up your Rolls."

"Of course. Silly of me, not to think of it."

"Not silly, darling. In character. You're a philosopher and I'm a writer, and between the two of us we're going to forget a lot of things; we'll just have to keep reminding each other, of what the other is forgetting."

They sat in the Rolls for a long time, holding hands, neither of them willing to see the end of the evening—and starting the car would have meant just that.

Besides Susan had some issues they had to discuss.

"Darling," she said, at length. "We've both been in a dream heaven—I'm so happy to say—but we've got to come down to Earth to make it last. Are you willing to discuss some issues today—or would you rather leave it for some other time?"

"No! Right now! I'm a military man—like your father and mine—at heart; there's nothing like planning for a battle and winning the war. I can't give up now!"

"Albert, I aced my 'A' levels, I've been admitted to Mamma's old college—and yours too I believe?—at Oxford. I want to get a degree in English Literature from Oxford. That will take at least three years. Would you be prepared to wait that long?"

He laughed. "You don't think, Susan, that all the time I was dreaming of marrying you, I didn't spend some time analysing the issues? Here's my suggestion. Ready for it?"

She nodded, happily. She had thought he might freak out at the very suggestion of her going at Oxford—instead he'd given it some thought.

"First we do get engaged right away. Before you go to Oxford, in two weeks time, I believe? Sort of establish my claim on you before all those undergraduates start salivating over you!"

She laughed heartily: "Like the way you were undressing me and salivating over me at the Queen's party, Albert? I told the family about it that evening— about you wanting to eat me for breakfast, or whatever—and we had a hearty laugh over it. And then Mamma said to make sure I told you what she said."

"And what did Julia Aunty say?"

"She said, and I quote: 'I can't see him having you for breakfast, or whatever. He might, with your permission, possibly, nibble on your big toe, but that would be about all.'"

Albert burst out laughing. "I can see where you get your writing skills from. Actually, dear, I'd love to kiss your toes. Could we manage that sometime?"

"Oh, Albert! Don't tell me you have a foot fetish?"

"As far as you are concerned, my love, I have a fetish about every part of you. Shall I start from the hair on your head and end up at your toes—or would you that I start at your toes and end up on the top of your head?"

"Neither. At least not today. At least not now. So what are your plans for my education, may I know?"

"You will be very busy, my love, with assignments and papers to write and exams to take. And I couldn't be in love with you, if I made your life difficult by demanding the rights of a fiancé. I have none; I don't want any. But you have to eat dinner—and my estate at Rathbone is not twenty minutes away from the centre of Oxford. Why don't we meet every evening at the dinner hour, on weekdays, and let me take you out to dinner? Would that be too much of an imposition on your time? Just one hour a day?"

"Albert," Susan said, "you must have a very high opinion of the speed at which I eat, if you think that I can wolf down my dinner in one hour. I need at least two—and if we're having dessert—it could be even longer. Is that agreed?"

"Dessert every single dinner, every single weekday!"

"What about weekends?"

"Well, dear, that may depend on whether you have papers due on the Monday, and need the weekend for work. But I'm at your command; you decide. If you have the weekend free, maybe we could come down to London, visit your family and mine; then I drive you back to Oxford on the Sunday night after—what have you told me—your reunion dinner?"

"Done! I'll just make sure to work like crazy on the weekdays, so that I can spend the weekends with you. Oh, Albert, what can I say—but thank you!"

She leaned over and kissed him on the mouth.

"Any other issues?" Albert asked.

"Albert, are you religious?"

"Susan, I have studied the philosophy of all religions, without belonging to any of them. You want to bring up our children Jewish?"

"Yes."

"On one condition."

"Oh? What is that?"

"That we have a large family. Do you know what I envied most when, as children, we all got together? It was that there were four of you, and Jane and I had only each other. Have a large family and we'll bring them all up Jewish. Agreed?"

"How large?" she asked apprehensively.

"Say four—or five?"

She mopped her brow in mock relief. "I thought you were going to insist on the entire cricket team! Done, Lord Albert."

"You know, I might just call you—in private, of course—my 'book and baby factory'."

"You wouldn't!"

"But that's what you will be, dear. One year you will have a book; the next year you will have a baby; the next year you will have a book; the next year you will have a baby.........get the picture?"

She nodded. "Okay by me, Lord Albert, so long as you learn how to change diapers."

"What?"

She laughed. "I might just call you—in private, of course—my 'diaper daddy'. Because that's what you will be, dear, after you've changed a few hundred diapers—or is it a few thousand?"

"Any other issues, Susan?"

"One last one; a minor one."

"Well let's hear it. When a person says: It's 'a minor one'—you know it's pretty major. So what is this last issue?" This time it was Albert who was apprehensive.

"That you keep your moustache forever. It tickled me when I was kissing you, and I found it ever so exciting!"

"Done!" he said, leaning towards her and kissing her full on the mouth.

When they reached the Hampstead flat, Albert let Susan go, shyly declining her invitation to come and break the good news, on two fronts, to the family.

She was engaged to Albert and her novel had been accepted for publication.

The congratulations and the outpouring of love and affection from her family were strictly for her, and not to be diluted by his presence in the room—no matter how welcome he might be. If he were there she could not give her undivided attention to them—for fear of ignoring him and so hurting him.

Only a philosopher could think the way he did!

She understood—thanked him for his graciousness—kissed him again, made arrangements to see him the next day, and tripped up the stairs, as if on a cloud.

CHAPTER 16

It was the end of September, and all four of the Samuelson children were looking forward with some anticipation—always tinged with a little dread—to the start of the new term.

The anticipation was common to all four of them. It was always exciting on the first day of class to meet others students with the same common interests, and meet the lecturers, some kindly and gracious, others so filled with their own worth to be positively obnoxious; yet all of them intricate—and sometimes secretive—maps of knowledge that needed careful study, to reach the chosen destination.

The dread was different for all four of them.

Ruth had the least dread of them all. She was going back—after a very exciting summer vacation; some would say too exciting!—to the last year of an undergraduate degree in Exercise Physiology and Sports Psychology. She knew the students who would be with her, and the lecturers, readers and even the two professors in the department who would be teaching her. Her dread was that, not being the most academic of girls, some of the papers, projects or other assignments might prove too challenging!

What she did not know—and might have caused her even more dread—was that the news had, somehow through the grapevine, reached the Head of the Dept. of Ruth's ordeal, and triumph, in foiling a terrorist plot against the Hampstead Reform Synagogue. It had been only her magnificent run through Hampstead Heath that had saved the lives of more than two hundred Jews—the last being a baby, a homeless man, and her parents—before the Synagogue had exploded behind them. Many had read of the fire in a synagogue, as reported in the London Press; the news that one of their students had given a practical demonstration of her prowess in the athletic field—isn't that what Exercise Physiology was all about?—to foil the plot, had her professors, readers, lecturers, and administrative staff—all the way up to the Chancellor of the University—drooling over Ruth, with well-merited respect and concern. That she would get her degree was a foregone conclusion! Would she make the British Women's Team at the next Olympics, in the Mile, was the thought uppermost in their minds?

Sarah's dread was more substantial. She was going to start post-graduate work in Structural Engineering at one of the world-recognised Research Institutions of higher learning. Would she be equal to it? Her 'A' levels—while being decent—were nowhere as excellent as David's or Susan's. She had a good, High-Second Class degree in Civil Engineering from London Polytechnic. Yet, she had been admitted to the Imperial College, because British post-graduate students were difficult to get; the Institution was flooded with First-Class students from overseas, from all over the world, begging for admission.

Susan's dread was the most terrifying of them all. She was going to a University for the first time—Oxford University, no less! She was going away from home for the first time. Would she suffer from tearful bouts of homesickness—as friends at school, with mock sadness, had mournfully assured her she would?

She was engaged to be married, in love, and missing Albert dreadfully already! Would she be able to cope with all the pressures of the engagement, and still perform to the standards she knew she was capable of?

What she did not know—and would have caused her even more dread—was that the news of the acceptance of her first novel by a London Publisher had, somehow through the grapevine, found its way to the Dons at the College. Some of the Dons, who would be teaching her, had published fiction, and welcomed the prospect of teaching a published writer and one so young; others who had desperately tried and failed to be published, looked on her achievement as being strictly because of her nobility and her contacts in the publishing industry! Almost subconsciously, they raised the standards that she would be required to meet in their classes. Had she known that she might have quit Oxford, and left it for good.

David's dread was not for himself. He was going to be a military man—like his father—and he tried hard not to dread anyone or anything. His dread was for how Rachel would cope with his absence at Sandhurst. It had been different when he was at Cambridge for three years, doing his Mathematics Tripos. Rachel would slip away, drive to Cambridge, have many joyous hours with David, and drive back before she was missed. She had confided in her parents and they had approved; the less Florenzo knew the better!

But this time it was different. Sandhurst was a military academy and David had far less freedom with his spare time than at Cambridge. He worried about her.

There were two others in the household who dreaded the start of the new term—Joshua and Julia.

Julia dreaded it more than Joshua.

Joshua missed his children, but only his son had been away. The other three had always been around to keep them company and 'hold their hands' when they felt miserable. Besides, Joshua went to work when the girls were away in school or college; poor Julia stayed at home and managed the cooking and the cleaning and missed all her children even as she cooked and cleaned!

What was heartening to all six of them, was that the term did not start for two weeks, and so they all had some time to be together, as a family.

It was Friday evening, after an early dinner, that Joshua reached for the car keys of the Mini for his series of Friday evening lectures on 'Military Strategy in the India/Pakistan Wars', given to the India Club of the East End of London. Attendance had been good and was increasing, because Joshua, having been in two wars, was able to incorporate personal stories into his talk, with more than just a historical perspective.

Julia was upset—with herself: "I'm so sorry, dear," she said, "I clean forgot about your Friday evening talks; I've made arrangements to meet Cecily in Putney. We're going to a talk on 'Flower Arrangements'. I'll call Cecily and cancel."

"Don't you dare!" Joshua said. "Flower arrangements take precedence by far—at least in my vocabulary—to my talk. I'll have no problems coming home; I've driven that way so often. You go and have a good time with Cecily. Tell her we'll soon all be related when Susan marries Albert."

Julia hesitated: "Why," she asked argumentatively, "do 'Flower Arrangements' take precedence over your 'Military Strategy in the India/Pakistan Wars', might I ask?"

"Shorter title," Joshua said. "The shorter the title the more important and interesting the talk—hence the precedence."

"Darling, you have problems seeing in the dark—and it will be dark when you return. Please?"

"Nonsense, dear! I can see perfectly well in the dark—my old military training. Do you think we fought wars only by daylight? When night fell, we shut shop?"

"May I say something?" Sarah said, seeing a 'quarrel' brewing between her parents.

They nodded to their eldest daughter, who had often mediated between them.

"David is with Rachel, Ruth is with Will, Susan is with Albert—I'm with nobody. Why don't I go along with Daddy to keep him from getting lost in the dark on the way back? Then Mummy, you can attend your talk on 'Flower Arrangements', with Cecily Aunty, with an easy mind—without worrying where Daddy is, and if he'll end up in Kent instead of in Hampstead."

They all laughed, but it resolved the problem.

So with Joshua driving and Sarah beside him, the two of them entered the East End of London, along Silver Street. The India Club of the East End was just round the corner.

The traffic had come to a halt at a red light, when Sarah saw, just up Silver Street, a restaurant called 'Kanska'. She touched Joshua on the arm.

"Pappa," she said. "See that restaurant, 'Kanska', up Silver Street? Would you mind very much if I got off here, and did not attend your lecture? I'll be in there; you can pick me up in the restaurant after you are through? Would you? Do you mind?"

"What a wonderful idea, Sarah! I thought to myself while we were driving down here: is it fair to subject my eldest daughter to the horror of listening to her father talk for 50 minutes, with 10 minutes for Questions and Answers, particularly when the poor girl has heard the same stories repeated, only Heaven knows how many times before? Say in an hour or so, dear?"

Sarah kissed him on the cheek, as he pulled into the curb. She alighted, and entered the restaurant.

It had a few customers; it was not empty. But seated at a table at the far end was His Grace, Lord Jacob, Duke of Trenton. His mother was not sitting beside him; Sarah had expected otherwise.

Jacob was sitting with a bowl of soup in front of him, his head down, staring at the tablecloth. He seemed, to Sarah, to be depressed.

Sarah went up to the cashier's desk. An elderly man was taking the orders and handling the till at the same time. There was no waitress service, but an elderly lady—his sister, perhaps,—was clearing away the soiled dishes from the other tables.

Sarah dropped her voice.

"Do you see that young man sitting at the end table there?" she said. "Do you know him?"

He shook his head. "He comes in here, with his mother, most Fridays, but I don't know them."

"That is His Grace, Lord Jacob, Duke of Trenton. His mother is Dowager Duchess of Trenton; is she not here today?"

"She was. She came in with him, but left only a few minutes ago. Perhaps she'll be back later. It is still early; we do not close for a while. Why do you ask?"

"It is a very old story—goes back to 1945—when a Jewish girl used to work here for your father. They were refugees from Auschwitz."

"I know! I know!" He cried excitedly. "My father told us the story, many times, how she got engaged to the Duke of Trenton in this very restaurant, at that very table—in his presence!"

He called out to his sister: "Ursula! Come! Come!"

She came immediately. Sarah repeated, very briefly, the story the Dowager Duchess had related to her at the Queen's party.

"So that is their grandson?" Ursula asked. "And his mother is Miriam's daughter? Why didn't they ever tell us? They could have eaten here, for free, every Friday of their lives!"

"That is why they didn't tell you," Sarah said, with a smile.

"The Duke left a thousand pounds for our father to arrange their marriage, and it was our father's deep regret—even to the day he died—that he had so much of it left over," the elderly man said.

"Would you do me a very small favour?" Sarah asked. "I am Lady Sarah Samuelson, great granddaughter of the eleventh Earl of Bromfield; my brother will be the twelfth Earl. I have met him and his mother."

"But of course," Ursula said. "What can we do? Oh! This is so exciting!"

"What I need is a bucket, with a little water in it, and a mop with a long handle—the sort his grandmother must have used. I also need a scarf."

The bucket, with a little water in it, and the mop were forthcoming immediately; the scarf took a little longer, as Ursula insisted on finding Sarah a brand-new, unused scarf from the flat upstairs, where brother and sister, both unmarried, had a living room, two bedrooms, a kitchen and the bathroom. The kitchens and the bathrooms for the restaurant were downstairs.

Sarah tied the scarf low down around her head, to hide her face, took the bucket and mop, and approached Jacob's table—as a cleaning woman might.

"Please, Sir," she said, tremulously, "please could you lift up your legs for just a minute so I could mop under your feet?"

He lifted his legs obediently, without protest, while she mopped the floor assiduously.

She stole a quick glance at him; he looked, at close quarters, both downcast and depressed.

He was a very handsome man, tall, but unlike other tall men, he was very well-built, with a powerful torso and superb biceps that tightened the arm sleeves of the shirt he was wearing. He had brown hair, piercing blue eyes, a semitic, slightly hooked nose, sideburns, a military moustache that was full on his upper lip, but did not curl into handlebars. She was sure that the rest of him that was seated, was also the body of an athlete, but in the more physical sports—rugby perhaps?

She withdrew the mop, placed it within the bucket, and had almost decided that what she had done was not appropriate; it was almost the nature of a prank on a sad figure, and unworthy of her, when he looked up at her and started to his feet, upsetting the bucket. The water sloshed all over the floor.

"Lady Sarah!" he exclaimed. "It is Lady Sarah, isn't it?"

She removed the scarf. Ursula, seeing what had occurred, came immediately to the rescue, mopping up the floor expertly, smiling deliciously at Sarah while retrieving the scarf from her.

Sarah curtseyed to the Duke. "I am so dreadfully sorry, for having played a 'prank' in, possibly, very poor taste on Your Grace; please forgive me. I will leave immediately."

Sarah curtseyed once more and would have turned around to leave the table, but he grabbed her by the arm and held her tight.

"Sit," he said. "Please sit. Don't leave me. I need to talk to someone; my thoughts overwhelm me! Please—for my sake, not yours—sit."

She sat down on the chair to his left; she had not noticed it before but the chair to his right had a woman's purse on it. It was his mother's chair before she had left the restaurant.

"Where is Lady Sophie?" Sarah asked. "She seems to have left her purse behind."

"Mummy has gone to the your father's lecture on 'Military Strategy in the India/Pakistan Wars'. You did not know it, but Mummy is a War Historian buff and loves such lectures; regrettably

I don't. Maybe not so regrettably, because I would not have met you here otherwise—would I? You are a very beautiful woman."

Sarah blushed. "You seem depressed, downcast. You wanted to talk to me; please do. I'm a very good listener."

"I don't know where to begin," he said, sadly.

"Perhaps, the Queen's party would be a good place to start?" Sarah said, gently.

"You know?"

"Yes. Not everything, but we know the essentials."

"We? Who all is 'we'?"

"The family. Our family. I'm so sorry."

"Everybody knew—and nobody told me? I feel so abandoned."

"Your Grace, everyone makes some mistakes—we all have."

"Please, will you do me a small favour?"

"Of course, Your Grace."

"Please stop calling me 'Your Grace'. My name is 'Jacob'. Otherwise I have to keep calling you, 'Lady Sarah'."

"Done! On one condition, Jacob."

"Oh? And what might that be, Sarah?"

"That when I ask you for a small favour this evening—you will return it?"

"Done! Now may I proceed with my sorry tale; you'll regret agreeing to listen to it."

"Are we talking about the same thing, Jacob? Are we talking about Jane?"

"Yes."

"And that she is a lesbian?"

"Yes."

"And that you did not know it at the Queen's party, because no one told you?"

"Yes."

"And that you fell head over heels in love with her because you like tall, slim, willowy models, and she broke your heart, and so you're sitting here, while I hold your hand, so that you can pour out your grief to me?"

Jacob burst out laughing.

"Sarah," he said, "am I telling you my story or are you telling me my story? Besides, it's not even true."

"What isn't true?"

"That you're holding my hand."

"I meant it figuratively; but if it makes the story more true, I'll hold it as you talk."

Sarah reached for his hand, lying on the table, and held it in hers. There was a tingle of excitement that went through the both of them. She trembled as she spoke: "There! Now what's untrue?"

"What's true is that I was attracted to her. Have you seen me? I'm built like a rugby player—which I am. She seemed so frail, almost ethereal, I was drawn to her—as I am sure many men have before me. What is untrue is that I fell 'head over heels in love with her'. That is so untrue!"

"I'm sorry, I apologise."

"No need for that, Sarah. That is the way it must have seemed to everyone in the room. It is true, I sent her a dozen red roses the next day, and a box of chocolates—she'd told me she liked soft centers—and asked her out to the theater. She chose—you can guess—'Lady Windermere's Fan' by Oscar Wilde. Was she trying out, perhaps, to discover her true sexuality—with me as the guinea pig? I don't know. But it was I who felt that something was missing in our relationship—there was no feeling, no love! So I asked for some answers from her—did she care for me? That is when she told me, as gently as she could, that she was not interested in men—but in a woman as a life's partner."

"She has found a partner," Sarah said, quietly. "One of her lesbian writers. I'm sorry Jacob, I really am."

"I'm not. My asking her for answers prevented me from making a very big mistake—one that I would have regretted for life. Forgive me?"

"Of course, Jacob. If you'll forgive me."

"Oh? And what indiscretion of yours do I need to forgive?"

He released her hand from his.

She laughed. "Indiscretion? No! But that is what most men automatically assume when a woman asks for forgiveness. Ah, ha! Must be an indiscretion. Sorry to disappoint you, dear. It is for being so ignorant about the way men think, that I ended up being an unwitting party to an Indian boy getting engaged to an Indian girl he does not love and—unless he has the courage to break it—is now condemned to living with her the rest of his life! That to me is as equally bad as Jane not telling you, at your very first meeting, that she was a lesbian."

"Want to tell me about it?" he said, gently.

"Yes, but you did promise me the return of one favour before the evening was out?"

He nodded.

"Will you, please, Jacob, hold my hand as I held yours?"

"I'll do better than that. I'll hold your hand in both of mine."

She told him all about Devinder, how they first met at Ayrton Hall, how she felt sorry for him, their lunch at India House, and the subsequent discovery that her mother had been a servant girl in her father's bungalow in Ajmer in India.

"It was the Rajput honour of a servant woman—his mother—that saved us from each other," Sarah said. "Her Colonel Saheb, Daddy, had plucked her from poverty, cared for her as his daughter, nurtured her into womanhood, got her married when she fell in love with Havaldar Mansingh of his regiment—whose life he had saved by a wise judgment call in a war with Pakistan. She could not, and would not, permit her son to lay a finger on the Colonel Saheb's daughter—for the sake of my happiness! But she, and his father, had no objections to his marrying the only daughter of the Indian

High Commissioner in London, for whom her Colonel Saheb now worked. That is Rajput honour."

She paused before she continued.

"It was in the mother; not in the son. Because he wanted to use me to break off his engagement to Premlata, by asking me to meet him in the Union Cafeteria, at the precise time she was to meet him. Fortunately, I was early and she was late; though I did tell him before I left that I considered it despicable of him to have tried to use me in that way."

She smiled at Jacob.

"And that, my dear, is my 'indiscretion'. Will you forgive me too?"

"Sarah, will you marry me? I ask only that you love me, be faithful to me, and bear me children—and an heir."

"Yes, darling, I will. I ask only that you love me, be faithful to me, and allow me to complete just a Master's in Civil Engineering at Imperial College, and then, perhaps, if possible, teach part-time at some low-level technical college, so that my education isn't wasted. I promise you I will not let my studies interfere in any way with my duties as a wife and mother. Please?"

"Only a Master's degree? I thought you were hell-bent on a Ph.D."

"Jacob, a Master's degree will take only two years. We can have a two-year engagement, and then be married right away. A Ph.D. would take forever! Mamma gave up her dreams of being a writer to marry Pappa and have the four of us. She needed a lot of courage to abandon her dreams, for the happiness of all of us—I can do no less."

"Sarah, I have a confession to make."

"Oh? Is it that time when you confess to me all your indiscretions?"

He laughed. "No, dear, much worse! My greatest folly was in not paying attention to my studies when I was in school. I've barely passed my 'O' levels. I wanted to be a professional rugby player, and I knew that Father had enough wealth to support me. Actually Father had a great business sense, which I've inherited, because I've done very well in the business world—without an education."

Sarah looked apprehensive.

"Anything the matter, dear?"

"That was Devinder's problem with Premlata—the Indian High Commissioner's daughter. She was a Harvard graduate with a Master's Degree in Business Administration. He felt inferior to her; ran her down in every way because she was better educated than he was. Jacob, is it going to be that way with us?"

"The man was raving mad! I will shout out your achievements from the roof tops! I'll be so proud of you, Sarah, you're going to be embarrassed by my pride in you."

"Thank you, Jacob. Strange isn't it? I would never have realised how fine a person you are—if I had not talked to you."

"And I you, my love. I might have gone through life turned off all women because of one woman—who had every right to choose her own lifestyle. But you all are not getting so easily off the hook, for leaving me in the dark. Who knew that piece of information? Who could have given it to me and didn't?"

"Jane's mother, Cecily Aunty, Mamma's dearest and oldest friend."

"Her own mother betrayed her?"

"Not betrayed, dear. Jane wanted the word spread when you showed your interest in her. Cecily Aunty saw me looking—with longing eyes—at you, and she couldn't keep it from Mamma."

"So that is when you knew?"

"No, actually. The Queen whispered, confidentially, to me that things were not what they seemed—I didn't understand it at all. I mentioned it to the family on the way back home—and that is when Mamma enlightened us."

"The Queen! She knew that Jane was a lesbian?"

"Darling, there were three women with Cecily Aunty, gossiping away. Let me give you a piece of confidential information—never to be repeated, you understand! Our Queen—God bless her—enjoys a bit of women's gossip as much as any of our mothers do. It must be pretty boring to be stuck with interviews with Ministers and Ambassadors all the time—don't you think?"

"So the Queen and Lady Julia were there. Who was the third lady who heard that delicious piece of gossip?"

Sarah was silent.

"I can't tell you, Jacob. I really can't. Please don't ask me."

"Sarah," he said, very gently, not upbraiding her; more like pleading with her, "darling, we're going to be married—we can't protect others from the two of us. Our first loyalty is to each other—no matter who the other person is—except your mother and father; that I will understand."

"Or yours?"

"Mine too. Wait a minute! My father is dead; you don't mean my mother is the other third person who was with Lady Cecily when she gave Jane's secret away?"

Sarah was silent.

She was saved from further explanation by Lady Sophie, Dowager Duchess of Trenton, walking in through the front entrance of the restaurant. Seeing Sarah, she came to her with outstretched arms. She folded Sarah in a warm and motherly embrace.

Jacob looked at his mother with angry eyes. Piercingly blue, they now had a fire in them, Sarah had not seen before. She thought: Dear God! Please let him not, ever, face me this way. What would I do?"

Jacob indicated the seat beside him, where her purse had been lying. "Sit!" he said.

She sat down not fully understanding his angry tone.

"Did you find out at the Queen's party that Lady Jane was a lesbian? And you never told me?"

Lady Sophie turned and looked at Sarah, with an enquiring look, as if to ask: 'How did he find out that I knew about Jane'?

Sarah hung her head; she did not reply.

Jacob saw her plight and softened—not to his mother, though.

"Before you say any harsh words to Lady Sarah, I want you to know that you are speaking to the future Duchess of Trenton. You answer me—don't look at her!"

"Future Duchess of Trenton?" Lady Sophie got up with a bound. She folded Sarah in another tight and warm embrace.

"My dearest girl! I'm so happy, I could cry. Was I harsh to you? Please forgive me. I will never ever raise my voice to you or berate you. I've wanted you ever since that day at the Queen's party. Only this lout had to get himself mixed up with a lesbian! Yes, it was Sarah who took me to meet her mother and Lady Cecily—how did you describe them?—two of the finest ladies in the kingdom. And they were! How many mothers would give away their daughter's secret to bring comfort to a friend's daughter? And before her Majesty, the Queen! Why did I not tell you? Because you're old enough now to make your own mistakes—and pay for them. So don't roll your eyes at me you big, no-good, grandson of a Duke—you deserve what you got from Lady Jane! That'll teach you to be more appreciative of fine girls, like Sarah. How she ever consented to be your wife is beyond me! Don't forget I'm a Jewish Mamma, and I'll take you to task even if you're eighty and I'm a hundred," she ended lamely.

Sarah burst out laughing. Jacob looked to her for sympathy; Lady Sophie looked to her for support. They both wanted her to adjudicate their quarrel.

"Jacob," she said quietly, "you shouldn't speak to your mother that way. Mothers raise us, love us, care for us; once in a while we have to forgive them, even if we think they are grossly in error. Will you apologize to Lady Sophie? Please, for my sake?"

"I'm sorry, Mamma. I got carried away thinking my own mother had betrayed me."

"Lady Sophie, would I have kept my only son in ignorance of such a damaging fact, knowing that he would be hurt in the end? I don't think so."

Lady Sophie put her head in her hands.

"You're right, Sarah," she said, softly. "I was wrong not to tell him immediately. I was recommending a very beautiful Jewish girl to him—you—and here he was with a tall, thin, lesbian. I was so upset, with pique and anger, I wasn't thinking straight. Would he have believed me? Why don't you ask him what his reaction would have been?"

"You're right, Mamma. I would have said: I don't believe you!"

"But I should still have told you, Jacob. It might at least have made you more wary when you were with her. Looked for some tell-tale signs. I'm sorry, dear. Forgive me?"

"Forgive me, too?"

They laughed as she stretched out her hand to him, and he kissed it.

"Mamma, do you have Grandmother's engagement ring—the one Grandfather gave her in this very room, at this very table?"

The dowager Duchess dug in her purse for it and fished it out.

"Please, Jacob," Sarah said, "could we wait just a few minutes more? Daddy will be coming here to get me. Could we wait for him?"

"Yes," Lady Sophie said. "He was in the Q&A session when I left; he should be along any minute now."

She had barely finished speaking, when Joshua came through the front entrance of the restaurant. He was not familiar with it, but Sarah called out: "Daddy, we're here!"

"Why, we have quite a gathering here," Joshua said.

Jacob courteously invited Joshua to sit across him in the fourth chair at the table. He then motioned to the brother and sister at the cashier's till—who had been watching the proceedings with undiluted interest—to come on over.

He drew the ring out from his pocket. He addressed the brother and sister.

"In 1945, you witnessed my Grandfather, Duke of Trenton, give this very ring to a refugee, Jewish maid, from Auschwitz—and made her my Grandmother. I'd like you to witness something along those lines today."

He leaned across to Sarah and slipped the ring onto her finger. They clapped; Ursula wiped a tear from her eye. Lady Sophie and Sir Joshua beamed in joy. Sarah leaned across and kissed Jacob on the mouth—a long, deliberate, passionate kiss that set them both on fire.

"Please, Sir," the brother said. "I have about 500 pounds of the money that your grandfather gave to my father for his marriage to Miriam. In the bank, it is now 4000 pounds. May I return the money?"

Jacob shook his head: "No," he said, "but I'll tell you what you can do. Why don't you donate it to the nearest soup kitchen for homeless, hungry people—men, women and children? Both your father and my grandfather would be delighted at your generosity."

They got up to leave; it was getting late. Both brother and sister urged them to linger. It was an evening they would never forget—a closure after so many years.

"There's one thing, Sarah," Joshua said, "that you will get from Jacob that Mamma couldn't get from me, that Rachel will not get from David, that Ruth will not get from Will, and that Susan will not get from Albert."

"Oh! You surprise me, Pappa. No one could be a more loving husband than you have been to Mamma all these years—she swears by it!"

Jacob understood. Joshua nodded to him in consent.

"What does Daddy mean, Jacob?" Sarah asked.

Jacob came and stood beside Sarah. He put one strong arm around her back, the other strong arm beneath her thighs and swept her into his arms, raising her, as if she was weightless, to his chest. She squealed in delight; then raised her head to his, and kissed him on the mouth.

He carried her across the threshold of the front entrance of the restaurant, and very gently stood her on her feet again, as the others came up, laughing and clapping, to join them.

"Oh, how I wish Mamma and the rest of my family had been here to see that," Sarah said.

"Darling," Jacob said, "whenever and wherever you want me to carry you in my arms, I will do so; it will be a joyous pleasure."

CHAPTER 17

That Sunday was to be their last reunion dinner until the Winter/ Christmas/Hanukah break when those who would be away would be—for certain—back home again. The term opened on Monday for David, Sarah and Ruth; Susan's term at Oxford would open a week later. After that, everyone could look forward, with anticipation, to Christmas and Hanukah.

Joshua insisted on a Christmas tree; they had had it for all the years when the children had been born because it meant so much to the old Earl of Bromfield. He loved to have presents under the tree for his granddaughter and his great grandchildren—and for his grandson-in-law too, he assured Joshua.

Joshua called it his Hanukah tree, and, with Julia's help, surreptitiously substituted a six-pointed Star of David, instead of a five-pointed star, at the top—for his mother's sake!

Peace reigned at the Holy time.

The type of presents for the children was a touchy one that had evolved on its own. At first, when the children had been young, it had been easy. All that Julia and Joshua—and mainly Julia—did was to take them window shopping to note the exclamations of delight when a child saw a train set or a special doll—which toy miraculously ended up under the tree.

With the children getting older it got more difficult.

The look of dismay, the screwing up of noses, or even outright tears, at receiving a present other than what was expected, so unnerved both Joshua and Julia—how could you have a child weeping at Hanukah time or on Christmas Day?—that they called a 'Council of War', with all four of the children in attendance, and announced that from the next year onwards each would receive an envelope hanging from the tree—all envelopes would contain exactly the same amount for each child. They could do with the money as they pleased. They could spend it all, or save it all to add it to their pocket money or birthdays gifts—which would also be money in envelopes—or spend part of it and save part of it in bank accounts that would be opened in each child's name, as a joint account with their mother. The amount in the envelope each year was the surprise!

No argument could result because after making the announcement, Joshua immediately announced: 'Troop dismissed'!

No argument would have resulted because all of the children preferred it that way. Susan and Ruth had no complaints because they got the same amount of money as David or Sarah. David and Sarah had no complaints because, on going to the shops, they found, to their glee, that gifts for the youngest children were priced more than the more mature things they wanted to buy.

Peace reigned throughout the year.

But that festival and those reunion dinners were still quite a few weeks away; this Sunday would be the last full reunion dinner before the terms commenced.

There were to be eighteen of them round that table. Joshua, as usual sat at one head with the eleventh Earl at the other. Julia sat beside Joshua and to his right. Then the arrangement changed from past practices. Cecily, Julia's oldest friend from the days of boarding school in Kent, sat next to Julia. This was the very first time, she would be attending one of their reunion dinners, and Julia wanted to make sure she was comfortable throughout the evening.

Cecily's son Albert, Earl of Rathbone, sat next to her, with Susan next to him.

Lady Sophie, Sarah and Jacob sat, in that order, next to Susan. Sarah wanted to be placed between the two so she could look after the needs of both her fiancé and her future mother-in-law with equal diligence.

That left only one seat vacant before the side was complete. It was for the one imponderable in the seating arrangement. They were not quite sure whether Florenzo would be coming or not. Lysa had informed Julia that Roberta and Alphonso had already left for Milan; Florenzo was angry and depressed. He would not be good company; yet Julia felt that the last thing the family should do was to ignore him by leaving him out of the dinner.

He had been invited, but his coming was uncertain.

As in dinners past, on the right side of the eleventh Earl was David—the twelfth Earl. Beside him, as always, was Rachel. Then the arrangement changed, with Lysa and Joe sitting beside their daughter.

Ruth still wanted to sit beside her Joe Uncle—they had had many fine conversations about her running in the past, and she felt that while she was an engaged girl, with her fiancé beside her, her affection for her Uncle was no less than ever before. So Will was beside her, with his brother Samuel beside him.

Beside Samuel and to Joshua's left—was Rehana.

Begum Nassem Banu had called Julia to inform her that Samuel and Rehana were engaged to be married—and how pleased she and Edward were about it! Could Rehana accompany Samuel to their reunion dinner?

Naseem Banu and Edward were promptly invited as well, but the offer was graciously declined. Sunday evening were visiting hours at the jail where Yusuf was still being held in protective custody; the officials said it was for his own safety, but his parents knew the real reason—and approved of it. It was to prevent him from fleeing the country, to Pakistan, before the trial of seven people, at which he had agreed to turn Crown's witness and give evidence against them.

He was too valuable to the Crown to disappear!

Even the menu had changed from previous dinners.

Sarah usually made her favourite dish which was a lamb biryani. This time she casually checked with Jacob as to what his favourite dish was—Indian or any other type of ethnic cooking—and found to her surprise that he loved Indian cooking, but his favourite dish was lightly spiced seekh kababs—which was minced lamb, tightly pressed onto stainless steel skewers, and grilled to a golden perfection in the grill of the oven, the skewers being turned over and over, to face the side of the electric element, for even heating. After removal from the skewers the long kababs were cut into about 10 pieces. She would make the rice as a separate dish.

Sarah estimated that, on an average, each would eat at least 4 pieces? That made for 72 kababs—or at least 7-8 skewers in the oven. She spent all afternoon on it.

Ruth made the same casual inquiries from Will, and found to her delight that Samuel was a 'fish and chip' lover. Since she had always made fried fish for her Joe Uncle, she merely doubled the number of pieces of fried fish at the meal. For Will she had his favourite dish, of course, which was chicken casserole with potatoes and onions.

Susan made the chappatis as usual. But casual inquiry with Albert, revealed that he did not particularly care for Italian food, and so while she would still be making the spaghetti and meat balls for Lysa Aunty, she would have to cater to Albert's tastes as well.

It turned out that Albert loved Indian cooking too—his favourite dish was prawn biryani. Susan knew how to make the spicy prawns, first marinating them in the spices and then lightly frying them to a golden perfection; the spicy rice was made separately and the cooked prawns then mixed in to make the biryani.

But making three major dishes for 18 people was more than she had bargained for.

She was overwhelmed, and almost in tears, when David came to her rescue. He told Rachel about Susan's plight. Rachel immediately offered to cook the spaghetti and meat balls with the Italian sauce—but at their house; not in the Italian restaurant.

When Susan gratefully received the offer of help, and inquired the reason for the change of cooking venue, Rachel coloured, and whispered softly: "Because it gives me more time with David, silly! I can spend the whole afternoon here with him—the cooking won't take an hour!"

How devious are the ways of love? Susan thought. It might just make a nice plot for her next novel?

Julia stuck to her tried and successful gulab jamuns: 'If anyone doesn't like it—and I know my husband and children do—they can just lump it!' she said to herself. Sometimes the hostess had to put her foot down or your guests could ride all over you. The girls were young, she thought; they'll learn soon enough. Of course, Joe would have his sugar-free apple pie as usual.

Joshua pitched in by preparing the raitha he'd made before. He could have let one of the girls make it—all four of them offered—but he abruptly turned them all down.

"Is he offended with us?" Susan asked her mother, anxiously. "Maybe, because I insisted on him making the raitha last time? Should I apologize to Daddy?"

Julia laughed. "You have to live with a man for twenty-five years, my dear child, before you can read his actions. Reading his mind is easy, but why he acts the way he does sometimes beats all logic! Shall I tell you why he wants to make the raitha—and why he'll take the best part of two days to do it—part now and part tomorrow?"

The girls gathered around; David and Rachel too.

"Tell me girls, where are we all working—David included, because David will be where Rachel is?"

"The kitchen," Susan said.

"And tell me where would your father be if he wasn't in here making the raitha with us?"

"In the living room or his bedroom or the study," Ruth said.

"And he would feel excluded," Sarah said.

"Now tell me, is a General in the Indian Army ever going to admit to his wife and children that he feels excluded and lonely, when they are in his own house, but in a different room—within calling distance? To be fair to Daddy," Julia continued, "he's getting old; he's over sixty years old, and soon you all will be leaving us and going away. He has never been afraid of the enemy, or dying, but the thought of you all leaving us, and the loneliness we will face, frightens him in a way no words can express."

For the first time, as she said this for Joshua, she faced it herself, and she broke down in tears and wept.

They had crowded round her and were consoling her when Joshua, his sleeves rolled up, walked into the kitchen. He saw Julia weeping at the dining table, and said: "Might I know why your mother is crying? Why are you making my wife cry?"

"It's all your fault, Daddy, for making Mummy cry!" Susan said, wagging her finger at him.

"My fault? I've only just come in the room. How can it be my fault?"

"By not having three or four more children after me. Then you would have had some child still at home after the four of us are married and have gone away. Now whose fault is that—if not yours?"

Joshua went and sat beside Julia, took her hand in his and put an arm round her shoulder; she leaned against him and sobbed.

"Don't cry, my love. You'll still have me; I'm all you had to start with. Sure it will be lonely round here; you can't live with children for the best part of twenty-four years, and have them move away to their own homes without feeling the loneliness and the desolation that lies ahead." It was only when the truth of his own words sank in, when the bleak day-to-day living it foretold hit him, that he took his hands away from her and put them on the dining table, with his head between them.

Julia looked at him. At first she thought he might be imitating her in jest—to make her feel better—until she shook him, and he refused to look up at them.

"Don't cry, my love," Julia said. "I'll still be here with you; I'll always be there for you—I promise."

The children stood as if transfixed and rooted to the floor, exactly where they were standing—like robots that would need a signal to come alive. It came when he realised that it was no use concealing his head any longer, and they saw his eyes brimming over with tears.

It was the first time, ever, in the all the years that they had lived with him, that any of his children had ever seen their father cry. After that all of them, including David and Rachel, were all over one or the other of them, cuddling their hands and arms and heads and backs and shoulders, to any part of their own bodies they could—to arms and face and head and chest and breasts. After savoring the moments with Sarah, Ruth and Susan cuddling him, Joshua shook himself free.

"Onions always make me cry! Now, who's been cutting onions on the dining table? How many times have I told you girls never to cut onions on the dining table? I put my head down and the onions did it!"

"It was Rachel," Ruth said seriously.

"Sorry, Pappa Joshua," Rachel said equally seriously. "The girls told me, but in the restaurant any table-top is suitable for onion-cutting. Forgive me?"

She said it so contritely, that they all—Joshua and Julia included—burst into laughter.

The episode was over, but the one and only memory they had ever had, of their father crying—they had seen their mother cry on several occasions—would stay in the minds of his children forever.

"Well, I'm ready to make the raitha. You know, I think I'll make a batch today and a batch tomorrow. Give you girls more time to use the kitchen, instead of having me hang around. On second thoughts, I'll even make tea for all of us—during the time you all are taking a break. I make a great cup of tea. Would anyone care for that?" he asked.

"Count me in, dear," Julia said. "You know, for me— all time is tea time!"

"I'd love a cup, Pappa," Susan said. "I'll even help you to set the table, if you wish?"

"Yes, I'd like that. Regular or decaf for you, Susan?"

"Regular, Daddy, please."

Joshua reached for the notebook near the telephone and the pen they used, to make notes on it while on the telephone.

"May this waiter take all your orders, please?"

"Decaf for me, Pappa," David said. "The caffeine keeps me awake at night."

"I reckon it's your dreams of this dear girl here, David, that are keeping you awake at night. Played havoc with my sleep too, when I was courting your mother. At least you have it better than I did."

"Oh?" Rachel asked. "And how so Pappa Joshua?"

"Because, dear girl, he already has you tightly sewn up—as his! Your Mamma Julia, was the granddaughter of the eleventh Earl of Bromfield—and I was a nobody. Don't forget that was twenty-six years ago—when Indians and Pakistanis and West Indians were still called 'bloody wogs'!"

"You weren't a nobody, dear," Julia said, mildly. "You had an MD, and were a practicing physician, besides being a Colonel in the Indian Army, with IMI, which Grandfather knew, but I didn't."

"Next order, please?"

Rachel opted for decaf too—she couldn't get to sleep either, and they all knew the reason why.

Ruth wanted green tea—it was healthier, she said.

Sarah wondered if her father could brew her a cup of coffee instead of tea? Jacob was a coffee lover and she felt she had to get used to it too—while getting him used to hot tea.

Joshua flashed them all a smile of warm gratitude; their orders would keep him in the kitchen, with them, for a long time.

Florenzo did come to that Sunday reunion dinner. He felt uncomfortable at first. He knew that the family had been given the news of Roberta's affair with Alphonzo, and their departure for Milan; nevertheless the aplomb with which he had so majestically displayed her photograph round the table, made him feel that, perhaps, Susan might be inwardly laughing at him, while outwardly showing her concern and sympathy.

He could not have been more wrong. Susan felt genuinely sorry for him. Nevertheless, Julia had taken the precaution of putting Florenzo on the same side of the table as Susan—and far away from her—so that no eye contact or direct conversation between them was possible. This was, of course, to save Susan any embarrassment as well; a reawakening of old desires in him—she had never felt any—was undesirable!

The girls had opted once again for their favourite fruity white wine, the riesling; the men had opted for scotch and soda; the older ladies were having a glass of sherry; the food was eaten with great gusto amid repeated exclamations of delight and compliments to the chef of the particular dish—be it Sarah or Ruth or Susan or Rachel. The dessert had not yet been eaten so Julia did not—with evident pride in her children's cooking skills—share, yet, in the compliments of the evening.

So it was that when everyone was in the jolliest of moods—the wine and the scotch and the sherry helped—and the dessert had just been served, that Joshua tinkled his glass of water with a fork, to draw the attention of one and all.

First he welcomed all of them to the reunion dinner; the introductions of the newcomers, to the rest of the table, had already been done when everyone had filled their very first plate with food from the counters.

"My Lords, Ladies, and Gentlemen, I know that you have enjoyed the culinary delights that the—Oh, so!—beloved ladies of my house have cooked up for us, and I hope that you will all leave this house as happy people. But for the evening to be the most memorable we can have, it is essential that we give vent to whatever we wish to say to ourselves and to each other. Perhaps I'll start with a frustration of my own, that was finally laid to rest by an incident I witnessed with my daughter Sarah and her fiancé Jacob."

He paused to smile benignly at the couple, who hadn't the faintest idea of what he was talking about. The thought uppermost in both their minds was—Pappa has had a drop too much!

"I am a slightly built man—I am not ashamed to admit—as you all can well see. I was not able to carry my bride across the threshold of a door to the marriage bed; she mercifully, being the gracious lady that she is, saved me the embarrassment of the moment by tripping across the threshold before we reached it. Darling, I may not have thanked you for that for twenty-five years, but I thank you today! But it was set to rest a few days ago when I saw Jacob do that effortlessly to Sarah—he did it for all of us men in this room today, because none of us has or will be able to do what he did; he did it for us all! Jacob and Sarah, please, for my sake, and for the sake of all the men in this room, will you do it once again?"

They both got up delightedly. It was not what they had been expected to be called upon to do—and they loved it! Jacob slid one arm behind Sarah's back; the other beneath the backs of her thighs, and lifted her effortlessly on to his chest. She raised her head, put her free hand—the one that was not squashed up against him—around the back of his head, and kissed him soundly on the mouth—while the entire dinner table burst into clapping and applause.

"When I heard Sarah say in 'Kanska' that she wished her Mamma and sisters could see what he'd done before me and Lady Sophie, I said to myself: And so they shall—and now they have."

The old Earl—from the other end of the table—tinkled his glass of water with his dessert spoon.

"You did say, Joshua, did you not, that the floor was ours?"

"Absolutely, Sir. Feel free!"

"Well, Joshua, then I would like to correct a statement you just made. You said: 'All of us men in this room today' did you not?"

"I believe I did."

"For your information, dear boy, I did that 65 years ago to Julia's grandmother. Did you know that I, too, was a rugby player, in days long gone by? Julia's grandmother was built like Julia—tall, elegant, very well-built and very beautiful; to me she was all that—and the lightest woman in the world!"

"I stand corrected," Joshua said, with a smile, raising his scotch to the old Earl, who responded with his own.

Surprisingly, the next tinkle on the water glass came from Jacob.

"I truly appreciate the applause that you just gave when I showed that I will carry Sarah over the threshold, when the time comes. But I would willingly give up my strength for an MD (raising his glass to Joshua), or a Mathematics Tripos from Cambridge University (raising his glass to David), or a degree in Military Science from Sandhurst, (raising his glass to Will), or a Business Degree from London University (raising his glass to Samuel), or a Diploma in catering (raising his glass to Florenzo), or a Degree in Philosophy from Oxford University (raising his glass to Albert). I barely passed my 'O' levels, I am ashamed to admit. So now you all know how proud I am of Sarah and her education—and she will be getting that Master's Degree from Imperial College, I promise you! As Pappa Joshua said, I did what I just did for all of us; so too, Sarah will be getting the degrees I never got—for the both of us."

"I begged Mamma Sophie to come and live with us—and she has agreed," Sarah said. "How else can I do it? Thank you, Mamma Sophie." And Sarah leaned across, hugged her, and kissed her on the cheek.

Rachel picked up courage, and tinkled on her glass of wine, to draw their attention.

"What I have to say is very brief. David and I have discussed this at length with Pappa and Mamma and Grandpa Romano and Great Grandfather—and they all have given our idea their blessings. I am yielding my half-share of the restaurant—Grandpa Romano had intended to leave a half-share to me—to Florenzo. He will be the sole beneficiary in their wills."

"What!" exclaimed Florenzo, who had been listening to the proceedings with a disinterested look. Suddenly he came alive again. "You don't want to share it with me, Rachel? Why? I want you to work with me!"

"Ah, Florenzo, but that is precisely the reason, I don't want it. I am going to be Lady Rachel, wife of the twelfth Earl of Bromfield. My husband, after his term at Sandhurst—and remember because he already has a degree from Cambridge, his training is very short—will need me to look after the estate at Bromfield. I am not available to run the restaurant; if you are going to run it all the time, you might as well be the full owner of it."

"Well, said, Rachel," the old Earl said. "And I'll need someone to run the House of Bromfield right now. I've talked to Lysa and Joe as well; you'll be coming to live at Bromfield from tomorrow—the day David goes to Sandhurst. Emma and Tomkins have known you since childhood; they could not be any happier than with David's choice of a wife! But you'll need all the help you can get to learn how to manage the servants, run the estate, and keep the accounts—as your Julia Aunty did for years, before she was married."

Florenzo tinkled his glass of water.

"I know that you feel sorry for me that Roberta fell in love with Alphonzo and has gone back, with him, to Milan. It was my fault! I thought I could get a girl to love me, and then initiate her into working for the restaurant. I was wrong. It works the other way round. I have now started to interview Italian girls in London—au pair girls who came here to learn English, like England, and would like to stay on—to cook and waitress at the restaurant. Perhaps, from the three that I will hire—to replace Alphonzo, Roberta and Rachel—one of them will give her heart to me as well?"

"You've got it wrong, dear," Lysa said, gently. "You will have to win her heart! Look around you, Florenzo. How many years has Rachel been in love with David, or Albert with Susan? They never gave up."

Rehana tinkled her glass of water with her fork.

"I can see what honesty in family matters means to you all—hearing all that I have heard here this evening. I am going to be part of this family, and I would like to share some of the discussions that Samuel and I have been having these past few days. I have talked to him—and he agrees."

She was under considerable nervous stress; Samuel held her hand. She drank some more water. As a good Muslim, she abstained from the wine—though she knew that her mother, Begum Naseem Banu enjoyed a glass of sherry as well as any Englishwoman!

"Samuel and I are going to be married. The question was where, and when? I've decided that since Ruth has been my lifelong friend, and since Samuel has been brought up Jewish, we will be married in Hampstead Reform Synagogue in a double wedding—Will to Ruth, and Samuel to me. The decision was mine—freely made. Samuel has not forced me into it."

The applause in the room was deafening.

"The more important decision was how we are going to bring up the children—in what faith? I followed Rachel's example. Yusuf's children will be brought up Muslim—no doubt of that!—so Mamma has one set of grandchildren in her faith. Daddy is Christian. So I talked it over with him, and this is what he said: 'Child you may want to think beyond me and Mamma—because we won't always be around. My sister Cecily has two children—Jane and Albert. Jane isn't going to have children of her own; Albert's children are going to be brought up Jewish. All of your children's cousins—whether from my side or from Samuel's side are going to be Jewish. Give them the closeness with their cousins they deserve. If you want them to be brought up according to my wishes, I'll say they ought to be Jewish—and Mamma and I will dance the Hava Nagila at your wedding!' And there you have it. Jacob's grandmother, Miriam, was right when she said: 'They did not win'. Not then; not now."

The silence in the room was the sadness within them all. It was broken only when Sarah tinkled her glass.

"I received a letter on Friday, at Ayrton Hall; I have not shared it with anyone—not even Jacob. Today I will share it, first with him, and then I'll ask him to read it out to all of you. It is from Devinder—from India."

She took an envelope from under her table napkin and, smilingly, handed it to a glum Jacob.

"Don't look so downcast, my love," Sarah said. "You'll only find a confirmation of all that I've already told you. Please, Jacob, read it silently first—so that you are the first to know, and then read it out to the family; they know the whole sorry tale. Then, please, return it to me; I would like it back."

He read it silently. As he read it, Sarah's eyes upon him, he broke into a gentle smile. Then, he leaned over and kissed her on the lips. He cleared his throat and read the letter out to the others around the table.

"It was mailed from India, about a week ago, and is addressed to Sarah at Ayrton Hall. It reads:

My Dear Sarah,

You will be surprised to receive this letter from India. I've given up my studies at Imperial College and returned home. Because I cancelled my admission before the term commenced, I did not lose much money. With a Bachelor's degree in Mechanical Engineering from Jodhpur University, I have found a very good-paying job already; my parents are very pleased!

I am writing to say how sorry I am that I tried to use you to break my engagement to Premlata—please forgive me. She came only a few minutes after you left and she came to break the engagement! She realised—as I did—that we were not suited to each other. My mother has found me a beautiful Rajput girl, eighteen years old, and we are going to be married shortly. She is not very educated—she passed her Secondary School Leaving Certificate (SSC) in the Second Class, two years ago. She is very proud of me and my education.

I would like to maintain communication with you. Please write to me at my office address, on the envelope, and I will maintain your confidence with my wife, my parents, and your family too. Love from afar! Yes?

I was always very fond of you; I'm sorry my mother had all her outdated ideas of Rajput honour—in this day and age! If I was good enough to marry the only daughter of the Indian High Commissioner, surely I was more than good enough for you—his Military Attache's daughter? Even if you were her Colonel Saheb's daughter! Love, Devinder." Jacob paused.

"The mother knows what Rajput honour is; the son, sadly, does not," Joshua said.

"Here's the letter, my love," Jacob said, placing it in its envelope and handing it back to her.

Sarah took a match box also from under her table napkin—she had obviously come well-prepared!—went to the fireplace, lit a match, held the envelope, with the letter in it, until it caught full flame, almost to her fingertips, before throwing it into the grate.

She walked back, smiling, to Jacob, kissed him on the lips, and resumed her seat at the table, to a family in silence.

This time the silence was broken by Susan's tinkle on her wine glass—so masterful that it had Julia wondering if she'd cracked it!

"You know that I've always wanted to be a writer—since my teenage years. God has been merciful to have given me a way with words. So I ask myself why, when I need that gift the most, do I find myself wanting in the words I should use to tell you of my decision that I am not going to Oxford University this term—or ever!"

There was an uproar at the table. It was what she had expected. She leaned towards Albert, and put her arm in his; he massaged it in affection. He had not known of her decision; yet, he didn't seem upset by it.

"May we know, why?" Joshua asked, gently. "The decision, my darling child, will always be yours, but have you thought it over carefully? Wouldn't you like to discuss it with all of us round the table?"

Susan smiled at her father. "Dear Pappa," she said, "I'll tell you why; it's the genes you gave me—not Mamma's genes, but yours! You are responsible for the decision I have taken. Now would you tell them, Daddy, why I am not going to Oxford University for a degree in English literature?"

The table burst into laughter.

"You mean," Florenzo said incredulously, "that Joshua Uncle will tell us why you've decided to let those 'A' levels of yours—the ones you aced!—go to rot?"

Joshua sighed. "You're right, dear, and Mamma knows it too—and we approve whole-heartedly. We wondered when you would tumble to it. Mercifully you've taken your decision before the term commenced, so you can cancel your admission—allowing some other fortunate student to take your place."

"Will somebody tell me," Albert said, mildly, "why it is that I, with a Master's degree in Philosophy from Oxford University, can't make out the reason for her withdrawal from Oxford, while her parents can?"

"Because Albert, my boy, you've got to live with this girl for eighteen years, before you can fathom her deep and intricate mind—and the way it works. But if it's any reassurance to you, Albert, you'll have a wonderful time getting to know her, and you'll not regret one moment of it!"

"Thank you, Pappa Joshua. That I have known for the past six years; that she has consented to marry me is all I ever wanted from her. Now, the floor is yours. Tell us why?"

"In military terms—it's called a 'focused war'. When fighting a war, there are only limited resources, and the demands on several fronts can be more than are available to the General in command. So he throws into one attack on one battlefront, everything he has. That breaks through enemy lines; he then encircles the enemy from behind, and wins the war—or whatever objective was important to him. Get it?"

Albert nodded.

"Susan wants to be a great writer—maybe change the way in which man thinks? She already has her first novel accepted for publication. Tell me, Albert, how is wasting—and I mean wasting—three years at Oxford going to help her become a better writer? She has read, prolifically, these past six years—ruined her eyes in the bargain, as you well know. Are her Dons at Oxford going to help her reach her goals in a 'focused war'? I don't think so; her Mamma doesn't think so, and—what is most important—she doesn't think so."

Joshua paused. No one spoke.

"Susan has already broken through enemy lines; now she cannot dilute her resources of time and energy on more than two fronts."

"Two?" Joe said. "I thought you said just one?"

"She is getting married; any daughter of mine would give her marriage the highest priority. Fortunately, for Susan, Albert is such an understanding person, she will have no difficulty juggling marriage and writing—but a degree from Oxford is just too encroaching on the other two. Have I got it right, dear?" Joshua said, looking at Susan.

"Perfectly, Pappa! I couldn't have put it any better than you did. It was Albert who gave me the idea."

"Did I, dear?" Albert said, mildly.

"When you called me your 'book and baby factory'. Remember? One year a book; the next year a baby; the next year a book; the next year a baby—shall I go on or does everyone get the picture?"

They burst into laughter, lifting their glasses to her in their congratulations.

"Of course, I retaliated immediately by calling him 'diaper daddy'! Tell me, Mamma," Susan said, turning to Julia, "how many times will Albert have to change diapers on the baby, before the child says: 'No more! I'm big enough now.'? Oh, and four or five children?"

Julia looked at Cecily; Cecily looked at Julia. Lysa looked at Sophie.

"A few hundred?" hazarded Julia.

"A few thousand?" hazarded Cecily.

"It depends on the children," said Lysa, getting into the spirit of it. "Shall we say a thousand, per baby?"

They all looked to Sophie.

"Why are you all looking to me?" Sophie asked, with a twinkle in her eye. "I've had only one baby. He was a twelve pound brute, but his diaper needs were no different. I had my Mamma Miriam's help too. Julia has had the most! Perhaps we should ask the General?"

"It seemed like thousands to me," Joshua said gravely. "Albert, my boy you've got your years ahead filled out for you—the 'diaper daddy'. She's made sure you grow old prematurely."

"It was my idea, Sir, to have a large family—not hers. But, I will have Mummy and Mamma Julia to help me, won't I? Sophie Aunty is going to help Sarah."

The three ladies groaned, though inwardly they glowed. Any contact, of any kind, with any grandchild, was most welcome!

This time it was Ruth who tinkled her wine glass to draw their attention.

"I think there is one little matter unsaid, and both Rehana and I would like for you to be aware of how we are going to handle it. Will, Samuel, Rehana and I have discussed it together—not separately—and so this is a joint decision." She stopped to let Rehana continue.

"Yusuf is my brother; I cannot abandon him. I love him—as Sarah and Ruth and Susan love David. As they will tell you, a sister's love is unconditional. God has been more merciful to them than he has been to me. But I have to play with the cards he dealt me. So Samuel and I discussed the matter before we got engaged—and he was most supportive of me. How can I thank you, darling?"

She leaned over towards him and kissed him full on the mouth. He put an arm around her, and this time it was he that continued: "We went along to see Yusuf last week—to tell him we were engaged. Rehana and I stood side by side, holding hands, while I told him I was Jewish and a 'Squigby'—Will's brother and Ruth's brother-in-law-to-be. He was stone-faced. He didn't say a word; we still don't know how he took it. But we told him the truth—all of it—that Rehana and I were to be married in the Hampstead Reform Synagogue, that our children would be brought up Jewish, that we would certainly meet with him, but that he would never meet Ruth or Will again—ever!"

"And that is how it stands—as of now," Rehana said. "As Joshua Uncle said a few minutes ago—a girl's first priority is her marriage. He was talking about Susan—but it applies to me too. Now, Yusuf has to take the steps needed to make Samuel and me comfortable with him, so that I can be a real sister, and Samuel a good brother-in-law, to him."

"Naseem Aunty has agreed to play the 'Scheduling Queen'," Ruth said with a laugh, "to ensure that our paths don't cross—as much for his sake as for ours! But when Will's and Samuel's children do come along, I'd like for them to be as close as the children of these two brothers—Pappa and Joe Uncle—have been over the past twenty, or so, years. Rehana and I have decided to make that our personal responsibiltity—no matter what!"

"Well said, Ruth!" Joshua said. "And Rehana, thank you for clearing away a few of the unsaid doubts lingering in our minds—you have been very gracious. We have to be able to forgive—otherwise we are less than human. Thanks to your Mamma, you, and Ruth, no one was killed or injured—and forgiveness will come easier than if it were otherwise."

Susan, who had left the table to get Cecily Aunty another of Julia's delicious gulab jamuns, was passing the window that overlooked the street, when she stopped and exclaimed: "There's a whole cavalcade of cars on Fitzjohn's Avenue below. I wonder who it could be? And visiting whom?"

The answer came almost immediately when the doorbell pealed in a strident tone.

It was Her Majesty, the Queen.

Every man and woman was on their feet, to welcome their distinguished visitor.

"Please sit," the Queen said. "I can't stay long. I'm off to some place in St. Albans to give an after dinner speech, and thought it a good idea to drop in and find out how my children are doing? Congratulations on all the engagements; Julia kept me fully informed."

The Queen chuckled, as she said softly: "On second thoughts, I'm a pretty good matchmaker, wouldn't you say? The only one I haven't met is the Countess of Bromfield. Come here child; give me a hug."

Rachel advanced shyly, curtsyed gracefully to the Queen, and was hugged by her. "And congratulations, my dearest Susan on having your novel accepted for publication. Come give me a hug too!"

Susan did just that, saying shyly: "You're in it, Elizabeth Aunty. I want you to know that before I give you a copy of the book."

"Am I, dear? That's wonderful!"

Before she could continue further, the royal equerry, obsequiously, pointed to his watch, urging her attention to the time; she silenced him with a withering glance.

"Where was I when I was interrupted? Ah, yes! I trust you have shown me in a good light, child?"

"Elizabeth Aunty how could I not show you in a good light, the way you are; a kindly, gracious monarch, warm and endearing—with a withering look!"

They all burst into laughter, the Queen no less amused than any of them. Even the equerry smiled. She wagged a finger at Susan. "Have I ever used my withering look on you? No, don't answer that. I'll find out for myself, when I read the book." She turned to Joshua. "We'll just have to get a session together—not on Jane Austen, but on Susan Samuelson; maybe rope the author in for further explanation, deeper analysis of characters and plot—fact and fiction?"

He bowed to her in acquiescence. "Your every wish, Elizabeth Aunty, is my command."

"Mine, too," Susan said, curtsying to the Queen. "I'd like that, if only to show to you, Elizabeth Aunty, that I could never depict you in a bad light; myself, perhaps—but you, never!"

"I hear," the Queen said, "that the first novel was called 'A Family at War'?"

"It was," Susan said. "It was pretty terrible! Albert reviewed it, anonymously, and told me what a ghastly writer I was!—so I punished him by getting engaged to him—but Sarah and David really made me see ambition in a light that makes us—even the poorest of us—worthy of it."

The Queen smiled, touched Susan's cheek, softly, in affection, and was about to turn towards the door, when she stopped and said: "So, Susan, what is the title of the published novel going to be?"

Susan smiled, and without a moment's hesitation said:

"Of Royalty and Commoners."